# It Would Be Funny. . . If It Wasn't My Life

## LISA DOW

McArthur & Company

Toronto

Published in Canada in 2008 by
McArthur & Company
322 King St. West, Suite 402
Toronto, ON
M5V 1J2
www.mcarthur-co.com

Library and Archives Canada Cataloguing in Publication

Dow, Lisa     It would be funny…if it wasn't my life / Lisa Dow.

ISBN 978-1-55278-742-7

I. Title.
PS8607.O987318 2008      C813'.6      C2008-903547-X

Cover and text design by Tania Craan
Printed in Canada by Transcontinental Printing

The publisher would like to acknowledge the financial support of the Government of
Canada through the Book Publishing Industry Development Program (BPIDP) and the
Canada Council for our publishing activities. The publisher further wishes to acknowl-
edge the financial support of the Ontario Arts Council for our publishing program.

10 9 8 7 6 5 4 3 2 1

To my dad
who watches over me always

*Larry E. Dow*
*1943 – 1996*

## Acknowledgments

Special thanks to:

*Hilary McMahon*, for being my brilliant agent and believing that every woman should have a Kit in her life.

*Kim McArthur*, for loving Kit enough to publisher her.

*Sandy Cardwell*, for living and breathing this book with me every day, from conception to print, and still taking my calls.

*Tim Metcalfe*, for your courier services, financial support and being my Number One Fan (but not in the scary Kathy Bates in *Misery* sorta way).

*Fernando Homen*, for being you.

*Dorothy Dow*, for being the most amazing mom ever and never once asking where the mortgage money was coming from.

*Sandra (Poytress) Morgan*, for the "social beverage experiments" and keeping me employed so I could pay the bills while I wrote.

*Toby Simon*, for believing in me a full decade before I believed in myself.

*Kathy (Kelly) McDermid*, for lending her nickname to this project and understanding my "adolescent crushes" on rock stars.

*Carly, Shelby* and *Jake Dow*, for whom I want to set a good example and be the best that I can be.

And to all my incredible family and friends who encourage and support me no matter how big my hair gets. I know I am very lucky to have you all in my life. Thank you.

# 1

I suppose I should have been worried. Melanie had been standing at my dining table for a full five minutes, staring, arms hanging limply by her side, mouth gaping open. I had never seen her speechless before. In fact, I'm not sure anyone had ever seen her speechless before. If I hadn't been starting to wonder if she'd ever recover, I might have found some humour in her frozen state. Lord knows she's seen me speechless on more occasions than I can count.

Mel isn't like me and that may be how we've managed to stay friends since preschool. They didn't call it preschool back then — it was simply home, where we stayed with our stay-at-home June Cleaver moms and we were neighbours. But we have been friends since before that first terrifying day on the big yellow schoolbus. Back in those days, school started when you were five and you only had to endure one year of kindergarten. I don't know if my germ-phobic, neat-freak personality could have withstood a second year of "sandbox." Whoever decided that bringing dirt inside and making you play in that dirt was important for developing fundamental social skills was sadly mistaken. Dirt and I have never been close, and failing sandbox in kindergarten still remains one of my most strongly guarded secrets. I think Mel has a better relationship with dirt and social situations — she passed sandbox. Mel is more driven than I'll ever be and is currently making a financial killing as one of the top-selling real estate agents in the area. She's a fast-talking go-getter who tells people how it is going to be, what properties to consider and how much to pay for them. Even in a state of shock Mel's hair is perfect. Like always. She is the most together perfect size four — a source of envy for me since I'll never be smaller than a six no matter how many miles I run a day — who wears exquisite Prada shoes and carries matching handbags. Seeing her in a state of shock is uncharted territory.

Is that movement? I think I see a small subtle shake of her head. Yes, she is shaking her head. She is trying to move her lips but no sound is coming out. This is a definite one-eighty from the determined non-stop talking woman who flew into my condo five minutes earlier. I knew it was Mel by the single rap on the door. Mel is no-nonsense and sees no point in wasted knocking. She's a one-knock gal — two if she's really excited and has just closed a huge deal (huge qualifies as a million dollars or better). There is one knock. I wander over to the door, unlock and open it. Mel flies into the room like a hurricane. Fast walking, four-inch-heel tapping, arms flailing, Prada handbag flying, head twisting, hair tossing and talking. This is how Mel always enters a room. Mel entered kindergarten the same way, only with less Prada. I think she was wearing Buster Brown black patent leather and toting a little brown-paper lunch bag back then.

"Where have you been? I've been calling and calling and you're not at work." Mel always asks multiple questions and doesn't leave time for answers. Mel knows me too well to actually require answers most of the time anyway.

"What is wrong with you? Are you still in your pajamas? You don't let men see those pajamas, do you? No wonder you're on the backside of thirty and still single. Is that a glass of wine in your hand? It's only ten thirty in the morning on a workday!" she exclaims and would continue but has to stop for breath.

"Thirty-one is not the backside of thirty and it's a lovely Australian Merlot, would you like some?" I manage while pushing the door closed behind her and glancing down at my red plaid flannel pants (circa 1996), my unmatched socks (one is blue with penguins on it, the other is red) and an orange t-shirt that features holes in both armpits and a Minnie Mouse decal on the front (it used to boast the word *flirting* in glitter but now reads *tin* because most of the glitter has peeled off). When I look up from the pajama assessment, I notice that Mel's perfectly coiffed long blonde hair is shinier than ever; she's just had her highlights done. The memory of the larger-than-life three-day unwashed mess I saw in the mirror earlier makes my head hurt.

"Australian or not, you never drink before lunch and never on a Monday. Why aren't you returning my calls? You could have been dead and you know I have no time for that sort of thing. The Corbetts are thinking Post Road and I have that Burrows fellow almost ready to make an offer on the Elm Street property. I can't possibly fit in a funeral!" She stops only for oxygen.

"I turned my ringer off," I slip in while she's inhaling and take a sip of wine. The dead thing does not offend me. I know she would make time for my funeral if I really were dead. She's only being dramatic.

"Well, obviously. But you never screen calls. Mr. Right could be calling *right now*. Why aren't you at work?"

"The condo market is drying up. You said so yourself," I state flatly, taking another sip of wine. "Are you sure you don't want a glass?"

"No and you shouldn't either," Mel takes the wineglass out of my hand and looks concerned. "I saw you Thursday at lunch, you were busy at work and excited about going to the hockey game. What happened? Did the Leafs lose? You know I don't follow hockey. Don't the Leafs always lose?" She reaches out and grabs my hand that had previously been holding the Merlot and assesses my fingers, "Oh my God! You're biting your fingernails again! You haven't bitten your nails since the third grade!"

Yes, I have been biting my nails again and I haven't been answering my phone, or even looking at caller ID for the past two days. I don't know how to have *this* conversation, or any of the other conversations I must have post-haste. I'm not normally a stick-my-head-in-the-sand kind of gal. I think I mentioned my relationship with sand earlier so I wouldn't go that route unless bodily forced or backed into a corner. Unfortunately, sand and I have bonded over the past couple of days and I'm burrowing in for a long stay if it means not dealing with the sticky situation in which I currently find myself. It has actually taken me the past two days of contemplation and nail biting to come up with the word *sticky*. I was referring to it as interesting but this situation rates a bit messier, so after trying out adjectives like devastating, horrific, ghastly, horrendous and gruesome I finally settled on sticky. No one has been maimed to this point, so the other adjectives just seem over the top, for now anyway. The situation could, of course, escalate. But currently, I'm thinking of it as sticky.

I can't even begin to explain to Mel what has transpired in the four days since I saw her last, so I take back my nail-bitten hand and point to the dining table of my sparsely furnished condo. Mel, determined to solve whatever is ailing me, get me back on track and still make her twelve o'clock lunch, taps across my hardwood floor to the table. I love my dining table. It's a seven-foot-long harvest table that I bought at the Amish Furniture Market just before I moved into the condo. I love the Amish. They are so dedicated to their culture and craft; it's all very commendable. Sadly, I didn't love the matching chairs, and believe matching was a complete misnomer, so I purchased the table only, obviously with the view to finding the perfect chairs at some point down the road. I've been travelling that road for almost a year now and still have not found the elusive perfect chairs. I did invest in two plastic Rubbermaid EZ Two-Step step stools that are currently doubling as chairs. The thought being that the non-slip Two-Steps will come in handy after I've found, fallen in love with, purchased and taken delivery of the aforementioned perfect chairs. The Two-Steps are scheduled to become much needed aids in reaching the top shelves of the cupboards in this condo with its impossibly high ceilings that challenge my five-foot-three stature on a daily basis, but currently they are acting as chairs.

I follow Mel to the table, where she now stands speechless beside the white Two-Step. I have a white one and a blue one. I couldn't commit to one colour when I bought them so I bought one of each. I take my wineglass out of Mel's hand, as she is in no state to argue or put up a fight, and I walk over to the cupboard, take another wineglass off the shelf and fill it from the open bottle of Merlot on the counter. As I top up my glass I notice the wine charm on Mel's glass reads "Comatose." Fitting, I decide, and almost smile for the first time in days.

Since Mel is trying to make words now and appears to be coming out of her original shock I walk over and place the Comatose wineglass in her hand. She looks up from the display on the table, makes confused eye contact and downs the contents of her wineglass in one long, loud swallow. I take the glass from her and walk back to the counter to refill it.

"What is all this? Tell me you robbed a jewellery store?" she finally stammers. The idea that I am a felon is easier for her to comprehend than what she suspects is the actual truth. I walk back to where Mel is standing and she readily accepts the wineglass again, but without downing the contents immediately as before.

We both turn back to the table where three velvet ring boxes stand open to display three very different but equally stunning, glittering diamond engagement rings. The boxes themselves are impressive enough, plush velvet in various colours, and the combined worth of their contents would be impressive if either of us had the wits about us to do the calculation. Beside the green-velvet ring box is a man's high-school signet ring with a very large, heavily scratched navy-coloured glass stone with the words "Central High '92" barely legible on the well-worn and somewhat misshapen band.

"Nope. The first three came with proposals," I manage, quietly.

"But you're single. You aren't even dating *one* person seriously, let alone four! You invented 'Sex with the Single Ex'! You can't even commit to kitchen chairs!" Mel's voice cracks and she sounds like she has dry mouth even though she has just made very short order of a glass of wine.

"Seems the Sex-with-the-Single-Ex plan didn't go as hoped," I state, trying to be as matter of fact as possible even though I don't feel that way.

Having had several days to absorb the insanity of my current sticky situation, I am able to lead Mel to the couch. I discovered over the past couple of days that not being near the "ring display" makes breathing and adjective assessing easier, and I have been giving the table a very wide berth while going to and from the kitchen to get After Eight mints. I have been carrying the wine bottle around the condo with me, but the After Eights have to stay in the fridge; they are so much nicer cold.

"But…" Mel manages as I help her get seated. I walk back to the fridge and grab the box of After Eights. I suspect it is going to be a long morning and Mel may not make her twelve o'clock, but the time has come to bring her up to speed on the sticky situation. I walk back to the couch and sit down beside her.

"Mint?" I ask Mel before I begin the story. Mel does not look impressed as she takes another sip of wine. I don't think she wants a mint. I take a sip of my wine and bite into an After Eight. The story I have to tell started long before last Thursday. If I had to decide when this particular sticky situation started brewing I'd have to say about three years ago.

# 2

I'm going to my first Toronto Maple Leafs game! This is huge. I've lived in Toronto for almost two years now and know that Leafs tickets are impossible to get and I'd never be able to afford them even if I could get them, especially since they made the move from the Gardens to the Air Canada Centre. I have to call Mel.

"One of the contractors, here at work, asked me to the Leafs game on Saturday," I shriek into the phone.

"What? Which one? Tell me you didn't accept! No, Kathryn Louise Jennings, I *forbid* you to go!" Mel hisses fiercely but quietly into the phone. Mel is working reception at a real estate office and her office manager, Grumpy Jim, frowns on her taking personal calls. This is the "Grumpy Jim's not here yet and I've got about thirty seconds to talk," or in this case "reprimand-you-like-a-child" whisper.

"Don't be silly! Of course I accepted! I really want to go."

"You're not in Kansas anymore, Dorothy! This is The Big City where you can't just be buddies with men, especially the seedy contractor types. Things are 'expected' here, especially for high-priced-sporting-events!" Mel's voice is high pitched and her words all run together which means Grumpy Jim is enroute to her desk, and before I can respond, "I'm sorry Mrs. Smith, Jackie's not in right now can I have her call you back?" Mel quips in her overly friendly singsongy Grumpy-Jim's-standing-here-and-glaring-at-me voice.

"Meet me at the Firkin after work, we'll talk then. Give Jim a big kiss for me!" I mock, knowing Mel can't retaliate verbally and is writing a fictitious telephone number on her pink While You Were Out memo pad.

"Ohhh, Mrs. Smith! Absolutely!" Mel gushes for Grumpy Jim's benefit.

It's Thursday and the Firkin is busy and smoky. Good Lord, we really need to start enforcing the smoking by-laws in this city, which apparently is not Kansas. I wonder if Kansas enforces smoking by-laws. I walk in and see Mel at one of our usual tables. She's smoking frantically and adding to the ambiance that will require me to wash my hair before I go to bed.

Mel likes to have a good view of the door; she says that it's important to be able to take note of who walks in and who leaves with whom. She maintains that she has to know everyone so that when her career picks up in real estate — she is currently taking courses to become a sales agent while working at the front desk of the real estate office — she'll be able to schmooze better. In reality Mel is a bit of a stargazer and I think she secretly hopes that Brad Pitt will walk into the Firkin someday. Mel has seen *Thelma and Louise* seventy-two times and she wore out her VHS copy and had to replace it with the DVD. I don't have the heart to tell her that Brad wouldn't be caught dead in our local pub, but she holds firm on her "seeing the door" policy and maintains Brad's not the reason anyway, especially since he left Jen for Angelina and not *her*.

"How's Grumpy Jim?" I inquire playfully as I walk up to the table and sit down, throwing my Roots knapsack purse on the floor under the table.

"Kit, how dare you call and just spring on me that you're going to the Leafs game with a *contractor!*" The word *contractor* takes on the same disdain we reserve for words such as Nazi and the names of the three domestic car manufacturers. "This is definitely an over-a-beer, break-it-to-me-gently, do-you-have-any-plans-on-Saturday-because-they'll-be-calling-you-to-identify-my-lifeless-remains sort of conversation. He's probably a mass *murderer*." She puts extra emphasis on murderer and takes another drag of her cigarette.

"He's not a murderer, he's an electrician and didn't you quit smoking?"

"Ha ha. Good try. You'll be playing the asthma card here in a second, but I'm being serious."

"If I play the asthma card it's because you're smoking like a chimney and you're not being serious, you're overreacting," I manage to get out just as Steve, our favourite server, sets down Mel's beer and asks if I'd like the usual. Steve always asks me even though I never change my order. I'm a Coors Light girl.

"Absolutely! Thank you. Oh Steve, before you leave, do you think all electricians are mass murderers?"

"Not all of them but wasn't Paul Bernardo an electrician?" Steve smiles.

"Paul Bernardo was an Amway salesman, but thanks for your help," I reply with a hint of sarcasm as Steve walks away to get my beer. "Anyway, it's *not* a date. I did some invoicing for him because his assistant was away and he's just saying thanks. Besides, he's married."

"Like that matters! Which one is the electrician anyway? Emilio? Claudio? Fabio? It's one of the swarthy Europeans. One of the *married* swarthy Europeans."

"All contractors are of European descent and you consider everyone who isn't Brad Pitt to be swarthy. I think you just like that word." I take Mel's beer from her hand and have a sip while I wait for mine to arrive. "It's Marc, actually, and he's only a little bit swarthy," I smile and take another sip of Mel's beer.

"I know his name is *Marco*," she puts extra emphasis on the o, "and I think you've been single too long and have lost all sense of reality."

"Mel, the only guy I've dated since I moved here is Rob-the-bike-courier. Remember him? You encouraged me to go for it and I did, only to discover that he was sleeping with every female between eighteen and fifty-five on his courier route! I'm not doing anything insane, I'm just going to a hockey game. I promise I'll be smart and careful. I don't want to date anyone anyway. You know I've never completely recovered from the Boob Man fiasco." In hindsight the whole Boob Man debacle is quite funny. After university I returned to North Bay to work and that's where I met Boob Man, as we affectionately refer to him now. We met my first week as a receptionist at an insurance firm and I was completely smitten. We stayed together forever. We took turns going to family holidays and everyone just assumed we'd get married, so when he asked a couple of years later I accepted. Unfortunately, a year after the ring was presented, during a heated discussion about what the main course should be at our wedding (I wanted chicken and he wanted roast beef), I made the mistake of asking him why he was marrying me anyway. Just to get the honest heat-of-the-moment answer — which I did not want to hear — of "I don't know! I guess because you've got great boobs." The engagement pretty much ended at that moment. I never told my parents about the boob thing. How do you actually say something like that out loud to your parents? All my friends know though, and my great boobs are the topic of many conversations and jokes.

Mel takes a long drag of her cigarette, but turns her head away from me to exhale, "Well, I hope the swarthy European knows that — the 'not dating' part not the 'boob' part — he probably already knows about your boobs," she laughs and seems argued out.

"Brad Pitt won't like you if you smoke. I read somewhere that he has asthma as well."

"You don't have to worry about it. You'll have been murdered by a swarthy gun-totin' European long before Brad breaks my chain-smokin' heart, baby!" Mel laughs. Steve brings my beer and we settle in to discuss more important things, like whether Brad had better hair in *Fight Club* or *Ocean's Eleven*.

# 3

After great deliberation and four complete outfit changes, I decide on the jeans with a long-sleeved black t-shirt combination, black boots, small black over-the-shoulder bag and black leather jacket to finish off the ensemble. Since moving to Toronto I have adopted "The City" fashion sense, and have eliminated all items from my wardrobe that are not denim or black. Toronto exudes black. I've heard that in Vancouver people wear colours other than black, but I've never seen it myself. I'm sure the Leafs don't care what I wear, but you never know when you might run into someone you know so it's best to look "Toronto chic" just in case.

My cell phone rings as I'm walking to meet Marco (yes, Mel was right — that is his name) at the pub around the corner from my apartment. I know the caller is Mel before I pick up. Mel is trying her best to convince me not to go and has called five times to reconfirm my cell phone number, which she knows by heart, the spelling of Marc's name, the seat location, a list of who to call when I turn up missing and whether or not I'm carrying mace. The answer is no to the mace. Firstly, I don't own mace and secondly, since I decided on the smaller purse, it wouldn't fit anyway.

"Hi Mel," I sigh into the phone.

"Don't sound like I'm an inconvenience, you'll be happy for the attention when you are lying beaten in an alley. Do you have your ID on you? And I don't mean in your purse. Any good murderer would remove it from your purse. Put it in the pocket of your jeans, and did you put a stickie on it with my name and number so the nice policeman who finds your rotting remains will know who to call?" Mel's voice goes singsongy at the end of her sentence and she emphasizes the word *nice*. Personally, I've only met one policeman in the city and he wasn't that nice because he gave me a parking ticket.

"My ID is in my pocket, as per your directions three phone calls ago. It's Saturday night. Don't you have anything else to do? Where's Triple D? Weren't you meant to see him tonight?" I try to change the subject from my imminent demise to a more worthy topic. Triple D is the guy Mel's been dating for a month. He's really nice but isn't so smart and his conversation topics are limited to contact sports, bodybuilding and the sales pitch for the protein drink mix he sells. I think Mel is dating him because he reminds her of a really muscular Brad Pitt, but she maintains he's delicious and intellectually stimulating *enough*. She nicknamed him Delicious Dave and shortly after meeting him I added the Dumb. He's been known as Triple D ever since and I some-times have to stop and think to remember his proper name.

"You won't believe it. Triple D is staying in to watch the hockey game. You know I don't do hockey," Mel huffs into the phone.

"Hockey is like our national anthem. You should at least feign interest. Go to his house and watch the game with him, you might see me on television. Besides, you can have intellectual conversation during the commercials," I laugh.

I have arrived at the pub and bid Mel goodbye only after promising three times to call the *second* I get home, even before I take off my shoes. She would actually prefer that I call from my cell as soon as the auto-lock lobby door closes behind me, but I'm going to make her wait until I enter the apartment.

I see Marc at a small table at the back and I wave as I make my way to the table past the crowded bar. I've known Marc for two years, since shortly after I started working at my current job as an assistant to a developer, Sebring Property Development. We started with a small project, Sebring I, to test the condo market viability, and Marc owns the electrical company that was hired for the job. Marc's company is now the electrical contractor on our second building project, surprisingly called Sebring II. As an assistant to a property developer, the only people I meet are contractors and Joyce, the lady who does our accounting and keeps track of sales. Joyce is wonderful and sweet and I just love her. Joyce brings me homemade cookies, tucks my hair behind my ear and pulls down my sweater if it slips up and shows too much midriff. She actually reminds me of Mrs. Doubtfire from Robin Williams' lesser-known comedy of the same name. Needless to say, Joyce and I don't run in the same midriff-baring crowd.

Marc is actually quite attractive, for an old guy. He's definitely the best-dressed contractor on our site and smells the nicest. If I had to make a guess I'd say he wears Calvin Klein's Eternity (the men's obviously). He has sandy brown hair just starting to go a little grey, olive skin, green eyes and exceptionally straight teeth. He could have modelled underwear in his younger days — well, if he were taller. He is past his underwear-modelling prime now though — I'm sure he's almost forty. I've heard a rumour through the building site that he has a crush on me but haven't had the rumour conclusively confirmed or denied. He asked me to the game after I did some invoicing for him, so I'm sure the game is just to say thanks. Well, that, and I've been bugging all the contractors with season tickets to take me, so one of them had to give in eventually; they probably drew straws and Marc got the short one.

I order a beer and we're going to have nachos before we go to the game. Conversation with Marc is always easy. Marc and his wife married young and have practically grown children (three, I think), a dog, a cat and a rabbit named Barry. I didn't ask who named the rabbit but in my head I assume the rabbit is white and Barry is for Barry White. That would make sense in my world. Unlike Marc's world of wife, kids he barely mentions, and mini-zoo, my world is an open book. Single. Briefly engaged. Intermittent stints of dating badly, then back to single.

Most of the guys who contract for Sebring Property

Development know about Rob-the-bike-courier, and because he's the only person I've dated since working with them he comes up often. Tonight is no exception.

"You are way too nice and smart to be dating bike couriers," Marc mentions out of the blue, while I'm trying to separate nachos from cheese but still get some cheese.

"No I'm not. He's a nice enough guy and smart too. He just hasn't found his niche. Beside, it's not like I meet a lot of eligible men working with Mr. Sebring and Joyce."

"The guy cheats on you and you can defend him?"

"Absolutely, I didn't want to keep him and we had some fun. At the end of the day that's pretty much what dating is. Sad but true," I say honestly since I no longer have hard feelings toward Rob. Oh, I'll never tell Mel that! It isn't often I get anything on her so I have to use what I can. Besides, Rob has some fairly large issues and a possible drug habit that I hadn't fully confirmed. I didn't want to deal with that in the long run so it was for the best that I caught him moving on, for lack of a better term.

"You're serious, aren't you?" Marc asks thoughtfully.

"Yep. Besides he was really fit from all that bike riding. He had a great six-pack. You could bounce quarters off it."

"On *that* note, we have to get going if we're going to actually see the game," Marc says as he motions for the bill.

# 4

Okay. *That* was the best thing ever. Better than bouncing quarters off Rob's six-pack. I love hockey. Before today I really liked hockey but now I love it! After the hockey strike last year, all hope is on this year for our beloved Leafs to finally bring home the cup. Sadly, not off to the best start, and another loss tonight but it was so exciting to actually be in the arena and feel like a part of the action.

"If I'd known you'd be this excited I would have taken you to a game long before now," Marc laughs.

"Well, it's not like I didn't bug you enough! But thanks for taking me now, I loved it!"

"I'll have to take you again sometime."

"I'm sure you have a lineup of friends and family who want to go, so I won't hold my breath. I know it's impossible to get tickets." I try to sound nonchalant but I really would like to see another game as I now fancy myself the Leafs' Number One Fan (but not in the scary Kathy Bates *Misery* sort of way).

"Good try, I know you're dying to go to another game. Besides, you seem to appreciate it more than any of my buddies. I've never seen such enthusiasm over a loss."

"I'm from North Bay, win or lose, the Leafs are big-time entertainment for me."

We've almost reached my apartment building. Marc offered to walk me after the game, and I actually have to think about how to end the evening. A handshake seems ridiculous. I see him every day at work and don't shake his hand there. I'm definitely not going to kiss him and the idea of hugging is ridiculous, so I decide a punch on the shoulder is the only respectable, virtue-saving way to go — it says "I had a great time but respect that you're married."

"This is you, right?" We've arrived at my building.

"Yep, this is me. Thanks so much again for a wonderful evening," I say as I reach out and punch Marc in the arm. Unfortunately, I misjudge how far away he is, and because arm punching isn't something I've spent much time doing since I was eight and Mel's brother Mike used to make us play Flinch, I actually hit him pretty hard and his whole shoulder moves backward and he almost loses his balance.

"Ouch! What was that for?" Marc asks, very confused while righting himself.

"Oh my gosh. Sorry about that. I was just trying to be cool like the rapper kids and say thanks man," I try to explain but I know I'm blushing from embarrassment.

"You make me laugh," Marc laughs, grabs me, pulls me to him and gives me a huge bear hug. He does smell nice and it's definitely Eternity; I know now for sure because I gave the same cologne to the Boob Man for our last Christmas together. Marc loosens the hug and reaches up to hold my head with both hands and bends down and kisses me on the forehead. "Thank you for a wonderful evening," he says quietly.

"No, thank you."

"Now get," Marc says while punching me in the arm — probably not as hard as I punched him, but it still smarts a little and I shout, a little too loudly, "OUCH!"

"Now we're even," he laughs and pushes me toward my walkway. I'm so happy from the excitement of the game and the great evening that I don't retaliate; instead, I wave and skip up the walkway swaying from side to side with my arms outstretched, not even caring who can see how silly I look. Today is a good day.

I decide to walk to work on Monday. I'm still giddy from the game and the fall weather is actually quite nice for walking; it beats the summer heat in the city. I escaped the wrath of Mel, who I think was secretly disappointed when I called her alive and well with my virtue intact after the game because I'm sure she had practised her "*Ah-ha*, told you so!" speech the whole time I was out. Mel has always watched out for me and feels responsible for me because she is six weeks older than I am and has lived in Toronto six months longer than I have. Mel does wear her more-experience-in-The-Big-City badge very proudly.

A block from work I stop at my favourite coffee shop, thinking about the workday ahead. Mr. Sebring is away so I have big plans to catch up on the filing.

"You look happy," I hear a familiar voice from behind. It's Marc, who has just followed me into the coffee shop.

"Hey you, this is a surprise," I say as we approach the counter. "What are you doing at this end of town? I thought you were working on my building today?"

"I've been at Sebring's building since seven o'clock," Marc laughs, "I'm heading to another job and thought I'd get my invoice in to you on the way." I order my flavoured coffee — butter pecan today — and Marc gets a regular non-flavoured coffee, which I don't understand because flavoured coffee is so much yummier. I have yet to find After Eight–flavoured coffee though.

"Mine, the company's, same thing really," I laugh. "Do you have the invoice with you? I can take it now."

"No, it's in the truck, but it's parked on the way. I'll walk you." Marc then turns to the coffee lady, "How much for both?"

"No, I'll buy the coffee. I owe you at least that since you took me to the game," I open my wallet, but Marc pushes my hands away and pays for the coffee.

"Well, thank you again," I reply as we turn, coffee in hand, and start toward the office.

"It's the least I can do. You make sure I get paid every month." I see Marc's truck parked up the street in a no-parking zone. It fascinates me that all the contractors who work for us manage to park illegally and never get ticketed. If I stay over a parking meter for two minutes in Nasty, I'm guaranteed a ticket. Nasty is my car. I needed a car quickly after Boob Man and I parted ways so I bought Nasty sight unseen from a mechanic friend of mine who called and told me the car was in good shape, the price was right and it was available immediately. I didn't think to ask what colour it was because, as he said, the price was right. Unfortunately, the day Mel and I picked her up, my only reaction was "Wow, that is one nasty colour of blue!" and Mel's response was "But not nearly as nasty as the pink decal down the side." Nasty is a great car and has required very few repairs but she is a magnet for parking tickets, probably because there isn't a traffic cop in town colour-blind enough to miss her. I should become a contractor. Apparently tickets aren't a concern for them and they all seem to drive trucks that are normal colours and decal-free.

We arrive at Marc's truck and he pulls the invoice out of his briefcase. Not a traffic cop in sight. Unbelievable. I guess if I didn't pay so many tickets I too would be able to afford Leafs season tickets.

"I'm taking the guys out for a few beers after work on Thursday, why don't you come along?" Marc asks casually.

"Are you sure? I can't imagine the guys want me hanging around. Isn't guy beer when you all vent about work, ergo the company I represent, and try to pick up 'dirty girls' in high-heeled red shoes?"

"No," Marc laughs, "we really just go out and drink beer. No one picks up dirty girls. Well, mostly no one."

"Okay, sure then, so long as no one will mind. Let me

know where you're going." I turn and start toward the office. This might be fun. I've never been invited out as one of the guys before. I make a mental note not to wear red shoes — not that I own any — but it's still a good reminder to oneself in general.

# 5

"Can I ask you something?" Marc asks very tentatively. He seems nervous and that's not generally how he comes across anymore. Marc and I have actually become good friends over the past six months. He is at the coffee shop near my office more mornings than can be considered coincidental, and Thursdays out with his employees have become a common occurrence. Mel even started coming out on boys' night Thursdays after she and Triple D broke up during a heated discussion over the remote control. I like all of Marc's employees except one, John, and even he is slightly fascinating, well, in a bad way. He is very opinionated and loud and I almost always end up in a discussion with him. Discussions with John never end well. He is an uncouth brute of a guy. Guy because at twenty-eight he isn't a man yet; he has floppy little boy hair and always wears t-shirts with multi-coloured horizontal stripes in a style only ever truly pulled off by Charlie Brown. John might almost be considered attractive if he wasn't such a know-it-all and didn't dress like a cartoon character. I think Mel secretly has a crush on John but is afraid to tell me because I find him so abrasive. I've noticed the way she looks at him and it isn't the same abhorrent way I look at him; it's quite the opposite. I haven't come out and asked Mel about it because I don't want to encourage a relationship in that direction. I'm hoping that after Triple D, who has no opinion about anything except the remote control, that she is just riding the pendulum to the other extreme and that this too shall pass.

"Of course, but if it's about your cheque, Joyce told me the cheques will be ready on Friday." But I suspect this isn't about getting paid. We are just sitting down in the front window of the coffee shop. I have managed — a feat I don't pull off often — to pay for both coffees.

"No, it's not about getting paid. What are you doing on Saturday?" Again Marc is behaving very nervously.

"Not much. Mel has several open houses. You know she passed her exam and is a proper real estate agent now, but other than that I might go for a long run, maybe along the bike path toward Ontario Place. Why?"

"Would you want to do something with me?" Marc blurts out in an atypically rushed sentence.

"What do you have in mind?" Intuitively, I know this conversation is going down a road I don't want to travel. "I'm guessing from the way you're acting this isn't about going to the Leafs game."

"No. Would you come to a wedding with me?" Marc finally blurts out the true question.

"Wedding? Like as your date?" I am completely confused and this conversation has not gone down a road, it has leapt onto the expressway and is travelling much faster than would be considered safe by even NASCAR standards.

"Yeah, I guess, like my date. Roger, my client who renovates century homes, is getting married and I think we'd have fun. The reception is downtown at the Sheraton." The way Marc is talking now I can tell he's feeling a little more confident.

My head is reeling. Marc is serious. This isn't a joke. He seriously just asked me on a date. This cannot be happening. Marc is married and as far as I know is still married in every sense of the word. This is a nightmare, not because I have to deal with Marc but because it means Mel is right and now I'll have to tell her she's right and I'll never live it down. Mel has been maintaining for months, since the first Thursday she came out with Marc and his employees, that Marc has a thing for me. I have to agree that I have noticed the "thing." Marc always sits near me and touches me a lot, not in a bad way, just my arm or my back. When we are walking back to the office from the coffee shop and I'm on the sidewalk close to the street he always puts his hand on the small of my back and crosses behind me so that he is walking nearest the street. I actually think it's nice and his small gestures have given me faith that maybe chivalry is not dead like I had come to believe during Rob-the-bike-courier days. Rob wouldn't try to save me if a car was careening out of control and venturing up on the sidewalk. Rob would use his bike-courier dexterity to save himself. I, on the other hand, would be roadkill.

Mel has warned me that this day would come, but I was sure (obviously now, naïve is the better word) that Marc would never cross the line. He knows I know he's married. Sure, I've never met his wife but I've never met any of the contractors' wives. The contractors all seem to live in the suburbs and only come downtown to work. Meeting wives and children is improbable given the distance of my office from their homes but I'm well aware of their existence.

I am staring at Marc with my mouth hanging open. It feels like I've been stationary for months but in reality it's only been a few seconds. I can't form words. The only thought in my head is "wow, this would be really funny if it wasn't happening to me." I know I'd find great humour in it if it were happening to Mel. I'm sure God is punishing me for something evil. I must have been a murderer in a previous life, a really good one or bad one, whichever. My mouth is incredibly dry.

"Ahh." I finally start to talk but the words get stuck in my throat so I take a sip of coffee larger than the temperature of the coffee would normally allow.

"No," I finally manage after I put the coffee cup down. "You are joking, right?" I try to give him an easy way out so we can both go on with our lives as if the past twenty seconds never happened.

"I'm completely serious. I want you to come with me." Marc is obviously a bit slow on the uptake and he didn't catch the lifeline.

"But you're married. Where I come from married people don't go on 'dates' with anyone other than their spouses, and I'm not your wife."

Now Marc looks shocked, although surely not as shocked

as I looked moments earlier. He must have guessed I'd say no. I've never given Marc any indication that we are more than friends and I don't even own red high-heeled shoes. I work, run long distances (I am currently considering a half-marathon), hang out with Mel, bake my own banana bread and vote in all elections. I haven't even been on a date with a *single* guy in more months than I care to count, let alone any married ones. I scan back in my less than newsworthy past to find one shred of evidence that would allow anyone to think I'd knowingly date a married man. Nothing. I've lived a fairly benign existence to this point and plan on keeping it that way.

"But I don't love my wife," Marc finally states matter-of-factly. "We haven't been close for years." This is news to me. Marc doesn't gush on about his wife but he has never implied that they were anything but happy.

"I love you," he says emphatically as he reaches out to grab my hand. I can tell by the look in his eyes that he does in fact mean it, or believes he means it.

I pull my hand back quickly and I know I'm going to throw up. My stress response, ever since I was five and was asked to recite the alphabet in front of the kindergarten class, is vomiting. It's just what I do. It's not pretty and Mel maintains it is completely juvenile but Mel's opinion aside, it remains a fact that I cannot change. I get up and rush to the washroom, hurdling two handbags and a briefcase, where I proceed to vomit the instant the door clicks shut behind me. As I stand, leaning over the sink rinsing my mouth after the vomiting has ceased,

I wonder why scenes like this one don't make it into movies like *Gone with the Wind*; surely with what Scarlett went through she must have tossed her cookies occasionally. What about *Casablanca*, when Ilsa finds out that her husband is alive and in a railway car outside of Paris but she can't tell the man she loves and has to arrange to disappear? Definitely enough stress there to induce a bit of vomiting.

Marc is knocking at the washroom door. "Kit, are you okay?" Marc started calling me Kit shortly after we went to the hockey game and I didn't mind then. Kit is my nickname and has been since Mel started calling me that when we were kids, but at work I'm always Kathryn. I rinse my mouth and open the washroom door. Marc is holding my coat and purse and what remains of my coffee. I reach to take my coat and purse from him as he starts to say something. I interrupt him but the only thing I can say is, "Don't." I push past him in the little hallway at the back of the coffee shop; with my coat over my arm I throw my purse over my shoulder and rush to the door, anxious for the routine of work and the safety of my office. Personal lives don't enter the offices of Sebring Property Development — it's an unspoken fact. The Sebring offices will be a wonderful escape from the reality of the past ten minutes.

# 6

"Love? He used *that* word. Love?" Mel has said *that* word over thirty times in the past fifteen minutes. I'm starting to get nauseous again.

"Yes. He used *that* word and please stop saying it or I'll vomit on your boots." I hope Mel will heed my warning as she is wearing a brand-new pair of Prada boots. Mel has never had enough money for expensive shoes but received her first official commission cheque today and went shopping at Holt Renfrew this afternoon. She actually pulls off Prada nicely and I can only guess what they cost, but that won't stop my stress vomit reaction. If she keeps it up I am going to throw up and I cannot guarantee the safety of the boots.

Mel insisted on meeting me at the Firkin after she called me at the office to tell me about the boots and I was not myself on the phone.

"Prada! Did you hear me? Good heavens. What's wrong with you? Did you get fired? Meet me at the Firkin after work. There is definitely something wrong with you," Mel had insisted emphatically not two hours ago.

I managed to get through the day with no Marc contact.

He called the office several times but I asked Joyce to answer the phones with the excuse that I was filing and wanted to get it all done. I suspect Joyce knew something was up but she did cover for me and I officially owe her one, maybe two. In truth I got very little accomplished at work and was happy for the end of the day to finally arrive so I could meet Mel. I know Mel will get a lot of mileage out of what happened this morning with Marc but there is nothing like the security of my best friend in a crowded, smoky bar full of strangers. What I really want is for this morning to have never happened so I can go back to the naïve me of yesterday who believed my friend Marc was a nice guy and not a philanderer.

"Even you wouldn't vomit on Prada. It would be sacrilegious." Mel is chewing gum in a less than ladylike fashion. It is stop-smoking gum. She picked up a pack after she bought the boots. Seems her newfound love of expensive footwear has finally caused Mel to re-evaluate her priorities and smoking has fallen off the list. I really thought she'd quit for Brad Pitt, but expensive footwear works too. I don't know how she is managing the taste of gum with beer, but since she isn't smoking I'm not about to ask.

"I won't say that *word* anymore, but you do know that I warned you. The way Marc looks at you, wow. I'd kill to have anyone look at me that way. Well maybe not. I caught Triple D looking at my boobs that way once, and it was a bit disturbing. Anyway, anyone who's seen Marc look at you saw this coming."

"Well, I didn't. He's married. This should never have 'come.'"

"I know. You are way too trusting and good; you have to try to be more evil and jaded like me. And you haven't spoken to him since? Aren't you going to have to at some point? He works for the same company. What are you going to say?" Despite the gum chewing Mel can still talk a mile a minute.

"Of course I'll have to talk to him. But right now avoidance seems to be working just fine. And you're not being any help. What *should* I say to him?" I implore. Mel is my savvy, streetwise, now Prada-wearing, friend; surely she must have some insight into how to handle this situation. Oh she claims to be all "worldly" but I can tell from the way she's going on that she is just as incapable of dealing with this situation as I am.

"Well, you did the right thing by saying no," Mel says as she puts her arm around my shoulders. "I might have added 'you two-timing scumbag' if I'd said it, but what you said is good too."

I laugh a little because I can picture what Mel would have done to Marc and part of me wishes I was more confident and fast-thinking, albeit less gum-chewing.

Mel continues, "Just stay consistent and keep saying no; and you're right, avoid the man as much as possible. You can say no thank you politely, which will allow you to work together until this project is over, and then hopefully the two-timing philandering bastard will disappear off the face of the earth forever," with a squeeze of my shoulders before digging in her purse for a new piece of gum.

"I wish I could disappear off the face of the earth forever," I sigh.

"Oh don't be silly," Mel quips as she pops the new piece of gum into her mouth, which I'm sure makes at least six pieces since we sat down (so no wonder she's chewing in such a cowlike fashion), "if you weren't here, you wouldn't get to see how it ends."

The morning after I met Mel at the Firkin to see her new boots (we don't speak of it as the time we met to discuss "that word"), I woke up early, in the sense that I hadn't actually fallen asleep, and took the subway to work. I didn't stop for coffee. I have no idea if Marc would try to find me at the coffee shop but decided in the middle of my sleepless night that maybe I should give up caffeine anyway. Walking to the subway, I try to convince myself that I am not avoiding Marc and I just want to catch up on all the work I didn't do yesterday, but even I can see through my transparent lie.

The subway is actually quite civilized at this time in the morning. Not so many frazzled people rushing around as during peak rush hour. I think I might make a point of getting to work earlier all the time. There are a lot of trench coat–wearing businessmen, stockbrokers I guess, getting to work before trading opens. I've never really understood the stock market. I should take a course to get a better understanding of stock brokering. Is it called stock brokering? My brain is whirling; anything to not think about the day ahead of me. There is a construction timeline meeting at the office this afternoon and Marc is scheduled to be in attendance. I hope he has the good sense to not show, but that wouldn't actually be good sense because it might jeopardize his contract. It would only be good sense in that I wouldn't have to see him.

My stop is next. I get up and move toward the door of the subway car. At the same time one of the trench coat wearers gets up and stands beside me. He's probably not a stockbroker, not the right stop for the Toronto Stock Exchange. Trench coat guy is actually kind of cute, well in a tired, it's-way-too-early-in-the-morning sort of way. He has short brown hair that looks like it could easily get severe bed-head, huge blue eyes and the longest eyelashes I've ever seen on a man. He also has an amazing smile. I know this because he has caught me staring at him.

"Good morning," he says politely, probably thinking I'm some sort of crazy woman.

"Good morning," I manage as the doors open and we step onto the platform together. Trench coat man turns and walks determinedly toward the exit but I slow my pace to walk behind because I'm using the same exit. I suspect trench coat man has a really nice butt under his trench coat and wonder why I didn't spend a little more time trying to tame my hair this morning. My hair, which is naturally larger-than-life and fit nicely into the eighties, needs a lot more attention since hairstyles of the 2000s have become brutal straight and flat. Taming it is no easy feat and this morning I just wasn't up to the task. No doubt trench coat man will be telling his co-workers about the crazy staring lady with the wild hair he saw on the subway.

As I approach my office, lost in thought about trench coat man and the stories he could tell, obviously embellishing in my mind and sort of laughing to myself, I realize I am actually enjoying the walk from the subway to my office and thinking heck, maybe today won't be so bad, when a person pops out from behind one of the pillars that holds up the building next to mine, and is directly in front of me. The scream is hideous. I am shaken completely through because I had no idea anyone was around. It feels like minutes go by but its only milliseconds until I realize that the person who has just taken ten years off my life is Marc.

"WHAT ARE YOU DOING?" I shriek at him, in a typically uncharacteristic fashion. I would never raise my voice in the street, especially this close to the building I work in.

"ARE YOU COMPLETELY INSANE?" The stress of being terrified brings tears to my eyes and I'm sure I'm going to cry. Of course crying is preferable to vomiting but neither is desired.

"I'm so sorry, I just wanted to talk to you." Marc reaches out to touch my arm, "I knew if you saw me..."

"*Don't touch me!*" I hiss, cutting him off and taking a step backward; anger has replaced the fear I felt moments before.

"In fact," I start to point my finger accusingly at him in sharp stabbing motions, "don't ever touch me or speak to me again!" I know the tears are about to flow now, too much adrenaline in too short a time, so I run toward my office door, digging in my purse for the pass card that is needed before and after working hours. Once in the safety of the lobby the tears flow freely and I don't look back at the door. I don't want to know if Marc followed me. I make a stop at the ladies' room to rinse my face and try to get back to normal. My heart is still beating a mile a minute and what little makeup I had on ten minutes ago is completely gone. As I wipe my face with one of the unforgiving industrial-grade paper towels I realize it's *not* going to be a good day and I have to do something about the Marc situation. I can't live like this.

# 7

The office is silent. I love the office when it's just me. I turn on the lights, hang up my coat and head to my desk to start the day. I turn on my computer and notice that the voicemail indicator on my phone is flashing. As I reach to pick up the phone it starts to ring. Caller ID, which I think is the most wonderful invention ever and quietly thank its inventor every time I'm able to avoid an unwanted call, tells me it's Marc calling. The past twenty-four hours have been the longest of my life. I could avoid Marc's call but then what? Another scare of a lifetime or, worse, he'll show up at my apartment. There's no one else in the office; this is the moment of truth. I shall take the bull by the horns and end this here and now. I pray for just a bit of Mel's fast-thinking, fast-talking savvy as I reach for the handset.

"What do you want?" I ask pointedly, doing away with any niceties like "hello."

"I just want to make sure you are okay. I think I gave you quite a scare."

"I'm fine and thanks for the apology. Oh wait, you didn't apologize." Sarcasm is the lowest form of communication but sometimes you have to use what you've got. "Why are you lurking in front of my building anyway?"

"I need to see you." Marc sounds a bit desperate, "Let's grab a coffee. We have to talk about yesterday."

"I don't drink coffee anymore, thanks to you, and no we don't have to talk. There's nothing more to say," I manage through clenched teeth. "You think I'm someone who would date a married man and I think you're a philandering jerk. See? No more left to say." The handset is halfway back to its cradle before I get the whole sentence out. Not as refined as Mel but I'm confident I have made my point — well, for twenty-three seconds until the telephone starts to ring again. Marc. Apparently on top of being a philanderer the man is a sucker for punishment. I'm learning more about this guy every second. Four rings and voicemail picks up. I sit down to open email, maybe there is a joke or if I forward a prayer to ten of my friends I'll win an outrageous amount of money, thereby allowing me to leave the country and the ringing phone. Marc again. Has the man got nothing better to do? He has a company to run, a wife and kids. A rabbit. Surely he can find something to do besides call me repeatedly. Voicemail picks up. I look to the ceiling and say a little thank you to the inventor of voicemail. I've been giving way too much credit to the caller ID guy. You have to give thanks for *all* the inventors of wonderful telephone functions. Except the damn ringer! Again with the ringing! I reach over and turn the volume down to minimum. I can't turn the volume completely off because I have the system's main phone and Mr. Sebring tells me it's impossible. A part of me thinks he made it up so I'd always be at his beck and call, but since it's before hours and no one knows I'm here, no harm done. I'm not going to get anything done with the ringing, so I decide to play some music on the outrageously expensive office stereo system that rarely gets used (so in reality I'm doing the company a favour because the components could seize up) and do some filing. I can file with frayed nerves, big hair, no makeup and ringing in my ears.

As the hour approaches nine o'clock and the start of the workday, I turn off the stereo and prepare for Joyce's arrival. I actually managed to get all the filing done so even if I accomplish nothing else today I can still say I did something. I pick up my handset and dial in for voicemail in-between rings.

"You have thirty-six messages," the voicemail lady tells me. I wish the voicemail lady could vet them for me.

"Kit, it's Marc..." is all I hear before I delete.

"Kit..." delete.

"You have to..." delete.

"This is ridiculous..." delete. And on. And on. After I've gone through all the messages only three of them actually pertain to work. So apparently, Marc doesn't have anything else to do except call my voicemail. The company voicemail. Damn. I haven't checked my cell phone. I haven't even turned it on for two days.

The telephone is ringing again, caller ID is telling me it's Marc but it's 9:08 and Joyce arrived while I was checking the endless voicemails and she can hear me from her office. I have to answer it.

"Good morning, Sebring Property Development. Kathryn speaking," I say in the most professional voice I can muster.

"Kit, we have to..." Marc starts.

"I'm sorry, Mr. Sebring isn't in right now but I'll gladly put you through to his voicemail," I interrupt, and then hang up without transferring the call.

Again. The phone is ringing again. The man has no shame. This time I actually do transfer him to Mr. Sebring's voicemail.

Again. I play the wrong-number card.

Again. Arrgh. This is just getting silly. I start picking up the handset and dropping it back in its cradle immediately. By 9:30 I give up on the idea that Marc is going to tire of this game; he really isn't getting it. I call my cell phone voicemail from Sebring's second line and erase the fifteen messages that are there, all but one from Marc, and wonder if I'm going to have to change my number. I return the three calls from the Sebring voicemail that are business-related and the whole time line one is ringing. I don't want to have to call in Joyce again after yesterday but she's going to realize something is going on. There is no way she hasn't noticed the incessant ringing.

I decide to act casual; I'll just carry on business as usual.

Mr. Sebring won't be in until this afternoon so it's a perfect time to tidy up his desk. The ringing phone is very faint in Mr. Sebring's office; his phone only rings on the private line or when Joyce or I call him.

"Do you want to talk about it?" Joyce is standing at the door of Mr. Sebring's office watching me gather up the contents of the outbox.

I look up at Joyce and start to cry. I always do that. I can hold it together just fine until someone asks "Is something wrong?" or "Are you okay?" and then the dam bursts. Any show of concern and I'm a flood. Joyce walks over to me and gives me a hug. She pulls a tissue from out of nowhere and tells me to wipe my eyes.

"So what's all this then," she asks. "I'm guessing it's Marc. It was really just a matter of time until he stepped in it. I suspected something like this was coming."

"Yes, it's stupid Marc. I suppose I saw it coming as well. I knew he had a crush on me but never expected this," I manage between wiping my eyes and blowing my nose. "I liked being friends with him. I didn't think he'd cross 'that' line."

"He finally told you he's in love with you, right?" How does she know these things? I can't answer, but manage a nod.

"Did he leave his wife yet?" Joyce asks more matter-of-factly than I would expect. The word *yet* hangs in the air.

"Yet?" I almost yell, "*Is* he planning to leave his wife? He'd better not leave her for me!"

"Oh probably not. Marc's like most men — they want the best of both worlds. He probably wouldn't dare rock the boat with the wife until he had you lined up to take her place, and who knows, maybe not even then." Again Joyce is talking in matter-of-fact tones as if this sort of thing happens every day. Surely this isn't a common occurrence, is it?

Joyce puts her arm around my shoulder and says, "Oh you'll be all right. I assume from all this that you aren't interested in pursuing a relationship with Marc, then?"

"Absolutely not, and I told him as much but he keeps calling. It's driving me crazy." I have to blow my nose again but the tissue I have is incredibly soggy. Joyce magically hands me a new one.

"I know. You're a good girl. You wouldn't do anything wrong. Besides, Marc isn't the type for you, too swarthy. Why don't I take the phones for a while?" I can't help but smile. I love Joyce.

"I might have to put Marc in his place, hope you don't mind?" Joyce says more than asks over her shoulder as she heads to my desk. I don't answer because I really don't mind and I know she'll do it no matter what I say. Marc isn't hearing me, but I know he won't mess with Joyce.

I wipe my face again, thankful that all the makeup is already gone, and get down to work on Mr. Sebring's desk. Mr. Sebring is a bit of a packrat with scatter tendencies so I always feel like I've accomplished something when I can see the colour of his desk. It's a lovely medium oak with nice grain, but you can't tell that right now.

Five minutes later, I've tidied, found the desk, have the contents of the out tray in my arms and approach my desk where Joyce is on the telephone. She is speaking to whom I can only assume is Marc.

"When you're a contractor it's nice to have good contacts in the office. I can't imagine what would happen if invoices went missing. I suppose cash flow would stop and that could affect even the most stable company, couldn't it?" Joyce is positively breezy in her manner of speech. I have just heard the sweetest woman in the world threaten someone's livelihood and she did it while grinning the whole time. I thank all the angels and saints that Joyce is on my side on this one. I'm a bit afraid of her right now.

Joyce pauses while Marc says something, but she is grinning and looking at her fingernails so obviously not paying much attention to whatever he is saying in his meagre defence.

"Oh, no! Don't be silly," Joyce laughs and throws her head back, "Kathryn doesn't tell me personal things. I have no idea what you're talking about. I'm just speaking hypothetically. But it would be a shame if someone got distracted by the telephone ringing off the hook and misplaced something important like an invoice." As Joyce is talking she stands up and reaches over to the shredder and shreds a blank piece of paper. I can't say absolutely for sure, but she did seem to lean down extra far so the phone was closer to the shredder. Does Joyce have Mafia ties? This is tantamount to sending someone's finger in the mail. Sweet, lovely Joyce has reached a whole new level in my eyes. No more Mrs. Doubtfire. She's now Clint Eastwood meets Al Pacino and I've never been so impressed.

"Well then, you have a lovely day," Joyce finishes the conversation and puts the handset down.

"There," she turned to me. "I don't think Mr. Marc will be calling much more today. Oh and I didn't mean I'd lose his invoice, I probably wouldn't do that." But the grin and the gleam in her eye say otherwise. "I think this afternoon when the construction meeting is going on you should be running some errands out of the office. I'll fix it up with Mr. Sebring."

"Joyce, is your dad in the Mafia by any chance?" I ask, laughing, as I put the stack of paper down on my desk.

"Oh don't be silly, dear," Joyce says matter-of-factly while pulling my shirt down, which had slid up to reveal a quarter of an inch of skin above my waistband, "people in the Mafia don't call it the Mafia, it's just 'the business.'"

Joyce pushes my hair back over my shoulder as she walks away from my desk and I know I'll never begrudge her pulling down my shirt again. There is a lot more to her lovable Mrs. Doubtfire exterior than I ever imagined. I think I know someone affiliated with the Mob — well, at least loosely affiliated. Maybe it's going to be a good day after all.

# 8

The next few days happen despite my praying to God, Buddha and that Indian God with all the arms, even though I don't know her name, for my life to come to a very abrupt yet peaceful end. I don't want to get hit by a streetcar or anything, I can't imagine my demise being at the hands of public transit, but a Lexus hit and run would be all right — well, provided I am actually killed and not left maimed. I don't think I could *do* maimed. Every day I wake up whole and alive I cringe. My morning stops for coffee have ceased so I've had to tackle the job of figuring out the coffee maker at work. Mr. Sebring loves gadgets and our office kitchen has not been spared his gadget-loving ways. When we remodelled the office Mr. Sebring acquired an All-in-One Coffee Machine. According to the manual, which rivals a paperback copy of *War and Peace* in volume, it makes espresso, cappuccino and coffee. The machine itself is the size of a Volkswagen Bug and we had to reconfigure the cabinetry in the kitchen to make room for it. Due to the overwhelming size and complex nature of the machine, neither Joyce nor I have ever taken the time to figure the thing out. The morning after Joyce showed her Mafia tendencies I tackled the coffee machine. Joyce arrived to find me in the kitchen on my hands and knees, sleeves rolled up, wiping up the water that covers the kitchen floor while the machine itself is making awful hissing noises and spitting out more water. Joyce didn't ask, but just turned around and went out to pick up coffee that day. It wasn't until Friday of that week that Joyce and I managed to make our first pot of coffee. Unfortunately, even after our victory, Joyce had to go out for coffees because the result was mud-esk.

Later that day, after we finally beat the machine but still can't successfully make coffee, I meet up with Mel at the Firkin. I can tell when I enter the pub that Mel is in uncharacteristically nervous form; she is obviously withholding information. I assume it is work-related because I had spoken to her after lunch and she seemed a bit stressed even then. Who knows, maybe she's started smoking again, but probably not; she is still chewing gum. Heck, maybe her Prada bill finally caught up with her.

"Well, I guess I have to tell you, you'll find out anyway and it really should come from me," she starts and I smile at her drama, what could possibly be so dire? "I have a date with someone I really like and you're not going to be happy."

"What are you talking about, who could I possibly object to you dating?" Wait, she can't possibly mean, "*Marc*! Tell me it isn't Marc!"

"*No. No.* Not that bad." Mel seems a bit relieved but I'm still confused; who could she possibly be talking about.

"Grumpy Jim? Mel tell me you wouldn't date your boss, he's married *and* grumpy!"

"No," Mel is laughing now. "It's John," she finally gets out.

"John? I can't even think of anyone named John." I am relieved because if I can't place him by name then how unhappy will I be about it, right?

Just then, as if I were living in a really bad B-rated movie, the door opens and in walks John followed by Marc. John looks around and sees Mel and waves. This can't be happening. Mel means obnoxious, know-it-all, in-your-face, Charlie-Brown-shirt-wearin' John who works for Marc. My best friend forever cannot be planning to date *that* person and he is *not* bringing the person I can't get away from fast enough to our bar. *We* drink here. This is our bar. This is our version of Cheers. They really do know our names here. Whenever Mel and I went out with Marc, back before the *word* ever happened, it was always elsewhere, never here.

"You invited them *here?*" My shock is obvious and my anger immediate. "Did you know he was bringing Marc or is that just a happy, happy coincidence?" I manage to hiss before John and Marc can hear me. To her credit Mel looks almost as shocked as I am, so I know she had no part in the setup. I have gathered up my coat and purse and am standing just as Marc and John get to the table. John leans over and kisses Mel on the cheek. *Ewww.* The situation is even more absurd than I can imagine and my desire to vomit on the two of them starts to take over. I see Mel has the deer-in-the-headlights look, so I refrain from vomiting. She really does seem shocked.

"Hello, Kit," Marc says while reaching out to touch my arm. I take a step backward and glare at him. It takes all of my strength not to throw the full glass of beer I am leaving on the table at him. I continue to stare at him in my best if-looks-could-kill glare and manage to get out, "I am just leaving." I step around Marc and practically sprint to the door. My head is spinning. I step out in the dreary fall evening and right in front of the Firkin I am lucky enough to see two people getting out of a cab that's pulled over directly behind Marc's illegally parked truck. I get the driver's attention and am pulling away from what can no longer be considered "our bar" in seconds. I spot Marc and Mel stepping out the door of the Firkin as the cab pulls away. My best friend has completely lost her mind and our favourite bar has been infiltrated by the enemy — well, by a philandering, swarthy contractor, in any case. Partial coffee maker success aside, it's been another bad day.

# 9

*Arrgh.* Another morning and I'm still alive. I know I'm alive because the ringing telephone is irritating me. The call is from Mel who can't apologize enough for Charlie Brown bringing Marc to *our* Firkin. Seems Charlie Brown didn't know anything about what had transpired between Marc and me and when Marc offered to drop him at the Firkin to meet Mel, he had accepted, not knowing there would be an issue. Mel told me that Marc stayed for one beer and tried to pry information from her, but she maintains she didn't offer up anything and she was openly hostile toward him, calling him a jerk on three separate occasions and *inadvertently* kicking him in the shins with her pointy Prada boots twice. Poor John, Mel's words not mine, was most confused. It must have been impossible for Mr. Know-It-All to sit idly by while Mel and Marc went at it, not knowing what it was all about. Mel no doubt filled him in after Marc left. She didn't mention if she took Mr. Know-It-All home. I really hope she didn't. Mel dating Charlie Brown could put a whole new spin on the situation even too unbearable for Joyce to shred better.

It's early so I take the time to tame my hair. I don't have nice hair. When I moved to Toronto I found a hairdresser, well, stylist I guess, and I told him I didn't have nice hair and that I have to blowdry it straight. He laughed and said that everyone says they have bad hair. After forty-five minutes of working with my hair he announced, "No, you're right, you do have really bad hair." He did a great job with the bad hair and I respect his honesty. He is still my stylist today. I don't know what I'll do if he ever moves — move with him I suppose. I sometimes imagine how nice it would be to wake up with Mel's perfect hair every day. I do envy Mel her hair but not her taste in men; I think she has worse taste in men than I do, if that's possible.

With hair done, makeup on, a little "I am a wonderful person despite my unfortunate taste in friends" pep talk to myself and a new box of After Eights in my purse I head to the subway. I'm visualizing a good day. I will be successful today and not let the idiots in the world get me down. I get on the subway and I know instantly it is going to be a good day and the visualizing is paying off. Cute Probably-Not-a-Stockbroker Long Eyelash Guy is on the subway and I have good hair. Yes. He's standing holding the next bar because there are no seats available. Now all I have to do is not stare. Damn, I'm staring while thinking about not staring. Read the advertisements. Oops, staring again. Cute Long Eyelash Guy is wearing a dark blue suit, crisp white shirt, a really nice silver-blue tie and a trench coat. Trench coats are a bit sexy, especially when they're not done up and the belt is hanging. Add a briefcase and wow, definitely sexy. Not the briefcase, the whole package. Must stop staring. Double damn, he caught me looking. I bet he smells nice too. Okay now I'm looking at my shoes and laughing to myself. It's official. I am a lunatic. I didn't visualize being insane, yet here I am, walking a slippery slope. I might as well just embrace the bad hair and wear it big every day; all crazy people have bad hair.

"You're happy this morning." Wow! Cute Long Eyelash Guy is talking to me. Stay calm. Must reply. Must form audible coherent sentence.

"Not really," blurts out of my mouth but then I continue, "I was just thinking it would be funny if it wasn't my life." It's official. I'm completely insane and now Cute Long Eyelash Guy knows it or strongly suspects.

"I bet it's not so bad. It's funny at least, right?" Cute Long Eyelash guy is still talking to me. Maybe he's insane too!

"Good point," I laugh, "it is indeed funny. Or it will be five years from now." The subway pulls up to our stop and we both move toward the door. As the doors open Cute Long Eyelash Guy says, "Your hair looks really nice today. You can't have a bad day with great hair, it doesn't happen." Then he grins the cutest grin *ever* and walks off the subway car. I am Jell-O. Cute Long Eyelash Guy noticed my hair, so must remember my bad hair, and he still spoke to me. And that smile! Wow! Cute Long Eyelash Guy remembers me. It *is* going to be a good day. We walk to the street level together and introduce ourselves before parting ways. His name is Derek Stanford and he has already made this a great day and it's not even nine o'clock yet. I suddenly have a newfound love for public transit and more surprisingly a renewed will to live. I can officially stop jumping in front of Lexuses, or would the plural be Lexi?

My newly discovered desire *not* to be killed by a Lexus makes me thirst for good coffee. Although Joyce and I have managed to make the impossible Volkswagen-sized coffee maker actually work, we have yet to make *good* coffee. We are getting close but what we make always tastes a bit like mud or how I imagine mud tastes. I'm starting to think the *does everything* coffee maker is more for show than for actually doing *anything*.

Throwing caution to the wind, where Marc is concerned, I decide to get coffee at the coffee shop; who knows, maybe Marc has tired of lurking there. I'm humming as I enter the coffee shop, no Marc in sight and the counter staff seem very pleased to see me. Jeannie seems very genuine when she says, "We've missed you! Where have you been?"

"My boss got us a new coffee maker," I laugh. "I felt I had to give it a try. But since I'm back you can guess how well that went!" Jeannie and I are making small talk when Marc does walk up behind me. I knew it was too good to be true, but am feeling invincible with my good hair and compliment from Derek Stanford, how cute is that name? I bet there's a number after it. I can do this; I can be civil to the philanderer.

"I thought you gave up coffee?" Marc asks.

"It wasn't working for me," I manage without any expletives, although I did think "you philandering bastard" in my head at the end of the sentence.

"Are we speaking again?"

"Only so much as I have to speak to you. I still think you're a complete idiot who ruined a perfectly good friendship for nothing." Damn, I was doing well until *idiot* slipped out. Oh well, what's one little backslide?

"Thanks, Jeannie," I say over the counter as I gather my purse and coffee and start toward the door.

"Can I ask you something?" Marc didn't order any coffee and is following me as I walk toward the office. Think happy thoughts.

"As long as it's not to accompany you anywhere, shoot." What the hell, I'm in a good mood and we have to speak at some point.

Long pause. Marc is speechless. I guess he was going to ask me to go somewhere with him. This is too funny. Marc is still trying to figure out how to ask me what he wanted to ask when we arrive at the Sebring building. I have my pass card out already and swipe the pad, open the door and say, "Well, have a great day then," and enter the safety of the lobby. I've never seen Marc speechless before. I was civil, I didn't have any breakdowns and I managed to make Marc uncomfortable. I think this is a victory, a very small one, but I'll take it.

# 10

Later that same afternoon, Mel asks, "So what do you think? Almost as great as talking to Cute Long Eyelash Guy and rendering Marc speechless in one day?"

Mel is excited and with good reason. She has maintained for ages that we have to get into the housing market, which is actually one of the reasons she became a realtor, and today she's showing me the house she wants us to buy as co-owners.

"It needs some work for sure, but the market is only going up and this is a good neighbourhood — not like the seedy one you currently live in. We'll make our money back plus some." Mel is right into the sales pitch and not drawing breath. "It's not attached so that's great for resale and it has a decent-sized yard and parking — all huge pluses for Toronto. There's no second bath but we can figure out something about that I'm sure. I can borrow from my parents and you have your inheritance from your grandfather that you've been sitting on for two years. You really should make your money work for…"

"Stop. Enough already, I'm sold. I'm in. I'm having a great day. I spoke to Cute Long Eyelash Guy so let's buy a house, fix it up and make oodles of money," I cut Mel off and laugh.

"But we'll need to set boyfriend boundaries. I don't want Charlie Brown here every night." Despite Mel's insistence on dating Charlie Brown, I have yet to grow any fonder of him and am starting to develop a phobia for all things striped.

"Don't call him that!" Mel laughs. "I almost called him that the other day. You're going to get me in trouble. Besides, you'll sing a different tune once Derek Stanford wants to hang out all the time." Mel says "Derek Stanford" in the singsongy playground voice from grade three.

"Fine, but I won't like it." I'm talking to the top of Mel's head as she is bent digging into her briefcase; and I have to be honest, who knew Prada even made briefcases? How many cows can one woman, who I know has never seen a cow up close, be surrounded by at one time?

Mel stands up with an offer to purchase and a bottle of champagne in one hand and two acrylic champagne flutes in the other. She is nothing if not prepared and in the "Bible According to Mel" you have to have the proper glass for the proper drink. She prefers glass glasses, but in this case acrylic is the more sensible choice. There will be no Dixie cups for Mel Melrose's champagne.

"Wow, you came prepared. What if I'd said no?" I say, in part fascination, part knowledge that Mel has never not gotten what she wanted.

"Oh, I was just getting started. I have the whole pitch ready, we're just getting to the champagne sooner than I expected. You were actually a pretty easy sell. I wish all my clients were so easy," Mel laughs as she uncorks the champagne with a loud pop.

"I may be easy, but I'm not cheap. Isn't the champagne a bit premature? We don't actually have the house yet." I'm new to this house game but I know the sellers have to agree to the offer.

"It isn't even officially on the market until tomorrow afternoon. I'll go in with an offer before it's listed, then the house is all but ours. Besides, getting you to agree to buy was the hard part; if not this house, there'll be another one soon enough." I love Mel's confidence and her new boots — yet another pair. Yes, I mock her but she does have great shoes and boots. Curses to my size-six feet. If only Mel and I were the same size, I could give my feet the occasional treat of expensive footwear — especially when all that Prada will be in the same house.

"You're staring at my boots, is there a mark on them?" Mel picks up her foot and starts looking at her boot.

"No, they're fine. I was wondering if there'll be room for me and all the Pradas in this little house. Are you going to have to rent a storage unit for the footwear?" I ask straightfaced. I'm not feeling one hundred percent normal but am starting to show signs of normalcy with my sardonic wit returning.

"Don't be a smart ass!" We clunk acrylic glasses of champagne and start planning a colour scheme for our almost new house.

The next day at work I realize how much I love my office.

It's just been freshly updated, the stone-tiled lobby is littered with expensive, exquisite-looking furniture with great clean lines and all our computers are the latest iMacs, which, aside from being the best on the market, are very compact and tidy. My desk is very neat. The office makes me happy — well, mostly. Sometimes when the filing pile is taller than I am I get a bit flustered; but since I'm on top of the filing I love the office today. I turn on lights and computers and bring the office to life, even turning on the stereo before the workday officially begins. I start the day by clearing off Mr. Sebring's desk. He worked late last night so there is dictation, new assignments and of course more filing overflowing his out tray. Mr. Sebring's office has floor-to-ceiling windows and amazing light; it's a great place to start the day.

The phone is ringing as I get back to my desk; caller ID tells me that it's Marc. Luckily I'm still riding the high of talking to Derek Cute Long Eyelash Guy yesterday — who sadly wasn't on the subway this morning — and being a property owner. Mel firmed up the offer this morning at 8:00 a.m.; Mel's efficiency is staggering. I throw caution to the wind and pick up the receiver.

"You remembered what you wanted to ask me yesterday," I quip. I have completely given up on telephone niceties when Marc calls the office.

"I know you don't want to go out with me, but could you meet me at the hockey game on Saturday night?" Marc manages but sounds flustered.

"No. Meeting you is the same as accompanying you." I'm not as stressed as I would have been a week ago, but this conversation is still awkward.

"It would mean a lot to me if you'd come to the game. I really miss seeing you, besides you love hockey." Marc sounds sincere, but I'm still not inclined to accept his proposal.

"Marc, you're married. I'm not. You have a whole life that doesn't involve me. I could justify hanging out with you when I thought we were both on the same 'beer-drinking-friend' page but not now. Apparently, I shouldn't have attended the first game because you read more into it than I ever intended and now I'm having a conversation I never intended," I state calmly and remarkably feel the same calm.

"This isn't about hockey games. I've been crazy about you since the first time I saw you. You were in the elevator in your grey suit. I think of you all the time. You're the first person I think about when I wake up in the morning and the last person I think about at the end of the day. I've never felt the way I feel about you with anyone. Good Lord, I feel like a fifteen-year-old kid again. I can't eat. I hardly sleep. I feel like I'm going crazy. If I don't talk to you for a day I get completely agitated and have to drive by your building hoping to get a glimpse of you. Please just come to the game with me. I'll be a complete gentleman. I promise," Marc pleads desperately. I feel awful for him but not bad enough to sacrifice my morals.

"Marc, I can't go with you. You have to see that. What if I go to the game? Then what? You'll get over this whole thing and we can go back to being friends? It doesn't work that way. I go to the game, and then next week it's another game or something else. That's not fair to you and it's certainly not fair to your wife. I've never thought of you as anything but a friend because I can't and you can't either. This 'thing,' whatever it is, has to end now."

"Don't you think I've tried to make it end?" Marc sounds terrible. "Do you think I like this? I'm practically a stalker. I know I'm no fun anymore. All my buddies are confused. My wife keeps asking me if we're going bankrupt because I'm so moody at home. I'm constantly yelling at the guys at work so they all hate me. I don't like feeling this way. I don't like being in love with you when I know we can't be together, but it doesn't change the fact that I do love you and I can't live without you."

"But you do live without me every day. We've never been together. If I ever gave you the impression I wanted more, I sincerely apologize. I really just wanted to be friends and I never thought of you as anything more. Really I didn't and I can't." I truly did just treat Marc like I treat Mel or any of my other friends. I just acted normal and nice. Maybe it's the nice part I should eliminate, but that will be difficult because generally I'm nice so my normal includes nice. I should get some pointers from Charlie Brown on being abrasive. I bet abrasive women don't have discussions like this one.

"What if I were single, if I left my wife?" Marc's desperation is becoming more apparent and I don't think he's in a good state to be making such an impulsive decision.

"Marc, you aren't single. Please don't do anything rash. Ask yourself if you would have left your marriage if you hadn't met me. You know the answer is no. We both know the answer is no. You were perfectly happy in your life before you started working for Sebring. Why would you give that up?" Trying to speak logically to Marc seems futile but I'm grabbing at anything right now. I can't be responsible for a marriage ending. I've been so busy trying to avoid him and wondering where I gave the wrong impression that the question of whether or not I'd actually date Marc, if he were single, has never crossed my mind. Deciding what I want isn't something I do well and making spur-of-the-moment decisions is definitely not my forte. I've been shopping for the perfect low-rise jeans for six months. I've tried on every pair by every manufacturer in the Greater Toronto Area and to no avail; my jeans are all quickly becoming unfashionably high-waisted. I'm not good at knowing what I want but I know instinctively what I don't want. I do not want to be responsible for a marriage breakup especially when I'm not 110 percent positive I want to spend my life with the person doing the breaking up.

"Besides," I continue, with a small degree of confidence, "I've never been in a relationship that lasted. I'd probably end up breaking your heart and then where would we be?" I try to make light of the situation while telling Marc nicely not to count on me.

"You don't have to love me back. I love you enough for both of us." Marc's sincerity is pulling at heartstrings I didn't even know I had. I'm not callous or anything, I'd just never had someone speak so honestly and sincerely to me before. The most heartfelt thing Boob Man ever said to me was, "Your boobs look great in that sweater; you should wear it more often" which I had accepted as a declaration of his undying love and devotion at the time. This is new territory for me. Tears are welling up. I know I have to end this conversation soon or I may do something I'll regret.

"I have to go. This is getting us nowhere." I put the phone down before Marc can say anything else. I flop down in my chair. I always have serious conversations while standing, preferably pacing, but in this case I don't have a portable phone or headset, and start to cry. Isn't it always the way, someone you don't love loves you with all their heart and the person you do love, or thought you loved at any rate, only thinks you have magnificent mammary glands. It is a funny old world.

# 11

I see Marc's truck outside my apartment building before I see him sitting on the wall of the planter by the entrance door. I worked later than I had planned; I just lost track of time, so I have no idea how long he's been outside my building.

"Been stalking long?" I ask, walking up to him.

"Not too long, about twenty minutes or so," Marc smiles but he looks terrible. He's obviously lost weight, he hasn't shaved in several days and he has bags under his eyes. "I can stalk longer if you have errands to run or anything."

"Isn't stalking a crime? And didn't your mother warn you to dress properly when stalking in January?" I lean against the wall beside him and fall easily back into conversation as if with an old friend. "It's been quite a ride. How are you doing?" I ask seriously. I am worried. Marc looks really sad.

"I just found out this morning the person I love most in the world doesn't love me back but I lived through the day, so yeah, I guess I'm doing okay." I know he means what he's saying and the sorrow in his voice is breaking my heart. "I'd rather be your friend than never see you again. I couldn't live with that."

"You must be frozen. Can I buy a friend a coffee? Or better, a beer?" I ask sincerely, trying to make him feel better even though I know it won't work. I know we could get into the whole discussion again but what would be the point. We both know where the other stands on the issue and the only thing that will mend a broken heart is time. There is no speedy recovery from something like this.

"I'd like that. Beer, I think. I could use a friend about now." I can tell he means it.

"Okay, to the pub!" I shout as Marc jumps down off the planter wall and we start to walk toward the pub around the corner. "You shouldn't sit on concrete in the cold, you'll get hemorrhoids. Didn't your mother give you any advice before she sent you out into the world?"

"She told me to always put on clean underwear," Marc smiles and punches me in the arm.

"Well, that is good advice. You look like hell by the way." I rub my newly bruised arm.

"Yeah, I'm getting that a lot lately," he laughs, "but I think I might keep the beard, what do you think?" I didn't realize how much I missed our fun banter until just now.

"I think you look like the Unabomber." We walk around the corner to the pub, chatting like old friends who didn't just have the weirdest couple of weeks ever. For all the drama that has transpired I suddenly feel that Marc and I have come full circle and are back where we started.

I find out from Marc, now that we're friends again, that Charlie Brown really does like Mel a lot, and he mentioned "*that* word" actually. In light of this information I have decided to cut Mel and Charlie Brown some slack. Some. I'm not going to completely stop bugging her and I think the nickname Charlie Brown is too perfect to lose, but I have decided to at least stop sneering at him when I'm in his presence. I may even ease up on the open hostility. Honestly, the things we do for friends. Visualizing having a civil conversation with Charlie Brown is not easy. I tried all the way to the subway and while I waited for the train, but every time Charlie Brown opens his mouth in my visualization I see my hands reaching out to grab him around the neck, then I'm squeezing and shaking him and screaming "Why can't you wear a t-shirt that is all one colour?" No. This is not productive visualizing. Oh, it brings a smile to my face sure, but it is not helping me achieve the kinder, gentler attitude I'm working toward.

I step on the train and no Derek Stanford. I haven't seen him in a week. I hope he's not avoiding me. As much as I'm sure I have the ability to repulse men, I hope he's not avoiding me only after one brief conversation. Maybe it's the hair; he may have issues with women with high-maintenance hair. He wouldn't be the first man who ran screaming from my hair. Or maybe a Lexus struck him down. It happens.

Visualize. I'm nice to Charlie Brown. Not working, I'm still strangling Charlie Brown. I feel the furrow of my brow and reach up to flatten it. Must relax forehead. Oh God, what if Mel stays with this character for any length of time. Surely I'll develop an ulcer. Visualize. Good thoughts.

Imagine the good things Charlie Brown must do. Marc says he is a tolerable employee. His work is excellent when he's assigned individual tasks but he has difficulty working with others, shocker there. Maybe he volunteers at the food bank, or helps to raise money for the homeless. Maybe there is a good side to Charlie Brown that I don't know. I shall endeavour to discover the goodness in Charlie Brown. My brow is still furrowed but I think I'm making headway. I can embrace Charlie Brown. Not in the physical way, *ewww*, more in the theoretical way, and it seems I'll get my chance sooner than I'd hoped.

"What are you doing on Sunday?" Mel asked me last night on the phone. I had called her to give her the update on Marc.

"It's Super Bowl Sunday! I'm doing what I do every Super Bowl Sunday, watching the Super Bowl," I laugh. Mel would never know when Super Bowl airs; her dislike of football is rivalled only by her dislike of hockey. Well, in truth, Mel has issues with most sporting activities. I did manage to get her to watch some of the luge competition during the last Winter Olympics. I think she has a healthy respect for the luge now, but that's pretty much where her sporting enthusiasm ends.

"Of course you're watching the Super Bowl. I wanted to know if you'd like to watch it with me?" Mel sounds serious and I almost spit the water I've just started to swallow.

"You what? Who the heck are *you* and what have you done with my friend Mel?" It is apparent to me that aliens have landed and abducted my friend Mel and replaced her with a clone, but a bad clone because the real Mel Melrose would not be caught dead dedicating an entire Sunday to a sporting event.

"No, seriously. I'm going to the sports bar near John's with him and his friends to watch the Super Bowl and I'd love it if you came along. You know, moral support." Mel is serious. Seriously insane, I decide immediately.

"Excuse me? You told Charlie Brown you like football? What were you thinking? You hate football. You hate all things that involve sweat. You don't even run for the streetcar! Surely even Charlie Brown can see through this one!" I am absolutely shocked that Mel believes she can pull this one off. Everyone who knows her knows she doesn't do sporting events. By some freak of nature, Mel is able to maintain a perfect size-four figure without even knowing gyms and public swimming pools exist. I used to suspect she didn't eat, unless in public, but I've seen her plow through a cheeseburger and, given the opportunity, she would happily sit down to an entire side of beef. Her metabolism must rival that of an Olympic athlete — there's a healthy dose of irony for you.

"No. Stop calling him that! I didn't pretend. He knows I don't run for streetcars. I just told him it's because of the heels. Okay, maybe I fibbed a little bit. But I really like him and I think me watching that silly game with him means a lot to him."

"Okay, start from the beginning. How did you get yourself into this? I really have to hear what transpired to get Mel to give up house selling to attend a televised sporting event, not even the real thing.

"I know it's bad but I lied and told him I like football and I can't get through this without you. I need you to come and be my moral support. I really, really like him. I like him enough to spend a Sunday at a bar with a bunch of jocks. Please!" Mel's desperation is most amusing. I know I'm going to end up going to the bar with Mel and Charlie Brown and that it's wrong to revel in her predicament but she rarely asks for help with anything so I'm going to revel a little.

"Mel, I love the Super Bowl. Asking me to watch it with Charlie Brown will be like poking my own eyes out. You can't seriously think you're going to pull this off? Do you even know who's playing?" I ask, knowing full well that she has no clue.

"Well, that's where you come in, how hard can it be? We can meet up tomorrow after work and you can tell me how the whole football thingy works. What could be easier? Who is playing anyway?"

"I'm poking my eyes out here, Mel. Do you care?"

"No you're not. It'll be fun."

"It's Pittsburgh and Seattle; the Steelers are favoured to win." I can't believe I'm telling Mel who's in the Super Bowl.

"Wait, Pittsburgh and Seattle. Okay. But who are the Steelers? Are there more than two teams?" Mel asks seriously.

It's going to be a long week getting Mel up to speed on this whole football "thingy."

"Mel, you're killing me! And you're going to owe me huge for this one!" I moan. She is a brilliant woman. How did she go her whole life without absorbing even one tidbit of sporting knowledge or trivia? Fascinating.

"Didn't I find the perfect house for us? Getting me up to speed on football is the least you can do," Mel says in her best mother singsongy voice.

Least I can do? Mel has no idea. I'm wondering if there is a *Football for Dummies* I can pick up for Mel as I surface from the subway into a sunny day. It's a chilly −4°C, but that's above average for January in Toronto.

"Kathryn Jennings." I hear my name and turn to see Cute Long Eyelash Guy Derek Stanford is calling me.

"Good morning." I can tell I'm blushing and am thankful for the subzero temperature, "I thought you might have left the country."

"I did actually, I was in New York. Our firm has an office there. It was crazy busy but I'm back now and I wanted to catch you on your way to work." I know I'm smiling too much as he talks to me.

"Well, you caught me, what can I do for you?"

"I was wondering if you'd like to have dinner with me tomorrow night?" Derek asks tentatively.

"Absolutely! I'd love to," I gush, probably a little over the top, but I don't care. I have a date with Derek Cute Long

Eyelash Guy. We exchange business cards and agree on time and place and part ways to our respective offices. I'm completely on cloud nine when I get to the office. Nothing will ruin my day, not even knowing that I'm going to have to spend a large portion of the evening coaching Mel on the basics of football, which I suspect will be a lot like teaching my mother how to set the clock on the VCR.

# 12

"No. The offence for the team that has the ball is on the field at the same time as the defence for the defending team. The offence tries to get past the other team's defence to get to the end zone." I am exhausted. Mel's brain does not *get* football it would seem.

"In hockey everyone is on the ice, so why aren't both the offence and the defence on the field?" Mel is sincere but if we can't get past who is on the field then I don't think we'll ever get through onside kickoffs.

"Because they're not playing hockey. They're playing football and that's just the way they play the game. Why couldn't Charlie Brown like tennis? You *get* tennis, don't you?" I'm looking for a ray of hope that Mel has some brain cells that can think sporty.

"No, not really, the scoring is a mess in tennis, and honestly Kit, you saw me in high school phys-ed, I wasn't exactly Maria Whoever-tilova." To her credit, Mel is both serious and correct; she was dismal at the physical education portion of our schooling. I go back to the pad of paper on the table in front of us.

"Okay, the offence has to try to get the ball from where

they start, the line of scrimmage, to the other team's end zone. In order to get the ball there the quarterback can either throw the ball to a player who is ahead or pass it off and have a player carry it." I hope this is sinking in but suspect by the vacant look in Mel's eyes that it is not even remotely getting through. I continue, "The offence gets four chances, or 'downs,' to attempt to move the ball forward ten yards. If they manage to get ten yards, then they get four more chances to go another ten yards, and so on."

"So how does the other team get the ball? Surely it's not that hard to move the ball ten yards?" Mel is asking a quality question. This is a good sign.

"It's actually not that easy, the defence for the other team is full of big, burley, mean men who try to stop that from happening. But if the defence can't stop them and the offence runs the ball all the way to the end zone they get a touchdown, *then* they have to *give* the ball to the other team so they can have a turn." I'm starting to get a bit excited; maybe Mel isn't hopeless.

"So, what's a touchdown again?" Mel asks, dashing all my hopes.

"A touchdown is when a team scores and the player who gets the touchdown does a little dance in the end zone. It's the equivalent to a goal in hockey." I can do this; surely some of this is sinking in.

"So, a touchdown is one point?" I give her credit for trying.

"No, a touchdown is worth six points and once the team

gets a touchdown they get to kick a field goal and if the ball goes though the upright poles they get an additional point, so seven in total," I explain, knowing the scoring is a bit confusing.

"Why is it seven? Wouldn't one make just as much sense?" This time Mel is asking a question we've probably all asked. Honestly, the whole six points plus one is strange.

"I guess to make it different from European football," I answer and it could be true.

"Well, how do the Europeans score football?" Mel is looking a bit pale now and has a deeply furrowed brow.

"European football is the same as our soccer, so one point per goal." The statement is out of my mouth before I can stop myself. Mel is not going to like the football/soccer mix-up. If she can't understand a touchdown, she's never going to understand how two completely different sports have the same name.

"*Arrgh!*" Mel throws her forehead onto the table and moans. "I'm not going to get this before Sunday!"

"You know what, it really is easier if I can explain it to you while there's a game being played and the players are wearing different-coloured uniforms. Why don't I explain it while the game's on?" I pat Mel's shoulder.

"John thinks I understand football. He's going to wonder why you're explaining everything."

"No, you said you *liked* it, you didn't say you understood it, did you?" I see an out if Mel didn't get herself in too deep.

"No, I just said I liked it," Mel lifts her head and perks up a little bit. She can see where I'm going with this line of thinking.

"We stand firm on the fact you *like* it but we casually mention that you're still learning the finer points of the game. Who knows, maybe Charlie Brown will be able to explain it better to you than I can and you two can really bond." I see the rest of the evenings this week magically freeing up.

"Do you think it'll work?" Mel looks more relaxed than she has since we sat down to talk football.

"Absolutely, most women don't understand football by choice. At least you're making an effort to understand something he likes. I think that'll go a long way." I don't add that she'll probably never really get it anyway. I think some things should just remain unspoken.

"That's a good point. At least I'm trying, right? Oh speaking of *trying*, have you heard from your mother lately?" Mel asks, changing the subject completely.

"Yeah, she's called a couple of times and has hinted that she wants to help us decorate the new house. I hear the hinting but I'm not letting on or giving her an inch. Why?"

"Oh that explains it. I got an envelope from my mother today that contains godawful paint chips and a stickie that says 'PEACH. I'm thinking peach!' I guess she means for our house, I thought she'd finally lost her mind completely," Mel laughs.

I arrive home that evening, defeated in my attempt to give Mel a modicum of understanding of American football but thankful that we hadn't delved into the differences between American and Canadian football. She's definitely not ready for that sort of confusion.

# 13

Goosebumps. That's the best way to describe my first date with Derek. He is absolutely perfect, charming and handsome. We meet at the restaurant. He'd made reservations and he is wearing tan khakis and a blue sweater. I am wearing a brand-new outfit, purchased on my lunch break, despite Mel's objection and argument that I have plenty of great clothes Derek has never seen. He is worth a new outfit. I don't want to wear something on my first date with Derek that I've worn before. That just doesn't seem right. The end result is a little black skirt, new tall black boots (not Prada) and a little white Liz Claiborne charmeuse silk blouse with a wide black leather belt.

Derek's hair is a little bit dishevelled from the wind but in a good way, and his eyes are more sparkly blue than I remembered and framed exquisitely by his superlong any-girl-would-kill-for eyelashes. As we are being seated, he puts his hand on my back and lets me walk in front. Goosebumps. Such a gentleman. He says I look beautiful, more goosebumps. He orders wine, a kind I'd never heard of but it is excellent. The food is perfect and conversation is easy. Derek is an investment banker, so not far off from a stockbroker and his office building is on the same street as the Sebring building. He graduated from university and went straight into banking. He travels occasionally for work but mostly works out of the Toronto office. The most amusing part of his workday is his rotating assistant. He is fairly new to this firm and therefore gets the "leftover" assistants, or the ones whom no one else likes. He's been with the firm for eight months and his longest-lasting assistant stayed six weeks, but she seemed good at her job and got snapped up by one of the senior bankers. He's currently on day four with Bianca; he doesn't think she'll last long, but not because she's getting "snapped up." Seems Bianca can't work the fax machine and faxes everything upside down so the intended recipient gets blank pages.

Derek was born and raised here in the city and went to private school. He is an only child and his retired parents travel all over the continent in their new RV. He loves sports, mostly football and hockey, and the amazing, most goosebumpy part, is that he runs. I've never dated anyone who ran but always imagined my life with a partner who would actually don running shoes and run beside me smiling and chatting like you see in television commercials. I just think it would be so cool to be one of those couples. Sure, Rob-the-bike-courier was fit, but that was his job. He took the occasional spin around the skateboard park but showed little interest in exercise outside of those two things (his apparent interest in having sex with women other than me aside). At least his infidelity proved he wasn't a complete slug.

After dinner, Derek walks me outside. We have decided to call it a night because it is late on a school night. Not wanting the evening to end, I'm not exactly proactive at hailing a cab and several go by as we continue to chat and laugh. I hadn't driven Nasty for two reasons. Firstly, I suspected I would have a drink with dinner and secondly, I don't like to introduce Nasty to potential boyfriends too early in the relationship. I fear that one look at her metallic blue sheen and blinding pink decal could scare many a potential suitor. Best they get to know me first and then meet Nasty later. Sadly, the cold temperature and wind of Canadian January start to make it impossible to linger much longer and Derek reaches out and bundles me up in his arms and gives me the most amazing bear hug ever. Suddenly the January wind doesn't seem nearly so chilly and in my invincibility I feel that I can stay here all night being wrapped in his arms. I stop breathing as he leans down to kiss me. Wow. I am shocked with a bolt of electricity that surges through me from my lips all the way down to my toes. Now I'm really not afraid of the cold any longer and want to throw off my clothes and get naked with Derek right there on the snowy sidewalk, even though all good dating etiquette books insist this is not appropriate behaviour for young ladies to engage in, especially on the first date. We smooch for some time but the weather and good judgment finally force us to say goodnight for real and concentrate on hailing our respective cabs.

The coffee shop is hopping the next morning but I hardly

notice because I'm still riding the high of my date last night. I practically trip over Marc without noticing it's him.

"Hey, I haven't seen you here in a while," I smile, probably too much, but I can't help it after last evening with Derek.

"I was hoping to see you. I need to pick up a set of drawings for the new building."

"You're going to bid on Sebring III?" I am surprised. The call for tenders went out last week and Marc had not picked up a package or even mentioned it when I'd seen him so I just assumed that he was going to pass on the project. I also assumed it was, in part, to distance himself from the company that I worked for, in light of the confession of love and the non-reciprocation issue.

"Yes, actually I am." Marc seems more confident now that he's told me he intends to bid.

"Do you think it's a good idea?" I'm hoping he'll know what I mean without me having to say "that we continue working together after all that's transpired."

"I think it'll be fine. We're friends again and I like working for Sebring." He seems to have put some thought into the idea of continuing to work for Sebring. I just hope he's okay with the idea of me dating "other" people. Even if Derek and I don't work out, the average project takes about two years to finish. That's a long time to work together if things get awkward. I think Marc is okay with not dating me so long as I'm not dating anyone, I don't know for sure that he will be quite so friendly once he finds out about Derek.

"Okay. Well, walk to the office with me and I'll get you a package." I have to provide the package, that is my job after all; but a part of me is very apprehensive about the thought of working with Marc for another two years. The walk to the office is pleasant. Marc catches me up on Barry the rabbit — seems he escaped and was located hiding behind the furnace. After unlocking the door, turning off the alarm, turning on the lights and hanging my jacket up I leave Marc in the foyer to go the War Room to get a copy of the tender package for him. The War Room really isn't a place where we plan wars, but is the catch-all room where piles of plans, addenda, samples and pretty much everything that doesn't have a proper place ends up, so it looks as though a war happened here and could possibly still be waging under the piles. It is impossible to keep this room neat and the disorganization of it all makes me a bit antsy whenever I have to spend extended periods of time here. I manage to locate all the plans and addenda in record time and am quite pleased with my accomplishment so early in the morning.

"Ta da!" I shout triumphantly as I come back to the foyer. "One tender package ready to go." Anyone who doesn't actually have to maneuver in the War Room has no idea of the magnitude of my accomplishment, but I will not deny myself the small victory. Marc, however, doesn't look pleased with the package. He takes it from me while assessing my suit up and down with the critical eye of a designer or high-end tailor.

"You're dating someone, aren't you?" He sounds hurt and dejected.

"What? What are you talking about?" I ask nervously as I pull the lapels of my jacket tighter across my chest to cover my blouse.

"That's your Vera Wang blouse. You haven't worn that blouse since you started dating Rob-the-bike-courier — that's your special occasion blouse." Marc still looks hurt but appears to be getting a bit angry as well.

"What are you talking about? I wear this more than just when I date. You don't see me every day!" I am both surprised and shocked that Marc has paid such close attention to my wardrobe and of the accuracy of his statement. This is my "I'm infatuated" blouse. How can he possibly know that? I've never even told Mel I have occasion clothing. It's a weird personal thing that I don't think I would even share with a therapist.

"You only wear that blouse when you're seeing someone. I know that because I love you enough to pay attention to things like that. So, are you dating someone?" Marc is officially angry now.

"Well, since you must know, yes, I went on a date last night and it went well. Are we officially seeing each other? No. Are we seeing each other again? Yes." I can't lie and know that telling Marc is the best thing, but if I had to decide whether to tell him or not, without him figuring it out, I might have decided to withhold the information for a while longer. Judging by the hurt look in his eyes I would have made the right decision. No one wants to hear that the person you care about is seeing someone else, especially so soon after your admission of love. I feel terrible, like I just accidentally kicked a puppy or dropped a friend's baby. I immediately wish I'd had the good sense to lie, but I know he would have seen right through me. He knows about the special occasion clothes, he would have known I was lying.

Marc doesn't say anything more. He just gives me that hurt it-would-have-been-better-if-you-shot-me-in-the-stomach look, turns around, walks out the door and slams it behind him.

Oh man! That didn't go very well. I look down at my blouse and say, "Damn you, Vera Wang, with your exquisite silk, classic fit and really cool collars."

# 14

I manage to get through the day without hurting anyone else's feelings or kicking any puppies. I am also able to fight off the overwhelming desire to vomit every time I think about the look on Marc's face. I think I'm making real headway with the stress vomit reaction. It probably helped that Derek and I emailed each other about a thousand times during the day. I know I didn't get much work done and suspect that Derek's company wasn't too impressed with his production either. I called Mel to tell her what happened with Marc and she wasn't nearly as sympathetic to his feeling as I was. She summarized her feelings in the statement "He just has to suck it up," which she made twenty-six times over the course of the telephone call. She also brought up the fact that he's married and has no business feeling anything about what I do or don't do. As much as I know she makes valid points, it is still difficult to know that I'm hurting someone. I did suggest to her that telling someone who looks at you like you just kicked them in the stomach, to "just suck it up," really isn't a good way to make friends and influence people. Mel did laugh at that point and conceded that maybe I'd handled this situation better than she would have. The rest of the conversation was pretty much dominated by which boots Mel should wear to the Super Bowl outing. She settled on tall black Prada, which took a bit of cunning on my part as she had her heart set on the bright pink ones, which I think would be wasted on the average football enthusiast.

I meet Derek at the bookstore after work and we walk around for hours, discussing books we've read, travel destinations we want to go to (while we are in the travel section, obviously) and our favourite authors. Derek compliments my hair and my blouse. Good work, Vera! We part ways with a lovely kiss, but not before Derek asks me what I am doing for Super Bowl. I explain the Mel situation to Derek and tell him that I really can't let her down on this one. Derek thinks it is nice that I am helping Mel and asks if it will be okay if he and his friends end up at the same sports bar. He even suggests that maybe he can help give Mel a few pointers on the game as well. So it is decided and I am over the moon. I'll have Derek with me and Mel won't feel abandoned in her time of need. I can't wait for Sunday.

The rest of the week flies by. Emails with Derek seem to increase daily and I'm sure if there is an award for most emails sent in a day (when we're suppose to be working) we'd definitely be in the running. I didn't see or hear from Marc; he delivers his quote for the new project to Joyce when I am at lunch, which I'm sure was planned to avoid seeing me. I am surprised that he even submitted a quote after the Vera Wang incident. I can only hope that he priced the job too high and some other contractor will be awarded the contract. When I'm not working-slash-emailing Derek, running on the treadmill or packing the contents of my apartment (the house deal closes three days after the Super Bowl), I'm having marathon telephone conversations with Derek. Conversation with Derek comes naturally and I've discovered that he is funny and sensitive and all the things you'd want in a partner. I can't wait for the weather to improve so we can start running outside together and get off our respective treadmills. I don't see Derek at the gym because he is a member at a different one. Gym fees being what they are, it is not at all feasible to go changing gyms just to be near a newfound romantic interest.

I try to time my morning subway trips to coincide with Derek's but that rarely happens because if you're even one minute behind schedule you're waiting for the next train. My hair and the whole taming process makes down-to-the-minute timing nearly impossible. We do try to meet up in the evenings when our schedules allow but that doesn't happen as often as I'd like. If the work needs to get done Derek and I are both the type who will stay and do it so there is no proper quitting-time. The only people who seem to adhere to any quitting-time schedule at all are the Train People. I call them the Train People because they ride downtown from the suburbs on the GO Train every day and their lives revolve around the train schedule. It is fascinating when it's not annoying. I've had several friends who started off as normal, partygoing downtown dwellers but who hooked up with significant others and immediately migrated to the suburbs to join the Cult of the Train People. On the rare occasion when you can coerce a Train Person into actually agreeing to stay late after work and meet up for a beer, the visit is always nerve-racking and irritating to the point that you want to tell them to "just go already." The Train People are so afraid of missing their train and having to wait for the next one that they spend the entire time they are supposed to be socializing and having fun doing the time check, which occurs about every twenty-two seconds. You're having a chat about little Billy's braces, the state of the world economy or your latest romance and the whole time the Train Person is wrist twisting and doing mental time calculations while feigning mild interest in the conversation. More often than not you can throw in a statement like "I think Jimmy Hoffa's at the next table" while the Train Person is doing mental time calculations and get the response "Yeah, me too." Okay, it's a little bit cruel, but it can be very amusing. The only thing more annoying than socializing with a Train Person is socializing with more than one Train Person, and God help you if they are travelling in different directions. The waitress comes by to see if you'd like another round of beverages and the panic begins. The downtown dwellers all order up, they're going home via streetcar or subway so they can just sit back and watch the show.

Train Person #1: "Hmm, let me see, I have to catch the

6:11," looks at his watch, sizes up the amount of beer still remaining in his glass, moves forward to the edge of his seat like he might jump up and sprint out the door at any second, checks his watch again, taps on the table while he calculates the time to walk from the bar to the train station, turns to Train Person #2, who is behaving in the exact same fashion, and continues, "What are you going to do?"

Train Person #2: "What time have you got?" resorting to the synchronized time check in order to put off making the call.

Train Person #1: "I've got 5:23" and you know that his timepiece is calibrated daily to match the exact second of the train station clock.

Train Person #2: "Yep, that's right, mine is one minute fast and I've got 5:24 and since I'm catching the 6:17 eastbound I've got a little more time. Yep. I think I can do it, I'll have another beer." The pressure is now completely on Train Person #1. His choices are bleak. He gets up now and is officially the first one to leave or he stays for another beer and runs the risk of missing his train and having to wait for the 7:11. Tough call. The downtown people start to get fidgety and move in their seats; in the time it's taken for the Train People to decide what they are doing, another round could have been delivered by the poor waitress subjected to their antics.

Train Person #1: "Nope, sorry guys (often the Train Person will bang the table at this point). Can't do it." He then looks at the waitress and says, "Just my bill, please. I have a train to catch." The Train Person always looks a bit defeated at this point and adds the train comment in order to imply, "I used to be more cool than this, but the train dictates my life now."

The collective sigh is audible. The thoughts running through the heads of the downtown dwellers are all similar to "Yay, one down, one to go," "Who invited the Train People anyway? They are so annoying" and "What happened to Train Person #1? He used to be so much fun." After Train Person #1 pays for his unfinished beer and sprints from the table, the downtown dwellers know they only have to endure the arm-twisting solo performance of Train Person #2 briefly until he too sprints out the door at precisely 6:08, still swallowing the last of his beer. After the Train People are gone, the downtown dwellers can finally sit back, relax and enjoy the evening, vowing, of course, never to invite the Train People again.

# 15

Super Bowl Sunday at a sports bar downtown pretty much guarantees a Train People–free event. They don't venture downtown on weekends because the weekend train schedule is completely unmanageable with fewer trains and longer wait intervals. The suburbanites have their Super Bowl parties in civilized family rooms and serve chili in bread bowls — unlike the downtown dwellers who tromp out in the cold and head to crowded bars and drink beer by the pitcher with several hundred strangers. But here we are. Mel and I have just arrived and have spotted Charlie Brown across the bar. How could we miss him really? He's wearing a blue-and-orange-striped short-sleeved t-shirt. Unfortunately, I think Charlie Brown has a tough time finding his preferred shirt in the long-sleeved winter version and must resort to wearing his summer stock even in the dead of winter. I look over to Mel as soon as I spot Charlie Brown and she too has seen him. Surprisingly, her face lights up and I can tell that she really, for some reason only known to Cupid, thinks Charlie Brown is wonderful. We muscle through the crowd — it's an hour before kickoff and the bar is already packed — to get to where Charlie Brown is with his friends. I recognize two of the guys from work, they work for Marc's company as well, and the other three Charlie Brown introduces as friends from college. I make a mental note that maybe Charlie's not so bad; he has managed to keep friends from college.

Mel is as nervous as a long-tailed cat in a room full of rocking chairs and keeps clutching onto my arm under the table. We are actually in a great spot to see the game, just off to the right side of the projection screen at a tall table so we can stand and move around. Mel's nervousness probably stems from being in a room that is filled with men who may sweat. Her aversion to sweat has become much more pronounced since she started the whole football charade. I'm trying to calm Mel down with soothing words and pry her grip from my arm as I'm fairly sure I will lose circulation soon, when I hear a very sexy voice that I recognize instantly behind me, "Hey Kathryn, you look great." It's Derek. He's here! Yay!

"Hey!" I turn around and manage to pry Mel's remaining fingers from my arm only because she too turns to see who has spoken to me. I try to act casual but I know my look of excitement upon seeing Derek gives me away and blows any chance of coolness out of the water. I'm wearing my heart on my sleeve these days. I just love being near him. I feel like I'm in high school again and Tim Taylor (the quarterback for our senior football team who was three years my senior and didn't know I existed) has just walked by me in the school hall. Derek introduces me to his friends Paul and John. I size up this second John and am happy to see that he is wearing a Steelers sweatshirt. I then introduce them to Mel and the Charlie Brown crowd, and surprisingly manage to remember all of Charlie's friends' names. The bar gets more crowded as kickoff approaches and Mel seems to relax a little. She manages to make conversation with Derek and laughs a couple of times. Derek gives Mel the advice of following the group of Seattle fans that are to our left, suggesting that if they cheer, you cheer. Mel isn't a Seattle fan obviously, but Charlie Brown is, so since she has *no* opinion it's best to adopt the opinion of the man you are trying to impress. I personally am cheering for Pittsburgh, but not wholeheartedly. I'm a Dolphins fan and honestly they are still regrouping since Dan Marino's retirement. Who knows, maybe next year will be the year of the Dolphin. The evening passes quickly. The Super Bowl is generally a four- or five-hour edge-of-your-seat ordeal but today it doesn't seem nearly long enough. Derek, who is considerably taller than I am, is able to stand behind me most of the game and see the screen over my head. It also allows him to whisper into my ear and make me giggle, so I'm happy that the game is a bit of a sleeper. The Seahawks manage to hold their own but never really find their stride, so Mel doesn't have to worry about straining her cheering voice. I completely miss one of Pittsburgh's touchdowns because I am whispering and giggling with Derek who is standing behind me holding my waist and squeezing me occasionally; it's a wonder I can concentrate at all actually. I decide before the half-time show that this is how you are meant to watch football. Mel actually seems to catch on to the game a little bit, and once Derek pointed out that the television network does the keeping track for us she seemed to relax considerably. Derek explained that the time remaining, the quarter, the down and yardage statistics are all right there across the top of the screen so if anyone asks what down they're on, just read it off the screen. We even practised asking Mel questions until she became a "genius screen reader." I think she actually had fun despite her misgivings about sports and sweat in general.

As for Mel and Charlie Brown, I have to admit that my dislike for Charlie Brown has actually kept me at arm's length where their relationship is concerned. I had hoped that Mel's infatuation with the opinionated would wear off, but after seeing them together for an entire evening they actually do seem well suited and they get along swimmingly. It truly is a mystery to me, but stranger things have happened in the guise of love. I make a vow to *really* put forth an effort to like Charlie Brown and not just the surface attempts I've been making of late. Mel and I are going to share a house in a few short days and it seems Charlie Brown is going to be a fixture in that house. I shall be kinder to Charlie Brown in the future. Perhaps I can convince Mel to get him a solid sweatshirt to wear at our place. I'll keep the heat low so he needs a sweater. I wonder if Prada makes men's sweats?

Near the end of the game, when the time factor makes it

physically impossible for the Seattle Seahawks to come back and win, the crowd begins to disperse. Charlie Brown is not happy that his team didn't win, but even he rallies. Mel is just thrilled that she managed to tolerate the entire televised sporting event without getting sweat upon. I don't think Mel will be spending very many Sunday afternoons next fall on the couch watching regular season games, but we might get her to attend another Super Bowl outing. Mel leans over to tell me that she and Charlie Brown are getting ready to go back to her place. I can tell by her grin that the loss of his team has not hindered Charlie Brown's libido. I know, I should stop calling him Charlie Brown but in reality that's probably not going to happen.

"Well, don't break a sweat!" I say playfully, getting as much mileage out of the sporting reference as possible. Derek had been talking to his friends but turns in time to hear my comment to Mel. When I look at him he is smiling in a very coy fashion that makes all my special parts start to feel a bit tingly. Breaking a sweat with Derek is something I've given a great deal of thought to in the past week. Mel and Charlie Brown bid us goodnight and Derek's friends follow shortly after, leaving Derek and me to finish the remaining inch of the last pitcher of beer. Charlie Brown's friends are still across the table but they are into a heated discussion of who would win a fight between Darth Vader and Spider-Man. Don't ask. I have no idea how it started or how they plan to determine who will be the victor. Light sabers aside, my money's on Spidey — less cape, more agile.

"So what did you think of the game?" Derek is so cute. Even when he asks me normal questions I get queasy.

"Not bad but it would have been better if Miami were playing." I did find the game a bit slow when I wasn't thinking about Derek's hands on my waist and loving that feeling.

"So I was wondering if I could take you home tonight, I'd love to see your apartment before you move out of it." Derek blushes a little bit so I suspect he's thinking about breaking a sweat as well.

"I'm not sure. I don't just go home with every man who asks, you know." I'm positive that I'm taking him home but I don't want to seem too eager, that's never attractive.

"About that. I was wondering if you'd like to be my girl-friend?" Derek is leaning with one elbow on the table and he just looks so adorable.

"Really?" In my entire history of dating, and that number is actually higher than you'd think considering my dating hiatus of late, not one of my significant others has ever asked me to be his girlfriend. It was always implied and we behaved girlfriend–boyfriend-y but it was never actually asked. This is the sweetest thing ever!

"Really. I think you are amazing and beautiful and would love to say you are my girlfriend the next time I introduce you to someone."

I'm quickly becoming Jell-O and playing hard to get is so not going to happen.

"I'd like that," I finally manage through my grin and hug him around his waist. He bends down to kiss me.

"Let's say we head out and I'll give you a tour of my apartment. There's one room in particular I'd like you to see," I hint. My tingly parts are dictating my actions now. Derek and I bid the Darth Vader–Spider-Man debaters a hasty goodbye, bundle up in our coats and rush off hand-in-hand to hail a cab.

The cab ride seems like forever but in reality traffic is moving well for the Super Bowl having just ended. Derek and I giggle in the backseat the whole way and I laugh a little too hard at everything he says. I pay the cab driver and we make a hasty retreat from the back seat. I almost fall on my butt when my foot makes contact with the fresh snow-covered ground because my dress boot does not have the traction of a proper winter boot, but Derek catches me and we are both thrown into another fit of laughter. We managed to slip and slide our way to the lobby and into the elevator, where Derek grabs me and starts kissing me in a most passionate way. I am halfway out of my jacket and my blouse is mostly undone by the time we get to my floor. I grab Derek's hand as the elevator doors open and we race down the hall to my apartment where I fumble with the keys and have a difficult time finding the lock because Derek is kissing the back of my neck and reaching around and fiddling with the button of my jeans. Giggling and excited, with my special parts tingling like mad, I manage to get the door open and Derek and I tumble inside and land on the terra cotta tiled floor. I think "that might hurt tomorrow" as I register my elbow hitting the floor harder than would generally be considered pleasant, but that thought immediately leaves my mind as I reach out with my toe and push the door closed behind us.

# 16

Getting to work the next day on time is a bit of a chore. Derek planned to get up early and go to his apartment to get dressed in proper work attire — seems Super Bowl attire isn't at all appropriate for investment banking. At the wind-down of our adventures last evening Derek was on the side of the bed that the alarm clock is on, and when the alarm went off he was unsure what to do to make it stop so I had to crawl over him to stop the buzzing. Since I hadn't taken the time to find any pajamas, underwear or other, crawling over Derek, who is also naked, leads to the logical conclusion that one often reaches when there is an extremely attractive, naked man in one's bed, and that leads to the thirty-minute late start to the day.

Knowing I have to go to the construction site later this afternoon and in light of the lateness of my start, I know I have to drive Nasty to work. However, the driver's door is frozen shut. The frozen driver's door is not a new occurrence in Nasty since it freezes nicely even in moderate tempera-tures. I drop my purse onto the icy sidewalk and go to the passenger door as I've done many times when combatting the frozen driver's door. I usually get in the passenger door, lean across to unlock the driver's door, and then push like *mad* to break the ice and open the driver's door. The process is not pretty, but it is effective. Today, of all days, the passenger door is *also* frozen shut. I go back around the car to my purse and find the de-icer that lives in it for just such occasions. The de-icer, which usually works on the passenger door, does not this time. I check my watch like a Train Person: time is ticking by at a rapid pace. I'm going to be really late if I don't do something quickly. So, yes, after as much deliberation as I can risk in light of the lateness of the hour, I finally accept that I must do the unthinkable — I must go through the trunk. The trunk never freezes shut.

Throwing all modesty aside, I hike myself into the trunk, butt in the air, dress boots flailing as I slither on my tummy through the seat opening (thank goodness for the back seat two-thirds split or I would never get my butt through). Then I pull myself across the back seat until I'm almost in the front passenger bucket seat before I can bend my legs around and under me. Once I'm out of the trunk and in the back seat, I have to contort myself, in what I know is not a ladylike fashion in any country, to maneuver over the stick shift and try and wiggle down into the driver's seat, which is really close to the steering wheel because of my five-foot-three vertical challenge. At this point, I say a silent thank you to Mother Nature for the frosted windows that make seeing into Nasty impossible while I perform my Cirque du Soleil routine from the back seat to the driver's seat. After what seems like forever I manage to get the door open from the inside, rub my now-bruised shoulder, gather up my purse off the sidewalk, scrape off the windows and get to work.

Despite the morning car adventure, I step off the elevator at work thinking, "I am a wanton sex goddess in true Bridget Jones fashion" and nothing, not even frozen Nasty, can ruin this day. In fact I wonder if my newly discovered contortionist skills will come in handy in the wanton sex goddess arena. Walking into the office, I remember that today is the day we award the contracts for the new Sebring project. I had forgotten about the meeting with all the Super Bowl hype, subsequent throws of passion and the frozen car adventure. The architects and engineers are assembling in the boardroom at 10:00 a.m. Joyce and I must tackle making coffee in the supersized machine from hell. I smile and remain undeterred. I am a wanton sex goddess with contortionist abilities and surely not every pot can taste like mud. We can do this. How hard is it to make coffee? Besides, Joyce and I have been making strides with the coffee machine. Well sort of.

I take a sip of the takeout coffee that Joyce brought for me as we stand in front of the machine that is making a new godawful howling noise never heard before. The concept is so easy and yet it eludes us. Water in, coffee out, surely it's that simple. We watch the coffee slowly fill the pot, our eyes not leaving the machine. Joyce asks without looking at me, "How was your Super Bowl get-together?"

"Excellent fun! Does that coffee look thick to you?" I

answer, not looking at her. We are both mesmerized by the globby coffee. "Oh, I officially have a boyfriend now."

"Yes. Very thick. Mudlike again. Congratulations. The cute fellow you met on the subway?" Joyce asks but doesn't take her eyes off the coffee either.

"Do you suppose it'll get thinner when there's more in the pot? Yes. It is the cutie from the subway. You'll love him," I answer, starting to worry about the coffee.

"I don't know if it gets much thinner than that. I'm sure I will. His name is Derek, right?" Joyce tilts her head to the right in a puzzled fashion.

"Yes. How about I run down to the corner and buy five large black coffees and we can transfer them to mugs?"

"Excellent idea," Joyce agrees as we walk out of the kitchen sipping our takeout coffees.

The meeting goes well and Joyce and I do not kill or maim anyone with our coffee since we went the store-bought route. I send a very large cosmic thank you to the inventor of the coffee shop and I include all things takeout; best to thank all the cosmic inventors. After the meeting I am given the list of the new project team and asked to draft the award letters. I'm not shocked that Marc's company is being awarded the electrical contract but I do cringe a little because it could be the start of a very long project for everyone involved. Joyce comes up behind me, looks at the list over my shoulder and says, "Oh, this might be a problem now that you're seeing Derek."

"Yes, it might." I look down at my "getting some" Nine West light-blue cotton blouse and wonder if Joyce knows about my occasion clothing.

Mel and I get the keys for our new house much earlier on moving day than we had imagined so we are able to complete the scrubbing, sweeping and vacuuming before the moving truck arrives. The house is about eighty years old and in desperate need of a more modern look. We decide that completely gutting and redoing the washroom to update it is a must and once that's done the kitchen will have to be renovated as well. We are going to have our work cut out for us but are actually looking forward to it with the optimism of youth and the ignorance of home-renovating novices. The moving truck arrives and we are in the house surrounded by boxes and furniture when Derek and Charlie Brown arrive to help us start our new adventure. Charlie Brown volunteers to set up the televisions and stereo which is a blessing because Mel and I are both hopeless with electronics and Derek and I tackle getting beds set up while Mel is left in charge of putting the kitchen in some sort of order. By eight o'clock that evening we are eating Chinese takeout, sipping on champagne that Mel magically pulled out of her Prada briefcase again and watching hockey on our working television. By ten o'clock Derek and I are christening the new bedroom and the new location does not seem to hinder our desire to be naked with each other, not that I suspected it would.

Settling back into life with Mel is easy. We've known each other our whole lives and understand each other's habits. I still ask Mel to come running with me and she still laughs maniacally at the suggestion of premeditated sweat. The only additions to our new living arrangement are the expensive footwear, the stop-smoking gum and the boyfriends who have different names. I could say that we are older and wiser, but the wiser part isn't necessarily accurate. We are older and now homeowners, so possibly older and more in debt would be more suitable.

# 17

Valentine's Day draws near. I hate Valentine's Day. A train wreck for single people because although every day seems like everyone on the planet is happy, in love and is *getting some* when you aren't, Valentine's Day puts a whole new level of pressure on you and not only are you still single, now everyone is pointing and laughing at you, or so it seems thanks to Hallmark. This year I'm dating so no one is actually pointing and laughing at me, but now I have the new couple Valentine's Day stress. What do you get for someone you just started dating? You don't want to seem overly sentimental but you can't appear completely non-sentimental. You can't spend too much money but you don't want to appear cheap. Flowers are an easy out for the guys, but I can't honestly say I've ever met a non-gay male who thinks getting flowers is a good thing. Chocolates. Again, easy out for the guys because 99.9 percent of women not only like chocolate but crave it like lunatics at least once a month, but do guys want chocolate? Not usually. A tie? Surely not. It's not Christmas and Derek's not my dad. Ties are out. There is always the t-shirt option and I've tried to impress on Mel that she should take this option where Charlie Brown is concerned, obviously I'm pointing out nice solid-coloured t-shirts with matching cuffs and necklines. Something Tommy Hilfiger, I suggest in the car on the way to work. But if Mel goes t-shirt then I can't because that says I have no imagination, even though t-shirt was my idea. It is such a conundrum. Did I mention I hate Valentine's Day?

A few days before Valentine's Day, I stop off at Derek's office on the way to work to drop off homemade peanut butter cookies. Mel feels that baking for a man so early in the relationship is the beginning of the demise but I honestly don't see where a few cookies could cause the downfall of a relationship. Everyone likes cookies and homemade are much better. Derek calls me later at work and thanks me for the cookies (see, no demise) and to tell me that he has made reservations at Mildred Pierce for dinner on Valentine's Day. I suddenly have a newfound love for Valentine's Day and all things romantic. Mildred Pierce is my absolute favourite restaurant. I love it there. I haven't even told Derek about my love, for Mildred Pierce not him, he must have asked Mel. I'm really glad I decided on the gift of cologne. It says I care, is expensive enough to say I care as much as you do, since I know I'm getting an amazing dinner, and it says I want to smell you. All is good and right in the world.

I wake up and roll over and hug Derek, who is conveniently in my bed and smell him. He always smells good, but tomorrow he'll smell even better. Today is Valentine's Day and it's going to be a great day. I'm so excited. Getting ready for work is a bit harried, as it always is when both Derek and Charlie Brown stay over. Four people and one bathroom — one ancient old bathroom with avocado fixtures — really brings the renovation to the foreground and Mel and I discuss it on the way to work. Possible financial destitution aside we must do something to remedy the situation and agree there is no time like the present. I am in charge of finding the hired help, which only makes sense because I work with construction contractors every day, and Mel is in charge of, well, being Mel. She will come in handy later to yell at the contractors if necessary. Mel can be much scarier than me.

Mel drops me at the coffee shop. I jump out of the car quick as a whip and we still get honked at in the nine seconds we're stopped. Rush hour, angry drivers, but nothing will mar this day. I'm going out for an amazing dinner.

"You look happy," Marc says as I come into the coffee shop.

"I thought you were mad at me?"

"We have to work together for the next couple of years. I knew you wouldn't stay single forever but I just wasn't ready for you to be dating so soon. I'm sorry I overreacted the other day."

"Thank you for the apology and you're forgiven. It is Valentine's Day after all, I'm feeling generous."

"You hate Valentine's Day," Marc knows me too well.

"I know, but Derek's taking me to Mildred Pierce for dinner so today I love Valentine's Day. Oh, speaking of food," I say as I reach into my purse to retrieve a box of After Eight mints and hand them to him, "Happy Valentine's Day."

"How'd you know you'd see me today? We weren't speaking, remember?"

"No. You weren't speaking to me and I wasn't expecting to see you. You'll notice the box is open. There are a few missing. Breakfast. Sorry about that."

"I can't believe you're giving me a partially eaten box of dinner mints," Marc laughs.

"Well, I figured I could get a new box before seeing you. I was hungry!" I laugh.

"Okay, thank you anyway. Can you stop at my truck on the way back to the office? I have some invoices for you," Marc asks as we walk toward his truck, which is illegally parked during the morning rush hour and no one is honking, cussing obscenities or giving him a ticket. Amazing. Marc opens the passenger side door and starts to hand me the longest flower box I've ever seen. The box has to be three feet long.

"This can't be invoices and if this box is for me you know I can't accept it." My eyes are huge in disbelief.

"Yes you can. If you don't they will die and it will all be your fault and you'll be a flower killer." Marc is grinning as he wraps my free arm around the massive box and gives me a kiss on the forehead.

"Marc, this is crazy. I can't accept these. Please take them back, give them to someone else." I'm pleading at this point and Marc is walking around the back of his truck, leaving me standing in the street with the massive box.

"Happy Valentine's Day," he yells over his shoulder as he jumps into his truck.

"Well, at least help me get my pass card out of my purse," I yell after him as he laughs, waves and pulls away.

Somehow I manage to get my pass card, get into the building and up the elevator and into the office without spilling my coffee or dropping the massive box. Once in the office I'm able to set the box down in the foyer, along with my coffee so I can get my boots and coat off — I will be so happy when there is no more snow on the ground — before I manhandle the massive box into the kitchen. When I untie the ribbon that is wrapped around the box the whole top of the box lifts two inches by itself due to the volume contained within. When I lift the lid the remainder of the way off, I discover two dozen of the longest-stemmed red roses I've ever seen. The stems are as long as my arm and the roses themselves are absolutely beautiful. The sight of them takes my breath away. Wow. This is the most romantic display of flowers I've ever seen and it's not from someone I've even dated. I feel like a beauty pageant queen as I try to put my arm underneath them to lift them into the sink. I think the beauty pageant people must remove the thorns on the actual pageant roses because I manage to poke and scratch myself a dozen times between the box and the sink, but I'm not deterred. I rummage around the vase cupboard for the perfect vase to put them in. Yes, there is a vase cupboard in our office kitchen. We have a fascinating company kitchen. The coffee machine the size of a small foreign car, a photocopier that does everything except type the actual documents, a full complement of fine bone china, place settings for twelve and a vase cupboard that contains thirty-seven vases of various sizes, shapes and colours. It's not whether I can find one that will work, it's which one, of the ones that will work, do I *want* to use. I always wondered about Mr. Sebring's vase collecting, but today, I finally get it. Mr. Sebring must have given his wife flowers once and not had the right vase. Since then, I'm sure all his houses and offices have vase collections to rival the one we have here. I finally understand his vase obsession and I'm really glad he has one or the roses would be in the cleaning lady's mop bucket. Not the best way to present the most beautiful of all flower displays.

After I select the perfect vase I go back to the box to find the white powder stuff that you put in the water. I'm not sure what it does exactly but I do know that I wouldn't dare *not* use it. It's called Fresh Flower Food, which is funny because aren't all fresh flowers really dead by virtue of being cut off from their real food supply? Anyway, like I said, you *have* to use it. What if it is indeed food and they will starve without it? Best to leave that sort of thing up to the flower people. When I find the Fresh Flower Food package it's taped to an envelope, which I presume is the card. I put the envelope on my desk and take the powder stuff back to the kitchen where I start to cut the stems under water. I read that your flowers last longer if you re-cut the stems under water after they've been in transit. There are a lot of roses and the process takes a while but the end result is extraordinary. I always suspected that roses were one of my favourite flowers but now I know they are my favourite. I put the flowers on the table in the foyer, which I can see perfectly from my desk and go back to clean up the kitchen. After I discard all the part stems, drain the sink and break up the box for recycling I return to my desk to start my day and open the envelope that came with the flowers. It does indeed contain a lovely card that is paperclipped to a second envelope. The card simply says "Because you make me smile"; okay, how nice is that? Marc has managed to take my breath away twice in one morning. When I open the second envelope Marc manages the impossible and my breath escapes me a third time. The second envelope contains two tickets to Saturday night's Leafs game and a stickie that reads "I know you won't go with me and I want you to see another game this year, so you can take what's-his-name."

After what seems an eternity I manage to get my breath back, gather my wits and dial Marc's cell phone.

"No, absolutely not! You are far too generous. The flowers are way more than I should accept but like you said, they're God's living, or dead…whatever, creatures but I cannot accept the hockey tickets. That's way too much and I don't deserve them. You know I don't," I blurt out as soon as Marc answers the phone.

"Just go to the game, have fun. Besides I'm out of town this weekend, they'll be wasted."

"No you aren't. You're just saying that so I won't give them back." I don't know for sure he's lying about going away but I suspect.

"No, I am going away. Use them. I won't take them back anyway and seriously the seats will sit empty."

"This is too much. I can't ever repay you, you know that." I suddenly feel really bad about giving him a box of partially-previously-enjoyed dinner mints.

"It's not about repayment, I'm just glad we're still friends after everything that's happened."

"Well, I'm glad we're friends too but you have to stop buying me things and that includes coffee," I say as sternly as possible considering I'm looking at two dozen stunning roses and holding two hockey tickets in my hand.

"You know I won't," Marc laughs, "Happy Valentine's Day," and he hangs up before I can say anything else.

# 18

By lunchtime, between emails to Derek and getting a bit of work done, I have devised a plan. It is a brilliant plan. I think I may actually have reached Suppa Genius status, similar to that of Wile E. Coyote from Road Runner cartoon fame. I will go to the coffee shop and pay in advance for a week's worth of coffees every week. This way Marc cannot possibly pay, as they will already be paid for, and I will finally be able to give something back to the friendship besides my winning smile, which I'm quite sure is closer to average than winning. Thank goodness for my staggering Wile E. Coyote intellect.

I am still revelling in my genius when Joyce and I venture outside at lunchtime into what our local meteorologist would describe as a snow squall. I like that word *squall*. I actually like all "qu" words: quail, quaint, equal — all big points in Scrabble. As for real squalls, however, as much as I like the word, I hate what the word translates into. Little bits of snow whipping around and around, pelting you in the face repeatedly making seeing and walking, two things you can generally do without thinking, virtually impossible. Winter in general is a pain, with the boots and coats and gloves but when the wind is whistling at you at gale force and makes

−13°C feel like −26°C you have to stop and wonder why we don't all just pack it in and move to the Carolinas.

The plan is to stop at the coffee shop and pay for a week's worth of coffees then go to the sub shop to grab lunch, then back to the office where it's warm and wind-free. There are a lot more pedestrians than I guessed would be out today, but Joyce and I trudge to the corner and wait for the light to change to green, which because of the gusts of wind seems like forever. I can see the coffee shop and am glad it is so close to the office. The light turns and Joyce and I start across the street with several other people, zigzagging around the pedestrians travelling in the other direction. Halfway across the intersection a gust of wind blows up and I am momentarily blinded by the snow but am able to focus in time to see a bike courier riding directly at me. I step to the right because Joyce and too many other people are on my left, but I don't sidestep fast enough and the bike courier tries to squeeze in-between Joyce and me, so we both end up being pushed out of the way. Fortunately, Joyce manages to keep her balance with the help of one of our fellow pedestrians, but I don't fare so well because I am on the outside of the crosswalk nearest the street and am pushed into oncoming traffic. The next several seconds pass with lightning speed but my mind thinks "Why are there bike couriers in February in Toronto in a snow squall?" I comprehend that I'm lying in the street at eye level with many pairs of winter boots with people in them, way up there; this can't be good. Just before I pass out cold, I register that I've been hit by a car and wonder if it is a Lexus.

I wake up briefly in the ambulance but just long enough to motion that I'm going to vomit and then do so. The movement involved to vomit into the little bag I am given, causes excruciating pain in my leg and chest, enough pain to make me vomit again before slipping back into the black abyss. The thought I manage to register before the blackness is "This really can't be good."

The next time I wake up I am in a hospital. There are a lot of people I don't know. I'll probably throw up again but the thought fades to blackness before I can do anything about it.

The third time I wake up I see Mel. She is a welcome sight but I can't talk. I am just too tired. I'll just close my eyes for a second then I'll say "hi."

The fourth time I wake up I'm thirsty. Very thirsty. Mel is still there but she looks tired now. I try to say hi but my mouth is too dry. I manage the word *water* and Mel holds a glass with a straw to my mouth. I try to move my arm to help but I can't because there is a severe pain in my chest. Once Mel is sure that I'm coherent she fills me in on the situation. I was indeed hit by a car. I am currently in recovery from surgery on my leg. My right femur is broken but has been repaired and I have a metal rod screwed to it and will be sporting a really awful scar. I have at least two broken ribs and possible whiplash. The good news is that I will be fine and should make a full recovery. The bad news is that my favourite Esprit black dress pants and sexy red Valentine's Day underwear with the stripperlike fringe had to be cut off and are a complete writeoff. Ditto for my favourite Nine West winter boots — well, the right one anyway.

I manage to ask Mel what time it is. My watch is not on my wrist. When she tells me it's after 6:00 p.m. I start to panic because surely Derek is going crazy wondering where I am. Mel assures me that Derek knows where I am and is actually in the waiting room with Joyce and Charlie Brown. She also mentions that our parents are driving down from North Bay. I want to ask Mel if the car that hit me was a Lexus but I am much too tired.

I wake up and it's light outside so it must be morning. I'll have to ask about my watch. I hate not knowing what time it is. My leg is in traction, but not in a cast, and I hurt all over. I honestly know now what they mean when they say "I feel like I've been hit by a truck," only in this case I'm sure it was a car. I'm waking up enough to know that I'm very thirsty again but look around and the water jug is out of reach. I don't want to buzz anyone and can't find the buzzer, if there is one, anyway. The room has two beds but the second one is vacant and I'm alone. I wonder if my parents have arrived and how Mel's doing at keeping peach paint off our walls. The door to my room opens quietly and Marc pokes his head in. I am thrilled to see anyone at this point, anyone who can hand me a drink.

"Hey, what brings you to this part of town?" I try to sound upbeat but know I sound hoarse and sleepy.

"You," Marc laughs, "did you think you'd win against a

Jetta?" Marc walks in and he's carrying two coffees. I love Marc. He is bringing me liquid.

"It was a Jetta?" I am crushed — I was so sure it was a Lexus. It would just be so much classier to get hit by a Lexus. "I probably didn't even scratch it, did I? Curses to the superior German engineering," I try to laugh. "Tell me one of those is for me," I ask Marc, eyeing the coffee cups.

"I thought I wasn't suppose to buy you coffee anymore?"

Damn. He has a point but I'm dying here, "Well, I'll make an exception this one time." I try to sound upbeat but I really do feel like I've been hit but a truck, or car as it were.

"Of course one's for you. I wasn't going to listen to you anyway," Marc starts to hand me a cup but I cringe as I lift my arm to accept it and he realizes I'm not sitting up enough so he puts the coffee on the table and starts to play with the controls to get me sitting more upright.

"Could you please hand me some water first, I'm really thirsty."

Marc pours me some water and hands it to me. I drink it in seconds and ask for another glass. We do this until the jug is empty then Marc hands me the coffee. Every inch of my body hurts.

"How did you know I was here?" I have no concept of time or what has happened in the outside world.

"I called the office yesterday and Mr. Sebring answered so I knew something was up, then I got hold of John and had him call Mel and I got the story from him. I also called Mel at your house last night and she seemed relieved to have someone to talk to. Seems all your folks have descended and are driving her crazy.

"Mel mentioned yesterday they were all coming and I'm sure crazy doesn't even begin to describe it." I take a sip of coffee and it's the best coffee I've ever had. I'm not sure if it's the near-death experience or the fact that I can't remember the last time I brushed my teeth, but this is good coffee.

"Ah, heaven, this coffee is really good. Thank you. Do you have the time? I don't have my watch." I realize then that I also don't have any clothes on, just one of the paper gown things under the blanket. I wonder where my stuff is.

"It's only 7:15 a.m. I wanted to see you before you get inundated with family and friends. Mel gave me your room number. She asked me to tell you that she'd be by later. I had to sweet-talk the nurse to get in this early, you know?" Marc laughs.

"Well, thank you." I inexplicably start to cry.

"Hey, are you okay? Do you want me to get a nurse or something?" Marc is honestly confused and concerned.

"No, I'm fine. I have no idea where this came from — the drugs I suppose." I try to laugh through the tears because I don't even know why I'm crying. Stress I guess, and if that's the case, then good for me for not throwing up the coffee.

"Well, you look pretty good considering." Marc is trying to be nice but I know, from the way that I feel, that I look like complete crap and I'm pretty sure there's vomit in my hair.

No one, and I don't care who you are, can look good with vomit in their hair.

"You're a very bad liar. I know I look like shit, but I do make this blue paper thing work, don't I?" I manage through fewer tears.

"Exactly, no one wears blue paper like you. You'll always have that."

"So, it looks like I was right, God doesn't want me to use your hockey tickets." I'm not sure where that comment came from, I had all but forgotten about the hockey tickets.

"You might be out of here by Saturday but you won't be in any shape to go to a hockey game. Give them to your dad and Mel's dad, they'll probably enjoy it. Here, and take this. Keep it until you're out of here," Marc says as he tries to hand me his watch.

"I am not taking your watch. You'll be late for all your meetings." Then I look at Marc's watch that he's holding out to me, "Oh, and it's a TAG Heuer! You have a *TAG*? How much money do you make?!" I digress briefly, then continue, "I'm not keeping a two-thousand-dollar watch. Are you insane? I can't cross the street without getting hit by a Jetta, there's no way I'm taking responsibility for a watch that costs more than the car I drive."

"It's a watch. I have two more at home." Marc puts the watch in my hand and leans over and kisses my forehead before striding toward the door, "I'll see you soon."

"Thanks for the coffee. You have *three* TAGs? We pay you

too much," I shout after him while admiring the most exquisite timepiece I've ever held. "Someday I'll have a TAG," I tell myself but I know that this is as close as I'm going to get for a very long time.

# 19

I manage to eat the muffin in the hospital breakfast and down the juice along with three more glasses of water before they arrive like locusts. I had no idea four people could consume a space like the parents did in my hospital room. Mom and Mrs. Melrose are in tears and rush to me like they've been in the desert for weeks and I am an oasis. The dads hang back at the end of my bed but still participate in the speed questions.

"Are you all right? You could have been killed!" That last bit is more statement than question.

"Why do you girls insist on living here in 'The City' and putting us through this torture?"

"Where did you get that coffee? Is that allowed?"

"Why don't you have a cast?

"When can we take you home?"

"What did the doctor say?"

"Do you have any vitamin E for the scar. I looked in your bathroom last night and there's no vitamin E." Again that last part isn't a question as much as an accusation that Mel and I aren't taking very good care of ourselves.

My head is spinning. Thank God Marc brought me the coffee. Not one of the parents seems concerned that I could be dehydrated or worse, have to go to the washroom. I look around my mother's perfectly coiffed hair at Mel, who is hanging back by the door, and she mouths the words, "I'm so sorry!" and shrugs and rolls her eyes. I know it's not her fault. If I were a parent I too would have come running when one of the nest flies off on her own and then gets run down by a car. A car has hit me, of course they are concerned. I just wonder how Mel and I are going to survive several days of "parenting."

"No seriously, where did you get that coffee? Are you allowed to have coffee?" Mom is pointing at the takeout cup Marc brought me.

"Mom, I broke my leg. I don't have an ulcer and they gave me coffee with breakfast," I manage. "How was the drive down?" I ask, trying to be upbeat and change the subject. Regrettably, just as it's out of my mouth I see Mel shaking her head and mouthing *no*. Too late.

The story of the trip starts, each parent getting equal time, Mel manages to catch my eye and mouth the word *coffee* and I nod. Luckily, after Mel slips out of the room I am able to zone out and play with the dials on Marc's watch, thereby missing the entire tale of the horrific trip to "The City" in "this weather." Our parents always call Toronto The City. They hate the fact that we live three and a half hours, in *good* weather, away from their protection. Any manner of tragedy can befall two young women living alone in The City and "*Look!* Now it *has!*"

My leg is aching. Oh, I say I'm as tough as the next gal and I'll be all "go on without me" if I get shot, but no, not really. I'm in pain and I need drugs. I look around me. These people want grandchildren!? Oh, I don't think so! I can only imagine the pain of childbirth but if it's half as bad as the pain I have right now, no, Mom, Dad, Mr. and Mrs. Melrose you are *so not* getting grandchildren from this womb.

"Mommy. I need drugs. My leg really hurts," I emphasize the "Mommy" part. I haven't called my mother that since I was four. She'll know I'm serious. And I am. I need serious drugs. Now.

"Bill, get a nurse! Poor Kathryn is in pain!" Mom shrieks at Dad, who, in complete panic grabs Mr. Melrose and they disappear into the hall. I hope they find drugs soon. Who would have thought being hit by a car could hurt so much. Oh, you imagine it will hurt, but you really have no idea.

I love Mel. Mel returns with coffee and brings one to me. She leans over and kisses my forehead and says, "I'm really glad you're okay. I was so worried yesterday when Joyce called me." Mel is starting to cry. I hate it when Mel cries. When Mel cries there is something really wrong in the world.

"Hey! No crying. We're going to need all of our mutual strength to get through this together," I say as my eyes survey the mothers at the foot of my bed who are discussing the uselessness of our fathers who have not returned with my drugs.

"I don't know where to begin," Mel exclaims in a half-whisper. "They're serious about redecorating; there's been talk of wallpaper borders."

"DRUGS! Mommy, I need drugs!" My shriek sends both mothers into the hallway after our "useless" fathers.

"Where? Where do they want to put wallpaper borders?" I turn frantically toward Mel, momentarily forgetting the pain in the leg and ribs.

"Everywhere, sweetie. Everywhere."

The drugs arrive but not without a palaver. When the nurse hands me the little cup containing drugs, sweet merciful drugs, I ask what they are. I have an allergy to sulpha, but it only shows up in antibiotics and I'm fairly sure these are painkillers, but I ask just to be sure, don't want any more vomiting if we can help it.

"Tylenol No. 3s," the nurse replies and I love her. Ah, codeine, sweet pain-relieving codeine. I start to raise the cup to my lips just as my mother shrieks, "NO! You're allergic to codeine!" and the nurse grabs the cup away from me.

"No *Mother*. That's Tia. Not me," I state emphatically as only one can who has been hit by a car and needs drugs immediately, while trying to get the little paper cup back from the nurse.

"No, I'm sure it's you," my mother is going to be killed. I will hire an assassin, whatever it takes.

"No. Mother I'm not allergic to codeine. Tia is. Remember when she broke her arm, that's when we found out about the allergy." I'm still trying to grab the drugs back from the nurse but have no reach since I'm in traction and have broken ribs so Mel steps in and is attacking the nurse from the other side, trying to get my drugs. I love Mel.

"No, I'm sure it's you." My mother is relentless and forget the assassin I'll kill her myself as soon as I can walk.

"*Mother!* It is not me. Tia has the allergy and the bracelet to prove it. Surely you remember the brouhaha over the silver versus the gold bracelet! How can we forget? She managed to get both out of you." I turn to my father, "Dad, I'm going to kill her!"

"I think maybe Kathryn has a point, Peggy. Seems to me the twins have the lion's share of the allergies." My quiet, laid-back dad is trying to be diplomatic when only brute force is going to work, but he is correct. Tia and Taryn, my twenty-one-year-old twin sisters, are, combined, allergic to a list of items that would rival the boy in the plastic bubble.

"DAD!" I scream, "get her out of here or I'm going to start cussing!"

Dad starts to manhandle Mom out of the room and Mr. Melrose grabs Mrs. Melrose and leads her out as well, I guess to avoid the aforementioned cussing. I'm sure they will comment later on me being the "handful" while the twins, despite their allergies, are the "adorable cute ones."

Mel manages to get the cup of drugs from the nurse and hand them off to me and is standing between the nurse and me with her arms outspread, defying the nurse to mess with her. I would laugh because Mel is dressed head to toe in Prada including her hot pink boots and the nurse looks afraid of her. The fact that Mel's in four-inch heels is an indication that the nurse could probably take her, but Mel does look fearsome. After this episode I might never get another drug as long as I'm here, but knowing these ones will dull the pain in fifteen to twenty minutes is all I can think about right now.

The nurse is leaving as Derek comes in. Derek. Oh no. Valentine's Day and I didn't even see him. He is carrying a beautiful bouquet of flowers and After Eight mints, the big box. He looks so handsome in his business suit and trench coat, except his jacket is off one shoulder.

"Kathryn, thank heavens! How are you? I'm so glad to see you finally. Do you know the people in the hall?" Poor Derek is flustered and has apparently met the parents. "The dark-haired woman grabbed me as I was trying to come in — she was muttering something about codeine?"

"Ah. Welcome to our hell!" Mel pats Derek on the shoulder then walks toward the door to give us some time alone.

"Sorry. Those are my parents and Mel's parents. They are usually quite normal," I am so happy to see him, and it helps that I know the drugs will be working soon but I have no control over the seemingly never-ending tears.

"Don't cry. I was just so worried. You look really pale. Is there anything I can do?"

"No. I just got some drugs so I'll feel a bit better soon, I hope. Sorry I ruined our first Valentine's Day." I really do feel absolutely awful. There was nothing I wanted more than to spend the evening with him, both at dinner and after. I hope my mother didn't really grab at him in the hallway. We've only been dating for a few weeks. I had hoped to keep him parent-free until at least Easter. This whole getting hit by a car thing, which was not a Lexus I might add, is really messing with my life.

"No. You don't get to worry about that. It was just a reservation that I was able to cancel. You were hit by a car! It's not like you chose to not see me. We'll go out when you're back up and around." Okay, it's official. I'm dating the sweetest man on the planet. Again, I want to ravish him and I reach out and touch his perfect chest. I've become very touchy-feely since meeting Derek. Mel even commented on it after the Super Bowl, but I don't care and Derek doesn't seem to mind.

"Okay. Thank you for being so great." I reach out to hold his hand. "Oh, and I apologize in advance for anything and everything my parents will do and say. They don't deal well with any sort of trauma."

"They're parents. Making you crazy is their job," Derek laughs. "Besides, you haven't met mine yet. What goes around comes around!" Derek bends down to kiss me and I curse the bike courier and the Jetta for putting me in traction and hindering my ability to do unspeakable things with my boyfriend.

# 20

The hospital stay is longer than I'd hoped. It is five days before they give me the go ahead to leave and after my appetite returned, around day three, the food is killing me as much as the pain in my leg. Mel is completely frazzled. At one point around day four I see her searching her Prada handbag in a frantic manner reminiscent of the old days when she'd misplaced her cigarettes. I ask her about it and she suddenly comes out of her frenzy and laughs. She has no idea what she is actually looking for and agrees, that yes, the parents are driving her back to nicotine and all vices in fact; she is sure she is drinking more. Derek keeps a close vigil, stopping by every day, and even seems quite at ease in the parents' presence. Mom and Dad both appear to like him and I can tell from the glint in my mother's eye and the way she laughs, touches his arm and coos his name that she is thinking "this might be the one to finally marry her." But as happy as my finally marrying would make her, this one will keep me in The City. She must be having mixed emotions about that. Dad to his credit, doesn't seem so anxious to get me married off and doesn't coo at Derek.

On day four, when my brain starts to become less foggy,

the magnitude of my situation finally hits me. A couple of days ago I was rushing around the city in crazed downtown-dweller fashion and training to run a half-marathon and now I'm lucky to get to the washroom unassisted. The recovery, full recovery to running, will be months the doctor says and maybe no running for a year. At one point I start to consider the complete disaster I am financially, now that I can't work, but try to forget that for the time being. The important things in my day now are when do I get more drugs and can someone help me to the washroom.

The trip home is not uneventful. I have to get dressed in order to leave the hospital, but nothing I own will go over the leg brace so Mel went to the secondhand store and picked up several pairs of "tear-away pants," the kind preferred by basketball players and strippers. In order to get into the tear-away pants I have to sit on the bottom and draw the front through my legs like a diaper then do up the top two domes and have someone else do up the remaining domes on the left leg and the bottom two domes on the right leg; it is not stylish by any stretch of the imagination but does get me out of the blue paper gown. The completely open side of the pants gives nice ventilation in the minus-whatever winter weather and I suddenly miss underwear. I can't get it on over the brace and putting on underwear when the brace is off is completely out of the question due to the pain factor. So commando it is. On top I wear a full-zippered sweatshirt. Again commando works best because my ribs still hurt and raising my hands above my head is almost as painful as any leg movement. If the pain hadn't forced me to toss all modesty out the window I'd feel positively naughty with all the nakedness going on.

Outside, getting my leg into an automobile when I can't bend it makes sitting up impossible. It is finally determined that the only way I can travel is to lie across the back seat of my dad's car, but getting in and out involves all the strength I can muster and the pain involved rivals the total of all the pain I'd ever had rolled into one. By the time I actually arrive at home I am too physically exhausted to even try to use crutches on the snow-covered ground and my dad and Mr. Melrose have to carry me into the house and get me to my room. Upon entering the house, I noticed a large number of flower bouquets and what appears to be the largest fruit basket I've ever seen. It is sitting on the floor of our kitchen and the leaves of the pineapple that is perched on the top of it are almost level with Mel's chin in her four-inch heels.

"Is that a fruit basket?" I ask Mel.

"Yep."

"Is that the largest fruit basket ever?"

"Oh I think so. I'm going to call the *Guinness World Records* people this afternoon to see for sure but I think we're in the running."

"I count four pineapples!" Even in excruciating pain I am amazed that one basket can house that many pineapples not to mention the other fruit it contains.

"And that's only one side," Mel laughs and follows us to my room.

"Where did the fruit come from?" I ask Mel after the dads have placed me on my bed and the moms manage to get me propped up and place pillows under my leg.

"The courier company that the little shit who threw you into traffic works for," Mel starts to tell me the tale. "Seems Joyce went nuts tracking the kid down. She went from office to office in all the nearby buildings until someone knew who he was, then she called the courier company he works for and they are going to pay half your wages until you're back to work and Mr. Sebring is going to keep paying you the other half so you won't be destitute before all this is over. Joyce mentioned something about rehab expenses too if you need them. She said she'd stop in this week to see you."

"Joyce found the guy? And they're paying my wages?" This solidifies my belief that Joyce does indeed have Mafia ties.

"Yep. I don't know how, but she got them to do it. I think Mr. Sebring might have gotten involved. He did lose his assistant for six weeks or longer. You, my dear, have one formidable ally in Joyce," Mel laughs. "We saved all the cards from the flowers and there's about twenty gift bags that all contain boxes of After Eights to go through when you're up to it."

"Here take these," Mel says as she shakes two painkillers from their bottle.

"Is it time for those?" My mother is worried that I'll become a raving drug addict from the painkillers.

"It's a bit early, but she's looking pretty pale from the trip. Are you in pain?" Mel turns to me.

"Quite a lot actually. You are a saint." I take the drugs readily.

"I'll get you some water and juice. Do you want anything to eat?"

"Maybe I'll have some fruit and After Eights later, after a little nap," I try to laugh.

"We'll be eating fruit for every meal and you may never have to buy After Eights again. It's good to have you home," I hear Mel say just before I close my eyes.

# 21

The next morning my parents bring me a large bowl of fruit salad and tell me they want to take me home for my recuperation, but are concerned about the trip. After seeing me in horrific pain just coming across town they don't know if they want to put me through that for the three plus hours that it will take to get me back up north. Inside I am jumping for joy, but manage to downplay my excitement. I absolutely don't want to leave Derek for six weeks. I'm sure I'd die without seeing him every day. My overactive libido would definitely suffer.

"I think you're right, Mom, I don't think I'd survive the trip," I say, but inside am thinking "happy, happy, joy, joy."

"But we have to get back home soon. Your father and Mr. Melrose have to get back to work and the twins will be home for reading week next week." My mom looks really concerned and I know she doesn't want to leave me.

"Mom, don't worry about me. I'll be fine. Besides, I'll just be in your way and would have to take one of the twins' bedrooms. At least here I'm not bothering anyone. Mel can just set me up on the couch beside the fruit basket and I'll be good as new in no time." I try to alleviate my mother's worry but I know I can't. Mothers worry, that's their job.

"I can call you all the time on the phone and I promise that as soon as I'm off the crutches Mel and I will make a trip up north. Maybe we'll bring Derek and John, that'll be fun." I try to smile through the pain and check the time on Marc's TAG to see if I can take more painkillers. Not yet.

"But what if you become a drug addict from all these drugs you're taking?" I can tell Mom's feeling better about leaving me and is back to the mother I know and love.

"Then you'll have something to tell the ladies at church, besides Mel and Derek will keep an eye on me. I've been very good about not taking them early. See I just checked and I can't have any yet. I'll be fine Mom. I promise."

Just before they leave my room, my dad leans over, kisses me on the forehead and says, "Oh, I forgot to say thanks for the hockey tickets. It was a great game. Maybe living in The City does have a few perks." Then he winks and leaves with my mom to return to the kitchen and tackle another pineapple. I hope there's a coconut in that basket, I'm starting to think making piña coladas for the neighbours is the only way we'll get through all that pineapple.

The big challenge today is getting me cleaned up. I can't take a proper bath or shower due to the stitches but I am desperate to wash my hair and get the hospital grime off me. Mel and the moms' help get me propped up over the kitchen sink with my leg supported by a chair. It is extremely painful but knowing that I'll have shiny clean, albeit much larger, hair after it's over makes it all worth it. My mom washes and conditions my hair like she did when I was little, but of course my hair wasn't nearly so unmanageable back then and she wasn't worried about bumping my healing leg. After my hair is wrapped in a towel I crutch to the washroom and do my best to clean up with a sink full of water and a washcloth. I'm not sure how much cleaner I am but I feel better than I did this morning. Completely exhausted, I spend the remainder of the day in my room going through gift bags and reading, or rather trying to read.

It's going to be a long six weeks I suspect. I hope I have fast-healing bones and the projected timeline is for the weakest people and I'll be a much faster healer than the average person. Unfortunately, if the amount of pain is any indication of how low my threshold is for pain, maybe I am average. The drugs always seem to wear off long before I'm scheduled for more. On the bright side, maybe I'm just well on my way to becoming the drug addict that my mother suspects I'll be by the end of this ordeal.

Derek stops in to see me on his way home from work. I can't help but smile just hearing his voice in the living room asking, "Is that a fruit basket?" This whole leg thing won't be over with soon enough. I just want to be back to normal and doing normal things, like meeting Derek after work, going to movies and having sex. I reach up and try to flatten my larger-than-life hair before Derek gets to my room. The last thing I want to do is share "the hair" with Derek this soon in the relationship. I had been making great strides in the taming arena before the Jetta interfered. Every girl wants to look her best for a sexy new boyfriend and big hair and tear-away pants is not exactly the statement I want to make. When Derek comes into my room after escaping the parents (my mother is still cooing at him), he looks relieved.

"Wow, you look a lot better," he says and sits beside me on the bed. "You looked so pale in the hospital."

"I'm feeling a bit better and managed to get cleaned up a little, but you're going to see bad hair for some time I'm afraid. I don't have the strength to tame the beast."

"How is it today?" Derek nods at my leg.

"More painful than I'd like. It's amazing how much pain can be concentrated in one spot. Occasionally I wiggle around so my ribs hurt and that makes the leg feel a bit better in comparison," I try to laugh.

"The important thing is you still have a sense of humour," Derek laughs and leans over and kisses me.

"I'm so sorry." I almost start to cry again.

"Hey, what are you sorry for? You didn't jump in front of that car, you were pushed, remember?"

"I know. I just want to have a normal life. We've only been dating for a few weeks and now I can't do anything fun. I can't even wash my own hair." I am quickly realizing that six weeks of this is going to be a long time and I wouldn't be surprised if Derek headed for the hills to find a girlfriend who can actually walk.

"Hey don't be silly. It's only a few weeks. It's nothing in

the scheme of things. I plan to stick around a lot longer than that. Sorry, you're stuck with me." Derek is being so sweet.

"Well, if that's the case, I hope you like fruit. How's Bianca doing?" I ask about Derek's assistant because it is an endless source of amusement.

"Oh, she's gone. She finally faxed something the right way around but she faxed it to the wrong person, and it was confidential. I have Janice now. So far she seems good, but she's only been at her desk since yesterday. Time will tell. Who knows, maybe this one's a keeper," Derek laughs because deep down he suspects otherwise.

"You'll have to keep me posted. You know I live vicariously through you. Well, for the next several weeks anyway."

Derek stays for over an hour but starts to leave when he sees how tired I'm getting. If this leg does nothing else, it will at least allow me to catch up on my rest. He leans over to kiss me and all my special parts start to tingle. I hold him as close as possible, given the way I have to sit, and whisper, "I'm going to be all over you like white on rice as soon as I can move."

"I'm never going to look at rice the same again," he laughs, "and I'm going to hold you to that," he whispers back and kisses me again and all I can think is this leg better heal mighty quickly because my mojo is going now, even with the gaggle of parents in the next room.

The next morning, Mom helps me with my washroom routine. I am confident that I can get to the toilet on my own now. It hurts like nobody's business but when the bladder calls, you answer. I also wash my face, brush my teeth and get my hair back into a scrunchie, again causing excruciating pain, but I try to downplay it because I know my parents are anxious to get home and I don't want them to worry about me. When I come out of the washroom, my dad and Mel have set up the couch with more traction pillows and have moved the DVD player to within reach of where I'll be sitting for the next six weeks so I can watch DVDs when daytime television becomes unbearable. They also bring me a little cooler for drinks and sandwiches and have a large fruit bowl within reach so I don't starve. They have thought of everything. The parents gather up their things and depart with only a few tears from my mother. I hear Mrs. Melrose on the way out say something like "well we didn't get around to that decorating and the living room would look much better with a floral wallpaper border." Mel and I make eye contact but stifle our laughter; we are both very glad they "didn't get around to the redecorating."

After the parents are herded into the car Mel comes back in to do the one last check that I have everything. I assure her that I'm fine as she checks the battery level on the portable telephone and hands me my cell phone just in case the portable dies.

"I'm not locking the door in case you fall and have to call 9-1-1," Mel yells from the front door as she's leaving at 10 a.m.

"Okay, but I won't be calling 9-1-1," I say, then add, "I hope!"

By lunchtime, Mel has called twice and Joyce, Derek and Charlie Brown have each called once. I must admit, reluctantly of course, that Charlie Brown isn't nearly as abrasive as I believed him to be when I first met him. He actually is a nice guy and does seem concerned for my wellbeing. I just hang up the phone from Charlie Brown when I hear a knock on the front door. I yell "come in" because there is no way I can make it to the door to be a gracious hostess. I press Stop on the DVD player and see Marc in the doorway.

"Hey, what brings you to this part of town?" I suspect full well that he's just here to check up on me but I don't mind; having a visitor is much preferable to sitting in front of the television.

"I was just in the area and thought I'd see how you were doing," Marc has a guilty look on his face so I know that's not true and I also know he doesn't have any jobs in this area, or didn't last week at any rate.

"Mel sent you, didn't she?" I laugh.

"Well, I did call her to see how you were doing and I mentioned that I could come by." He shoots me the little-boy-caught-with-his-hand-in-the-cookie-jar grin.

"Well, you're off the hook this time, but only because I'm happy for the company."

"I wasn't sure what the parent status was so thought I'd check with Mel. She was very happy I said I'd come by. I think she feels guilty for having to go to work."

"No sense in both of us sitting here watching movies. One of us should be making a living, right?"

"I heard you're going to get paid through all this. That's a good thing," Marc seems happy that my financial status is not that of a soon-to-be homeless person.

"It's a very good thing, what a relief. Paying the bills is much more stressful when you don't have an income. You can come in and sit down. If you want a drink or anything you can grab something from the fridge, or my little cooler here," I say as I pat my cooler of beverages. "Sorry I'm not the best hostess these days."

"No, I'm okay." Marc starts to sit down on the chair across from me.

"Oh wait, before you sit down, your watch is in my room on my side table, you should grab it now so I don't forget to give it back to you." I direct Marc to my bedroom from my post on the couch so he can retrieve his watch.

"Did you get yours back?" Marc asks as he returns to the living room and sits down.

"No, it was smashed by the Jetta, but it wasn't an expensive watch anyway. I'm back to the plastic Ironman that I wear for running, but that's fine for now. I'll get a new one when I get back on my feet, or foot rather."

Marc only visits for a half-hour but it's a nice break from television and movies.

# 22

The highlights of the next six weeks are three trips to the doctor, one to get my stitches removed and two separate occasions for x-rays. Since Mel, Derek and I all drive small two-door cars and Charlie Brown drives a small truck, Marc has to be called and I have to be loaded into his truck on all three occasions.

Around the middle of week five of my confinement, Mel and I discuss it and decide since I haven't shaved my legs in so long I might as well wax them. In theory this is a good idea; in practice it's completely the opposite of good. I've never actually put wax on my any part of my body then voluntarily ripped it off, and since I can't bend I leave Mel in charge of the ripping-off part. As she rips the first strip off my good leg, I scream "Mother of Pearl" and my only thought is "Painkillers are my friend, I can't imagine doing this completely lucid." I stick with it though — well, I have no choice since I am covered in wax and bits of cloth. Mel, on the other hand, doesn't seem to notice my shrieking and goes about her part like a crazed dominatrix. If she were wearing her high black boots the picture would be complete. Mel is so into it that by the end of the second leg she's figuring out when we should do the second round. I'm not completely sure I'm as excited about the second waxing as Mel is; I think subconsciously she resents having to take care of me and this is a bit of payback. Who am I to deny her such pleasure when she's been cooking, cleaning and doing my laundry for weeks?

By week six and the third trip to the doctor, my leg is feeling better and the ribs are well on the way to healing so the trip isn't nearly as exhausting as the previous two excursions. The doctor gives me the good news that I'm able to go back to work part-time. I can't wait to call Joyce and Mel and share the joy. Joyce is pleased and can't wait to get me back even if it's only for a few hours a day. I tell her I'll be in Monday morning, then call Mel who is also happy to hear my news but raises a very good point.

"Did you get a smaller brace?" Mel asks.

"Nope, same one. Why?"

"Well, what are you going to wear to work? You can't possibly go to the office in tear-away pants that are half open all the time. We'll have to find you some skirts with a lot of flare!" Mel is completely on top of my wardrobe issues long before I realize I have wardrobe issues. "Don't you worry, I'll come up with something."

As it turns out, I have very good reason to worry.

"You can't be serious." I look up at Mel from the couch where Derek and I are sitting watching the news. I'm not generally one to watch newscasts but since my confinement I have taken great pleasure in seeing what is going on in the world. Mel came in from work and handed me a large plastic bag and said "problem solved" with all the confidence in the world. However, when I opened the bag my thought was "no, problems just beginning."The bag contained five pleated plaid skirts — well, kilts actually — like the ones that high-school girls wear to, well, high school. These five actually looked like they had been shortened — probably by aforementioned high-school girls who wanted to expose their legs to the high-school boys.

"Did you strip schoolchildren on your way home?" I ask Mel as I hold up the very short, red plaid shirt.

"No, but that would have been cheaper. I should have thought of that." Mel is being serious. This apparently is not a joke. "See, they're perfect," Mel continues. "Tight around the waist so they don't fall down and then loads of flare to get over the top of the huge brace. Win, win!"

"I don't think they'll have to flare much. Look how short they are. The hem won't even make it to the top of the brace!" I've never been much of a mini-skirt girl and I'm not sure starting that trend while hopping around on one foot is a good idea.

"Oh, don't be silly. You wear your skirts far too long anyway. This will be liberating." Mel seems very pleased with herself, then turns to Derek, "What do you think, Derek, am I a genius, or what?"

Derek who has been sitting quietly saying nothing is staring at me, while I stand on one leg with the red plaid skirt held in front of me demonstrating that the hem does not reach the top of the brace, with his mouth hanging open and he doesn't answer Mel.

"See! Even my boyfriend thinks I look like a stripper!" I emphasize to Mel.

"Wow," Derek finally utters practically drooling.

"Just add little pigtails and *voilà*, stripper!" I continue incredulously.

Mel laughs, "Well then, you should be able to get all the construction guys to bend over backward for you."

"Well, I hope so since *I* won't be bending over for anything!" Just then Charlie Brown comes into the room and stands behind Derek and adopts the same hanging-open mouth before uttering, "Great skirt, Kit. Get yourself a push-up bra and pigtails and then we're talking!" Charlie Brown's excitement is a little too obvious.

"I'll get you back for this," I say to Mel. "I don't know how but I will."

"You'll be fine! A little bit of short skirt will do you the world of good, besides I didn't get you the matching ties, count your blessings!"

"I don't think the world is ready for me in short plaid skirts, with or without the matching ties." I turn and crutch to my bedroom with the bag of skirts in hand and Derek follows me with his mouth still hanging open. Derek closes the bedroom door behind us, takes my crutches, pushes me down on the bed and starts kissing me.

"Maybe we should try one of those little skirts on so I can take it off," he laughs while he starts removing my tear-away pants and leg brace.

"Well, maybe short little skirts *are* a good thing," I laugh and let Derek have his way with me before dinner. We had discovered about a week before that without the brace, depending on the way I hold my leg, sex is indeed finally achievable. Oh it is awkward, but definitely achievable and well worth the effort.

# 23

Monday is a big day. Getting to work is a lot more difficult than I remember. Six weeks of not getting ready for work would make one rusty, even with two working legs. I decided on Sunday that despite my complete abhorrence for the multi-coloured very short kilts, Mel is right, they really are the only thing that will fit over the brace and since I have lost several pounds over the healing period, thanks to all the fruit, I'm sure none of my other clothes fit right now anyway. I send a thank you to the inventors of the removable brace into the heavens. Since I am able to remove the thing, I am able to get tights on under the brace and kilts so as not to flash my bottom all over the city. The fact that it's March and temperatures are still dipping well below zero makes the tights an added warmth bonus. When I crutch out of my bedroom, ready to face the day in my kilt, black tights and white blouse, Mel takes my photo before I can even register that she is standing there.

"Memories!" Mel laughs as she puts her arm around my shoulder, "You look so cute!"

"No I don't and I'll be sure to use that picture as evidence when I'm on trial for killing you."

"You look great. Oh come on, you'll look back on this ten years from now and laugh," Mel laughs.

"I'd laugh harder if you were on the crutches wearing the child-sized skirt," I say, wholeheartedly crutching my way to the kitchen. Just then Charlie Brown walks out of the kitchen eating his bowl of Frosted Flakes. Not only does he have an affinity for little boy t-shirts, that same little boy theme carries over to his choice of breakfast food.

"That's what I'm talking about! Lose the tights, Kit, and you're in business!" Charlie Brown gets out between slurps.

"But no business I want to be in!" I smirk back. "Mel! You're dating a deviant!" I yell to Mel in the washroom.

"I know," Mel yells back, "isn't he yummy!"

"Oh YEAH!" the deviant yells out from the couch where he is watching *Breakfast Television*. "Yummy" is not the word I'd use but then again, who am I to say, I'm the one standing on crutches dressed like a stripper.

I'm practically exhausted by the time I wiggle into and then out of Mel's car and manage to get my kilt-wearing, knapsack-carrying, barely covered butt up the elevator and to my desk. Since I'm on crutches the only way I can carry my wallet, drugs and fruity snacks is in a knapsack. So not only am I dressed like a saucy high-school student I'm also accessorized like one. The only thing that would truly complete the picture would be bright pink bubblegum-flavoured lipgloss of the extra shiny variety. My return to the office is well known between Joyce and Marc, and the morning brings a parade of contractors all coming by to welcome me back. I suspect my outfit has something to do with the parade and am sure that Charlie Brown let the entire construction site know what I've been reduced to wearing. I really should try and sue the courier company for humiliation. I wonder if that would stick. Mr. Sebring seems pleased to have me back — well, after he almost snapped his head off at his neck giving my outfit the double take — and I spent most of the morning finding things for him in the files. I have devised a filing system that a child could utilize but both Joyce and Mr. Sebring still refuse to try to find anything, probably out of fear of messing up my system so that no one, including me, would be able to locate anything. I suppose it is better with just one set of fingers in the filing drawers. But after six weeks the filing on my desk does tend to add up and the pile, which is probably as tall as I am, is surely a health and safety issue. If the pile falls over someone could be killed. Thankfully Joyce has changed my voicemail and has been fielding all the calls. My email is a disaster to the tune of "you have 347 emails" (none of them from Derek because he knew I wasn't in the office and his are the only emails I look forward to). I have set a goal of getting email cleaned up before the week's end, but having only half-days will make my goal tough to achieve.

Marc comes into the office around 12:30 p.m. and offers to drive me home.

"Wow, John said I had to come by and see what you were

wearing," Marc blurts out after he is finally able to close his gaping mouth.

"Yeah, yeah. I look like a schoolgirl-slash-stripper. Come by every day this week, I have the same outfit in five colours," I laugh. "It's Mel's idea of an April Fool's joke I think."

"Wow, five different colours, this week's shaping up better than I thought." Marc suggests going out for lunch but I have to confess that I am completely exhausted, my leg is throbbing and I really just can't wait to get home, and back to my bed. The bed I couldn't leave fast enough is now calling me back home. I call Mel to let her know she's off the hook for driving me, then Marc takes me home ending my first day back in the real world. The real world, I decide as my head hits the pillow, is not meant for people who only have one good leg. The real world is definitely made for able-bodied two-legged creatures, like monkeys. Maybe I can find a monkey to wear the silly skirts and do my job. The skirts might be the right length for an average-sized monkey. I'll look into it as soon as I wake up.

The first two weeks of April fly by. Being back to work takes all my energy and I spend a great deal of time sleeping when I'm not hopping around in really short skirts. Easter approaches and the parents are ready to face another trip to The City. They decide to come to Toronto on Good Friday, have dinner with Mel and me and continue on to Kingston on Saturday and take the twins out for dinner there.

Mel's brother Mike, who moved to Atlanta years ago, is

spared all parental-accompanied Easter festivities. When we were growing up Mel and I never gave Mike much thought or notice. He was four years older than us and so far ahead in school that we never ran in the same crowds. Now, however, we revere Mike Melrose as a sort of parent-escaping genius with the brightness to foresee the future of parental visitation and the brilliance to get his butt transferred to a distance far enough away to deter if not ensure a mostly parentless existence. It's not that our parents are awful. I think they're pretty much like everyone else's parents except there are just so many of them. We were neighbours growing up and our parents are best friends with each other, so instead of having two parents to love and suffocate us, we each have four parents — they completely bought into the theory that "it takes a village to raise a child." Our dads stay fairly focused but the moms can be a handful. The moms feel that Mel and I have gone completely off course by moving to The City and are "getting up to Lord knows what" (their phrase, not ours). The moms would like us to settle down, get married and have babies so there is no way I can tell any of them I have the maternal instincts of a sea turtle. I think I can safely assume Mel isn't even in sea turtle mode. Mel might actually eat her young if they interfered with a real estate deal. I hope the twins have maternal instincts or the mothers are in for a very unwelcome surprise.

As soon as we finalized the Good Friday dinner with the parents, Mel and I decide that with my leg, we will make dinner here and limit the parents' exposure to The City. I am able to get around better but going anywhere is still a fairly major production. Much easier to stay here, inside, where I can't slip a crutch on snow or ice which is sadly still lingering on most of the city streets. We decide on roast beef and although it's not a traditional Easter feast it will be a lovely dinner, provided there are no battles over who makes the gravy. The gravy is always a bone of contention. Everyone who makes gravy has their own way of making it and everyone believes their way is the right way. Mom and Mrs. Melrose are very good friends, both are wonderful cooks and both make a fine gravy, but I've seen them almost come to fisticuffs over cornstarch versus flour. Mel and I decide to have the gravy ready before they arrive so as to avoid the mad rush for the kitchen that could result in injury. Best to ply them both with wine and keep the gravy discussions to a minimum.

Friday arrives and the parents descend like piranhas on a wounded carp. The arrival of four people, each with a driving horror to tell, and enough foodstuffs to fill a small cornerstore in hand, is no small event. Charlie Brown and Derek had arrived earlier and we are each a glass of wine into it before the parents' arrival so that makes it all seem more manageable. I'm not saying that we need to have alcohol to have a good time, but it does lessen the stress of family functions.

"Mother, we *do* have grocery stores here," Mel tells her mother as she takes the second bag of groceries from her and a third bag from her dad.

"Oh, but they aren't as good as at home. There's real meat in that one." Mel's mom points at one of the bags in Mel's hand.

"What constitutes real meat?" Mel asks the question but I can tell from the look on her face she regrets it the second it's out of her mouth.

"Don't get me started! I saw a story on the news about what they pass off as meat in 'big cities' and I'm sure what you get here is not real," Mel's mother starts. Mel rolls her eyes and turns into the kitchen with the "real meat" and her mother follows her, giving a full account of the story she heard, although some of the facts she is spouting didn't seem possible. Charlie Brown, ever the kiss-up, follows them into the kitchen and I hear him claim "to have seen the same program" and I'm pretty sure he is making it up. Besides sports, and the traffic segment on *Breakfast Television*, I've never seen Charlie Brown watch anything even remotely resembling informative television.

Derek and I offer Mom, Dad and Mr. Melrose drinks then Derek goes to get them from the kitchen. I can't carry anything so I'm fairly useless in the hostess arena.

"Kathryn, what are you wearing?" My mother is staring at my skirt in disbelief.

"A skirt." I'm actually getting quite used to the constant draft on my bottom after two weeks of short plaid skirts and didn't think much of putting it on for the dining occasion. I actually thought a skirt was much nicer than the tear-away pants. Besides, Derek seems to have taken a real shine to the skirts.

"But isn't that a child's skirt?" I knew Mel picked them up in the children's section.

"Probably. Mel picked them up for me since I'm not able to get out and shop. I have to wear something to work that goes over this brace. Nothing else works until I get a smaller brace or lose this one altogether," I explain.

"Well, if you weren't wearing tights I'd be able to see your underwear!" My mother is in the same shock I experienced two weeks ago.

"Coincidentally, I'm not wearing any underwear." I try to make light of the short skirt situation but get the look of horror and "KATHRYN!" hissed at me from my mother just as Mel, Mrs. Melrose, Charlie Brown and Derek come back into the room with drinks. Yes, ply them with alcohol, all of us in fact, that's how to weather a family dinner.

Dinner goes remarkably smoothly and the entire family gets used to my short skirt. Of course, it helps that I'm sitting and no one can see it. The gravy is not an issue because Mel made me stir it while she put in the thickener. I turned my head so as not to see if she used flour or cornstarch. Luckily, between the length of my skirt and the four bottles of wine consumed, the issue of how the gravy was made was narrowly averted.

Derek and Charlie Brown both have their own family commitments the next day so they go home after dinner to their respective apartments and reluctantly leave us with our overnight guests. Derek and I have become inseparable and take turns staying over with each other most nights, despite the leg issue. The parents get our rooms and I get the couch because of my leg, leaving Mel on an air mattress on the floor at my head. Mel and I giggle into the night until one of our mothers yells at us to "go to sleep already." It's just like being back in high school only now I have the uniform.

# 24

Saturday morning, after the moms make us a huge breakfast that includes real meat and we wish our parents well on the next leg of their journey, Mel and I finally discuss the house renovations. My run-in with the Jetta put all plans on hold and we haven't even mentioned the renovations since that fateful day. Now that I'm hobbling around in short plaid skirts and the fruit basket is no longer a fixture, the need for renovations is back to being very obvious. Charlie Brown has given the wiring the onceover and the electrical panel must be updated along with some of the wiring. Mel assures me we will make the money back plus some when we sell the house and the upgrades are necessary. I, on the other hand, see a lot of construction on a daily basis and realize, needed or not, we will be living in a complete disaster zone for some time before all the updates are completed. We agree to forge ahead and Mel is going to talk to Charlie Brown about starting the electrical upgrades as soon as possible. I will start asking the contractors I know for help with the plumbing and drywall repairs. Mel and I both agree that the living room, dining room and kitchen doorways must be enlarged into archways to make the living area seem like one big space. Mel has also arranged for three window companies to come in and give us prices on replacing all the windows in the house. We both suspect this is going to be a very costly venture but will only help in the resale.

Mel and I spend the remainder of the day looking through home and lifestyle magazines Mel borrowed from her office, deciding what look we want to have for our house. The one universal truth about construction that I've found is "with construction comes dust" so we decide that all non-essentials must be boxed and taken to the basement and covered in plastic until the renovations are over. Non-essentials will also include Mel's ultrasuede couch and all television and stereo equipment; once the destruction of walls begins we will officially be minimalists living in similar fashion to monks, although I suspect I won't become a vegetarian. I really don't care for the texture of tofu.

Monday, after the Easter weekend, my doctor gives me the go-ahead to start putting weight on my right foot when it feels comfortable and the okay to start back to work full-time. When you are healthy and two-legged, you don't pay much attention to things like going to work or walking, but as a one-legged crutch person this is extraordinary news indeed and calls for a celebration. I call Derek and Mel and we agree to meet at the Firkin after work to celebrate my first all-day adventure at the office. I am finally catching up on emails and filing and am able to push myself around the office on my chair faster than I can crutch so am making headway all around. My short skirts are quite normal now and are no longer drawing such large crowds to the office. I've actually become quite comfortable showing off all my legs and most of my bottom to the public around me. I hope this doesn't make me some sort of exhibitionist and pray that I will someday be able to transition back to normal-length skirts, possibly a nice dress pant, without having to seek therapy.

When we meet up at the Firkin, Charlie Brown is the last to arrive and he looks a bit frazzled. I've never seen Charlie Brown look anything but overconfident. It is strange to see him look vulnerable. My heart goes out to him a little when I see his look of consternation.

"Hey, what's up?" Mel asks Charlie Brown. She has also noticed his demeanour.

"Seems I'm in charge of Kit's condo site for a few days," Charlie Brown blurts out, but then looks a bit worried because as an employee of the developer, I may not have been a person who should hear this tidbit.

"What? Where's Marc?" Mel and I ask almost in the same breath.

"Gone. He gave me the company cell phone and told me I was in charge for a couple of days. Seems he's got something personal going on."

"Like personal health-related?" I too am worried, both about the construction site and Marc.

"I don't know. He didn't say. He looked healthy enough, stressed out, but otherwise healthy." Charlie Brown is more concerned than all the rest of us put together, and with good reason — he's now running Marc's company.

"Did he give you a contact number?" I am suddenly in full panic.

"No. *I'm* it. It's going to be a heck of a long week."

"You'll be fine," I offer as support, "Sebring II is wrapping up and you don't start at Sebring III for a couple of months. What else do you guys have on the go?" I try to make things sound fine in spite of the fact that I'm freaking out inside.

"Just two other little jobs. Actually, I guess I can send a couple of guys over to your house tomorrow. Marc said to keep the guys busy." Charlie Brown sounds better now that he's making plans for the other employees.

"That'd be great." Mel's glad that Charlie Brown is feeling better about the situation, so encourages him, "You have a key; do what you have to do."

"Yep, there's no time like the present to start the renovations," I add.

We spend the rest of the evening eating nachos and wings and trying to be normal but all of us are wondering what the heck is going on with Marc. Even Derek, who has only met Marc on two occasions, picks up on the concern the rest of us are feeling. It's not like Marc to take off for a couple of days without notifying all the parties' involved and leaving contact numbers. This must be something major.

# 25

The next day, Mel and I arrive home to what appears to be a "war zone." Charlie Brown has embraced his new position as leader of Marc's company and stepped it up a notch. Charlie Brown is now our personal General Contractor. Seems he's had a very large garbage bin delivered to our driveway. The huge bin is being filled with plaster, doors and doorframes that were affixed to our house this morning. The new electrical panel is installed in the basement and working. Charlie Brown has arranged for one of Bruno's employees, Bruno being the drywall contactor at that condo construction site, to work with him to insulate and drywall where plaster used to be. He has the plumber working out a plan to convert our existing washroom and storage cupboard into two separate washrooms, one off each bedroom, and has ordered kitchen cabinetry because one of the cabinet makers we deal with at work has an overrun and is selling them off at cost.

Charlie Brown is more hyper than I've ever seen him and is talking at a speed that would rival Mel. It would be funny if it wasn't just a little bit scary. Either Charlie Brown is spending way too much time with Mel or he's suffering a nervous breakdown.

"You said you'd look at the electrical! What the heck is all this? You've torn the place apart and..." Mel starts to give Charlie Brown "what for" but I interrupt her when I notice Charlie Brown's eyes look very glassy and I haven't seen him blink since we arrived.

"Have you eaten anything today?" I ask Charlie Brown. His glassy eyes are open far too wide and he is shaking.

"I had some coffee earlier," Charlie Brown blurts out, again at a speed that would rival most fast-talkers.

"How many coffees did you have?" I ask but suspect the number is higher than I'd like to hear.

"Oh I don't know. Ten." Charlie Brown's wide-open non-blinking eyes scan the room for something to do.

"I'm going to order some pizza for you and the other guys." I try to make it sound like I'm being nice and helpful but really I'm worried that Charlie Brown is going to collapse on his first day of taking care of Marc's business and then where will my electrical contracting be at work, not to mention our now-demolished house? Charlie Brown and I agreed last night to tell Mr. Sebring, Joyce and all the other contractors at the site that Marc was called away on a family emergency. There is no need to raise concern yet — we hope anyway. Now that I see what the pressure of running the company might do to Charlie Brown, I really wish Marc had left a contact number. Having Marc reassure me right now would be a good thing. I'm not sure I can keep an eye on Charlie Brown while hopping on one foot in a skirt far too short for the average six year old and living in squalor. As I dial the telephone to order pizza for our workers, two of them walk past me carrying the bathtub outside to the garbage bin in the driveway. I hate that bathtub, the finish completely wore through at least a decade ago, but seeing it walk by me and knowing the renovations are now in the hands of a man who is hyped up on nothing but caffeine and power makes me shudder just a little.

The pizza arrives at the same time as Derek. Right after placing the pizza order I called Derek for moral support and to ask him if I could sleep at his place tonight since our house currently has no working washroom and the kitchen sink may or may not have walked by me as well. I curse my still non-functional leg as I try to maneuver in the construction zone that I now call home. I have avoided the sites at work simply because crutches and construction debris do not mix well. Put a crutch on the wrong piece of debris and you could be back where you were eight weeks ago. Now that I find myself living in a construction zone, I'm glad I've avoided the ones at work. I quietly thank God for Derek who is going to take me out of this tonight and back to his nice apartment that is not undergoing renovations. Derek takes the pizzas into the kitchen and gets beer and Coke out of the fridge for the workers. Mel is frantically moving small things downstairs and out of the work zone and pops her head into the kitchen where Derek and I are smooching after slicing the pizzas.

"You two are worse than rabbits. If you can tear yourselves apart I need a hand covering the couch." Mel has located some old blankets to cover the couch since it will likely remain in the living area now that construction is way ahead of schedule, thanks to caffeine-hyped Charlie Brown.

The week flies by but still with no word from Marc. Mel and I go by the house every day after work to see how Charlie Brown is doing, and the work is progressing much faster than I ever imagined. Although Charlie Brown is still manic, he is less so than the first day. Since Mel is staying with him at his apartment she is making him healthy lunches and snacks that she packs in a large cooler bag for him to take to work. As for caffeine intake, Mel and I both feel that he's still drinking far too much coffee but at least he appears to be eating. Things are getting done and despite my abhorrence for his dress sense, I have to give him credit for running Marc's company fairly effectively in Marc's absence.

By the end of the week, we have walls and roughed-in plumbing for two washrooms where one used to co-exist with a storage closet, upgraded electrical, and new kitchen cabinets set in place but not yet installed. The countertop has been ordered but may take two weeks to be delivered. The windows are being installed next week. Charlie Brown is getting the work done but is not a very good money man. Mel has asked him several times how much things are costing and how we should be paying but he always manages to change the subject and not answer. We suspect that he doesn't have a clue about the costs and we are trying to keep track ourselves so that we can tell Marc when he gets back in order to pay for all the material and work. Yesterday, being Thursday, all Marc's employees handed their pay sheets to Charlie Brown while Mel and I were at the house and he looked absolutely shocked. I quickly gathered from his reaction that Marc had not left provisions for paying the staff.

"John, did Marc leave you signed cheques to pay the guys?" I ask but already know the answer.

"No. I don't have any way to pay for anything, certainly not an entire payroll." He has the deer-in-the-headlights look and is starting to visibly shake again.

"The guys know that Marc is away. We'll just explain it to them and tell them they will get paid on Monday," Mel says matter-of-factly.

"But what if Marc isn't back by Monday?" Charlie Brown, although manic, has a valid point.

"Good point, we can't keep the guys waiting in good faith just to tell them again on Monday 'Oops, sorry guys, Marc's not back yet.'" Now I'm starting to feel sick to my stomach. Where the hell is Marc? It just isn't right to leave poor Charlie Brown in this predicament.

"Marc hasn't even called you?" Mel has been openly hostile about Marc's disappearance to me but has managed to control her emotions when she's with Charlie Brown because I was able to convince her that she isn't helping poor Charlie by harping about the obvious.

"Okay. We can't help what is or isn't. Marc isn't here. How are we going to deal with this situation?" I interrupt Mel who is about to launch into another of her "irresponsible Marc" spiels.

"I can't deal with it. I don't have enough money for a payroll. I don't have enough money to cover my own rent and I'm not getting paid either." Charlie Brown is starting to see the magnitude of the situation.

"We can figure this out." I am optimistic and am devising a plan of sorts in my head. "John, do you know how much the guys even make?"

"Mostly and they'll tell me if I ask. Why?" Charlie Brown looks confused but is at least coming out of panic mode.

"You figure out how much the payroll will be roughly and Mel and I will figure out how much money we have set aside for the renovations. We have to pay for them at some point anyway. We can keep track of what we pay the guys and it can come off the total we owe Marc at the end of this." I scan Mel's face for a visible reaction and she doesn't give one because she is considering what I've just said.

"That might work." Charlie Brown is coming around to the idea.

"It might, but what about deductions and taxes?" Mel is one step ahead of me as usual.

"Joyce has the deduction book at work. We can figure out what each guy will make and I'll do the deductions at work tomorrow morning first thing, write the cheques on our account, then John can pick up the cheques and have them to the guys by day's end." I breathe a sigh of relief as it's all coming together.

"There will be a hold on personal cheques." Mel has another good point since she deals with personal cheques all the time in her job.

"We'll have to get them certified then, not much else we can do." The plan's not perfect but will keep Marc's business running and our renovations continuing for another week.

Charlie Brown does the math and figures out the pay sheets and the total is around ten thousand dollars. Mel and I have assessed our renovation fund and we can cover the ten thousand dollars but just barely. I really hope Marc is back soon because we were planning on paying the bulk of the renovation costs with our line of credit. I'm not sure where the bank stands on certifying cheques that are written on a credit line. If Marc's not back by next Friday we could have a mutiny on our hands.

The next morning I get to work early with the names and amounts due for each employee, I find Joyce's tax deduction book and figure out how much the government should get, prepare a spreadsheet to give to Marc when he gets back that shows hours, rates of pay (in case any of the guys gave themselves raises in Marc's absence) and the deductions I figured out (I don't have a clue how to pay the government, Marc will have to do that upon his return). I'm fairly sure I read the deduction book correctly but I'll let Marc check everything. After I determine what each employee should be paid, I write out the cheques and photocopy them, again to show Marc what we did. I call Mel because she has agreed to go to the bank and get the cheques certified this morning between clients and will meet Charlie Brown for lunch. Meeting for lunch was my idea. I know Mel isn't having much quality time with Charlie Brown these days so I suggested they go out to lunch and bill Marc when he gets back.

The process goes well and I get a report back from Mel in the afternoon that Marc's workers are all paid and are very happy that we managed to figure it out. I know Charlie Brown's life would have been hell if we hadn't found a way to pay them. I'm certain he would have no employees next week; no one works for free.

Friday night after work I meet Mel, squirm my still-braced leg into the car and go off to purchase the paint for the house. Painting is our domain; we don't want the added expense of paying someone to do what we can do. Ideally, of course, I would be functioning on two legs and would be able to do some of the work. Instead, I will be hopping and hobbling and leaving the brunt of the work to Mel.

"I could call my parents to come and help," I laugh to Mel in the car.

"Oh no you won't!" Mel laughs back, "Our decorating might take a bit longer, but at least we will escape wallpaper border–free!" Mel is being wonderful about my leg and taking on all the extra work.

# 26

The paint is purchased and paid for with Mel's credit card. Mel drops me off at Derek's apartment on her way to our house to find Charlie Brown and tear him away from the renovation. He is really doing a wonderful job but both Mel and I are worried that he is being too involved in it with the added responsibility of running Marc's company. He seems loath to leave our house and always seems to be thinking of a million things at once when you speak to him. Mel is taking him out to see a movie in the hope of giving his brain a break from the pressure.

I manage to get the door unlocked and start the hobble up the stairs to Derek's second-floor apartment. I never noticed what a pain the stairs were before crutches. I miss running up stairs. The first time I was here I ran up the stairs. Heck, at this point I'd throw complete caution to the wind and run with scissors and sharp sticks.

"Hey you! Are you home?" I yell out to the apartment as I struggle to get out of my knapsack. I won't miss the knapsack after all this is over either. I know that logically it's the only way to carry anything when on crutches but it is such a pain. My blouse always bunches up and, I'm not sure, but I think it hikes up my already shorter-than-necessary skirts. The most annoying part is that I have to actually put the knapsack on my back even if I'm only going a few feet because it gets much too heavy and awkward in a hand that is also trying to manage a crutch. I know I'm still in crutch-world for some time because putting weight on my foot is not progressing as quickly as I'd hoped. The longest I can actually put my toes to the ground is twenty minutes and I can only do that for a maximum of three times per day. After twenty minutes the pain is severe and I'm back to crutch-land. Crutch-world and crutch-land are like Disney World and Disneyland, surprisingly similar with few notable differences, and you don't want to be in either place when it snows.

It appears that Derek isn't home yet so I crutch to the bedroom to get out of my work-slash-stripper outfit and into my tear-away pants. I am starting to leave the brace off more and more during the evenings, so of late I've been able to button the entire side of my tear-away pants and not leave my leg exposed to the outside world. As I crutch toward the bedroom I notice the bed has been made. Derek and I were late this morning and since my morning ritual takes much longer than it used to, we didn't have time to make the bed or do the breakfast dishes. Derek must have been home at some point and made the bed. What a sweetheart. When I fully enter the bedroom there is a beautiful black dress lying on the bed and a note that reads "Please put this on and be downstairs at 7:30 p.m. Love, Derek."

The dress is amazing. It's a poly blend and has an empire waist and full-flowing skirt to accommodate my leg and a crisscross front with satin edging. Wow. I also notice that Derek must have gone to my house to get my shoes because one of my dress pairs is on the floor beside the bed with a package of new pantyhose tucked in between them. Wow.

A quick glance at the clock indicates that I'll be pressed for time just to get ready and hobble downstairs; it's 7:05 p.m. No time to shower or wonder what Derek is up to, just a quick wash up and refresh of the makeup. This is so exciting. I haven't been dressed up since I can remember and the mystery adds a very exciting element to the adventure. I have definitely never had a man purchase a dress for me. The one Derek selected is stunning and of a proper, respectable, parent-approving length.

I manage to get a hasty cleanup, teeth brushed and refresh powder, eye makeup and lipstick before quickly jumping into the pantyhose (which in reality is more of a struggle than a jump). As I pull the pantyhose up over the lengthy scar on my leg I notice how hideous and apparent it is through the sheer nylon. I've been wearing tights to work in an attempt to maintain some modesty and they are thick enough that no one can see through them, or I hope anyway, because that would be embarrassing if I've been thinking all these weeks no one can see my panties but in reality they can. I've been using the vitamin E according to my mother's instructions but am going to have to step it up. The entire leg-recovery process is taking much longer and is far more frustrating than I'd ever imagined. Brushing thoughts of slow recovery aside, I remove the tags from the dress and slide it on. It is fabulous. I feel like a princess and twirl — well, the best I can given the one-legged circumstances. The brace is not even contemplated.

After I slip on my shoes I realize that they have a considerably higher heel than I'm used to while crutching so I venture down the stairs very slowly and cautiously. Wouldn't want Derek to find me in a heap at the bottom; I think that would be considered poor form. At the bottom of the stairs I glance at my watch and it's exactly 7:31 p.m. I smile to myself and think "not bad for an invalid" just as the door opens and Derek steps into the foyer. He looks amazing. He's not wearing one of his work suits but rather a nice pair of khakis, a turtleneck and a sports jacket I don't remember seeing before. He is so handsome. I throw my arms around his neck as best I can, considering I'm balancing crutches under my armpits.

"You are the absolute best!" I say just before I kiss him. Then kiss him again.

"You look amazing," he manages between kisses.

"I have you to thank for that. Thank you." I get in a couple more kisses and start to think heading back upstairs to the bedroom might be fun.

Derek breaks away from smooching me, but not without a bit of a struggle.

"Your chariot awaits," he announces and gestures with a small bow as if I were royalty.

I start to giggle and think, "Wow, how cute is that?" when Derek pushes the door open and I see a shiny black stretch limousine parked in front of the house.

"Wow." I immediately stop giggling and am in complete shock. This is the most exciting date I've ever been on and it hasn't even started yet. Derek is absolutely the most romantic boyfriend I've ever had, not to mention the most handsome. My stomach is doing somersaults and I can't seem to make the crutches work.

"Are you okay?" Derek asks because, as he will tell me later, I've gone completely white and look a bit faint.

"Yes, I'm fine. I'm just a bit overwhelmed. What did I do to deserve all this?" I manage to stammer as I'm starting to get my wits about me and think I might cry at this point. Tears of joy and surprise, not tears of "you great big jerk" like I've cried with boyfriends of the past.

"Well, you're the most beautiful person I've ever known, inside and out. You've been an absolute superstar through the broken leg, you're doing more than your share to help Marc and John, but mostly I can't express how much I, and probably most of the downtown district, have enjoyed the short skirts," Derek laughs when he says the last part about the skirts.

"Oh well, so long as it's just to celebrate the short skirts!"

Derek and I get into the limo, which is larger inside than my residence room was at university, and head for Mildred Pierce to celebrate Valentine's Day nine weeks after the fact.

We have a leisurely dinner, which includes two bottles of

wine and a conversation about Derek's new assistant. Apparently, Janice ran off with a Latino "businessman" who has a mouth full of gold-capped teeth and a licence plate that reads "JAWS" on his bright purple Cadillac. Derek's new assistant, Carie (pronounced like *car* with an *e* on the end), was formerly a dog groomer but had to find other work when her clippers got the best of her while grooming an award-winning Chow named Chester. Derek doesn't know the full story but the best in show Chow may never compete again. Derek mentioned that although he's not sure what pet therapy costs, Carie may have to take a second job, as well as work for him, in order to pay for just half of Chester's recovery.

Over dessert Derek gives me an envelope and says "Happy Valentine's Day." As I accept it I realize with the car accident and subsequent recovery period, which is still ongoing, I never gave Derek his gift. I have a gift of cologne for him under my now very dusty bed at home. I wonder if unopened cologne goes bad? The envelope contains a homemade gift certificate for a four-day trip to Las Vegas to see the Cirque du Soleil show "*O.*"

"I had arranged with Joyce and Mr. Sebring for the time off and it would have been this weekend, but circumstances being what they were I thought it would be better to wait until you can walk, so that's why it's a cheesy gift certificate," Derek laughs.

"What? This is way too much. I thought the dinner was my

gift." I am surprised and suddenly feel even worse for ruining the real occasion, not that I did so intentionally.

"No, don't be silly. Besides, I want to go to Vegas with you. I want to do everything with you."

"So, when do you want to go?"

"When you can walk. There is so much to do and see, but it all requires walking. Let's wait and go in November. You'll be walking by then,"

"That sounds great!" It's official, I am dating the sweetest man on earth.

After our amazing meal Derek and I head home in the limo — but do a drive around downtown first, no point being in a limo if you can't enjoy the ride — where we watch *Casablanca*, my favourite movie of all time. Derek has claimed in the past that he hates the movie, but I'm completely convinced he was mixing it up with another movie when he claimed hatred. I mean who could hate *Casablanca*?

# 27

Derek and I sleep in a bit on Saturday morning, then I have to have my way with him, again. You can't take a girl out to dinner in a limo and give her a trip to Vegas and not expect to be sexually set upon repeatedly. It was his own fault really; he brought it on himself. By 10 a.m., unfortunately, I have to think about getting to my house for the paint party. Mel won't be pleased if I don't show up to lend my token support; Lord knows that's about all I have to offer. Derek drops me off at home on his way to the office but not before I steal a few more kisses and promise to defile him later.

When I crutch into the house the first thing I notice is that Mel is a "sight." I wish Derek had come in with me to see her. She is dressed in overalls, not a look I've seen on Mel ever, not even as a child would she be caught dead in overalls. Mel has always been a girly-girl and coveralls, even when they were considered the height of fashion, would not be donned, but there she stands. Denim coveralls, I'd guess two sizes too big for her petite size-four frame, a formerly white t-shirt, which fits and I'm sure is a name brand, but the real sight to behold is her usually perfectly coiffed hair piled in a messy bun on the top of her head and the shower cap she is wearing. I've never seen Mel in a shower cap; I've hardly ever seen her hair up, and when I have it was in an expensive, time-consuming updo coiffed by a posh stylist at an overpriced salon. Mel is not a woman who pulls her hair up, voluntarily, without high-paid help. I suspect she has no idea what I mean when I ask her if she's seen my pony holder. I think she imagines I have a horse halter in my bedroom.

As for the paint, there is some on the kitchen wall, but there appears to be more on Mel herself. I'm not quite sure how this happened, but seeing her standing there in her outfit and shower cap, covered in paint and holding a paintbrush will always bring the thought "if only I had my camera" whenever I recall it.

"How's it going?" I manage while holding back what I know is going to be a long, hard, tear-producing belly laugh.

"I got off to a bit of a rough start, but I'm making headway now." The determination in Mel's voice adds even more humour to the sight before me.

"Well, you look good doing it!" I get out in a broken sentence between gales of laughter, wiping my eyes and crutching over to where Mel is standing.

"Painting isn't as easy as it looks, but I'll figure it out." Mel is downright driven at this point.

"Well, if anyone can, *you* can," I get out while wiping my eyes. At this point I notice that Mel is wearing designer running shoes that were obviously brand new at the start of the day before her run in with the paint. "Are those Prada running shoes?" I ask in disbelief.

"Polo. You don't *paint* in Prada. Oh, I brought extra shower caps. You'll want to cover your hair. The paint roller seems to fight back but I'm having better luck with the brush," Mel says with a seriousness that makes me start to laugh again. She is an absolute riot, mostly because she's not trying to be.

"Okay, the rolling is probably better for me with the bum leg anyway. No way I can climb a ladder," I say as I balance my crutches in a corner and limp to the stove where I see the package of shower caps. "Oh, what the hell?" I think and start to put one on, "It's going to be a long day, might as well make it fun."

"Trust me, you'll be glad for that shower cap," Mel says from atop her ladder as I start to re-roll the wall that Mel had battled with and apparently lost.

"I'm certainly glad for yours!" I laugh as I roll over a very noticeable run and try to make it blend.

When Charlie Brown trips in the front door about an hour later, Mel seems to be getting the hang of the brush and I have resorted to rolling from Mel's desk chair which is on wheels so I can push myself around with the good leg. My run-in with the Jetta is proving more of a nuisance than I ever could have imagined.

"Looking good, ladies. Nice hats!" Charlie Brown laughs when he sees us. For all Charlie Brown's faults he can be funny occasionally. I hate to admit it to myself but I think I'm finally warming up to good ol' Charlie Brown.

"Yeah, it's all about the fashion," I manage as I too start to laugh. Mel still does not see the humour in her outfit or the shower caps.

"Give me that before you hurt yourself again," Charlie Brown says as he takes the roller out of my hand and starts to roll the top part of the wall that I can't reach from Mel's chair, even with the extender on the roller pole.

"You're a good man, John, no matter what all the other people say," I laugh.

"Well, let's see what the people say when they hear about your hat," Charlie Brown laughs.

"You won't be laughing when you have paint in your hair," Mel adds from the ladder, again in complete seriousness, which starts Charlie Brown and me laughing more.

The morning flies by filled with jokes and laughter and we are starting to see progress. Mel is determinedly manhandling the ladder every time she has to move it to continue cutting in the ceiling but seems to be improving at a rapid rate. Charlie Brown has all but taken over the rolling and I have to admit, is doing a much better job with two good legs than I was with the limp or the chair. I have resorted to sitting on my behind with a scraper and wet rag and am cleaning up the floor behind the painters extraordinaire.

"I was going to stay away longer, but coming back to this makes cutting the trip short very worthwhile." Marc's familiar and seemingly long-lost voice says from the doorway.

"Oh my God! *You're back!*" Charlie Brown tosses the paint roller in my general direction as he scrambles toward Marc. Luckily I'm able to catch the roller before it hits the floor but have to catch the actual roller itself, which is covered in paint.

When Charlie Brown gets to Marc he throws his arms around Marc's neck and hugs him in a way that men don't generally hug. I'm not sure but I think there are tears; I guess running Marc's company took more out of poor Charlie Brown than Mel and I thought.

"Well, if I had any idea I'd get this reaction I would have rushed back sooner," Marc says as he awkwardly pats Charlie Brown's back.

"I was so worried, man!" Charlie Brown muffles into Marc's shoulder.

"Well, I'm back now. You can let go." It's obvious Marc is starting to feel a bit uncomfortable in Charlie Brown's embrace. Charlie Brown does let go, but only for a split second before he grabs Marc again and says, "I'm so glad you're back!"

I've never seen anyone quite so overcome with emotion and judging from the look on Marc's face neither has he. It's making me a bit uncomfortable so I decide to deal with the paint that's oozing through my fingers and starting to run down my arm. I manage to get the roller back into the paint tray and the rag I'm using to clean up spills wrapped around my paint-dripping hand but I can't get myself up off the floor with only one useable hand and one useable leg. Mel is off the ladder now and turns from witnessing her boyfriend's unusual display of undying love to give me a hand getting up off the floor.

"I've never seen him so…happy," Mel says quietly to me.

"I know. I almost prefer the caffeine-freaked-out version to this one. He just seems so vulnerable," I whisper as Mel and I stand staring at the display. Charlie Brown's back is to us so we can see the look on Marc's face and it's registering the same disbelief we are feeling. Marc smiles, stretches out his arms and shrugs in an "I don't know what to do" motion.

"It's okay, John. I'm back now." Marc takes hold of Charlie Brown's arms and unfolds them from his neck.

"Don't do that again, man!" Charlie Brown does step back at this point, getting hold of himself, "I was really worried."

"Okay, it's a deal," Marc looks a little more comfortable now that Charlie Brown isn't attached to him any longer, even though he is still not his confident self.

"Well, that was *awkward!*" Mel states. "I'm getting a beer. Marc, would you like one?"

"Sure, that would be great."

Mel turns to Charlie Brown and says, "I'll just bring you one. You look like you could use one."

Mel follows me into the kitchen to get beer and I try to wash some of the paint off my hand in one of the buckets of water we are using for cleanup. We don't have any running water on this floor with the renovations so Mel has to bring buckets for me from the laundry sink because it's easier than me trying to get up and down the basement stairs every time I need to wash up, which seems to be frequently. Mel takes beer to the guys and then comes back to the kitchen.

"I think I'll hang here for a bit while the boys get caught up. They're talking shop now that Crybaby has regained his composure," Mel laughs.

"Perfect timing, can you hand me my crutches, my leg is killing me and don't be so hard on him. He's not really a cry-baby, he was just overcome with emotion."

"He was *crying*, I'm sure of it." Mel hands me my crutches and grabs the buckets to head downstairs and refresh them.

Marc stays long enough for one beer, to ask if Mel's shoes are Prada and to catch up with John on what happened in his absence. Charlie Brown explains about the payroll and Marc thanks us and says he'll figure out what the difference is for our renovation and we'll work it out when everything is done. Nothing is said about the reason for Marc's disappearance and none of us ask. I guess we'll hear about it if Marc ever wants to tell us.

# 28

The three weeks following Marc's return are filled with construction and more construction — construction at work and more construction and renovating at home every evening and weekend. The new windows are installed and, surprisingly, Mel and I, with help from Charlie Brown, get the paint finished before the tile installer arrives to tile the kitchen and bathroom floors and bathtub surrounds.

By the middle of May our home renovation is complete. Mel's couch has been professionally cleaned but still looks a fright and Derek's assistant, Carie, has moved to Argentina, where apparently you can groom Chows without previous references. She has been replaced by Jennifer, who adorned her desk with fourteen framed photos of her cats on her first day. Chester, the Chow, is still in therapy, or was when Carie left, so we may never know if he will ever be able to return to the show circuit.

We plan a thank you barbecue and party for the workers, especially Charlie Brown, who, despite his mini-breakdown when Marc reappeared, did a great job with the renovation and didn't charge us for his labour. I guess there are perks to dating an electrician, albeit a caffeine-freaked-out one who breaks down easily. I suggested getting Charlie Brown a very large, pineapple-wrought fruit basket but Mel vetoed that idea for fear of being redundant and Charlie Brown has an aversion to pointy fruit; he maintains that anything that can fight back isn't worth the effort. We finally decide to get him a custom-made plaque that reads "World's Greatest Contractor."

The Saturday of the party we prepare salads and put beer in coolers because our fridge can't hold enough for all the workers. Charlie Brown insists on being the actual meat chef and wants to barbecue even though we told him it was his party and he didn't have to do any work. It's the man and the open flame thing. Men feel obliged to cook if the flame is open. Put that same piece of meat in a frying pan and try to get any excitement out of that same man — it can't be done.

I am still wearing the brace on my leg to work, but when I'm home I try to keep it off as much as possible and am enjoying my old clothes again. When I crutch out of my room in jeans, Mel almost doesn't recognize me and Charlie Brown asks, "But you're still going to wear those little skirts, right?"

"You did a great job on the house, but you're still a deviant," I reply as I crutch by him to the kitchen. I think Charlie Brown and I understand each other better now.

Derek cannot attend the party because he is working in the New York office again. He flew out yesterday and is coming back next Saturday. This is the first trip to New York he has had to make since we started dating. He goes there four or five times a year. He's only been gone for twenty-four hours and I'm already having withdrawal. I don't know how I'm going to last a full week. It's really not right to separate people who are newly dating and madly in love. There should be a law about that.

"Hey, you're wearing jeans!" Marc says when he gets to our house. He seems pleased to see me out of the brace and finally into a normal pair of pants.

"I know, at this rate I'll be running in no time," I laugh but know that running is still a long way off.

"The house looks great. I guess John came through for you," Marc comments.

"Yep. I was worried but it all came together — well, except maybe Mel's painting," I laugh.

"I heard that! Hi Marc," Mel states as she walks by us with a tray of nachos for the guys who are in the living room.

"Can I take a look at the washrooms?" Marc asks.

"Sure I'll give you the tour," and we start to head to the renovated washrooms. They are actually very nice now; there is a full four-piece bath off Mel's room — the master bedroom, even though it isn't much larger than mine — and a full washroom off my bedroom, but it has two doors so is ensuite-slash-main washroom for guests. The third bedroom, which only received a fresh coat of paint job, acts as Mel's office. Mel does a lot more work from home than I do. When Marc and I walk past Mel's office, he sees a framed photo of Mel and me in our painting outfits, including shower caps, and he goes to have a better look. Charlie Brown took the photo and had it blown up to an 8 x 10. I guess he intuitively knows that he'll never see Mel so casually dressed again.

"You two are hilarious," Marc laughs as he looks at the photo.

"Oh yeah! We'll set fashion on its ear!"

"You never asked where I was when I was away," Marc turns to me and states seriously.

"No. I figure you'll tell me if you want me to know. There has been a great deal of speculation, and a lot of people asked me what I knew. It was actually nice to be able to say I didn't know anything," I answer honestly. Marc is my friend, but taking off like he did was very uncharacteristic of him so I know the reason must be major and he may not ever want to tell me.

"What is the most common speculation?" Marc asks.

"Gay love affair. Met the man for you and had to run off to Vegas to see the 'shows.' You know, the usual sort of thing."

"Ah, the gay affair. Not that there's anything wrong with that!" Marc laughs, quoting the famous line from Seinfeld. "But it wasn't an affair, gay or otherwise."

"Well, I'm glad to hear that. Although if you did have a gay lover he might be able to give Charlie Brown a few fashion tips."

"My wife left me," Marc states in the same nonchalant fashion one asks to "please pass the salt."

I am shocked, visibly shocked, and cannot organize the

million thoughts going through my head in time to say anything even remotely supportive.

"She told me she's known for a long time that I haven't been happy so she went out and found herself a used car salesman named *Dwayne*." Marc says "Dwayne" as if it leaves a bad taste in his mouth.

I'm still absorbing Marc's announcement. "Never trust a man with a name beginning with *DW*," I blurt out, then start to laugh nervously. "I'm sorry. I don't know where that came from. That was most inappropriate." I do have a thing about *DW* names. I mean why didn't the parents of these people just lose the *D*? Wayne is a respectable name in itself. Wight is a little strange but still preferable to Dwight. Dwyer is just a silly first name. I have similar thoughts about *LL* names. Lloyd is a name I cannot say without pronouncing both *L*s. LeLoyd.

Marc laughs, "Well, I don't like him and he's a complete idiot."

"So you've met him?"

"Yeah. He's slimy, just like you'd expect a used car salesman to be," Marc states more resignedly than emotionally.

"How are you doing?" I feel terrible for Marc. He was obviously blindsided by this event and he does look the worse for it. I have noticed that he has lost some weight but just now noticed how much and how sad he seems. He has been hiding it well at work but I haven't seen much of him since the first day he got back.

"I'll be okay. I'm living with a buddy of mine but I have to find my own place soon. She wants the house." Marc is defeated and I don't know anything to say to help him feel better.

"I am so sorry. Is there anything I can do?" I ask sincerely but suspect that this is one of those things that no one can do much about.

"No. Maybe just don't tell anyone for now. News will get out soon enough but I'm not ready to answer questions just yet."

"Absolutely. I won't even tell Mel. I promise."

"Oh, you know what? Maybe there is one thing you can do for me," Marc asks as we start to make our way back to the party.

"Sure. Anything. What?"

"You could agree to go on a date with me now that I'm single."

"Well, I'll have to ask my boyfriend, but he seems fairly set in his ways and might not want to share."

"Where is good old what's-his-name?"

"*Derek* is in New York for work and you know is name."

"Oh yeah, DWerek!" Marc laughs as he adds a *W* into Derek's name.

"You're an idiot!" I laugh as we join the party that is in full swing in the living room.

# 29

The summer flies by uneventfully. Work at Sebring is crazy busy and Marc is relentless about asking me out. It is funny now and just part of our everyday conversation.

"Will you go out with me?" Marc asks at least three times a week and I have an array of replies. The challenge is finding new ones. I have replied things like:

"Nah, I have to wash my hair."

"Nah, I'd just break your heart."

"Nah, but I might consider it if your truck was a nasty shade of blue."

"Nah, I don't date construction types."

"Did hell freeze over!?"

"Call me tomorrow, if I'm not wearing a short skirt I will for sure."

"Oh my gosh, are you the last remaining man on earth?"

Marc knows I'm seeing Derek and that I would never do anything to harm that relationship so he takes my replies in the fun manner in which they're meant and I'm quite sure he asks now just to see if I can come up with something new every time.

Mel is making amazing progress with her real estate

career and is vying for top sales in her office but had a harried couple of days in July after she was positive she saw Brad Pitt going into the subway. She was really busy at work and not eating properly so I'm not completely convinced she wasn't hallucinating. Her encounter with Brad led to two full days underground, riding the subway lines in an attempt to see him again. The two days underground resulted in one broken Prada heel, two days behind at work and a proposition to have "her world rocked" by a teenage punk rocker with a Mohawk but sadly, no Brad. For the record, Mel chose not to have her world rocked.

Derek's assistant, Jennifer, was let go from the firm for taking too many personal days to care for her perpetually sick cats, and was replaced by Hilda. Hilda is a formidable bodybuilder and I suspect she frightens Derek even though he won't admit it.

Marc is feeling better, has gained back a few pounds and bought a house close to his wife's house and when I say his "wife's house" I mean his old house. He's still pretty sensitive to the topic of the house, where Dwayne now lives with Marc's wife, youngest child, cat, dog and Barry the rabbit. News of Marc's separation got out a few weeks after he confided in me at the barbecue. Marc called Charlie Brown to come and get him after he was detained by the police for a scuffle at a bar with a man named Dwight, who apparently provoked Marc, but in reality I'm sure the *DW* name was enough to set Marc off and start the fisticuffs. Marc was not charged or harmed in any way but had to pay for some damages and send an apology letter to Dwight Dwyer. Honestly, the man is looking for trouble walking around with *two DW* names. I wonder if Dwight hangs out with a guy named Lloyd Llewellyn?

Mel and I had to make the trek up north to visit the parents. We put it off as long as we could but when Mike, Mel's brother, was making the trip from Georgia, the pressure and guilt were too great and we had to succumb. Charlie Brown and Derek joined us, so it wasn't completely unbearable. We actually had a great time, although we'll never let the parents know. On the Saturday night of the weekend the four of us, Mike and the twins went to see a band called Kevin, and had an amazing time. Mike Melrose is an absolute riot with a very sarcastic wit and the twins are a lot of fun when out in public and not tormenting our parents. As sad as this sounds, our outing to Kevin was the first social we're-all-old-enough-to-drink-beer outing with my sisters. The twins have been at university and I've been in Toronto so we haven't had the chance to socialize since they became of legal drinking age. In truth, the ten-year age gap has not made for close sister bonding; I'm much closer to Mel than to my own flesh and blood.

It is Tia's idea to go and see the band Kevin. The band had played at one of the bars the students frequented in Kingston last semester and Tia has a crush on the drummer, so when she heard that they were playing in North Bay she insisted we all go. The parents were appalled that we wanted to "go out" when we are meant to be home "visiting," but the twins, who have Mom and Dad and Mr. and Mrs. Melrose wrapped around their fingers, convinced them to let us go. It's the batting of the four identical huge brown, puppy-dog eyes and superlong eyelashes. No one can resist them. I'm quite sure neither of them ever completed an essay in high school but they both had straight As. They are incredibly beautiful girls and there are two of them. They are a formidable force when they work together. But no matter how they managed, the twins got us the approval to go see the band.

Kevin is a strange name for a band, even by Toronto standards. Tia filled us in on how the band got its name. Apparently, when they were hired for their first gig they had not yet decided on a name so the lead singer gave his first name as the contact. Then before they could decide on a name and get back to the host venue, they were already on posters as Kevin. So it stuck and the band that might have been known as Magic Eightball, Massive Heart Attack or something equally pithy, is now known simply as Kevin.

The band was actually very good; they did covers of The Tragically Hip, U2, Blue Rodeo and the Cure and their original stuff wasn't bad either. During one of the breaks Tia and Taryn, who had been hanging out by the stage as groupies, returned to introduce us to the drummer, Ben, and the lead guitarist, Jeff. They seemed like nice guys but didn't get a chance to say very much with the twins in full giddy force. The twins spoke their own language as toddlers and as adults can finish each other's sentences, so unless you have an experienced ear when with them, you can miss entire thoughts and get very confused. Sometimes it's best to just sit quietly when they are in high gear.

As the twins are rattling on, and the rest of us stand staring at them in awe, occasionally sipping our drinks, we hear a voice from behind us say, "Hey, it's the twins from Kingston!" and the lead singer, Kevin, joins our circle. The fact that Kevin remembers the twins is actually quite impressive since the band must meet hundreds of people. But like I said, Tia and Taryn are beautiful and there are two of them. I suppose an encounter with the twins is not easily forgotten, especially after Tia set her sights on Ben.

Kevin is older than the other band members, early thirties I would guess compared to Ben and Jeff's early twenties, and is very attractive up close. He has messy brown hair and clear almost see-through blue eyes. The twins go wild when he steps into the circle, both talking at once and waving their arms.

"Ladies, ladies," Kevin interjects, "remember we had to talk in Kingston. You have to speak one at a time." The twins burst out in nervous giggles as Kevin asks, "Are they always like this?" generally to the whole group.

"Yes," we all answer in unison. I think Ben and Jeff, who hardly know the twins, joined our affirmative chorus.

"They were born like this," I add and put out my hand to shake Kevin's. I introduce myself as the twins' sister and introduce everyone else around the circle. Charlie Brown, Mike and Derek take drink orders and leave to go to the bar after Derek asks me if he can borrow twenty bucks — seems he didn't get to the bank machine again.

"So you're the sister; are there two of you as well?" Kevin asks seriously.

"Oh thank God, *no!*" Mel interjects.

"Hey, I'm not that bad, but no, there is only one of me."

"Why the crutches?" Kevin nods down to my bent, but brace-free leg.

"Run-in with a Jetta last February. The Jetta won that round but I have its number."

"Good luck with the leg, and the sisters!" Kevin laughs and playfully punches Tia on the shoulder as the band heads back to the stage.

The rest of the evening goes well. The highlight for Tia is a kiss at the evening's end and a promise from Ben to stay in touch. I don't think I've ever seen my sister so excited and that's saying a lot because the twins excite easily and frequently.

By July, the physiotherapy on my leg is making a difference. I can now walk for longer periods of time, and although my crutches are still handy, I don't need them all the time. It is a sad day for the entire construction team at the new building when I get the okay from the doctor to remove the brace permanently. The official word that the short skirts "were no longer" travelled like wildfire throughout the Sebring III construction site and Marc called me to confirm the rumour. I joined some of the team for beer after work that day in memory of the skirts; it was a wake of sorts. Charlie Brown took the loss especially hard and didn't speak to me for two days. I think that since Charlie Brown let his emotions flow so freely when Marc returned last spring, he's had a difficult time keeping them in check. I'm back to my old clothes and the parade of contractors through our office has slowed up considerably. Even Joyce commented that more invoices arrive by mail and fax and aren't hand-delivered anymore. The era of the short skirt is over and inside I feel the warm glow of achievement I'm sure one only feels after being rescued from a desert island.

In early August Derek discovered that his bodybuilding assistant Hilda is in rehab after being disqualified from one of her competitions for steroids and "other drug abuses." I think Derek is relieved and mentioned that his new assistant, Felicity, has pink hair that he described as "the same pink of Mel's boots." I haven't gotten a look at her yet, but think I will stop by Derek's office one day next week.

The twins come to stay with Mel and me for the Labour Day weekend on their way back to school in Kingston. Tia has been maintaining a long-distance relationship with Ben, the drummer from Kevin, and the band is playing in Toronto both Saturday and Sunday nights on the weekend. I ask Taryn about Jeff from the band and whether or not she is interested in him, but she maintains she is still playing the field. Derek is in New York for work again, so Charlie Brown, Mel and I join the twins on their Saturday-night outing to see the band. We invite Marc but he declines. Charlie Brown thinks Marc has a girlfriend but her existence has yet to be confirmed. I am happy for Marc if it's true. He has been in a funk since his wife moved on with Dwayne so this might be just what the doctor ordered.

Kevin plays well and the bar is crowded. The band has a large following in the Toronto area it seems. Tia is over the moon to be in the same room as Ben. She took ages getting ready to come here, and managed three complete outfit changes in the time it took me to put on jeans and a t-shirt. Mel, who is like a sister to the twins as well, ended up lending Tia a top and her favourite pink Prada boots.

During a break, Tia brings Ben to find us to borrow money from me for beer. The twins have worked all summer and are on their way back to university so I'm sure she has money but in typical Tia fashion, she did not go to the bank machine before coming out tonight. I think she's taking lessons from Derek.

"Oh yeah, me too please," Taryn adds right after Tia asks for money.

"What do you girls do at school when I'm not with you to hand out twenties?" I ask as I reach in my pocket for a second twenty-dollar bill.

The twins look at each other and start to laugh, then they throw their hair over their shoulders in the most synchronized of moves, put their cheeks together and start to bat their eyelids. "We do this!" they say, again in synchronized twin fashion.

"Of course you do. Go. Buy beer!" The twins say thanks in unison as they leave with Ben and head to the bar.

"Hey! It's the sister but with no crutches," I hear Kevin say before I see him.

"Hi. Yep, I'm back on my own two feet," I laugh as Kevin steps into view.

"I saw the twins and hoped I would see you," Kevin says.

"Really? With the twins around I don't usually get much notice. I'm used to being overshadowed by them," I laugh again.

"Oh, they're larger than life all right, but you're someone who isn't easily forgotten," Kevin says seriously.

"Thank you, that's the nicest thing I've heard all day." I know I'm starting to blush.

"Where's your boyfriend? Don't tell me you got back on two feet and dumped him?"

"No, we're still together. He's in New York for work, but I spoke to him today and he wishes he were here."

"Well, I'm glad I had you to myself for a few minutes," Kevin leans over and kisses me on the cheek then mumbles "Oh, gotta go," and makes a hasty retreat for the stage before I can object to his kiss.

"Wow! What was all that about?" Mel asks inquisitively as she and Charlie Brown return from the bar and she hands me a beer.

"I'm not sure, I think I have an admirer," I say, still a bit in shock but very flattered.

"Isn't the groupie thing supposed to be the other way around?" Charlie Brown asks.

"Apparently, not when our friend Kit is around," Mel laughs.

"Yeah, right! Maybe if she were in one of her short skirts. Most guys would be all over that," Charlie Brown laughs as the band starts their next set.

"I admit I like him a bit better than before you started dating him, but he's still a deviant," I state flatly to Mel.

# 30

I arrive at the Firkin after work, rubbing my hands together to warm them up. It's chilly even for October and I forgot to grab my gloves this morning on my way out the door.

"Okay, what's your news?" I ask Mel as I sit down. Mel had called me this afternoon with the promise of exciting news.

"I have a buyer!" Mel is obviously excited, chewing her stop-smoking gum with exaggerated jaw movements and shifting in her seat.

"You always have buyers, that's why you're one of the top salespeople in the area. What's special about this one?"

"No, not a regular buyer. One who wants to buy *our* house." Mel is almost jumping off her seat.

"What? Our house? Is our house for sale?" I am stunned. I had no idea we were even considering selling. I have just gotten used to where everything lives in our new kitchen.

"Everything's for sale in a market this hot." Mel is not deterred by my unenthusiastic response.

"How hot?" For Mel to be this excited there must be a major financial incentive.

"Fifty thousand dollars each after we pay off the renovation line of credit and get our initial investments back hot."

Mel can hardly contain herself. "Not bad for a few months' work."

"You're kidding?! Who would pay that much for our house?" I'm feeling Mel's excitement but don't want to get swept up in it unless it's actual fact. The deflation of losing fifty thousand dollars, even an imaginary fifty thousand you just learned about thirty seconds ago, could be devastating.

"I have a buyer. They told me what they wanted and I knew our house was perfect. Of course I took them to a bunch of other places first so that when they saw ours they'd be in love. It's the perfect house for them, they love it and they want it." Mel is standing now and hugging me.

"Oh my God. You *are* the best little salesperson in the world." I jump up and Mel and I are hugging and jumping in a little circle when Steve comes to our table with our beer.

"Well, you two seem happy," Steve laughs. "I don't usually get a response like this for bringing beer."

"Well, you should," Mel jokes back and gives Steve a hug for good measure.

"Today is a very good day," I laugh as Mel and I sit down and clink glasses.

Mel goes on to tell me the potential buyers want a long closing and are looking at February, Valentine's Day to be exact. I have no problem with a long closing; in fact, I think I prefer the long closing so I can get my head completely around the idea of selling the house we just renovated.

I ask Mel what she wants to do about getting a new house.

The flip went well this time so does she want to do the same thing again? She mentions that she and Charlie Brown have talked about moving in together. I suspected the answer and I'm fine with going my own way, although I will miss having Mel in my world every day. I'll just have to speak to her on the telephone more. As for Charlie Brown being Mel's life partner, I know they are happy together so, despite my misgivings about Charlie Brown's dress sense, I have to give the nod of approval. Whether or not our parents will give Mel the nod of approval for "living in sin" remains to be seen.

"Oh, Marc is seeing someone. I asked him this morning at coffee," I tell Mel because the rumour is now confirmed.

"Good for him, what's her name?"

"He won't tell me so either she has a really funny name that we will tease him about or he's just being cautious." I give Mel my theories.

"Or he's waiting for you to agree to date him and then he'll drop her like a hot potato."

"No he wouldn't."

"Oh yes he would. What did you say today when he asked you out?" Mel looks knowingly at me. She knows Marc asks me out every time he sees me.

"Brain tumour caused by cell phone, only six months to live," I answer resignedly. Maybe Mel is right about Marc's reason for not telling me his girlfriend's name. Damn, I hate it when she's right.

"See? I don't know why you argue with me. A waste of time really." Mel is just gloating now.

I stop by Derek's office the next day after work to meet him for dinner but mostly to get a look at his assistant, Felicity, and her pink hair. Unfortunately, I don't get to see the pink hair because it's blue now. Felicity is a beautiful girl with deep blue eyes, so the blue hair is actually quite stunning and complimentary and I don't mind it at all. I can see where pink might have been a bit over the top though. Derek seems less nervous around Felicity than he was with Hilda. Even I have to admit Hilda was a bit scary so can't blame him for his fear; sometimes a little bit of fear is a good thing.

I fill Derek in on the sale of the house and Mel and Charlie Brown moving in together. Derek quite likes Charlie Brown and mentions that he thinks they will be happy living together. Besides Mel's immediate family and me, I haven't been able to picture Mel cohabiting with anyone, but I do think that she and Charlie Brown will be able to make it work. When Derek asks what I'm thinking of doing when the house sells, I tell him honestly, on my own, I won't be able to manage a mortgage without getting housemates and the idea of living with strangers isn't appealing so I might just invest the money I made and go back to renting, unless I can find a really super deal, but that's not likely based on the little bit I know about the current "hot" market.

Joyce is grinning when I get back from lunch the following day. She looks a bit like the cat that swallowed the canary so I know something is up.

"I have news," Joyce says in her singsongy fashion as she pulls down my shirt, which has slid up above my waistband.

"I would have guessed by the look on your face," I laugh. "So what's the news?"

"Mr. Sebring just told me that he wants to sell the model suite at the Sebring II building."

"You're kidding! Really?" I am very excited, as Joyce expected I would be. I absolutely love the model suite at Sebring II. When it was being built I loved it, even before it had walls. It is a corner unit on one of the high floors and it has floor-to-ceiling windows so the view is fantastic. After Mr. Sebring had it decorated to use as the model suite to sell the remaining units in that building, I loved it even more, if that's possible. Mr. Sebring has exceptional taste in décor, I think I mentioned the vase collection, and it would be my dream home — well, condo.

"Why is he selling it?" I am a bit confused because I thought Mr. Sebring was keeping it for himself.

"Apparently he likes the model suite at Sebring III better so he's selling the one at Sebring II. He just told me before you got back. I told him not to list it yet as I might have a buyer for him," Joyce smiles.

"I would love to live there but I know I can't afford it on my own. How much is he asking for it?" I ask Joyce but I know that any number she gives me is going to be too much. With a single income even the smallest suite at Sebring II is out of my price range and the suite in question is one of the biggest ones. When Joyce tells me the price I cringe but it's not as bad I thought. Maybe I can call my parents to be silent investors although I'm not sure how silent they would be. I tell Joyce not to do anything just yet, I'm going to crunch some numbers and see if I can figure out how to make them work. I call Mel and tell her the news. She knows exactly the condominium I mean because I took her to see it when we started selling that building, and even Mel, who prefers houses to condos, had to agree it is fabulous.

"I'll work on the numbers as well, but on your own I'm not sure how you'll pull it off. Even if you sell Nasty and all the rest of your worldly possessions, you'll have to give up food." Mel isn't being mean-spirited, she's being practical. The condo is out of my price range but if anyone can help make it work, it's Mel.

After work I get the key from Joyce and go to the Sebring II building to see the model-suite condominium again. My hope in doing so is to discover that the condo isn't as great as I remember and then I won't want to live there and I'll get it out of my system. Sadly, that's not the case. As I walk around the open-concept condo with the superhigh ceilings, I still love it as much as I did when we built it. It is big and bright and perfect. Damn, coming here did not produce the result I was hoping to achieve; it's quite the opposite, actually. Now I can't imagine going back to renting a small apartment like I did before Mel and I bought the house. I really want to live here. I can see myself living here. I wonder how I can pull this off.

# 31

Derek comes by the house just as Mel and I are heading out the door to go back and see the condo again. After crunching numbers for an hour and reaching the realization that there is no way to stretch my salary to afford the condo, I suggest to Mel that she and Charlie Brown might want to consider living there. I know Mel prefers houses but the condo is fabulous and if I can't have it I'd love to see someone I love live there.

"Hey ladies, where are you off to?" Derek asks.

"One of the condos at work just came on the market and I have the key. I'm taking Mel to see it so she will buy it and I can visit her there. Do you want to tag along?" I'd love for Derek to see the condo; he's never been in this model suite and in fact has never been in Sebring II. I would like to show him what we build so he can get an idea of what it is I do at work when I'm not emailing him. In actual fact, I'd like to throw him down in the foyer of the most amazing condo ever and have my way with him but Mel might not like that. She generally sneers when we can't keep our hands off each other so I'm sure she'd do more than sneer if we actually "did it" on a tiled foyer floor while she was present.

"Sure." Derek's easy going and will join in on anything that seems remotely fun.

The tour is finished — the condo is not huge but spacious for a condo. The washroom is exquisite. The tile shower has a frameless glass wall and six showerheads for the full-body shower. Of course, my mind wanders when Derek whispers a suggestion about the full-body shower. Everything is granite and upgraded and the automatic blind system to cover the huge windows is included in the purchase price. Mel and Derek are both impressed by the finishes.

"What do you think?" I ask Mel. "It's amazing, isn't it?"

"It's as great as I remember, once you get in it," replies Mel, "but you know I don't like elevators." Mel has a point with the elevator thing. If anyone is going to get stuck in an elevator, it's Mel. She has been stuck in more elevators than anyone I know and this condominium is on the tenth floor. She'd be stuck a lot.

"Oh right, the elevator thing," I laugh. "And I suppose with all Charlie Brown's work equipment you'll need more storage anyway. It's probably best to get a place that has a basement or a garage, or both."

"If it were on the ground or second floor I'd be all over it!" Mel laughs.

"Only then the view would be greatly diminished, you'd be looking into the condo across the alley," Derek adds peeking down to the shorter building beside Sebring II.

"I guess I'll just have to befriend the buyers and get my

butt invited over occasionally if I want to spend time here," I laugh.

"Hey, unless the buyer is a good-looking, single guy," Derek laughs.

"Well, you might be out of luck if the guy can afford this condo and he invites me over to use his shower," I laugh back as we turn off the lights and start to lock up.

"Are you okay in the elevator, Mel, or should we wait for you while you walk down the stairs in those boots?" Derek is being Mr. Funny this evening.

"Smart ass!" Mel says as she punches him in the arm.

"Well, I won't be happy if we get stuck in the elevator and I'll blame you. I might even have to use the heel of your boot to pry the door open."

When the elevator doors open on the ground level, Mel breathes an audible sigh of relief knowing she's "free" and the heels of her boots are safe from Derek.

Later, when Derek and I are lying in bed, he asks, "Kathryn, that condo you showed Mel, you want to buy it, right?"

"I did, well I do, but I can't afford it so I thought if I can't have it, it'd be cool if Mel did," I answer sleepily.

"You have a great down payment though, from this house, right?" Derek is being Mr. Inquisitive now.

"Yeah, but the mortgage, taxes and condo fees are the problem. I don't make enough money to carry it month to month and I can't imagine getting a housemate to share the expenses. It's a nice condo, but will seem pretty small if you don't love your housemate." Derek and I haven't ever discussed finances before. We know roughly what the other earns and I know how much rent Derek pays at his apartment but when it comes to actually seeing each other's bank statements, we've never been that intimate and I suspect Derek's might be a nightmare so haven't asked. I don't want to burst the bubble just yet.

"Would you love me if I were your housemate?"

"Don't be silly. I love you no matter what you are."

"What if we buy it together?"

"What? What did you just say?" I suddenly don't feel sleepy anymore and I'm not completely sure I heard him correctly.

"Well, think about it. I love you, you love me, we see each other almost every day and you stay at my place or I stay at yours. I haven't been able to save a down payment but I do pay a hefty amount of rent every month that would be better spent on a mortgage. We use your down payment, combine incomes and we have enough to get the condo," Derek says matter-of-factly.

"But then we'd be living together. Are you ready to live with me?" I ask tentatively. Derek and I have a great time and I know I love him but we've never even come close to discussing living together or where this relationship is going.

"I love you. You know that. I think it'd be great," Derek states, again, matter-of-factly.

"Really?" I'm positively in shock. Sixty seconds ago I was on my way to dreamland to dream about a condo I can't afford and now I might actually be getting that same condo in real life.

"Really. I think we're good together. It will be an exciting adventure," Derek says sweetly and rolls over to kiss me.

"But what about the elevator?"

"I'll carry one of Mel's boots in my briefcase in order to pry open any feisty doors," Derek laughs and kisses me again. I remind Derek that the full-body shower will be ours all the time and suddenly neither of us has sleeping in mind any longer.

I kiss Derek goodbye at the subway stop the next morning and we head our separate ways toward our respective office buildings. Derek is going to look into mortgage rates and qualifications with one of his co-workers at the bank and then we'll figure out what we want to do. I'm so happy. I literally skip to the coffee shop. I notice that I'm skipping because it hurts my healing leg a little bit, but it doesn't stop me. I'm on cloud nine.

"You look happy this morning," Marc says as he follows me into the coffee shop.

"How long were you behind me?" I ask, slightly embarrassed.

"Long enough to see you skipping. You were skipping, right? Not just walking funny?"

"Yes, I was skipping. It's a free country. I can skip if I want to."

"I didn't say I didn't like it," Marc laughs. "It's sorta cute actually, seeing a grown woman skip, I mean."

"Whatever. I'm buying coffee this morning," I announce.

"No you aren't. I always buy your coffee," Marc says protective of his coffee-buying territory.

"Yes I am because I have huge news and I'm happy, happy, happy." I put money on the counter, "So you don't have a choice."

"Happy, happy, happy?" Marc laughs, "Well in that case I'll let you buy me coffee but only this once. Why are you so happy?"

"I'm going to buy the model suite at Sebring II — you know, the corner unit with the amazing view." I can hardly contain my excitement.

"Is it for sale? I thought Mr. Sebring was keeping that one."

"Nope, he likes the one at Sebring III better. I think he prefers the location actually, but either way, he's selling it and I'm talking to him this morning about buying it."

"Wow! That is great news. You love that unit." Marc seems pleased for me.

"I know it's perfect!" I could not take the smile off my face if I wanted to as I collect my change and start to prepare my coffee. I still like cream in my coffee despite the fact that it's adding millions of calories to my weekly caloric intake.

"You must be getting an amazing deal from Mr. Sebring to afford it on your own." Marc is doing the math in his head.

"I am getting a deal, but Derek's buying it with me, so that makes it much more affordable."

"You're buying a condo with what's-his-name?" Marc doesn't seem happy for me anymore and, in fact, suddenly seems a little bit angry. "You hardly know him."

"Sorry?" I'm completely taken aback with Marc's response.

"You can't move in with someone you hardly know." Marc is not backing down on his position even though I've given him the opportunity to realize that he is completely out of line.

"I'll have known him for over a year when we get the condo and I love him. How long did you know your wife before you married her?" I come back defensively, the smile officially removed from my face. I have no idea how long Marc knew his ex-wife before they married but hope it was a short engagement for the sake of my argument.

"That's hardly the point. What's-his-name isn't good enough for you and you can't possibly love him." Marc is raising his voice now.

"Newsflash, I DO love him. But it's a good thing I'm not marrying him, isn't it? I suspect that when it all falls apart, splitting up a condo is easier than splitting up a marriage that resulted in three children. How is the divorce going, by the way?" I am furious with Marc but even I know that I've crossed a line with that last comment. People in the coffee shop are staring now so I pick up my coffee and start to walk toward the door. If I leave now I may get out without saying something else that I will regret. I do, however, stop just before stepping out the door, turn back to Marc and say, "Oh, for the last time, his name is Derek."

It takes all my strength not to break into tears on my walk back to the office. I went from being happier than I've ever been to being completely defeated in a few short minutes. I know in my heart Marc is just being protective and probably a little jealous but he can be such a hothead and say the dumbest things. I haven't badmouthed his mystery girlfriend with the stupid name or no name at all for that matter. At least he's met Derek and I've told him Derek's name, repeatedly. "He makes me so mad! See if I buy him coffee again" I think as I step onto the elevator at work. Yeah, that'll teach him.

I call Mel as soon as I get settled at my desk. I'm the first one in so I have a few minutes before the others arrive.

"You actually said that about his divorce?" Mel is surprised by my lack of self-control.

"Yes I did. I feel bad about it now but he deserved it. Who is he to be telling me what I can and can't do?" I am worked up into a tizzy at this point. "Arrgh, I'm just so angry with him!"

"I'm getting that," Mel laughs a little bit. "But why are you so angry? He has the right to his opinion. I don't agree with him, but it is his opinion."

"And this is helping how? You've been with Charlie Brown the same amount of time. Did he say anything to you or Charlie?" I ask, knowing full well Marc congratulated Charlie Brown because Mel told me he had.

"Well, he's not crazy in love with me or John, is he?" Mel hits the nail on the head with that comment.

"Loving someone is no excuse for giving up all form of

manners and civilized behaviour. We are what we are. Marc would still be married if his wife hadn't jumped ship with good old Dwayne so he's in no position to be critiquing my life or what I do or don't do with my boyfriend. Maybe if he'd gotten his shit together we could be a couple but we're not. I'm with Derek and he's with the mystery no-name girl. Life is going on," I speed-talk angrily into the telephone and almost start to cry again.

"I know, Kit. He has no right to say anything. He's just hurting because it didn't work out with you and him and you know that."

"Well, it would be really nice if he'd realize that being a complete bonehead is not helping the situation. For some reason he seems to think that this situation is all about him and that he can say anything to me, no matter how inappropriate. He seems to be under the mistaken impression that I have no feelings at all." At this point I do start to cry.

"I think he thinks you are tougher than you really are. You do give the impression of being tough as nails. I don't think he knows the situation with the two of you bothers you as much as it does. Have you ever told him?" If Mel wasn't making so much money as a realtor I'd suggest she go back to school to be a therapist. She really is good at seeing the big picture.

"No, you know I haven't. It's not something you just chat about. When he first asked me out he was married and off limits, and I didn't feel anything romantic for him. Then by the time he was single and I realized that I might like him, I was with Derek so it's a non-issue."

"Well, I think you're madder at Marc than you would be at anyone else for saying the same thing because you care about Marc more than you admit." I start to interrupt Mel at this point but she bulldozes ahead, "You know I'm right and it's okay. You're allowed to care about him. Timing has just not been in your favour where he's concerned. You have to ask yourself if moving in with Derek is the one hundred percent right thing to do, because if it isn't, now is the time to get out. Do you care about Marc enough to break up with Derek? Don't answer now but absolutely give it some thought, okay?" Mel is done with her spiel and she said it so eloquently I'm sure she'd been rehearsing it for just such an occasion.

"But Marc is such a jerk!"

"I know and I'm sure he thinks you're a jerk right now as well; the divorce comment might have been a little over the top." Mel is right and she's starting to annoy me.

"Kit, just give it some thought when you aren't so mad. For some reason you and Marc seem destined for 'something,' Lord only knows what, but it's something, so you have to consider it. Okay?"

"Okay, fine. I'll consider what you've said, but Marc is still a big stupidhead," I come back in true childlike fashion.

"Well, that's mature. I can see why Marc has undying love for you," Mel laughs.

I know Mel is right and it is time that I actually allow

myself to think about Marc as more than a friend. Can it be that Marc is the one for me and not Derek? Marc has been my most ardent pursuer. I know I care about him, but the question is how much?

# 32

Derek calls with great news. His friend at work, Pete, handles mortgages and he's going to give us a great mortgage interest rate and pre-approve us so we can put the offer in on the condo. I've met Pete a couple of times. His parents, whom I've never met but would like to, gave the poor man the moniker Peter Peterson. I would love to meet the people who thought this was a good idea. The redundancy alone should be a good reason not to double-name a child, but since I've never had children I guess I'm not in a position to judge. Pete is a really nice person despite his unfortunate name and he's giving us a great mortgage rate, so I give his parents credit for raising him well.

After I speak to Derek I tell Mr. Sebring that I am interested in purchasing the model suite at Sebring II and he seems pleased. I think he is happy that the condo will be going to someone he knows. Like me, Mr. Sebring has a soft spot in his heart for this particular suite. Since I write all the offers that do not have agents involved, Mr. Sebring tells me to put the offer together and get it to him this week. By lunchtime it seems Derek and I have the condominium and financing all wrapped up and we are going to be cohabiting in February of next year.

I'm just leaving my physiotherapy appointment when the magnitude of the day's events hits me. In a few short months I'm going to be living with my perfect boyfriend, in the perfect condo and have the perfect life, right? Will it really be perfect? Maybe I was just so in love with and determined to get the condo, I didn't give living with Derek enough thought. Maybe Marc's right and it is a huge mistake. Maybe I'll hate it and want to kill myself after two weeks. Maybe Derek is truly evil and in cahoots with Satan and walks the three-headed dog on his lunch hour; he does have questionable personal money-managing skills for an investment banker. My mind is spinning at a frenzied pace as I limp toward the subway; my leg always gets sore and irritated after the physiotherapist works his magic. My imagination is running away with me and I'm visualizing Derek with little horns sprouting amongst his perfect little boy hair, wearing a red leather suit and tossing our grocery money into the street, when my thoughts are interrupted by the ringing of my cell phone.

"Hello," I say into the phone at the top of the subway stairs. I don't have caller ID on my cell so I have no idea who it is.

"Hey, babe! Congratulations. We're going to own a condo. Want to go out and celebrate?" It's Derek and he sounds normal. Normal and sweet and the man I love. Whew. No horns.

"Absolutely. Where are you?" I ask. No point heading home if Derek is downtown.

"Just leaving the office. Let's meet up in the lobby and we can grab some dinner." Derek is so sweet. I can't believe I was just thinking evil, awful thoughts about him. I feel guilty for thinking bad things but worse for caring about Marc. What is wrong with me? I have a wonderful life and an amazing boyfriend. I can't screw this up. Even if I were madly and crazy in love with Marc, which I'm not, I can't date him anyway. We have to work together on Sebring III for at least another year and probably longer. If Marc and I did get together and date, it would mess up the work dynamic and I can't jeopardize my job. Besides, Marc is seeing mystery no-name girl and I would never interfere with his relationship. No. I'm doing the absolute right thing. I'm going on with my life as I should and letting any feelings I had, or have, for Marc go. This is the right thing. I'm going to buy the condo with Derek and live happily ever after, just like the fairy tales say.

I smile at Derek as I enter the lobby of his office building. He meets me with a hug and a kiss and pulls a red rose out of his jacket. The rose has a ribbon wrapped around the stem with a little plastic house affixed to the end that looks like it might have once belonged in a game of Monopoly.

"To our new house," Derek laughs and hands me the rose.

"You are so sweet and romantic," I say as I accept the rose and kiss him again. This feels good and I know I am making the right decision. I love the man in front of me now. My stomach still gets butterflies when I see him and he makes me happy, truly happy. I've never felt this way about anyone, not even Boob Man.

After dinner, Derek and I part ways at the subway. Derek is going home to his own apartment because he has to get packed and catch an early flight to New York. This is a shorter trip, only four days but will still be about four days too long. As I meander from the subway to the house I think about my situation and the roller coaster of emotion the day has brought. I'm still not happy with Marc but not nearly as angry as I was this morning. I'm excited to be getting the condo and very content that Derek and I are going to start a life together.

When I enter the house, Charlie Brown has obviously arrived just ahead of me and he's standing in the living room telling Mel what a terrible day he's had.

"Marc was such a complete jerk today," I hear him telling Mel. "He yelled at me three times and everyone else at least once. I think he even yelled at some of the other contractors. He was an absolute grizzly bear."

I walk into the room and vow in my head to say nothing about Marc and his obvious personality disorder but then Charlie Brown turns to me and asks, "Kit, are the payments late or something? Do you know why Marc is being such a jerk?"

"Besides that fact that he's a complete idiot who likes to voice absurd opinions on matters that don't concern him in the fashion of a sadistic dictator or drunken slob? No, I can't think of any reason why he'd be a jerk at work." Damn. That just slipped out. Maybe I'm still more upset with Marc than I thought. I must work on hiding my emotions a little better. I walk past Mel and Charlie Brown and venture no further comment. I do hear Charlie Brown say, "Well, that explains a lot!" to Mel as I close the bathroom door.

The standoff with Marc lasts weeks but it seems longer because I refuse to speak to him, even for work-related issues. Charlie Brown is not happy as his work environment worsens and he implores me to just call Marc and apologize. I refuse to call Marc on the grounds he started this little argument with his boorish behaviour and lack of manners, so he'll have to be the one to apologize. Charlie Brown is pulling his hair out and looks terrible. I can tell he isn't sleeping well and I'd feel bad for him if I was getting any sleep myself. As it is, he can suffer like the rest of us. It's not my fault Marc can't control his emotions at work. On the morning of day three of my standoff with Marc I'm in the kitchen trying to get our coffee maker to work and slamming things around when Mel comes into the kitchen and depresses the Delay button on the coffee maker and it suddenly starts to gurgle. I've had to resort to taking coffee in a travel mug because I refuse to go to the coffee shop on the slim chance I might run into Marc, and Joyce and I have completely given up on the coffee machine at work.

"This is getting silly now. You can't even work the coffee

maker. It's time to talk to him and clear the air," Mel says seriously.

"If he calls me I'll clear the air but I'm not calling him. He started it."

"What are we? Twelve? Just call him."

"If *I* give in first Marc will think it is okay to say any stupid thing he wants to me any time he wants. I'm going to buy the condo and live with Derek. I can't have Marc badmouthing the man I love and plan to spend my life with at every turn. If I give in I'll be sending the message that what he did was okay and it isn't. If I don't defend Derek to Marc now, Marc will never respect Derek and that is not respecting me. I cannot be friends with someone who doesn't respect me."

"You'd give up being friends with Marc over this?" Mel is surprised.

"He isn't being a friend so I won't be giving anything up, will I?" I have given the situation a lot of thought. "Mel, Derek has to know how Marc feels about me. God, everyone knows, but Derek has never asked me not to see Marc and he has never said one bad thing about Marc. Not one. I'm making the right choice."

"So you're never going to tell Marc that you care about him the way he cares about you?"

"No. I care about him but I'm not in love with him. Maybe I could have been if things were different but Marc and I have terrible timing, you said so yourself. It's never going to be, and maybe it's better for everyone if Marc and I *aren't* friends anymore."

"I don't know, maybe you're right," Mel agrees and I know that she too is realizing that unrequited love doesn't make for stable lasting friendships among the unrequited lovers. "Do you want a ride to work?"

"No thanks. I'll take the subway. I need some time alone after wrestling with the coffee maker." I try to smile but my heart is breaking.

# 33

Mel and I decided that Thanksgiving weekend might be a good time to tell our parents about the sale of the house and our wayward souls planning to live in sin. These little announcements sit better on a full stomach. We invite both sets of parents to come and stay for the weekend and include the twins. It's much closer for them to come to Toronto than to head all the way to North Bay for a long weekend and, as Tia mentioned in the course of our telephone conversation, Kevin is playing in Toronto on the Saturday night so she was hoping to stay at our house anyway. Seems Tia and Ben are still a long-distance item.

Mel and I are nervous about telling the parents our plans. Our parents have been pretty good sports about us showing no signs of marriage, save my failed attempt several years ago, but we both know that deep down they are anxious for us to be settled and begin producing grandchildren. Mel actually calls Mike to see if he will come for the weekend. We both think that Mike has a calming effect on our parents and that he will be a good ally to have in our camp. When Mel explains the situation to Mike on the telephone I can hear him laughing across the room. I take his gales of laughter to be a good indication that he will not be joining us for turkey at Thanksgiving. According to Mel's account after she gets off the phone, Mike wishes us both well and suggests we prepare last wills and testaments before we tell the folks. Aside from the will preparation, Mike has no further advice to offer.

Mike's ridicule aside, we forge ahead with our plan. We have to tell our parents at some point so it might as well be together and with our "sinful" boyfriends present. The twins arrive by train on Friday evening and I pick them up at the train station. Mel and I have a nice visit with them and tell them about the house and my new condo with Derek and Mel's plan to live with Charlie Brown when they find the right house to buy. The twins take the news well and are very happy for us. When we ask their opinion of what they think the parents will say, Taryn answers, "I don't think it will be *good...*" and Tia finishes her thought with "...so why don't you wait until we leave to see Kevin before you tell them tomorrow night!" Our siblings' support is staggering. I suddenly envy only children.

Mel and I spend Saturday morning preparing a feast for the family. Our parents are arriving this afternoon and we are going to have the big dinner tonight before the twins go out to see Kevin, and then have leftovers for the rest of the weekend. The leftover part of the plan only makes sense if our parents don't disown us and leave immediately following our announcement. The good thing about the distance to North Bay is that the length of the drive will deter them from making a round trip in one day and if they stay overnight surely they will mellow enough to endure the entire weekend.

The parents arrive in a flurry, each talking about the drive and the weather, which was perfect here but they maintain was terrible up north. Derek and Charlie Brown are both already here; we made them come early so we would present a united front, the appearance of which will come in handy later but goes unnoticed right now. Charlie Brown and Mel give the parents the tour of the renovations, which they have not seen until now, and Derek and I open the wine. Charlie Brown leads the dads downstairs to show them the new electrical panel and describe the renovation issues in depth and Mel brings the moms back to the kitchen where we hand them each a glass of wine. Derek leaves to go downstairs and join the men.

"So what's new?" Mrs. Melrose asks but then continues before either of us can answer, "Kathryn, you're walking well. I'm glad to see it."

"Thank you, it's been a long recovery but it's coming. I'm hoping to be jogging again soon." So far, so good.

"Well, you want to get strong, you might be walking down an aisle soon," my mom adds with a wink and Mel and I, who had both just taken sips of wine, almost spit the wine across the room. After Mel regains her composure and I'm still coughing, Mel asks, "What? What are you talking about?"

"Oh just tell us! Mike called last night and mentioned that we were in for a great surprise when we got here. We just can't wait. Which one of you is getting married?" I haven't seen Mrs. Melrose this excited since her lawn bowling team won the championship seven years ago.

"Neither of us is getting married. We sold the house," Mel explains. "By the way, when I see Mike again I'm going to kill him so his demise won't be a surprise because I just told you about it."

"You sold the house? That's the surprise? Well, that's not much of a surprise. Oh no! Did you girls have a falling out?" My mom seems quite deflated.

"No! Absolutely not. I got a great deal on a condo." I've regained my composure and have finally stopped coughing.

"And because I hate elevators, I'm going to buy a new house," Mel adds.

Our mothers look sad and defeated. They really thought one of us was getting married. They have nothing to say about our relocation news. It appears they could care less where we live. We could have said we were planning to be homeless and live in cardboard boxes and they would not have flinched. They want a wedding. The silence is getting awkward and uncomfortable so I nervously take another sip of wine. Mel, who believes in fixing all things broken announces, "But Kit might be getting engaged, she and Derek bought the condo together!" It's at this point I actually *do* spit wine all over our mothers.

The shriek from my mother is deafening and it isn't just because she is now covered in wine. She said she wanted a surprise, but I guess maybe she didn't really. Mrs. Melrose is shocked but finds the strength to console my mother by patting her on the shoulder and saying "there, there" while giving me a death stare.

After quickly brushing the wine off my shirt, I punch Mel in the arm and say, "What the hell!? What happened to waiting until after dinner?"

Poor Mel looks terrible. I could tell the minute the words were out of her mouth that she hadn't intended to say what she said, but once it was out, there was no going back. She was just trying to break the awkward silence, which she did succeed in doing.

"Well, you are in love and you *might* get engaged," Mel whispers to me.

"Yeah and I might *not*. And what about you? I am *not* going down alone!" I whisper emphatically so it isn't much of a whisper.

Our fathers and boyfriends are in the kitchen with us now, having rushed upstairs when they heard the shrieking. The twins, who I think may have overheard Mel's announcement, have wisely disappeared.

"Well, what's all this then?" my dad asks. "Spilled some wine, did we?" The poor man has no idea what he's in for as the mothers pounce all over him with news of my soon-to-be sinful lifestyle. Derek and Charlie Brown, having figured out what's going on, start to back out of the kitchen.

Mrs. Melrose shoots me another "thank God you're not my

child" look and I snap, "Oh yeah, well Mel and John are house shopping together — they just haven't bought one yet!"

Mel shoots me a glare, but she can't say anything because she sacrificed me first. At this point, Derek and Charlie Brown take giant steps backward and Mel yells at them to "Get back here, you snivelling cowards!" and they stop in their tracks but don't make any advances back toward the kitchen. All four parents are now yelling and pointing and I hear Mrs. Melrose shriek, "Where did we go wrong?" and I know it's going to be a long evening. Mel, Charlie Brown, Derek and I say nothing. We can't get a word in anyway. It's probably best to let them have their rant. I reach behind me and grab the open bottle of wine from the counter and refill my glass and Mel's, then hand the bottle past the cluster of parents to Charlie Brown. We're in for a long night; we might as well have another glass of wine.

By the time we sit down to dinner it's almost eight o'clock. Everyone is exhausted. The ranting went on for what seemed like forever, but once that stopped the lecturing began and that made us miss the ranting. I won't go into the entire lecture, Lord knows reliving it would be a nightmare, but the general points were that Mel and I have been living in The City too long, we have developed questionable morals, and our biological clocks are ticking. Mr. Melrose made mention of "No one will buy the cow if they can get the milk for free" but I'm not even going to dignify that little tidbit with a second thought.

After the lecturing the dads seem a bit better with the situation than the moms. I think the moms must have spent more time developing the "one of us is getting married" idea, so they are more devastated than the dads, who just think we are morally corrupt. If Mike hadn't planted the wedding idea the whole living together discussion might have gone more smoothly. As it is, the twins, who have done nothing wrong in the eyes of the parents, are forbidden to go out and see Kevin because they cannot be "traipsing all over The City being corrupted like your sister and Mel." The negotiations continue throughout the entire meal and at one point the twins would be allowed to go only if all the parents went with them. It was Charlie Brown who was actually able to convince the mothers that Kevin might not play music they wanted to hear for an entire evening, so it was finally determined that the twins could go out but would be dropped off and picked up by the fathers. There would be no traipsing, gallivanting or carousing for the twins. They would be properly chaperoned for the remainder of the weekend and possibly the rest of their lives. Mel and I mouth "I'm sorry" to the twins, repeatedly, but judging from Tia's steely stare I'm pretty sure Mel and I are going to have to go shopping next week and put together an eye-popping apology package for them.

The only upside of the dinner discussion and upheaval is that neither mother makes any comment or disparaging remark about the gravy.

After dinner, when the dads are getting ready to protectively drive the twins to the Kevin show, it becomes apparent that since neither the dads nor the twins live in Toronto or have any sense of where they are going, one of us has to go and direct them. The four Toronto dwellers are slow to offer to ride along. We'd all like the chance to escape the moms but no one wants to be alone with the dads either, in case it's an ambush. It could be a long drive downtown and back if you're being lectured. Dad's car won't allow for two more people so it's one of us to the potential slaughter. The moms are the scarier force at this point, having been denied the wedding of their dreams, so Derek offers to ride along with the dads. I watch in awe as the man I love puts on his brave face and plods toward the car as if drudging off to war.

A few minutes later, I'm quite glad Derek isn't here to witness the next installment of mother mania. After the twins leave with their chaperones and Derek the tour guide, the mothers start talking amongst themselves and speculating about what is to become of them now that they have the "worst daughters in the civilized world." Mel and I start to clean up the dinner table since we aren't being asked to partake in the conversation which is currently centring on how the boyfriends "who refuse to marry us" should be addressed and introduced. Charlie Brown is refilling wineglasses when Mrs. Melrose corners him with a direct question.

"Well, I just don't know what to do with you. What do I call *you*? My daughter's '*live in*'?" Mrs. Melrose is obviously agitated and Charlie Brown, whose opinionated demeanour leaves little room for the finer points of diplomacy, replies, "Oh, I don't know. How about the 'sin-in-law'?"

The shrieks being emitted from the mothers are louder and longer than when Mel first hung me out to dry earlier this afternoon. Mel manages to get Charlie Brown out of harm's way and into the kitchen but sadly the damage is done. Mel and I both think Charlie Brown's answer is quite funny but we dare not let the mothers know since they obviously find no humour in it at all. To Charlie Brown's credit, he's making Derek look good and judging by the looks my mother is shooting in Charlie Brown's general direction, I think she is quite pleased that I'm not "shacking up with *that* one." Derek is off giving directions and being helpful whereas Mel's friend is being vile and trying to impose levity where there ought to be none. All in all, despite our sinful ways, Derek and I might come out of this the less sinful of the two couples. Mrs. Melrose, who was a little too eager to pity my mother earlier this afternoon, is now looking a little pale. I guess the thought of having Charlie Brown as a sin-in-law will take some getting used to.

Due to lack of sleeping space, Mel and I had originally thought we might go to our respective boyfriends' houses and leave our house for the parents and the twins, but in light of the way the news of our cohabitation plans was met, we decide to rough it on the living-room floor with the twins. We give Tia the couch because we feel awful about ruining her weekend with Ben, and Taryn, Mel and I line up sleeping bags on the floor. In whispers, Mel and I apologize to the twins for the way the announcement came out and I stress that it is Mel's fault for not waiting until they were safely out the door on their way to see Kevin, which results in a kick from Mel. Taryn, who didn't have her weekend ruined, laughs and says, "Ah, no worries. After this I can run off and join the circus and I'll still be considered the good one. You girls are lowering the bar for us, so technically we owe you!" We all laugh, which results in being yelled at to "keep it down out there" by one of the dads.

Monday doesn't come soon enough. The stress around the house is almost unbearable and I worry that my healing leg will snap again under the pressure. I ask my parents a couple of times if they'd like to see the condominium we're buying and they refuse to even acknowledge its existence, let alone go there to see it. Mrs. Melrose looks the worse for wear. I think Charlie Brown may have pushed her over the limit with the sin-in-law comment. She refuses to eat and is certain that Mel is going to have children out of wedlock. I don't have the heart to tell her that Mel is probably using three types of birth control at once. Mentioning birth control at this point would definitely not be advisable. Unlike Charlie Brown, I have the ability to *not* say everything that pops into my head.

Mel and I stand at the door and wave goodbye to our parents. We both have the full knowledge that we may well be disowned but are happy that the worst is over.

"I think that went pretty well," Mel says sarcastically as we both fall onto the couch.

"It could have been worse. Not!"

"Do you think they'll ever speak to us again?"

"In a perfect world no, but I think they're going to want to get some mileage on the guilt. We are, after all, ruining their good reputations and community standing," I answer confidently. Oh, there will be guilt, lots and lots of guilt.

The weekend after the Thanksgiving parent fiasco, as we now affectionately refer to it, Derek and I had planned to go to Las Vegas but it didn't exactly work out as planned.

"So you're not going?" Mel asks from the other end of the phone.

"Nope. Seems Derek's credit card is a bit overextended and he can't afford the trip," I explain what Derek had told me earlier.

"You could afford it though."

"Yes, but with the condo closing coming up there will be unexpected expenses and we need to get a kitchen table. It's probably best we don't go, and keep what money we have for the move."

"Well, that's a huge drag. Derek really has to figure out his finances. He's a bit of a disaster for an investment banker," Mel states the obvious.

"Exactly, I've made a mental note to sign him up for a Living Within Your Means seminar but he might need the whole weekend retreat." Mel and I get a great laugh out of that one.

# 34

It's been a month since I've spoken to Marc, who Charlie Brown maintains is still being terribly miserable at work. If Marc and I have to speak about work-related matters we go through other people, and when I say other people I mean Charlie Brown. Charlie Brown is not pleased with his position as middleman and does mention it would be nice if "we could all just get along" on a daily basis. My response to Charlie Brown is always, "It'd also be nice if your boss wasn't a jerk." I sometimes change up the word *jerk* for other descriptive nouns and occasionally I add an adjective, but you get the idea. Arrgh, this whole argument is playing havoc with my caffeine intake.

I survey the coffee shop quickly as I walk in, just to make sure Marc isn't lying in ambush. I don't see anyone I recognize except one of the ladies who works on the floor below me in our building. I nod and say good morning to her. I think her name is Beth but I'm not one hundred percent sure so I don't say her name. I get my coffee, pay and turn around from the counter to leave and almost walk directly into a man's chest. I manage not to spill coffee on this person because the lid is securely fastened to the paper cup. The man is taller than I am so I'm eye level with the knot of his tie. I vaguely feel that I should recognize this chest and these shoulders. I start to look up toward the head that owns this body when I hear the voice that belongs to the chest, "Kit Jennings, wow, it's been ages. How are you?"

There standing before me in a complete suit and tie, carrying a briefcase, is Rob-the-bike-courier.

When I speak about my relationship with Rob-the-bike-courier, or did speak of it, because I haven't even given Rob a thought in well over a year, I never mention the manner in which we broke up. It's one of those things that you just don't tell people. I did tell people that Rob was unfaithful but never expanded on how I discovered his infidelity. Standing here in the coffee shop six inches from the chest and shoulders I used to massage and the six-pack I used to bounce quarters off, it all comes flooding back in nauseating waves.

Rob and I dated for five months. It was five great months back when we were both in a party frame of mind. We went out almost every night. Rob introduced me to great new bands and clubs that I'd never heard of before I met him. Rob convinced me to go bungee jumping and hang out at the skateboard park. If you'd told me I was going to break my leg I would have guessed it'd be on a skateboard ramp. I am far too old to be competing with teenagers at anything, let alone skateboarding. We basically tackled extreme sports (extreme to me anyway), listened to great music, had sex and drank way too much beer together. At the time I was infatuated with Rob and overlooked some of the inconsistencies in the relationship. Rob was often late to meet me and occasionally seemed "not himself." I didn't have the opportunity to figure out if he was using drugs or to what extent before the relationship ended, after which his drug use was no longer my concern.

The last time I saw Rob, or rather Rob's butt, was a Thursday afternoon almost two years ago. At the time Rob lived in a dingy apartment building in the west end that had questionable security. The front door of the building was almost never locked, so vagrants, door-to-door salespeople and girlfriends could easily walk in unannounced.

On that fateful day in May, I had planned to meet Rob at a club downtown much later in the evening but happened to be near his apartment in the afternoon. I was in the west end picking up a custom-ordered glass vase for Mr. Sebring, so decided to pop in and see if Rob was home from work yet. I walked into the building unannounced because it was unlocked as usual and walked down the hallway to Rob's apartment. Rob's apartment door was slightly ajar, which I thought was very odd and I was worried he had been robbed, not that he had much to steal save his skateboard collection. Listening at the door and hearing nothing, I had to assume that if Rob had been burgled the perpetrators were long gone. Then in true Nancy Drew fashion, I slowly pushed the door open and looked around. Rob was not notoriously neat so the apartment at first glance appeared to have been vandalized but in reality was just normal messy Rob. All four skateboards were lined up against the wall. I let out an audible sigh of relief just as I heard a noise from the bedroom. Assuming Rob was in there and probably just getting out of the shower, I started toward the bedroom and was just about to yell out Rob's name when I saw it, larger than life, Rob's butt. Rob's butt, doing with someone else what I believed he and I only did to each other, in the bedroom I'd painted for him not two weekends before.

I stepped back around the corner to regain my composure in shock and embarrassment because seeing people having sex is always embarrassing for the person who sees it, or should be anyway, depends on the person I guess. My mouth was terribly dry and I could not think straight. I felt like I might vomit and the first thing I thought was "Why did I pick Firelove Red to paint Rob's walls? Sure, I wanted to ignite passion, but with *me*, not other people!"

I made myself calm down and asked myself, "Okay, what are you going to do?" I'm not good with confrontation. I can hold my own if forced to but to actually walk into Rob's bedroom and confront him? No, that wasn't going to happen. I tend to vomit and/or cry in these situations and you never want to give the impression of weepy girlfriend. No. This situation required a bit more finesse and class — well, as much class as you can muster after seeing your boyfriend fornicating with some other woman. God, I hope it's a woman. I shuddered. Okay, wipe that thought out of your head and think. Must do something classy, yet get my point across, without any drama. Think. I looked around Rob's messy living room and it hit me.

I reached blindly into my purse and grabbed the first lipstick I could feel. I carry two lipsticks at all times because you never know if you are going to want to be light and summery or dark and mysterious. The tube I grabbed was Clinque's Blushing Nude, fitting since I'd just seen Rob's nude butt up to no good. I walked to the mirror hanging above Rob's faux fireplace and wrote "Oh isn't THIS just NICE!" I tossed the ruined lipstick tube on the mantel and turned to leave, but noticed Rob's skateboards lined up near the door. I grabbed the one closest to me and with the skateboard under my arm I left, ensuring that I slammed the door behind me so as to interrupt Rob's lovemaking. Needless to say I did not go to the club as originally planned and instead spent the evening drinking a bottle of wine, bastardizing the scene depicted on Rob's skateboard with a Super Sharpie, and discussing with Mel the hideous behaviour of men in general and bike couriers in particular. Rob tried to call me that night but I did not pick up and had Mel erase the messages without listening to them. A small part of me was curious as to what excuse Rob might come up with to try and save his skin, but ultimately he was having sex with someone other than me, so no excuse or apology would suffice. Hell, he probably just wanted to ask about his missing skateboard.

The morning after "Rob's butt," I went to the coffee shop

for much-needed caffeine. You don't sleep well when you've just caught your boyfriend in bed with another woman and I was determined to think it was a woman because the other option was just too overwhelming. While I was waiting in the coffee line, I overheard the conversation the two ladies in front of me were having. I recognized one of the women who worked in the building across from ours. She was attractive, with blonde bobbed hair, medium build, I'd guess in her mid-forties and judging from the rings, married. The other lady was also vaguely familiar. I recognized her from getting coffee and had admired her long black leather jacket in the past.

"Well it was the most startling thing," I heard the blonde lady say. "It wasn't *bad*, just completely unexpected."

"Okay, let me get this straight, you had just finished having sex and he slapped your bottom and asked, 'Who's your daddy?'" the lady in the black coat asked.

At this point my mind jumped into fifth gear. Rob-the-bike-courier did something similar to me when we were first dating. I immediately put a stop to bottom slapping and threatened him with severe maiming if he ever did it again, which to his credit he refrained from doing, but how odd? Had all men everywhere completely lost their minds? Was there a "Who's your daddy?" epidemic in the city? This poor woman was probably years into her marriage and suddenly her hubby's slapping her ass and asking her who her daddy is? Maybe *SportsLine* or one of the other sporting highlight shows was sending some subliminal who's your daddy programming that was affecting their poor, tiny, easily influenced male minds.

"Yes. It was actually a bit exciting," the blonde lady was smiling, so obviously she was not as anti-butt-slapping as I was.

"Wait a minute! Is your mystery lover Rob-the-bike-courier?" the lady in the long leather coat asked excitedly and not as quietly as I'm sure she intended to ask.

"How do you know?" the blonde lady now had that shocked, deer-in-the-headlights look.

"Because he did that same thing to *me*!" the lady in leather responded and started to laugh.

Oh this was just great! My boyfriend, Rob-the-bike-courier, was apparently doing more than delivering packages to every woman in the financial district of downtown Toronto. I felt the bile rising and I knew I was going to vomit. I ran out of the coffee shop but didn't make it back to the office and had to vomit in one of the decorative planters outside our building.

I spent the best part of the morning carrying coffee carafes of water downstairs to dilute the mess I made in the shrubbery. Later, after the shrubbery was in better form, I reflected on the situation. As disheartening as it was that the person I thought I cared about was fornicating with women all over town, it was less disturbing than the idea that all men everywhere were slapping women on the asses and asking "Who's your daddy?"

So now, standing in the coffee shop toe to toe with the man whose butt I haven't seen since that fateful day, I'm at a loss for words. I know as soon as I walk away I'll think of thirty different pithy comebacks but right now I've got nothing.

"Rob-the-bike-courier. It has been a long time and yet, not nearly long enough," I manage, then step around Rob to leave. I get out the door before I turn completely pale and lose all my composure. I don't have feelings for Rob any longer but I was completely unprepared to see him again. Toronto is such a large city; you can walk around for weeks and months fairly secure in the fact that you will never see anyone you know, let alone run face to chest with an ex-lover. I stop momentarily to assess the vomiting situation. Although I feel I *could* vomit, I think I'll be able to ride this encounter out without doing so. I continue walking toward the office confident that I'll kick this nervous stomach habit yet.

As soon as I get settled at the office I call Mel's cell phone to tell her about my coffee-shop encounter and Mel laughs heartily and asks, "Did you slap him on the ass and ask 'Who's your daddy?' as you walked out the door?"

"No, but that would have been funny," I answer. Again, you always think of the really great comebacks after the situation is long over.

"I bet he looks great in a suit. Was he in good form or drugged out?" Mel is most curious for details.

"It was eight o'clock in the morning so he wasn't drugged

out and he is pretty cute in a suit. I guess he's not working as a bike courier any longer."

"No, he's probably finally embraced his calling and is working as a high-paid escort. Oh look it up on the Internet! I bet it's called Who's Your Daddy Escort Service." Mel is in hysterics at her own joke.

"No doubt! And you are very funny this morning, but I have to get back to work. See you at home tonight."

# 35

As I'm shutting down my computer and getting my desk tidied to leave for the day, the telephone rings and it's Derek calling.

"Hey, how was your day? Are you up for meeting me at the Firkin for a beer?" Derek is skipping the gym so something must be up.

"Absolutely, I don't generally drink on Mondays but I can be convinced if it's with my handsome boyfriend," I laugh and we arrange to meet in thirty minutes.

I can tell something is bothering Derek when I enter the pub. He does not look his normal happy self and is fidgeting with a paper beer coaster. Derek is not a fidgety person. Skipping the gym, meeting for drinks on a Monday and he is fidgeting. This is not good. I approach the table tentatively, my first concern is for the mortgage being arranged by Pete Peterson, but I try to remain optimistic.

"Hey handsome, what's up?" I ask as I sit down across from Derek at one of Mel's regular tables near the door.

Steve looks up from the bar and asks if I'll have the usual and I nod yes.

"Well, I had a big day at work." Derek stands up and kisses

me as I am getting settled. "I had a surprise meeting with my boss and Ross from New York." Derek starts right in with what's on his mind, so I don't venture any input and let him continue.

"Seems I've been 'noticed,' but in a good way," Derek clarifies so I don't think he's been embezzling from the company. "It seems they want me in New York."

"All this drama, I thought it was something big," I laugh nervously and breathe a sigh of relief. "You always go to New York, so when do you leave this time?"

"No Kathryn, they want me in New York permanently. They want me to move there." Derek is the perfect mix of ecstatic and miserable.

"Oh" is pretty much all I can muster. The man I love and am planning to live with is moving to another country. Okay, it's a close country but it's hardly in the same condo.

"I don't have to let them know until tomorrow and I wanted to talk to you, obviously. This will change our plans a little bit." Derek is speaking faster. I can tell he really wants this move and has been worried about how to tell me. A part of me, the good part, wants to say okay whatever makes you happy, but the other part, the selfish part, wants to scream "Don't leave *me*. Move into the condo with *me* and be happy with *me*." I take a sip of the beer Steve has placed in front of me without me noticing but find it difficult to swallow.

"Is it a promotion?" I find myself interested despite the voice in my head screaming, "Don't go!"

"Yes, a great one. Two pay grades, a corner office and an assistant who speaks English, has normal hair and can type." Derek is excited. Now I know for sure he wants to go.

"Okay," I can't believe I'm having this conversation, "when do you leave?"

"The first of next month, but the company is going to pay all the moving expenses." Derek has lost the miserable portion of his demeanour and is completely ecstatic. Apparently it was the telling me part that was upsetting him, the leaving me part does not seem to be an issue since he has yet to mention the condo, or us, or the fact that we'll be living in different countries.

"The first of the month as in next week? Are you serious?"

"I know, one of the New York guys had a nervous break-down or something and they need the accounts covered," Derek says in his pro-company voice.

"Well, a nervous breakdown! I guess you'd better go then. Mr. Sebring will get me out of the agreement to purchase the condo but you'll have to deal with Pete." I try to be matter of fact when my heart is breaking. How Derek can just spring this on me when we had plans is completely unfathomable. I can't believe this is happening. This morning I was part of the happiest couple ever and nine hours later the man I love tells me he's moving to New York in the same voice he uses to order pizza with extra cheese.

I fear tears will be upon me soon and I'm fairly certain there will be vomiting, so I start to put on my jacket.

"What? Hey, where are you going?"

"I'm going home and you're moving to New York." I'm upset and starting to get angry; the man in front of me seems to want his cake and to eat it too.

"No. Well, yes. The job is permanent but only for six months to see if it's going to work. They're putting me up in a hotel and I can fly home every weekend if I want. If it's working after that then we'll have to decide what to do, but we're still good. We can go ahead with the condo and I can still pay my share. If we decide New York is working after six months we can sell it or whatever. We'll figure it out." Derek is standing with his hand on my arm.

"Why didn't you say that in the beginning?" I'm starting to cry now, "I thought you were just leaving forever."

"No. I'm not leaving forever. I'm so sorry. I was worried all day about how to tell you and then I screwed it up completely anyway." Derek seems sincere and I believe him. It can't be easy telling your girlfriend you're moving to another country, even if it's only for six months.

"But what about in six months, we'll be in the same boat only we'll own the condo by then? Not to mention I'll be completely insane because I won't be seeing you every day."

"We'll figure it out. Besides you might love New York and the company will guarantee the sale of the condo at market value so technically we could make money." Derek seems to have it all figured out and he's right, I might like New York. It's bigger than Toronto and the chances of walking directly into the chest of one of your ex-lovers would be greatly lessened.

# 36

The rest of the week is completely harried. Derek is trying to wrap up things at work, decide what he'll have to take to New York, pack the remaining things and get his furniture and unneeded effects into storage. We spend as much time as possible together and I take three days off work to spend time with him and to help with the packing. We decide what furniture will be necessary for the condo and put that into storage last.

I take Derek to the airport on the day he flies out. I generally don't take him to the airport when he's going to New York for a few days but knowing I won't see him for at least two weeks makes the drive to the airport together seem important. We get to spend a few more minutes together before we start living a long-distance relationship. We talked about it and decided that every second weekend for visits is the best idea; flying home every Friday night then leaving again every Sunday would be way too much for Derek on top of learning a new job and discovering a new city.

I usually love the airport because if you're at the airport you are generally going on a trip so it's a great place. The airport, however, isn't quite so charming when you are sending the man you love to live in another country. I don't park the car or go into the terminal with Derek because that's just going to be harder on both of us. Instead I drop him at the departures level. I get out of the car and help him get his bags out of Nasty's trunk. I'm on autopilot, which is fitting since I'm at the airport. I know as soon as I get back in the car I will be starting a whole new life and I'm loath to leave the old one. I have no difficulty functioning as a single person, but a single person isn't contending with long-distance phone calls and emails to sustain a relationship. A single person is single. This is going to be a strange six months.

I give Derek a huge hug and a kiss I hope he'll remember for the next two weeks. I want to say something deep but nothing comes to mind. I'm happy for him and sad that he's leaving. I'm a veritable goulash of emotions.

"I'm really going to miss you." Derek is sad as well, I can tell from his voice.

"Not as much as I'm going to miss you." I know Derek will be so busy learning his new job that he won't have the same time on his hands I will. I'll be doing the exact same things I did before only without him.

"I'll call you as soon as I get there. I love you." Derek kisses me again and I notice we are getting looks from the security person who tells you to hurry up when you've been parked in the dropoff too long but I can't let go of his hand.

"I love you too." Derek drops my hand, turns and walks

toward the terminal and I get into the car and start my life apart from him.

I find the weeks between visits with Derek go a lot faster when I work more. I originally thought I'd just do it for the first couple of weeks until I got used to him not being around, but I don't seem to be getting used to it as fast as I'd hoped. Being at home means I stand a good chance of spending time with Mel and Charlie Brown and, honestly, spending time with a nauseatingly happy couple makes me sad. Charlie Brown, to his credit, is being a great sport about my moping around and tries to watch football with me on Sundays when Mel's hosting open houses.

"You have to eat anyway," Mel is saying into the phone. "You can't work overtime every day; you're going to raise the bar so high even *you* won't be able to meet it once Derek comes back." I know Mel has a point. I've been getting to work early and working late most evenings. I've even started coming back to work after my physiotherapy appointments. I do spend some of the time emailing with Derek but more time working.

"You haven't been out for a beer with me in five weeks. It's Friday night, for heaven's sake. Besides, I have new boots to show you." Mel says the last part in her singsongy voice and I start to laugh.

"You always have new boots, what's new about that? Didn't you just buy a pair on Monday? How many pairs of boots do two feet need?"

"Those were proper winter boots. *These* are wonderful dress boots, completely different things."

"No. I look terrible. I will go home now, I promise, but I'm not going out. You and Charlie Brown go and have a great time." I want to go out in public like I want to poke my own eyes out with a fork. Well, actually if those were the two choices, the fork option might be preferable.

"No. Your birthday is next week and I'm not going to be around to take you out for a birthday drink on the actual day."

"Good, because I'm not celebrating my birthday this year. We already had this little chat, didn't we? No party. No big deal."

"The only party going on here is your private little pity party and this is one drink. You can't hide out forever."

"I'm not hiding out. I go out when Derek's home. We just went out for dinner last weekend, remember?" I know Mel remembers because she got a heel caught in a subway grate and scratched the leather on her lime green boots. I don't acknowledge her "pity party" comment because I'm quite enjoying my little pity party, thank you very much!

"Yes, but this is the Firkin, after work. We haven't done that in ages. Steve is asking about you. I saw him last week and he thinks you're mad at him." Mel is trying her hand at the mother-guilt but it's not working.

"You're making that up. Steve is a bartender; if I'm not there that's just less work for him. He's probably happy I'm not a regular anymore. Besides, I drink too much anyway; it's time I cut back." Two can play the guilt game. Surely she'll have to back down so as not to further corrupt me and send me spiralling into rehab.

"You haven't had a drink since last weekend, but good try." Mel doesn't fall for the guilt either. We really must stop trying it with each other; neither of us ever falls for it.

"I'm coming by your office. I will drag you kicking and screaming. I don't care. I'm not going to let the fact that Derek is working in New York ruin *my* social life." I hate it when she's adamant like this. I know she's serious and won't let it go. I might as well bite the bullet.

"Fine. I'll go but only for one beer then I'm out of there, deal?"

"Deal. I'll be there in twenty minutes, we'll walk over together." Mel is coming to walk me so I don't escape.

"I hate you," I say cheerfully into the phone.

"Oh don't be silly, you love me too much to hate me."

Mel meets me in the lobby of my office building. She seems very excited, far too excited to be just going to the Firkin for a drink after work on a Friday, even with the new boots, which are black by the way. How Mel can distinguish the difference between pairs of black boots — I think this makes pair number eight — would make a fascinating documentary akin to how a mother bear tells her cubs apart.

"I think I may have found the house I want to buy. I just heard about it from one of the other realtors. I'm getting a look at it tomorrow." Mel explains the jump in her step and it makes sense. Mel gets very excited about real estate. I ask location and particulars as we walk to the bar. I am happy for Mel but I'm tired and not in a particularly party frame of mind. The idea of sitting through a beer makes me sleepy. I can't believe I let Mel coerce me into this. One drink, then I go home.

I'm still not used to the idea of the long-distance relationship with Derek. Derek seems to love his new job and is loving New York. I suspect when the trial six months are up we are going to have to decide what to do and I'm almost positive Derek is going to want New York. The idea of being a long-distance couple indefinitely is nauseating but the idea of leaving and moving to be with Derek is equally nauseating. I've spent the past five weeks being very nauseous. I'm thinking about how nauseous I feel right this second as Mel opens the door to the Firkin and laughs, "After you, since you haven't been here in a hundred years."

I step into the bar and am thinking how crowded it is for a Friday evening, when the throng yells "*Surprise!*" Mother of Pearl. It's a surprise party for me! I am going to kill Mel. I told her *explicitly* no birthday parties and definitely no surprises. I obviously must work harder on my firm voice because she doesn't listen to me. My first thought, after picturing Mel's bloodied and lifeless body on the floor, is "I hope my hair looks okay." I've lost interest in taming my hair in the mornings since Derek moved and honestly can't tell you what it looks like now. The fact that I don't comb or brush or even think about my hair during the workday is an indication that it probably looks like hell and here I am the centre of attention. My third thought is the same as my first, Mel's bloodied, lifeless body lying on the floor in front of me. Just then Derek pushes through two of Marc's employees and starts to walk toward me. Oh my God! Derek is here! This isn't his weekend to be here. I suddenly don't hate Mel any longer and am absolutely thrilled. Derek gives me a huge hug and picks me up and kisses me. Despite my abhorrence for surprise birthday parties this is one surprise I'm actually enjoying.

"This is amazing. I didn't know you were coming home this weekend! Why didn't you tell me?" I'm thinking had I known of Derek's impending arrival I would have definitely done my hair.

"If I'd told you, you wouldn't have been surprised," Derek laughs and kisses me again.

"Okay you two," Mel interrupts, "there's a roomful of people to see Kit and you two rabbits have the rest of the weekend to be all over each other."

Derek laughs and puts me down. I look around and see so many people I know as well as a lot of the construction team, including Joyce. Taryn and Tia start toward me, with Ben and Kevin from the band Kevin, and give me hugs.

"Happy Birthday," they say in unison.

"Thank you both for coming." I didn't expect to see the twins until Christmas break and am really surprised they made the trip during exams.

"Kevin and Ben." I am very surprised to see Kevin. Ben I

assume wants to spend the evening with Tia. "This is a great surprise, thank you for coming out."

"Kevin is our entertainment," Mel mentions from beside me, "we couldn't fit the whole band in so Kevin is going to play solo for us."

"Well, an extra thank you then," I say as I turn back to Kevin. Just then Derek returns from the bar and hands me a beer and says, "Happy Birthday."

I start to walk toward some of the construction crew and realize that I'm still dressed in my work suit from the office so turn back to Mel and say, "I can't believe you pulled this off and got me here but mostly I can't believe you didn't think to bring me a change of clothes."

"Oh, sorry about that," Mel laughs. "I did bring you clothes; they are in my briefcase." She laughs and hands over the briefcase.

"I'll be right back." I hand Mel my beer and head to the ladies' room. The Firkin's ladies' room isn't the most convenient place to change clothing but if it will get me into a pair of jeans and out of my suit it will work just fine. Mel did well selecting my clothes; she brought my favourite jeans and a little Roots sweater. I bundle up my suit and try to put it into Mel's briefcase as neatly as possible but realize that no amount of neatness is going to keep it from requiring a trip to the dry cleaners. I apply some lipstick and try to tame my hair but have to give up as it's no use without a proper flatiron and styling products. After admitting hair defeat, I gather up Mel's

Prada briefcase and my purse and step out of the ladies' room. Marc, who I have not seen or heard from since the coffee shop argument more than two months ago, is lurking outside the men's room.

"Wow, I haven't seen you in ages. How are you?" I ask Marc, smiling wider than I should, considering I'm supposed to be mad at him. I guess the two-month absence did its job because I am no longer angry with him and have resigned myself to the fact that we may never be close friends again. Standing two feet away from Marc is actually quite nice and I realize that I have missed having him around. Unrequited love or not, he is someone who's company I enjoy.

"Yeah, it's been a while." Marc seems nervous.

"Charlie Brown tells me work is going well." I try to make small talk.

"Look, I'm really sorry about the last conversation we had. I know I was completely out of line and I said some things I shouldn't have," Marc says after a short pause and seems sincere.

"I'm as much to blame. I shouldn't have flown off the handle. You were only stating your opinion." I know I overreacted and since apologies are going around I might as well get mine in too.

"John tells me Derek got transferred to New York." Marc is slightly more relaxed but still nervous.

"Yep, but we're making it work." I smile at the fact that Marc actually used Derek's name. That's a first.

"Are you going to move there?"

"We haven't thought that far ahead. We still have a few months before we have to make any decisions. I know Derek loves his new job so that will be a large part of the decision I suppose, when we get that far."

Suddenly, talking to Marc about the possibility of leaving Toronto to move to New York, I feel nauseous again. The idea of leaving my job, Mel, the twins and even the insanity of my parents seems surreal. Don't get me wrong, I would love to sleep in the same bed as my boyfriend every night. Lord knows I want nothing more, but as much as living in New York will ensure I don't see cheating ex-boyfriends it will also ensure I don't see my friends and the people I care about as well.

"Are you okay? You look a bit pale." Marc has reached out and grabbed my arm because I'm a bit lightheaded and have started to tip over.

"No, I'm fine. Must be all the excitement of yet another birthday," I try to laugh and regain my composure, or what composure one can gain while walking around with big hair.

"Maybe you should go and sit down for a minute."

"Yeah, maybe. Thanks." I start to walk away but stop and turn back to Marc, "Thanks for coming today. It really means a lot to me to have you here. Friends?" I put my hand out and Marc reaches for it.

"Friends." Marc squeezes my hand and holds it a little longer than a friend might.

The party lasts much longer than my avowed "one beer" and we close the Firkin. The Firkin doesn't usually have live music but Mel arranged for Kevin to play in our favourite corner — there is only room for a bar stool and Kevin with his guitar. Having the whole band play would have been great but, room being what it is, they would have had to set up on the sidewalk outside and since it's December that's probably not good for their equipment. Kevin is amazing and plays all our requests, even the ones he scowls at before he starts to play. He throws in a few of his own and even dedicates one of his original ballads to me in honour of my birthday. Tia is thrilled that Ben isn't working and sticks to him like glue all evening. Taryn is a major hit with the guys from the construction team and spends the evening dodging wandering hands.

Having everyone together at the Firkin turns out to be a wonderful evening and I'm glad that Mel planned it as a surprise because I never would have gone along with the party idea. I'm not a huge fan of my birthday and was in no rush to celebrate this one, especially with Derek being in New York and the thought of what that means to us constantly on my mind.

"You did well," I laugh to Mel.

"I know!" Mel is nothing if not modest. "I knew you'd never agree to anything because you're a complete party-pooper but I had to do something great. This might be your last birthday in Toronto with me. Next year you might be an uppity Manhattan type who has no time for your less lofty Toronto friends."

"I know, you guys will all be toast as soon as I get a taste of the New York lifestyle. You'll call and I'll say, Mel? Mel who?" I laugh but inside I feel nauseous again and hope I don't vomit.

"I'm glad Marc showed up. It was touch and go all week. He was determined not to show but John told him about Derek being transferred and the fact that you'd likely be leaving Toronto in a few months so it was time he swallowed his larger-than-life pride and apologize. Did he?"

"Yes, we both did and it was about time." I am glad Marc is back in my life. Somehow everything just seems right when he's around.

"Good. I see Taryn is a hit with the fellas," Mel laughs.

"Gee, do you think? I should probably go and spell Marc off, he's been babysitting for hours." Marc had been running interference for Taryn for most of the evening.

"I'll go. Marc's guys are afraid of me," Mel laughs and taps toward the bar in her new boots to help Marc control his "hands-on" employees.

At the end of the evening, Tia approaches me with Ben in tow and asks if she can stay at Ben's house tonight. My immediate reaction is "no, absolutely not!" but Derek squeezes my hand and gives me the "you were in university once" look and I realize I'm on the fast track to becoming my mother. I agree to let Tia go home with Ben but only after Ben writes all his particulars on a business card and Tia takes my cell phone and promises three times to call me first thing in the morning so

I can come and pick her up. Tia and Taryn are only staying in Toronto for one night and are planning to take the train back to Kingston tomorrow afternoon. Taryn has had too much to drink so will definitely be coming home with me despite the promises I've had from Marc's employees to "take care of her." I politely decline their generous offers and suspect Taryn will have a very big headache tomorrow.

After Kevin packs up his guitar I give him a big hug.

"Thank you so much for taking time out to come here tonight." I am genuinely thrilled Mel arranged for him to be here.

"Are you kidding? It was great and I'm glad I could be here for your birthday."

As Derek and I try to bundle Taryn up whilst peeling the boys off her, Marc leans over and whispers, "Happy Birthday, I missed you," in my ear.

I don't respond but look up and smile at him. I'm glad he's back in my world.

# 37

I awake on Saturday morning in a panic about Tia and start calling her on my cell phone at the crack of dawn and am ready to call the police to track down the murderous Ben who, up until now, I quite liked and didn't consider even remotely sinister, when she finally calls me. Seems the battery on the cell phone was low so she turned it off. I am just glad she is alive and well. The parent brigade would never let Mel or me live it down if something happened to one of the twins while they were in our care. Taryn, on the other hand, looks the worse for wear. Poor thing has a hangover the size of the CN Tower. I made her take vitamin B before going to bed. I heard once that will help in hangover recovery, but I don't think it did much to help poor Taryn. She is still the colour of bright white printer paper when we drop her and Tia off at the train station. Luckily, Tia is in better shape or I would have insisted on driving them back to Kingston myself.

Derek and I spend a quiet Saturday. We stay in all day, watch three old movies, have "wanton sex" several times and order Chinese food for dinner. Derek leaves on an early plane on Sunday morning because he has some work to do before Monday and a new week begins. After I drop him at the airport I can't stomach returning home to a house without him in it so I head downtown to do some shopping. Christmas is just around the corner and I haven't even begun to think about gifts. I did, however, come up with an idea for Tia after Friday night. Tia, who up until now has shown no musical inclination besides playing CDs, seems quite struck with the whole band scene so I think I'll get her a tambourine for Christmas. Who knows, Ben and Kevin might let her play in the band if she becomes proficient with it. I'm standing on Queen Street wondering where one might purchase a tambourine when I hear a familiar voice.

"Kathryn Jennings, we meet again," Rob-the-bike-courier says as he grabs my arm lightly. "Don't go running off. Please."

"Rob. I can go months and not see anyone I know and here you are again," I say, resigned to the fact that if I am going to have to speak to this person at some point, it might as well be now.

"I really want to apologize for what happened with us." Rob sounds sincere but at this point what happened is so long over, does it really matter?

"Thank you for apologizing, but it's really not necessary. That was a long time ago." I have no hard feelings but don't know if I particularly want to socialize with this person either.

"No. It is necessary. My behaviour toward you was selfish and reprehensible. I didn't want to hurt you but I managed to nonetheless." Rob is being sweet and a part of me would love to hear his side of the story.

"Well, I definitely would have preferred that you break up with me before you started 'playing the field,' but whatever." I shiver involuntarily.

"You're freezing. Can I buy you a coffee? I'd really like to try to talk to you."

"No, I don't think that's a good idea. Let's let sleeping dogs lie."

"I know. I was a terrible human being but I am doing better now. Please?" Any excuse he plans to offer for sleeping with every woman on his courier route really should be heard. I can't for the life of me imagine anything other than "I'm a man-tramp who thrives on slapping a variety of asses while shouting 'Who's your daddy?'"

"Okay, but I reserve the right to leave at any point." My better judgment loses out to unbridled curiosity, which we all know killed the cat, but if I don't hear Rob out I will wonder for weeks what he might have told me. If nothing else, it will be something Mel and I can laugh about later.

Over coffee, Rob tells me his story, during which it becomes apparent I didn't know Rob very well at all. Rob, it turns out is a lawyer, and was a lawyer even when he was working as a bike courier. The summer before I met Rob he had been in a car accident — he was driving and a drunk driver hit him, which resulted in his good friend and colleague being killed. Rob hadn't been drinking and it wasn't his fault but the guilt of having been the driver in the accident that led to his friend's death was too much for him. He couldn't return to the firm where he and his friend had worked together and started into a downward spiral. Following the accident, Rob quit his job, became a bike courier and started skateboarding and experimenting with drugs.

By way of explaining his appetite for a variety of female acquaintances, Rob apologized again and said it was a combination of the constant black abyss he was living in trying to deal with the guilt combined with the drugs. He maintained that his behaviour at the time was circumstance-driven and that now he has his life completely under control. He went on to tell me the fateful day I found him in his compromising position was the day he finally took stock and realized that his actions had consequences. Apparently, he checked into rehab and finally found a good therapist who helped him get his life back on track. I didn't ask if he finished what I had interrupted before he checked into rehab because it would probably be considered an inappropriate question.

"Wow. So you're doing better now, then?" I ask when Rob finishes apologizing for the tenth time.

"Yeah, things are going well. I'm back at work, at a different firm. I still couldn't go back to the old one, too many people who know what happened. Seemed best to start off fresh."

"And the drugs?" I ask, because that is a problem he could carry with him.

"I'm fine. I was just experimenting and managed to get out before I was in too deep. I haven't touched anything harder than a beer since that last day you saw me." I can tell Rob is telling the truth.

"Well, I didn't see you so much as your butt in the air," I laugh and Rob joins in.

"Kit, the worst part was hurting you. You're great. I absolutely adore you and have since we first met. I just wish I'd been in a better place back then. I would have treated you better."

"No worries. You're in a better place now and I'm seeing a really nice guy so it all worked out." I honestly am glad that Rob has his life back together.

"Can we be friends? I'd really like it if we could."

"Maybe. The jury's still out until I see the new improved you in action. I'm still not happy with what you did, but if you want to you can start impressing me with your 'changed ways' by helping me find a tambourine for my sister for Christmas."

Rob and I spend the afternoon together walking and shopping and I do manage to locate and purchase a tambourine with his help. He is much more musically inclined than I am so knows his way around a music store. Well, he knows where to find music stores wherein he then knows his way around.

# 38

Monday is my actual birthday. I stop for a coffee, confident in the fact that if I run into anyone I know, Marc and Rob included, I'm in good shape because I'm currently on speaking terms with everyone. I am actually very happy that I can frequent the coffee shop again. Bringing my own coffee has been a pain and cuts into the allotted hair-taming time, which based on Friday's hair and the mess I looked at the party, is time I can't afford to lose.

I get my coffee and am walking toward the office on this brisk December morning, thinking that it looks like it might snow when Marc's truck pulls up to the curb beside me.

"Hey birthday girl." Marc gets my attention that was focused on the starting signs of winter.

"Good morning."

"I wanted to meet you for coffee this morning but I'm short-handed. John is taking the morning off," Marc explains why he's sitting in his nice warm truck and talking to me on the cold street.

"I know. He and Mel are looking at the 'perfect' house. Mel wants to put an offer in this morning if Charlie Brown agrees. Seems they're serious about living in sin."

"Well, I can't let your birthday go unnoticed so I got you a little something." Marc reaches to the passenger seat and tries to hand me a small gift bag through the open window.

"Thank you for thinking of me but I can't accept that. Being friends again is gift enough."

"No, you have to take it. I got it for you ages ago so the exchange time has expired. I got it when you'd been hit by the car and was going to give it to you as soon as you were back on your feet, but there's never been an appropriate time, so now you have to take it because it's your birthday," Marc explains. "It's not big; it's just something I thought you should have."

"No. You're being silly. I don't need anything. You can buy me a coffee later this week."

Marc gives me the give-me-a-break look and says, "I always buy you coffee. If you don't take it, I'm going to drop it out this window and then it will break."

"Fine." I call his bluff but he one-ups me and does drop it. I manage to grab it with my coffee-free hand just before it hits the ground

Marc smiles his "I win" grin and shouts "Happy Birthday" as he starts to pull away from the curb.

"Arrgh! I'm going to give it back," I yell after him as he pulls into traffic. I make a mental note that no one honked at him the whole time he was parked. Fascinating.

I take the beautiful little gift bag, along with my coffee and hustle to the building to escape the chilly morning. I peek in the gift bag and move the tissue paper a little as I ride up the elevator but am determined not to look at what's inside. I am going to give it back to Marc so it doesn't matter what it is, right? I get unbundled from my winter wear and open the office, then I put the gift bag under my desk so I will not be tempted to look into it. I turn my computer on and start to sort through the mail and try *not* to think about the gift bag. Joyce comes in and we chat for a bit and she hands me my birthday present. Joyce and I always exchange donuts for birthdays. My favourite is Boston Cream and I am thrilled when I open the bag to find one. I didn't have breakfast this morning in anticipation of my birthday donut. Joyce and I are constantly, as most women are, weight conscious so we decided donuts are outlawed unless it's a birthday occasion. A couple of years ago we did increase the birthdays celebrated at the office to include the Queen's birthday, Lincoln's birthday and we then added Alexander Graham Bell — he did invent the telephone and it is a much-relied-upon instrument we couldn't possibly live without. A Boston Cream in his name is the perfect way to pay homage.

By ten o'clock I've checked my emails (there were several birthday wishes), eaten my birthday donut and fielded a dozen telephone calls but still the little bag under my desk is driving me to distraction. It's making me insane. I *must* know what's in the bag. Honestly, what is wrong with me? I'm not going to keep it. I didn't expect it. I don't need to know what's in the bag. But I do! Okay, I'll just peek and get it over with. I'll see the bath beads, or whatever it is, then I can get back to work, right? It will be a good thing. I'll get my brain back on my job and everyone will benefit. I bring the bag out from under my desk, set it on my lap, move the tissue paper aside and peek inside. Damn. It's wrapped. I can't just peek at those bath beads because they are wrapped in really nice silver paper. I could just shake the box. If I shake the box, I'll know it's bath beads and then I can get down to work. I reach in and pull out the box, which feels quite substantial, not a bath bead box, although perhaps high-end bath beads come in substantial boxes. I'm not a bath bead gal so I really can't speak with any certainty on their packaging. Maybe it's bath beads from Holt Renfrew. That would be exciting. I could keep bath beads from Holts, right? I mean, Marc is definitely not a bath bead guy, or I hope he's not a bath bead guy. I guess the right thing to do would be to give the bath beads back so Marc could give them to his girlfriend. She's probably a bath bead person, more so than Marc anyway.

The voice in my head says, "I can't unwrap it, whatever it is, so just put it back and get on with your day." I hate the voice. I put the silver-wrapped box back into the gift bag and under my desk. I am determined to be strong and not let my curiosity get the best of me, but I'm not doing very well.

By eleven o'clock I'm a mess. I *must* know what's in the bag. I have convinced myself that I can just carefully open a corner of the wrapping and peek in, which I do. The result is the side of a box with no writing on it to give any indication what hides inside. By eleven fifteen I finally admit defeat and in a Boston Cream sugar-induced frenzy I tear the silver wrap off the box and stop immediately. The box is substantial and the top of it has the TAG Heuer logo on it. I know Marc did *not* buy me a very expensive watch. He said he has three, which he does. I've seen them all since he mentioned it, so he must have just re-used one of his boxes for the bath beads. I carefully open the box and peek inside.

Oh my God. It is a watch. It's a real watch. A real TAG Heuer. It's the most beautiful thing I've ever seen. I take my eyes off it for a few seconds to glance down at my current watch, the Timex Ironman with the plastic band. Gee, no comparison really. The TAG is stunning. I love it. I should never have opened it. Now I don't want to give it back. I can't keep it, end of story. I can't be accepting gifts of expensive jewellery (are watches considered jewellery?) from men other than my boyfriend. I can't. It's just not the *done* thing. I close the box and put it back into the bag. The silver giftwrap is unsalvageable so I toss it into the recycling. I immediately take the box back out of the bag. I have to try the watch on. I know I'm not keeping it but I have the opportunity to put the most expensive watch I'll ever be this close to on my wrist. I have to put it on.

I get the watch out of the box, figure out the clasp and trade the Ironman for the TAG Heuer. Surprisingly the TAG fits, which is strange because it's the bracelet-type band and those always have to be resized. The moment I close the clasp I know that putting the watch on was a huge mistake. Giving the watch back now is going to be an exercise that will command much more willpower than this morning has shown me capable of producing. I reluctantly take the TAG off and put it back into the box. I know I have to give it back to Marc but at least I will be able to say I had a really nice watch once, even it if was for just a day.

Mel calls during the day and we agree to meet at the Firkin after work for a birthday-slash-new-house celebration. Charlie Brown loves the house Mel found and they put an offer in this morning. Mel is confident they will get the house and she's very excited. Mel loves it when a real estate deal goes right.

I bring the gift of high-end jewellery with me to the Firkin on the chance that Marc attends with Charlie Brown. I don't feel particularly comfortable carrying an expensive watch around but I have to in order to return it.

"Happy birthday," Mel yells at me as soon as I walk into the bar.

"Happy homeowning," I shout as I start to take off my coat and sit down. Marc is in attendance and is sitting with his back to me. After I get my coat off I set the gift bag down in front of him and say, "You dropped this in the street this morning."

"What is it?" Mel is more curious than I am, if that's possible.

"It is a birthday gift from Marc, but I didn't open it," I say grinning because anyone who knows me knows I couldn't resist opening it.

Marc peeks in the bag and says, "Yes you did!"

I laugh, "Okay, I opened it and I love it and it's the most beautiful thing I've ever seen but I can't keep it."

"What is it?" Mel practically squeals as she reaches across and grabs the bag from in front of Marc.

In one motion Mel has the tissue paper out of the bag, the box out of the bag and the box open in front of her.

"Wow! This is stunning. If you don't want it, can I have it?" Mel asks emphatically, tossing any good manners our parents instilled in her out the window for her love of shiny things.

"NO!" Marc and I say together and Marc reaches across the table and snatches the box back from in front of Mel and starts to remove the watch from the box.

"It's for Kit. I got it for her after the accident and didn't have a good enough reason to give it to her. Now that it's almost been a year and she's in no hurry to replace that godawful Ironman, this is the perfect time." Marc has the Ironman off and is putting the TAG on my wrist.

"I'm not keeping it," I laugh, "and the Ironman isn't *that* bad!" I feign hurt feelings.

"Yes it is," Mel states, not helping with the return idea.

"Okay, I'll admit the Ironman has seen better days and I promise to replace it, but I can't keep this one, it's far too generous a gift," I say, admiring the stunning timepiece on my wrist.

"Yes you can." Marc is not going along with the return idea either.

"It costs more than my car so *no* I can't." I start to take it back off my wrist but Marc puts his hand over the watch and says, "It's already been sized and I threw the extra links away, I can't return it and the only other person it will fit is Mel. Do you want me to give it to Mel?"

"I know you didn't throw the links away. What about your girlfriend? Surely she'd like a tremendously expensive watch."

"Nope. She has really fat wrists. She's a really nice girl but she has really fat wrists. It'd never fit her," Marc states dryly and we all start to laugh. Marc leans over and grabs the back of my head and pulls me toward him to kiss my forehead, "Keep it. I want you to have it and besides you can't be moving to Manhattan wearing a plastic Ironman, the New Yorkers will run you out of town before you have a chance to unpack."

I know no amount of arguing is going to win this one. I'm going to keep the watch.

"Can I try it on?" Mel pipes up from across the table.

"*No!*" Marc, Charlie Brown and I say in unison again and we all laugh.

"I don't want you to get used to one of those. I don't own the company like Marc does." Charlie Brown furrows his brow suspecting that all his worldly savings may now be going toward expensive watches for Mel.

# 39

Christmas arrives much sooner than I'd like. Derek is home for a week over the break but has to spend time with his family as I do with mine. We decide that it's best if Mel and I go up north and Derek and Charlie Brown stay in Toronto and do their family visits while we do ours. I haven't told my parents yet about Derek's transfer and think it's best if I do so alone. The twins are already in North Bay, having finished exams mid-month, and according to their emails they are completely bored already.

Mel and I head north at noon on Christmas Eve and the trip home is uneventful. I guess driving excitement only happens to our parents when they drive to and from Toronto. Upon arrival we are met with excited, happy parents. I guess they are finally getting used to the idea of sins-in-law despite their initial shock and dismay. The moment I see Tia she is full of questions about the band Kevin and whether or not I've seen Ben. Unfortunately, I have to report that I haven't been out much and haven't seen the band Kevin or Kevin since my birthday weekend.

Mike Melrose arrives with his girlfriend Samantha shortly after Mel and I do. It's great to see them again or it was great to see them again until Samantha, a gorgeous, petite redhead who blushes easily, flashed a diamond engagement ring the size of a small kitchen appliance at Mr. and Mrs. Melrose. The shrieks from Mrs. Melrose are rivalled only by the gasp of disappointment from my mother. Mel, who had just handed me a glass of wine, whispers "Damn" under her breath. Now that Mike has given Mrs. Melrose the engagement she was so desperate for, this doesn't bode well for Mel and her soon-to-be-sinful lifestyle. To her credit, Mel is not deterred and rallies quickly despite her initial reaction and is able to hand me her glass of wine and give her brother and Samantha the required hugs of congratulations. I see her whisper in Mike's ear and he laughs heartily so I'm sure she threatened him with maiming or death. My mother, on the other hand, looks pale. She too is able to rally like Mel but can't completely hide her disappointment that Mrs. Melrose is getting the first wedding. My mother and Mrs. Melrose are best friends but despite their friendship the wedding rivalry started when one of our classmates, who was raised three doors down from the Melrose house, got married two summers ago. Since then, our mothers have not been very subtle in their desire for weddings and chubby, happy grandbabies. Our fathers are a little more wedding-phobic, especially my dad, who sees the expense of three weddings and is in no rush to break into the savings account.

Mel, who can usually produce champagne from her Prada briefcase, doesn't this time. It's Mike who produces two bottles, and the twins offer to go and get glasses from our house next door so we can all have flutes. Mel's insistence on the proper glass according to the drink comes straight-line from her mother who is currently beside herself with delight and keeps squealing. I could probably produce acrylic margarita glasses and Mrs. Melrose would go along with it today, but in keeping with the holiday spirit I don't attempt such a faux pas.

The Christmas Eve celebration of Mike's engagement goes on into the night. Samantha is thrilled with her ring and keeps glancing at it and playing with it on her finger. She tells us the ring is from Tiffany's and came in the identifiable blue box. Mel starts to compliment Mike on his amazing taste when Taryn says, "I can't wait to go to Tiffany's. Kit, after you move to New York you can take us shopping."

My mother, who was actually making strides toward recovery after the engagement announcement, turns visibly pale again and asks Taryn what she's talking about? Taryn immediately knows she's said too much and puts her hand over her mouth while her eyes grow wide.

"I'm not moving to New York. Well not for now anyway," I start to explain. I'm not upset with Taryn. I had to tell them about Derek's transfer and the potential New York move at some point over the holiday. I go on to explain the details of Derek's transfer and stress we are still getting the condo and that if everything goes well I may move to New York at some point. My mother, who a few minutes ago I thought may not survive this holiday, starts to look better and says, "So you won't be living together then if Derek is in New York."

"No, I guess not, just weekends, but we are buying the condo together." I don't really know where she's going with this.

"And in order to move to New York, you'd have to get married, right? You won't be able to work otherwise." My mother has peeled off the layers of what is potentially bad news and has found her own silver lining. The possibility of me moving to New York has given her new hope and she is envisioning a wedding of her own to rival that of Mrs. Melrose.

"Married? We haven't thought that far ahead, but I guess if I do move and want to work in the States we'll have to give it some thought." The leap my mother has made has taken me to places I haven't even considered. The news that her child will be moving from one "city" to a much larger "city" did not produce the negative reaction I thought it might. Instead I fear we'll be buying *Bride* magazine and discussing flower arrangements.

"Well, I'm glad you won't be 'living together' at any rate." My mother gets the jab in and Mrs. Melrose shoots Mel a scowl.

"Yes we will, or we would be, if Derek wasn't in New York." I am determined to defend my position and help Mel out in the process. "We will be on weekends."

"But not full-time, and you're thinking about getting married, so that's good." My mother is only hearing what she wants to hear at this point so there is no talking to her. The good news is she's taking Mike's engagement news better than before, even if her reasons are fanciful and borderline delusional.

"More champagne?" Mel asks as she tips the bottle to refill my glass.

"Absolutely. Thank you." I look at Mel and we roll our eyes in unison.

"I want to be a bridesmaid at your lavish New York wedding," Mel adds quietly so only I can hear.

"I don't think Prada makes nasty, puffy taffeta dresses, do they?" I whisper back and we laugh out loud.

By Boxing Day, when Mel and I head home to Toronto, I am tired. The holiday was very nice but very busy. Tia loves the tambourine and she and Taryn regaled us all with very bad karaoke for most of Christmas Day. The tambourine, although a great idea, is louder and more annoying than I ever could have anticipated. I'm quite glad the tambourine will be returning with the twins to Kingston and will not become a fixture in our house. I'm sure that given the opportunity Charlie Brown could be very annoying with such an instrument so best not to give him the opportunity.

Derek and Charlie Brown are coming to our house this evening to have our own Christmas celebration. The food consensus is no turkey. We are planning to order in and watch movies. Mel and I want to watch old classic movies but the boys want something more violent with guns and action. We are quite certain we will be watching action because we left the boys in charge of getting the movies. It doesn't matter what we watch, it will just be nice to be home.

Derek and Charlie Brown are both at our house by the time we arrive. They've picked out a selection of movies, not all action. Derek follows me as I take my bag into my bedroom to unpack and I find a small Tiffany's signature blue box on my bed. My first inclination is to panic. Could my mother be right? Is Derek thinking about marriage? We haven't even talked about it.

"Merry Christmas." Derek picks up the box and hands it to me.

"Thank you," I say as I accept the box and give him a kiss. I untie the white ribbon and open the box. Inside is a beautiful gold bracelet. It's stunning.

"I love it," I say as I get it out of the box and present my wrist for Derek to help me put it on. I hand Derek his gift and I start to retell the story of Mike's engagement and the comedy of conversation that led to my mother now believing that we are thinking about getting married. When I get to the part where my mother claims that we too will be getting married soon, Derek asks, "You told her we aren't, right?" in a tone that makes me think he has no intention of getting married any time soon, if ever.

"Of course I told her. We haven't even talked about it," I snap back at him. I am still surprised by Derek's reaction. Apparently, he has no inclination to marry but if we are going to live in the same American city, marriage might have to be considered, especially if he wants me to get a job. Odd.

"Oh, I'm sorry, I didn't mean we'll never get married, it's just not something I've thought about much," Derek apologizes.

He must have realized that his tone had thrown me off and that this conversation was going nowhere but downhill if he didn't clarify his statement. I don't venture any further comments as Derek opens the Christmas gift I got him. It's a watch. Not a TAG Heuer unfortunately — TAGs are not in my soon-to-be-condo-owner budget.

# 40

The January blahs hit hard as soon as the Christmas break is over and the world returns to work, and Derek and I living in separate cities. My motivation to pack for the move to the condo is lessened greatly by the fact that as soon as I move, which is scheduled for February 14th, I will be completely alone every evening. I won't have Mel with me to help make the time pass while I wait for the next visit with Derek, but on the other hand I won't have Mel mocking me about my marathon telephone conversations with Derek and about baking cookies and putting together care packages for him either.

My physiotherapy is going well and I'm back at the gym but I'm not running yet. I really must start considering other hobbies. Macramé. Now there's a hobby that doesn't get much press these days. I wonder if there is a macramé club or guild I can join. I've never really done any before but how hard can it be? You tie knots in string. I can get knots in lots of things; surely I can handle knot tying. I'll have to look into that after the move.

Over the Christmas break Derek and I decided that because of our workloads we will only be able to fit in one visit during the month of January and two in February. Derek is planning to take a long weekend the week we move so that means he has to work harder in January and his workload is already greater with the new job. You can romanticize long-distance relationships all day long, but the reality is that they are hard and fairly lonely for both people involved. Derek is already getting restless in his hotel and is looking for an apartment, which is not going to be cheap in Manhattan. The company will pay a portion, but I'm not sure how we are going to be able to afford both the condo and an apartment. I guess we'll just have to figure it out.

The last Sunday in January is a no-Derek weekend and I'm lying in bed contemplating what's left to pack and possible hobbies to take up, when Mel comes into my room.

"Glassblowing. I could make vases and things," I say to Mel as she sits on the side of my bed and hands me a coffee.

"You really do need a life but glassblowing is not for you with the asthma. You'll get halfway through something and lose your breath and then where will you be?"

"Good point. I guess I'll have to keep thinking."

"What are you doing today?" Mel asks. Surely she's being funny. She knows I don't do much except sit by the phone and make care packages for Derek.

"I have a new cranberry and white chocolate cookie recipe I want to try, why?"

"Because that's ridiculous. You bake for that man far too often. Besides I'm taking the day off, no open houses. Let's do something fun." Mel is excited — she never takes time off.

"Did you have anything in mind? I'm up for whatever!" I too am excited now. This will be a nice change from the ordinary.

"Well, you need a table for the condo, right?"

"Yes, but you know I've been looking for months to no avail." Derek doesn't have a dining table and the one here belongs to Mel. The condo is very open concept so the living and dining areas are one room and it will look odd if we don't have a table, not to mention it will make cozy candlelit dinners impossible. Sitting with a plate on your lap in front of the television is just not conducive to romance, or good digestion for that matter.

"Let's do a road trip to St. Jacobs near Kitchener. Surely we'll find tables there. The Amish make lovely furniture." Mel might be on to something.

An hour later, Mel and I are on the road headed toward Amish country.

# 41

Mel drops me off at home around 3 p.m. after the road trip and heads to Charlie Brown's for the evening. I'm excited to call Derek and tell him about the amazing table I have found for the condo. It is absolutely perfect and even Mel had to agree that "it's the one." I arranged for delivery the Friday after move in. Mel didn't buy any furniture but she did buy six pounds of fudge. She couldn't decide which flavour she wanted so she bought six different ones. At first I thought she was being completely insane, but we sampled them all on the drive home and each was as good as the last so in hindsight I think she did the wise thing by purchasing all the flavours.

I listen to the messages on the phone. Derek left one early this afternoon and he sounds rather down. I hope he's not having a bad day. He had mentioned that he planned to work all weekend — maybe things aren't going very well.

"Hey handsome," I say cheerfully when he answers his cell, "what's up? You sound down."

"No, not at all, it's quite the opposite actually, I finally know what this whole 'love thing' is all about." Derek does sound better but I'm a bit confused.

"What do you mean?" I say, nervously laughing, "we've been in love for a year, what are you just figuring out?"

"No, we haven't actually. I've met someone extraordinary. Her name is Tiffany Abernathy. She's a debutante from Atlanta. I'm doing some work on her father's portfolio. I met her on Tuesday. Kit, she's absolutely adorable and I can't wait for you to meet her." My mind is reeling. The man for whom I purchased the "perfect" table is telling me he's in love with someone named Tiffany and he called me Kit for the first time ever.

"Tuesday? Debutante? What are you talking about? Do they even *make* debutantes anymore? It's 2007 for God's sake, surely women today know how demeaning that is!" Yes, my relationship is possibly over and instead of saying something poignant to win back my man the first thing I say involves my opinion on the demeaning practice of "coming out," in the non-gay sense of the term, and being presented to society like a prime cut of meat at a barbecue.

"Kit. She's perfect. Tiffy was first runner-up in the Ms. Georgia pageant." Derek is offering this material to me like he's a used car salesman and I'm actually interested in the hunk of junk he's selling.

"Tiffy? What? What are you talking about?" The man I love, who has refused, up until this moment, to call me by my nickname for some reason known only to him and his therapist, is calling someone Tiffy and tossing my nickname in for good measure.

"Tiffy's a virgin. Isn't that sexy?" Oh my God! Derek has officially raised the bar, or lowered it, for Insane Things You Say When You're Dumping Someone to an all-time high or low, whichever. At this point I should remain speechless or hang up because this conversation has nowhere to go but downhill.

"How old is she? Twelve? Has she never been to an all-you-can-drink keg party? Surely someone in all of Georgia got her drunk and took advantage of her. It's a big state." I am indignant and my inability to comprehend the magnitude of this situation is allowing Derek the opportunity to speak again.

"She's twenty-two and tall," and it's official. He's crossed the line with the tall crack. I've never been self-conscious about my height and most days am quite happy with my compact five-foot-three-inch frame, but there is not a vertically challenged woman alive who doesn't at some point in her life wish she were tall and willowy like Elizabeth Hurley. Bastard. The virgin crack was one thing, but short comments will not be tolerated. Unfortunately, while I'm trying to close my hanging-open mouth and find just the right comeback he continues, "I'm going to ask her to marry me at dinner."

"You don't even want to get married! What dinner?" I manage although my mouth has gone completely dry and the short insinuation has taken a back seat.

"Tonight at dinner," Derek laughs. "I was going to wait until Valentine's Day but I just can't wait." I cannot believe the man I love is saying these awful things to me and doing it while laughing. He has just torn my life into little bits, thrown them on the floor and is laughing while he stomps on them. Little bits. Stomp. Stomp. Stomp.

"What about us? We're buying a condo on Valentine's Day. You remember, two weeks from now. You and me. Together. The papers are already signed." I feel myself going into what I'd have to describe as shock-denial. A part of me is actually hoping I can talk some sense into him and he'll come back to me, but a larger part of me knows that I'll never be able to get this conversation out of my head. Ever.

"Oh yeah, that." He says "that" as if I mentioned he left a sweatshirt in my car. "Well, like you said, it's all signed up so we have to close the deal. How about you just deal with it, we'll figure out my part of the down payment later. You can write me a cheque or something."

"Write you a cheque?" I'm officially in shock but have a definite opinion on this matter. "I'll write you a cheque when…" I was about to say "hell freezes over" or "they find your rotting corpse" but never get the chance because Derek cuts me off with, "Sure Kit, whatever. Look I've got to run. See you later." Then click. Click. See you *later*? Click. See you in hell is more like it, you cheating bastard, or not. Can you be a cheating bastard if the other woman in question is a virgin? I turn the phone off and put it down. Baby steps. Just get a grip.

I look around the house at all the packed boxes ready to be moved to our shiny new condo. Mel's boxes are in the living room and mine have taken over the dining room. We're meant to move to our condo in sixteen days, Derek's and mine. Me. Not Tiffy. What the hell kind of name is Tiffy anyway? It's the name of a spoiled Shih Tzu, that's what it is. Then it hits me. I can feel my stomach churning and the bile rising in my throat. I run to the washroom, zigzagging around boxes, with my hand over my mouth. The mastery of not vomiting for lesser stresses is one thing, but there is no way I am going to get through this situation without tossing my cookies at least a couple of times.

I'm not sure what time Mel arrives home. It is dark. I haven't left the washroom since the vomiting started and Mel must have assumed I was out because she is completely startled when she comes into the washroom and sees me hanging over the toilet, hair in a scrunchie, surrounded by wadded-up toilet paper. After the initial vomit the crying started. I tried to get a grip, blow my nose and make it stop but after I blew my nose about five hundred times and it was sore from the blowing I just let it free flow along with the tears.

"Oh good Lord! What's wrong with you? Do you have food poisoning? I told you not to eat that sausage dog, but you have to be the adventurous one. Well, look where that's got you now."

I look up at Mel but can't bring myself to tell her what transpired with Derek so I just shake my head.

"Did someone die? Someone *must* have died. I should call Derek in New York." Mel is determined to make things right and turns to walk toward the phone.

"NO," I manage. "Can you get me a glass of water, please?" Mel, happy to have a vocation, hurries to the kitchen while I try to regroup. When she returns I'm sitting on the floor leaning against the bathtub. I can only imagine how dreadful I must look but I don't care. Mel hands me the water then takes the mouthwash out of the vanity and pours some into a second glass she brought from the kitchen. She hands me the mouthwash and says, "Here. Rinse and spit. You'll taste better." I'm on autopilot and would probably dance a jig if Mel told me to and she is right, I do taste better.

I hand Mel back the empty mouthwash glass and start to open my mouth to speak and tell her what happened but the tears start flowing like a river. I can barely make a sound let alone form words. Mel crouches down in front of me and looks really concerned.

"Okay. Calm down. You have to tell me what happened."

"Derek dumped me," I get out between sobs, before I turn back to the toilet and start to dry heave again.

"Sweetie, that doesn't make any sense. Are you sure?"

"He's going to ask someone else to marry him. So yeah, I'm pretty sure."

"But you can't keep your hands off each other. You bought a condo together. You baked him all those cookies. He loves *you*." Mel is where I was a while ago. It's going to take her some time to catch up.

"Mel, you're not helping," I say into the toilet so it has that hollow sound to it.

# 42

Mel calls Joyce for me the next morning to tell her I have food poisoning and won't be in today. There is no way I can get to work. I haven't left the washroom all night and am starting to get shaky from lack of nourishment. The only thing I've consumed in the last twelve hours is water. Mel stayed with me a good portion of the night and slowly, in very short segments between sobs and dry heaves, I was able to tell her the entire conversation I'd had with Derek. Mel is wonderful, of course, and calls Derek all sorts of nasty names with me. We decide that his act of treachery and deceit requires a one-of-a-kind particularly nasty name. We spent quite a bit of time on it and finally decide on The Bastard Cock-Lick. We aren't entirely sure it is completely accurate but in light of The Bastard's ability to shock us, we decide it could very well be appropriate. We really have no idea what he's been "licking" in New York so are covering all the bases. Early this morning we determine that the name Derek shall no longer be uttered and the only way "that person" will be referred to in the future is as The Bastard Cock-Lick or The Bastard if we are in delicate company. I can hear Mel on the telephone from my newfound home in the washroom and assume she's working from home today.

"What's the plan, then?" Mel is at the doorway of the bathroom.

"Death by starvation." I have actually given my demise a great deal of thought in the past twelve hours. Everyone will say nice things like "But she was so young."

"That's not very proactive, is it? As your best friend and realtor, I have to tell you that this is not an attractive look for you." Oh no, it hits me, she's not even giving me twenty-four hours to wallow in self-pity. "Moving men will be here on Wednesday, you've already booked Thursday and Friday off, so you're going to have to go to work tomorrow. It's only one day and thinking about other things is probably a good thing. You can do this. Start thinking about showering, we're going to the pub for dinner." She turns around and walks away.

"I'm not going anywhere for dinner," I yell after her.

"Yes, you are. It will be good practice for tomorrow. Besides, I'm going out for dinner and I'm not leaving you here alone." There is no arguing with that woman.

"I don't like your new shoes," I yell.

"You're taking your Bastard anger out on my shoes. Get in the shower."

I did think about the shower but it seemed like a lot of work, so all I did was think for a very long time. At 4 p.m. Mel is back at the washroom door with my towel and brush in hand.

"Either you get in voluntarily or the shoes and I will man-handle you in. And you don't want to see that." Mel speaks in a very serious tone. Mel is the fixer of all things broken. She likes her world in perfect order. Mel has sent many a co-worker home in tears simply by being brutally honest. When Mel wants something "fixed" she'll resort to whatever means necessary. If that means being scary, she can be very scary. The Mel in front of me was both serious and a little bit scary.

"Fine. But I won't like it." The shower actually feels refreshing. Maybe Mel has a point on this one; of course, I'll never tell her that. The shower is so nice that I actually don't want to get out. I sit down in the tub to let the shower water fall on my head as if I were in a rainstorm and I have a nice little cry and pity myself for my current sad set of circumstances.

"You've been in there forever. Are you crying in there?" There is no escaping Mel who is back in the washroom with me.

"Is there no privacy left in the world? Of course, I'm crying. The shower was your idea. I was perfectly happy crying on the bathroom floor."

"Have you washed your hair?" Mel sounds like the mother of a six year old, which I suppose makes me the six year old.

"Yessss." I can't believe she's doing this.

"All soap residue gone?"

"Yes, Mel! I'm shiny clean!"

"Okay, sorry about this." Then she flushes the toilet and the water cascading on my head turns incredibly hot. I scream, jump up and slam myself against the back wall of the shower. Mel's hand reaches in and turns off the water, then my towel comes in past the curtain where I'm standing. I grab the towel and hold it in front of me, throw the shower curtain open and shriek, "You are truly evil!"

Mel, laughing, turns on her heel and says over her shoulder, "Yeah, I know. Get ready. We're out of here in fifteen minutes."

"I really, really hate you and your shoes," I yell after her and start to dry off.

True to her word, Mel had me out the door in fifteen minutes but it wasn't pretty. I did manage to get dressed in my oldest jeans that have the butt ripped out of them. I am wearing long boxer shorts underneath, and my ratty old university sweatshirt with the frayed cuffs. My hair is completely on its own at this point and has become its own entity. The allotted fifteen minutes' preparation time gave me no time to tame. I towel-dried and had intended to comb it, but got sidetracked when Mel insisted I find socks, so I left the house with wet, uncombed hair. Mel, who generally cares about appearances, allowed it on the grounds that she knew if she made a big deal I would fight to stay home.

The fact that I know people at the pub should have concerned me, but in my state of shock-denial-defeat, I am able to completely zone out. Mel sits me down at one of our favourite tables, she facing the door, me with my back to it. When Steve comes over to the table, he looks at me and makes a noticeable head shake and his eyes pop open wider;

he is too polite to say anything about my appearance but I can tell by the way he's looking at me he's a bit shocked. Mel orders us each a beer and nachos as if everything is perfectly normal and she's not sitting across the table from someone who looks as though she just escaped from a mental institution. Mel knows I love nachos and I think she's hoping to entice me into eating something. Mel is chatting away to me like we're here after work on a normal day, not even acknowledging that my life is a complete disaster. Steve brings our beer and looks at me strangely again but still doesn't say anything. I suddenly feel really tired. I put my head on the table beside my beer, which I can't even contemplate drinking. My hair has started to dry now and has reached epic proportions, its volume expanding exponentially as it dries in the pub's warmth.

"You really shouldn't put your face on the table, someone might have had sex on it over lunch. Besides, your hair is blocking the aisle and people are afraid to walk by you." Mel is actually quite funny and I would laugh if I had the strength. I lift my head to tell Mel I hate her, just as Charlie Brown and Marc arrive at the table. Perfect. An audience for the big-haired freak show. Marc is standing beside me and looks at my hair. Horrified is the only way to describe his expression. All Charlie Brown can do is stare with his mouth slightly open.

"Hey guys," Mel says normally as if it were any other day and I look sane.

"Joyce told me you were sick today. What are you doing out?" Marc actually does seem concerned and not just about my hair. "You do look horrible."

"Thanks. I am sick. Dictator Mel made me come out. She's the spawn of Satan."

"Best thing for you!" Mel quips. I don't ever remember her being so Stepford Wife-ish. Charlie Brown and Marc both look at each other and shrug.

"Mel won't let me stay home alone. She's afraid I'll kill myself and the resulting police inquiry will screw up the house sale."

"Exactly," Mel says in her most annoying singsongy voice as she reaches into her magic Prada handbag and pulls out a scrunchie, a brush and some mascara and hands them to me. "Now why don't you go and try to freshen up and maybe do something with your hair." Mel moves her hands in a large circle around her head for emphasis as she says the word *hair*.

During our conversation Charlie Brown and Marc are both still fascinated and confused, their heads moving in unison back and forth as they follow the conversation.

I stand up willingly. "You're just getting rid of me so you can tell the guys the horror that has become my life."

"Unless you'd rather," Mel's singsongy voice follows me as I walk toward the ladies' room. I give Mel the finger over my shoulder but am not completely sure she sees it through my hair. I take my time in the ladies' room. When I first look in the mirror and see my hair, I actually have to smile. It hasn't been this big in a very long time. I try to brush it but that just seems to make it larger. When I stand back I can actually centre myself in the mirror so my hair goes off both sides. I manage to run my fingers through it and can fix it in the back with the scrunchie into a very untidy bun. After three attempts I get the bun so it actually looks respectable. I contemplate putting on the mascara but immediately decide against it. I'm sure I'm not finished crying and there's no point having big black raccoon eyes so it's not even worth the effort. I do splash water on my face and wipe away the tears that have started to fall completely involuntarily again and dry my face with the front of my sweatshirt with no concern for the state of my skin or my sweatshirt. I linger in the ladies' room, reading a poster about "STDs and You!" (which could be me except I won't be having sex ever again). I don't want to return to the table mid-story because I know I won't be able to stomach hearing the truth spoken aloud. My brain wanders to having to tell my parents what happened and I feel tears welling up again. Okay, time to get back to the table. Telling the family can wait until I have a firmer grip on the situation myself. I give myself one last look in the mirror and decide that Mel's right, although I won't ever tell her that. I have to go to work tomorrow. I have to face the world, so why not start now. It will be easier with people I actually know so I'll go back to the table and be my normal self, or as normal as I can be with this crazy hair.

I gather up Mel's Prada purse accessories, open the washroom door and step right into Marc.

"Ahh!" I scream before I register who it is. "You have *got* to stop doing that. You've just taken another year off my life and since I don't plan on living another year, I could be dying right now!" I punch him in the arm for good measure, but realize after by the look on his face and the soreness of my hand, that I hit him much harder than I had planned.

"Mel told us what happened," Marc says while rubbing his now very sore arm. "I always suspected what's-his-name was a jerk."

"He goes by The Bastard Cock-Lick now, actually." I pause to wipe away tears — they seem endless.

"Your hair looks really nice now," Marc lies, "and I like your ripped jeans, very sexy."

"Okay, you're lying about the hair and you'd say I was sexy if I was wearing a garbage bag."

"Good point. For the record, I think what's-his-name is an idiot and he'll regret what he's done very soon. Just wait, he'll be back on your doorstep before you know it."

"Well, thank God I'm moving then, because if he shows up knocking on my door any time soon I'll kill him," the tears still free-flowing.

"Yeah, I felt some of that rage a minute ago, I believe you could take him right about now," Marc laughs and rubs his arm again. Marc wipes away my tears with the sleeve of his shirt and asks, "Do you want me to take you home, or do you want to try a beer?"

"Beer. I can do this. He won't beat me, right?" I ask tentatively.

"Right. You're better than him. Come on." Marc puts his

arm across my shoulders and we head back to the table so I can start my new life of big hair and beer.

I manage to hold it together for one beer and even to laugh a couple of times. Everyone is a bit awkward but I'm able to stumble through the next hour with fewer tears, so I chalk it up as a success, my first success as a single gal *again*. The highlight of the evening is actually Charlie Brown who tells me, in all seriousness, "This chick, Derek said she was first runner-up at a pageant? Remember Kit, first runner-up is just the first loser. Derek's with a loser right now." Then Mel mentions that Derek is a bit of a financial nightmare and I'm probably better off. I have to agree on both points. After the success of finishing my beer, Marc offers to drive me home and Mel agrees to let him. Mel's been crazy busy at work and she and Charlie Brown haven't seen each other much and have both ordered another beer.

"I will be home soon and will be driving you to the office in the morning," she shouts at my back as I walk toward the door. I give her the finger over my shoulder and she sees it this time because my hair is up.

"I'm glad you're feeling better," she laughs.

On the way home I'm sitting across from Marc in his new truck and I'm finally able to get The Bastard off my mind for a few minutes. Marc's new truck is huge, I've seen it from the outside but I've never been in it. I could lie across the front seat and neither my head nor feet would touch either door — amazing. How does he park this thing?

"Are you feeling all right? You're being awfully quiet." Marc is always so nice to me. I know he's genuinely worried about me.

"I was just wondering if I can live in your truck when I become homeless, it's big enough for both of us and I promise I won't get in your way."

"You won't be homeless. You'll be fine." Marc is ever the optimist.

"Time will tell I suppose, but we qualified for the mortgage based on both our salaries and The Bastard's salary was the lion's share." Reality about my financial situation had dawned on me immediately after The Bastard's announcement, but being dumped for a ditzy debutante had taken the forefront for the past twenty-four hours. In two weeks I move into a condo I can't afford. Period. Full stop. I guess a second job and roommates are going to have to be my first priority but I don't want to think about that right now.

"What about the down payment?" Marc isn't asking to be nosey. I know he really is worried about me.

"Oh, The Bastard threw in five thousand dollars, which I'm pretty sure he got from his grandfather, but the rest is mine from the sale of this house. The beauty is that since he's on the mortgage he'll get half the proceeds when I sell it. Luckily I'll be bankrupt long before that happens." I am resigned to the fact that I may be going down financially but when I do, I'm taking The Bastard investment banker with me. That'll learn him!

"No you won't. You'll be fine. You're a fighter. I've seen it firsthand. Don't let this guy beat you. He will come crawling back, and when he does, don't you want to be in a position to tell him to hit the road?"

"I'd like him to be run over by a thousand concrete trucks, is that the same thing?" I'm smiling at the thought of Derek being squashed in the street.

"Close enough for now," Marc laughs. "At least I recognize a bit of the fight that I know is in you."

"I'd like to be driving the first truck."

"There's the Kit I know and love and do you know what?"

"What?"

"I, for one, am very glad you won't be moving to New York."

"That makes two of us." I smile a little. This is the only good thing to come out of being dumped; I won't have to make a relocation decision anytime soon and I'm glad I'll be staying in Toronto indefinitely.

# 43

I manage to get out of bed and into the shower after Mel removes all the blankets from my room and leaves me freezing. She really is a pain in the ass. I can't even contemplate taming my hair, so I comb it wet into a semi-tidy bun at the back of my head. I'm staring into my closet at the few outfits I haven't packed and decide on my newest blue suit. The blue suit is so new that it has no special-occasion clothing status attached to it so is perfect for feeling suicidal. I shall wear it every time I feel this awful. It's officially my "feeling suicidal" suit and will probably double as my "chequebook-balancing" outfit, as I'm sure I'll be feeling suicidal while doing that little task in the near future. Obviously, I will have to decide on the method of aforementioned suicide because getting hit by a car is not nearly as romantic as I'd envisioned before I was actually hit by a car.

Mel drives me all the way to work and stays parked in front of the building, defying all manner of horn honking and morning rush-hour cussing in order to ensure that I actually walk into the building and get on the elevator. I'm sure she stayed there for some time after I disappeared into the elevator just to ensure that I didn't escape and go back home, find my blankets she'd hidden and crawl back under them.

Filing. It truly is the bane of my existence and a hateful job, but today I shall get the whole pile completed. I will beat the filing, then I will beat The Bastard Cock-Lick, with my bare hands, until he's bloodied. Yes. It will be a good day. Workwise I'm not in bad shape considering I missed yesterday. I suppose all the long hours I've been keeping while I pined for my boyfriend, who so obviously was not pining for me, has kept me up to date at work. This is a good thing because I fully expect this whole "personal setback" will affect my work performance for the next few weeks at least. Joyce comments that I look terrible and whatever I ate must have been nasty. I'm glad Mel used the food-poisoning excuse, good cover. Must remember that one the next time I'm dumped by the man I thought was in love with me. Uh-oh, tears. Must think happy thoughts, fluffy kittens, happy, chocolate ice cream on a sunny day, happy, balaclavas that one might pull over one's head before committing a crime, such as beating an ex-boyfriend to a pulp, no, not so happy and yet I find myself smiling. I probably can't take Mel along for the beating as I'm not sure balaclavas come in hot pink, or if Prada even makes them.

Marc calls at 11:30 a.m. to see what I'm doing for lunch.

"Nothing. I'm planning death by starvation so eating goes against everything I'm working toward."

"Okay, what if I promise not to feed you?"

"Sounds good. What do you have in mind? Jumping off a tall building might be fun."

"You're insane, do you know that?" Marc doesn't wait for me to comment before continuing, "Be downstairs at 12:30. I'll pick you up out front."

At the allotted meeting time, I jump into Marc's truck, and I literally do have to jump. Marc's truck is very tall and I'm not so tall, as The Bastard so bluntly pointed out.

"So where to? Is the lake frozen? Oh, you could drown me!" I've never thought drowning would be the way I'd want to meet my end, but today it doesn't look so bad.

"Worse. I'm taking you to a financial institution."

"For lunch? Are we going to crash someone's retirement party and eat their little triangle sandwiches? I think that's bad form." I am serious. I do think it's bad form.

"You are completely insane! No. Not for lunch. I want you to meet my banker. You're starving yourself anyway."

"I'm sure your banker's nice and everything but couldn't this wait until I'm not suicidal?" Then I have another thought, "What the...? You aren't trying to set me up, are you? I refuse to date another banker!"

"Stop already! No, I'm not setting you up. Please, just trust me." Marc seems to be getting frustrated with me but I have to be honest, he's the one who started this whole blind date with his banker thing only two days after I've been dumped for a ditzy debutante. He really is bringing it on himself.

"Can you get out of your mortgage?" Marc asks.

"I don't know. Why would I? I need to close the deal so I

need the mortgage. Don't they go hand in hand?" I'm not a financial wiz or anything but I'm pretty sure I have this part right.

"Yes they do, but will your bank let you not use the mortgage you've arranged if we get you another one?"

"I guess, The Bastard's friend Pete arranged it so I'm sure he could un-arrange it. I don't know, I haven't asked." I'm starting to see where Marc is going with his course of questions. "But I can't qualify for a mortgage this large on my own."

"You don't have to. I'll buy the condo with you," Marc states matter-of-factly.

"What? And you called me insane!" Even in my state of semi-awareness I'm able to spot lunacy when it's sitting right beside me.

"No. It makes perfect sense. I'm always looking for investments and can't go wrong with real estate. I'll match your down payment and that will lower the mortgage payments to where you can afford them on your own. No strings attached and when you sell it, if you sell it, you give me back my investment plus half of any profit." Marc has obviously put some thought into my condo dilemma.

I sit quietly beside Marc in his truck contemplating what he has just said. I am completely overwhelmed he would do this for me. It's just so nice. Who does such nice things?

Marc takes my silence as negative and continues, "Or we can try to get you out of the whole deal altogether if you'd rather."

"No, I have to live somewhere and if I can swing it I'd like it to be in the condo. I just don't know if I'm comfortable tying up your money. That doesn't seem right. What if you want to use your money for something else?"

"No worries. I have enough money and if there's a problem, we'll figure it out then. We can always sell the condo, right?" Marc does seem to have it all figured out.

"Why are you being so nice to me?" I start to cry again.

"The stunt what's-his-name pulled on you is unconscionable. I just want you to be in a position where you don't have to deal with him when he comes back and I know he *will* be back. This way you are standing on your own and you don't need him for anything and you'll be in a much better position." Marc reaches over and grabs my wrist and fiddles with my watch.

"You really think he'll be back?"

"He'll be back. Whatever crap he's pulling he hasn't put any thought into it. He'll regret his decision soon enough. Why, would you take him back?"

"Absolutely not. If he's capable of something like this once, he'll do it again. Thank you, by the way, for everything. You shouldn't be this nice to me."

"It's not about you, I just want to keep an eye on the TAG," Marc taps the face of my watch.

"Oh it's all about the TAG, is it?" I laugh despite my tears.

"It's *always* about the TAG," Marc laughs with me.

By the end of the day it's all settled. Marc's bank is going to mortgage the condo and I'll be able to make the payments on my own. Marc, who told me that he would match my down payment when we were in the truck, in reality matched and doubled my down payment, so the condo is well within my single means and I can afford to buy food should I decide not to starve to death. I put a call into Rob-the-bike-courier slash real estate lawyer to get his take on getting out of the mortgage Derek and I had arranged. I tried not to tell him what had happened but he knew instinctively by my voice that something was up and offered to come to my office immediately. I was able to calm him by filling him in briefly on the situation without going into too much detail. Rob faxed me a release and had me call Pete Peterson and request that he sign it and fax it back. When I spoke to Pete, he had no idea what Derek had done, and when I told him he was more than helpful and assured me there would be no problem. I had the release signed and back by the end of the day. Mr. Sebring allowed me to execute a new agreement with him taking Derek's name off the agreement and Rob did the legwork with Mr. Sebring's lawyer. All in all, it is a very busy day but by the end of it, The Bastard Cock-Lick is no longer a part of the condo or my world.

# 44

For the next ten weeks I exist entirely in a fog. The Super Bowl happens. I spend it sitting on the couch with Mel and Charlie Brown. I vaguely remember Indianapolis won but can't recall any details. The move happens, my new table, less the chairs, is delivered on schedule, and my hair just gets bigger. I lose all interest in personal hair taming and by moving day have decided "bigger is better." In fact, I spend hours brushing it to make it bigger and frizzier. My hair has become my new hobby. Forget macramé, I've got huge hair.

Five weeks after the move Mel, Charlie Brown and Marc come to the condo to unpack for me because I have shown no inclination to do so myself. Charlie Brown threatens to unpack my panties and other dainties and to everyone's dismay I don't even lift an eyebrow. Charlie Brown in my panty drawer would normally send me into a tailspin but now fighting Charlie Brown just seems like too much effort.

"You don't have any food," Marc states emphatically when he looks into my mostly empty fridge.

"*Hellooooo?* There's beer in there AND After Eights in the butter thingy," I respond defensively.

"You can't live on beer and dinner mints. What real food are you eating?"

"I don't know. I had nachos a while ago." I really can't remember what I ate last or when. Eating has not been a priority. I haven't tamed my hair for heaven's sake; surely they must realize that food is lower on the priority list than hair. People actually see my hair.

"You had nachos with us yesterday at the Firkin and you only ate one chip. I was watching you." Marc is visibly angry now and his raised voice is enough to get Charlie Brown to tear himself away from my panty drawer and come into the kitchen.

"Whatever. I'll eat soon. I promise." I'm in no state to argue with Marc. Let's face it, I'm rather weak — I've only eaten one chip and a couple of After Eights in the past several days.

"You have got to snap out of this. When stupid what's-his-face comes back do you want him to see you like this?" Marc is pulling out the tough-love father card and he's doing it well so I'm guessing he's played it before on his children.

"No, I just can't get back on track," I start to cry again.

"Kit, you're getting way too skinny." Mel has joined in to what I now realize is not just good friends helping me unpack but some sort of planned intervention. Damn, I should have seen it coming.

"How much do you weigh?" Mel continues. "Well, it doesn't matter. I can tell you're approaching car accident skinny and that means that none of your clothes are going to fit and you know what that means?" Mel raises her eyebrow in a you-brought-this-conversation-on-yourself manner.

"It means back to the short skirts, baby! Yahoo!" Charlie Brown answers the question for me with the added fist pump in the air.

"See? Do you want John in your office every day looking at your butt?" Mel could so be a mother. If Mel and Marc raised children together those kids would have no end of interventions. They both seem to be thriving on this conversation.

"Exactly," Marc starts to add his intervention wisdom but gets interrupted by Charlie Brown returning on a run from my bedroom waving the little red plaid schoolgirl kilt.

"Oh here Kit, put it on! Oh, and I found a little red thong in your panty drawer, wear it too!"

Ignoring Charlie Brown I turn to Mel, "That man is just *not* right."

"I know and if you don't snap out of it I'm going to leave him here to watch out for you for a couple of days. How would that be?" Mel says in her singsongy voice. She is evil to the core.

"I hate you. I hate you all" is the only comeback I can think of as I grab the kilt out of Charlie Brown's hand.

"And she's back." Marc twists open a beer while Charlie Brown tries to wrestle the kilt back from me. The intervention went a little way toward getting me out of my "being dumped funk" but my appetite still didn't return and my hair still didn't warrant any attention.

On the Thursday A.I. (After Intervention) I ran into Marc and Mel outside my condo building, literally. I had gone to a lunch physiotherapy appointment when I got the news that finally seemed to snap me out of the dumped funk. Near the end of my appointment, which I had almost cancelled for lack of enthusiasm and large hair, the therapist said, and I will remember these words forever, "Let's get you on the treadmill and see if you can run." At first I thought I was hallucinating and I asked him to repeat himself, but he had said the word *run*. I've never hugged my physiotherapist before. I think I caught us both off guard when I jumped up and embraced him. It was a bit awkward really but I haven't run in over a year, so kinder words have never been spoken. My life is pretty much in the toilet, I look a fright being all big-haired and accident-skinny but I can run again. Of course, it's not all butterflies and chocolate éclairs. I have to start off with slow short runs but it's a beginning. In my excitement I call my hair stylist to get an appointment and he can fit me in this afternoon. So I call Joyce and tell her I'm taking the afternoon off and head to the stylist; then, with my new tamed hair, I head home to attempt my first little run. It's at the end of the run when I literally run into Marc and Mel who are pacing together outside my condo building.

"Hey guys. What are you doing here?"

"Looking for you! We were worried sick!" Mel doesn't know whether to hug me or hit me.

"I called the office and Joyce said you took the afternoon off so I called Mel and here we are worried to death! Where have you been?" Marc is using his angry dad voice.

"What do you mean? Look at me! I'm running." I remain undeterred by their attitudes. Surely they have better things to do than pace outside my condo. Don't they have jobs to do, companies to run, things like that?

"I see that but you're supposed to be at work. I thought you were off killing yourself or something." Mel is not pleased that she had to take time off and worry about me when I'm obviously fine.

"Mel," I grab her by the shoulders and give her a little shake, "I'm running, not walking, running." I stretch out the word *running* because they don't seem to be getting it. I guess my not being able to run wasn't as important to them as it was to me.

"Oh my God! You are! You are running!" Mel finally clues in and excitedly hugs me. "And your hair!? Oh my God, it smells nice and it isn't huge!" I think Mel is more pleased about my hair than the running, but she's pleased so I'll take it. It's a definite improvement over the scowl of a few moments ago.

"Yep, I got the word that I could start running again and I couldn't wait. It was only two kilometres but I'm not complaining."

"How's the leg?" Marc finally understands the magnitude of what running means to me and joins the conversation without his angry eyes.

"A bit sore but nothing like it was after the accident. Oh and guess what?" I ask excitedly.

"Something besides running and hair maintenance? I don't know if I can handle anything else," Mel says in what I'm sure is sarcasm.

"I'm hungry. Really hungry so I'm going to get some food," I laugh. My stomach was gurgling the whole run. I guess running on coffee alone isn't a great idea.

"I think I might have a chip under the seat of my truck. That should fill you up," Marc laughs as we start into the lobby of my building.

"You can buy me nachos *and* a beer for that comment, mister!"

"Gladly, anything to see you eat something." Marc hugs me around the shoulders.

"So what possessed you to get your hair done finally?" Mel asks. "Couldn't fit through the subway train doors anymore?"

# 45

My breakup with The Bastard Cock-Lick finally became common knowledge around the time I got my running legs back. The Bastard's parents, or I hope it was his parents and not him, thought it would be appropriate to put an announcement in the Toronto paper even though the wedding had taken place in New York. I have no idea what the little announcement might have cost but it wasn't really little. How much does a quarter page run in the *Toronto Star* these days? There was a photo as well — again, to ensure that no one missed the news. Seems there were over four hundred guests in attendance, the bride veered away from the traditional satin and wore linen and they served duck. Duck isn't a choice I might have made but I can only assume Tiffy's father is a hunter and he personally gunned down the poor unsuspecting birds to feed the hoards at his daughter's nuptial gala, thereby personalizing the enormous event.

Mel rallies the troops the day the announcement hit the paper and I am forced to meet her, Charlie Brown and Marc at the Firkin. I would have been happy to go home and slit my wrists but it seems Mel is wise to the wrist-slitting plan and insists on keeping me busy in times of crisis. Unfortunately, in light of the reason for us all being together, it is very awkward. Everyone wants to comment on the wedding announcement but no one wants to be the first to mention it, even though we all know it's why we're together in the first place. Luckily, or not so luckily, Charlie Brown, who seems to lack any sense of propriety, breaks through the awkwardness and simply blurts out, "Sucks about The Bastard's wedding announcement, Kit!" I almost spit beer out my nose and Marc almost chokes. Mel smacks Charlie Brown who seems shocked and gives her the what-did-I-do? look.

"Yes. Yes it does." I really have nothing to say about the whole thing.

"It couldn't have been much of a wedding despite what that paper says; they threw it together in a few weeks — besides, the bride looks high maintenance. I'm sure she'll be a handful." Mel tries to make me feel better.

"Oh, she'll be a handful all right, a handful of boobs! Did you get a look at those in the picture? They're huge!" This last comment gets Charlie Brown hauled off, not too politely, to the bar with Marc, leaving Mel and me alone at the table.

"Bringing good old Charlie Brown on the 'cheer-up mission' maybe wasn't such a good idea, eh?" I start to laugh. Charlie Brown can always come up with the absolute wrong thing to say. How he's managed to get through his life this long without offending the wrong person and getting beaten to death is a mystery.

My parents take the news of my breakup with The Bastard

harder than I imagined they would. I thought they'd be pleased I would not be living in sin because that seemed to be a stumbling block for them a few months ago; but no, instead my mother seems devastated. She didn't come right out and say it but I think her upset stems mainly from the fact that since I'm single again, she may never get the wedding she's so desperate to throw. Oh, don't get me wrong, living in sin is still *very bad* but at least it's a step closer to the white taffeta gala. With Mel dating and Mike engaged, mother sees that Mrs. Melrose might have two weddings under her belt before she gets a single one. I think secretly my mother would have liked to have been invited to The Bastard's wedding — she is crackers for a wedding.

Mel and Charlie Brown renovate their new house. This house renovation is considerably larger than the one Mel and I did, so Mel and Charlie Brown move into my guest room. As much as the condo seems a bit crowded, especially in the morning when Charlie Brown is sitting on a Rubbermaid Two-Step, always the blue one, watching *Breakfast Television* and eating Count Chocula breakfast cereal, it is nice to have company and not be alone all the time. Charlie Brown has a distinct opinion about the Two-Steps and considers the white one to be too feminine for him. The fact that he squeezes his butt cheeks between the edges of the blue one is fine and doesn't impede his manliness, but you won't find his butt squished on the white one. No, that would be wrong.

I spend most evenings and weekends at Mel and Charlie

Brown's new house helping where I can. I can actually be helpful this time around because I can hold *and* direct a broom at the same time, something that is terribly difficult while balancing on crutches. Charlie Brown is much less stressed this time around so either he's better when *not* running Marc's company or Mel is tossing Prozac into his Count Chocula.

One Friday in late July, near the end of the renovation, we decide not to go out for drinks but to forge ahead on the painting. Mel and I meet at the house after work and are breaking out rollers and brushes when Charlie Brown and Marc arrive. Marc hasn't been around much and we all assume he's busy in his relationship with mystery no-name-girl so we don't bug him about it. Besides, helping friends and co-workers with home renovations really isn't most people's cup of tea. There are a shocking number of friends who say "good luck with that" and you don't hear from them until the celebratory renovation-completed party. Seeing Marc on a Friday is actually a nice surprise.

"Hey you! No date tonight?" I ask playfully. Mel and I have found our painting rhythm and painting isn't nearly the adventure it was at our house.

"Nope, not tonight. I'm here to help." Marc looks tired but it is Friday and most people look tired after a long week of work.

"Not anytime soon, either," Charlie Brown interjects as he starts to walk by us toward the kitchen, "he got dumped!"

Mel, who is standing behind me and gets to register what Charlie Brown has just said before he's past her, punches Charlie Brown in the arm on his way by, which stops Charlie Brown dead in his tracks and he gives her the what-did-I-do? look. I am surprised, both that Marc got dumped but more so that Charlie Brown seems to have no tact whatsoever. I am glad Charlie Brown chose electrician as a career and not doctor. I can't imagine his bedside manner or delivery of bad news to patients and their families. Sitting behind his desk in his white lab coat announcing to a terminally ill person, "Yep, you're gonna die. You've got three weeks max!" then slapping the file shut and yelling "Next." Mel follows Charlie Brown into the kitchen where I can only assume she is trying to hammer some sensitivity into him. I wonder sometimes if she doesn't stay with Charlie Brown because he's a "work in progress." Mel will not fail. If Charlie Brown ever develops into a well-mannered human being I suspect the relationship will end because Mel will no longer have anything to work on besides his fashion sense, and that's one hurdle even Mel will never clear.

"That's a bummer," I say to Marc after Charlie Brown is safely out of hearing range.

"Not so bad. She wasn't the one for me for a lifetime and I probably wasn't putting as much into the relationship as I could have."

"So you just treated her bad until she dumped you?" I smile.

"Something like that."

"That's always a safe route to take. They can't hate you for breaking up with them in that case. I can honestly say that I know how you feel, if that helps. Paintbrush or roller?" I hold up one of each utensil. Might as well get Marc working so he doesn't dwell on his girl problems — that was Mel's theory with me at any rate. It's much nicer to be on the work-encouraging end of things as opposed to being the one made to work.

"Roller! I'm not cutting in," Marc laughs and we get down to the business of painting.

Marc doesn't get much paint rolling done before Mel and Charlie Brown return and Mel takes over and frees Marc up to help Mr. Sensitive install the upper kitchen cabinets. I tease Mel most of the evening about Charlie Brown's sensitive side or lack thereof. I'm not sure she appreciates my sense of humour. I suspect she's fighting a losing battle trying to get Charlie Brown to understand people's feelings but she maintains that he's made strides already. The obvious question to ask is, "How bad was he before?" but again, she did not think I was very funny. The evening passes without further sensitivity issues and it's actually a lot of fun to have Marc in the trenches with us.

# 46

The renovations at Mel and Charlie Brown's house are well in hand and they move back to their house the week after the paint party. It's been nice having them at my condo but it's also nice to get the place to myself and be able to run around naked if I so desire, not that I do it often with the floor-to-ceiling windows, but it is nice to know I *can* if I want to.

The twins, who would have invited themselves to stay whether Mel was still in my guest room or not, are descending this weekend under the guise of seeing my condo and Mel's new house, but I know it's really to see Kevin. Tia and Ben are still seeing each other, which I know is a record long relationship for Tia. Who knows, maybe Mom will get her wedding yet.

I see Marc a couple of times for coffee and he seems to be getting back to his usual happy self after his breakup. I suppose his recovery is speedier than mine because he at least saw it coming and was actually maneuvering the relationship down the breakup path. I have not heard one word from The Bastard so can only assume married life is everything he hoped it would be, had he actually aspired to be married before meeting the large-breasted-beauty-queen-first-loser.

On Friday, at lunchtime, I'm leaving the office for the day, having booked the afternoon off to spend it with the twins, when I bump into Marc coming into my building.

"Hey, what are you doing here? I thought I got all your invoices yesterday."

"I wanted to see you. Are you leaving for the day?" Marc is surprised to see me taking the afternoon off. I've been a work junkie since the breakup and normally don't leave until long after the closing bell unless I'm helping Mel with her house.

"Yep, I took the afternoon off to spend it with the twins. They're driving down from North Bay for the weekend. We're going shopping on Queen Street," I explain the afternoon off.

"Oh, I wanted to talk to you about something but it can wait." Marc seems a bit agitated.

"Shoot! You came all this way you might as well ask. No sense wasting a trip."

"Oh…well…" Marc is starting to stammer. "You don't have to answer. In fact, don't answer, just think about it." Marc is fast-talking now. Oh oh. "I was wondering if you'd like to go out on a date with me. You know, a proper date, not just a beer after work. Don't answer, just say you'll think about it," Marc blurts the whole thought out and I'm really glad he stressed "don't answer" because I couldn't even if I wanted to. A proper date with Marc could be the start of something. Something I'm not sure I want to tackle, or do I?

"Okay. I will think about it. I'm not completely sure I'm ready to go on 'proper dates' just yet, but I promise to give it some thought. It might actually be nice to finally see if we could 'work,'" I say with more confidence than I feel.

"Whew. Good." Marc's face lights up, presumably because I didn't call him a masher and smack him with my purse. I walk Marc outside to his illegally parked truck before heading home to meet the twins at the condo.

The twins have a great weekend and are the stars at the Kevin show. Tia, who seems to have embraced the tambourine wholeheartedly, is actually on stage playing it for a few songs. She is on cloud nine and in rare excited form, which gets Taryn wound up as well. Once the twins get excited, whether it's real or imagined, someone could get inadvertently stepped on with a three-inch heel so it's best to give them a wide berth. During a break and after the twins flurry of excitement Kevin approached us, "Hey Kit, Tia tells me that the band has you to thank for the tambourine."

"Why yes you do!"

"Well, thank you," Kevin laughs but also does an eye-roll.

"You're welcome!" I know Kevin isn't impressed but he is being good-humoured about the whole tambourine thing.

"Are you here alone with the twins?" Kevin looks around.

"Yes, Derek and I broke up a while ago. So it's just me and *them*!" I gesture toward the twins.

"I'm sorry to hear that, the Derek part, not the twins. Are you okay?"

"Absolutely. It was probably for the best." I am able to talk about the breakup now without getting weepy or vomiting. I am making huge strides in the recovery department.

"Well, he's an idiot to let you go," Kevin squeezes my arm then checks his watch and excuses himself to go and rustle up the other band members for the next set.

I didn't give much thought to Marc's date offer until Sunday after the twins leave to return to North Bay. I walk the twins to Mom's car, which they had borrowed for the drive to Toronto, and instead of going back to my now-empty condo I decide to go for a walk along the harbourfront. It is bright and sunny and a beautiful day to enjoy the city. Deciding what to do about Marc isn't easy. I haven't given the idea of dating him any thought at all since a couple of days right after our fight last fall, but he was dating someone else so it wasn't even real consideration. I know I care about Marc — he is one of my best friends, we are currently both single, that's a first, and we do own a condo together. But will we be tempting fate and potentially ruining a great friendship that might otherwise last the test of time? Is status quo better than the potential for more? More could turn out to be much less. Could Marc and I date, see each other naked, and then be friends again if the relationship didn't work? Well, Rob and I are slowly becoming friends again, and I've seen him naked. I've bounced quarters off his abdomen, for heaven's sake, and now we occasionally have coffee together. Marc and I might be able to maintain a friendship if the relationship goes wrong, but what if we can't? Is unrequited love better than love gone sour? We are friends and we own real estate together, surely these are the cornerstones for something wonderful? I've never owned real estate with anyone except Mel, so that must mean something. My brain whirls for over an hour while I walk. Every possible scenario, good and bad, concerning a potential date goes through my head. Finally, after the hour, as I approach mental exhaustion, I sit down on a bench near the water. I am a firm believer in "going with your gut" because mine is so sensitive. Generally, in my case, vomiting is bad and not vomiting is good. So I sit quietly and pose the question out loud, "Do I go on a date with Marc, potentially starting a relationship and ruining a friendship?" and I wait. I assess my gut and realize that it is not upset or even close to vomiting. It is actually a little bit excited. "He has kids. Am I stepmonster material?" Assess gut. A little more action down there, I've never been in the stepmonster role before since I've never dated anyone with kids. But, still no vomiting. I have my answer. No vomiting. I will go on a date with Marc. I feel better already and can't wait to call Marc and tell him. This could be the start of something good.

# 47

We are going on a date. A proper date, not just drinks after work with the guys. We are going to dinner and a movie on Thursday night. I am very excited. I have a date. The fog that has been following me around for the months since The Bastard dumped me suddenly feels lighter. I have a date. When I told Mel that I am going on a date with Marc her response was positive. Well, it was something like "Mother of Pearl, it's about time!" but I took that as positive reinforcement. I asked her not to mention it to Charlie Brown because I don't want anything to be awkward for Marc at work. Marc will tell Charlie Brown himself.

I rush home from work on Thursday to get ready for my date. I have a date with Marc! I have a quick shower to get the city grime off but am careful not to get my hair wet. Once wet, the hair process can take an hour and I don't have an hour, best to just leave it and go with today's work hair. Work hair is not perfect but a definite improvement from breakup hair. I redo my makeup and pluck my eyebrows, which I noticed in the mirrored elevator at work had gotten completely out of hand. I could give Oscar the Grouch a run for his money in the unibrow department. I decide on my favourite jeans that have a butt in them, and a plain white t-shirt and my brown sandals. I switch purses to my fun-little-summer-purse, spray on some perfume and have five minutes to spare. Not bad. I feel confident. This is going to go well — I mean I'm ready on time, I have two distinct eyebrows and I look pretty good if I do say so myself. Marc said he would buzz up when he got here but I decide to head down to the lobby and wait; besides, he should be here by the time I get downstairs.

I get downstairs and no Marc. Strange, he's not usually late for things, not work things anyway. Oh well, he's probably stuck in traffic. I sit on the planter edge in front of the building for what seems likes ages, look at my watch, it's only been five minutes. I must be just nervous about the date. I pace up and down in front of the building, counting the sidewalk tiles and figuring out the square footage of the area between the door and the street. Look at my watch again. I am becoming a Train Person. At this rate Marc would never make it as a Train Person, best he keep his truck in good running condition. Ten more minutes have passed for a total of fifteen. Marc is fifteen minutes late. Not terrible by bad traffic standards, but still not making a great impression for a first date. I take my cell phone out of my purse. No missed calls. I turn it on to see if it's working and getting reception. Yes, it's working. I decide to call Marc's cell phone; if he's really stuck in traffic I can offer to meet him at the restaurant and save him the time of picking me up. Strange, my call goes directly to voicemail. He must be on the phone, probably a work problem. I leave a voicemail telling him I'm waiting downstairs.

By the time Marc is fifty minutes late, I've pulled all the weeds out of the planter, filed my nails in public, something I would never normally do, befriended four dogs and their owners and turned down two propositions to "get busy." After the second proposition I decide Marc probably is not coming and he must have had some medical emergency. Surely, if he were able to pick up his phone and dial he would have called. He must be incapacitated. Heart attacks and strokes are prevalent in men with stressful jobs — I hope he's all right. In a panic I return to the condo and call Mel.

"He hasn't shown up yet? Something bad must have happened. Marc would walk on hot coals to get to a date with you." Mel is as shocked as I am.

"And his phone is going directly to voicemail." I was concerned before Mel mentioned, "Marc would never miss a chance to take you out." Now I'm really concerned. "What should I do?"

"There's not much you can do; if he's in a hospital it could be any of a number and finding him would be impossible. I guess we have to wait until tomorrow and then surely someone at work will know what happened." Mel is right, there isn't anything to do. Even if I found out what hospital he is in I'd never be able to get any information because I'm not family.

"You're right. I'll call you if I hear anything." I resign myself to waiting by the phone all night.

"Me too, if John hears anything about Marc I'll let you know."

The next morning I am exhausted. I have not slept more than an hour all night worrying about Marc. Every time the phone rang I jumped out of my skin but it was never Marc. I had calls from my mother, Mel and a person trying to sell me half-priced Viagara, but no Marc. I manage to get ready for work. I consider calling in sick except I know my best chance of hearing anything about Marc will be at work. I stumble out of the coffee shop with my extra-large coffee, knowing my eyes are red and bloodshot because I can't focus properly, and stumble right into Marc.

"Oh my God! You're alive!" I hug him in my excitement to see him alive. "What happened? I was so worried!"

"I'm really sorry about last night. I want to make it up to you. I got stuck with one of the kids. He got into some trouble and I had to bail him out." Marc seems sincere in his apology and if it was one of his kids in trouble I understand the priority.

"Why didn't you call me? I was worried sick." I know I'm not in a position to say anything about him not showing up since it was child-related but I have to address the bad manners of not calling.

"I know I was going to but I got stuck with his lawyer and by the time I was out it was too late to call."

"You honestly think at ten o'clock I just said 'oh well' and went to bed and slept? Look at me! I haven't slept all night. I was awake and a call would have been the decent thing to do." I'm a little put out by Marc's lame excuse for not calling.

"I know. I screwed up. I should have called. I'm sorry," Marc grabs my shoulders and seems sincere. "Can we try again? I really want to take you out, I promise I'll show up and if I can't for any reason I will call."

"I don't know, Marc. I'm not completely thrilled about the idea of dating again in the first place and now that you've stood me up to *supposedly* bail out a child you never mention. I can't say I'm very anxious to try it again. I deserved a phone call. Period. If I don't qualify for a phone call when you aren't showing I'm not sure I'm that high on your list of priorities." I am a mess of emotions. I'm thrilled that Marc is alive after believing he must be dead, but very frustrated and angry that he had the ability to let me know what was going on and chose not to. Who does that to someone? Especially to someone he claims to "love more than anything." It's all very strange. I know my volcano of emotions is going to erupt in tears or vomit or both momentarily so I simply shake loose of Marc's hands and storm toward the office building. I don't turn around when he calls my name.

"He could have called you but he just *didn't?*" Mel is as shocked as I am. "He follows you around for over a year, buys you expensive jewellery, bails you out of the condo mess, finally gets a chance to date you then stands you up and *chooses* not to call to explain himself?"

"Yep, that's pretty much it." I am still angry but have

already cried the pent-up flood of tears and have cleaned up my streaked face.

"Did he say what the kid did?"

"Nope, and I didn't ask. I can't even remember the last time he mentioned any of his kids. I always had the impression his wife, and now Dwayne, do most of the kid stuff. It's very odd that the night we have a date he's suddenly in the running for father of the year," I share my theory about Marc's parenting skills or lack thereof.

"And he wants another chance?" Mel is fuming. If Marc thinks I'm mad he doesn't want to run into Mel today.

"Yep."

"You told him to go screw himself, right?"

"Not as eloquently as you, but that was the message," I laugh but think Mel's way would have got a better response. Well, Marc would have had a more comical look on his face anyway.

After work, at the Firkin, I repeat the events of my day to Mel before Charlie Brown gets there. At 10 a.m. a courier arrived with what was obviously a flower box. The box contained a dozen long-stemmed red roses and a card that read "I am really, really sorry. Please give me another chance." The card wasn't signed but could only have been from Marc. I put the flowers in a vase on the office foyer table, tossed the card into the recycling box and got on with my day. At 11 a.m. another courier arrived with another box of roses. The card had a similar note. I added the twelve new roses to the previous vase and tossed the card. The day continued in that fashion. For seven hours, every hour on the hour, another box of a dozen long-stemmed red roses arrived with a card professing sorrow and regret. The office looked like a flower shop or funeral home, depending on your state of mind.

"You're kidding? Every hour on the hour?" Mel is impressed with the display of flower affection.

"He's still an insensitive ass. One phone call would have saved him a lot of money." I'm less moved than Mel seems to be but I am the one who was up all night worrying.

"So where are the flowers? Did you leave them at work?"

"Mel, it's eighty-four roses! I can't just be hauling them all over town. Besides I don't have enough vases at home anyway." I had considered bringing one dozen home but then thought better of it. I don't need a reminder that Marc stood me up and I may actually be well on the way to becoming a spinster cat-lady.

"Point. I bet they'd be heavy and awkward."

"I can take you by the office and get you some if you want." I do feel bad the flowers will bloom over the weekend in an empty office and no one will get to enjoy them.

"No. That's fine. So what are you going to do?"

"Leave them at the office. I'll deal with the dead leaves on Monday." I thought I'd made this fairly clear.

"Not with the roses, silly, with Marc!"

"Oh that. No plans. I'm in no hurry to get stood up

again." I am seriously not in any hurry to try dating anyone ever again but I don't tell Mel this last part.

"He did show a pretty major display of affection and remorse today. Maybe he was just trying to be considerate last night by not calling you too late. It might not hurt to give him one more chance," Mel gives me her Mel-knows-best look.

"Mel, I can't do it. A few months ago the man I loved dumped me to marry a bimbo, then I take a chance, which I think is a sure thing, just to be stood up. You know what? My ego can't take another mishap right now!" As I'm explaining this to Mel I realize I am more upset about being stood up than I thought. I feel like I'm going to cry but I know if I start I won't be able to stop. Before Mel can respond Charlie Brown comes in and sits down beside her.

"Oh man, I need a beer! You wouldn't believe the day I had. Marc was in a severely foul mood. That guy makes me crazy sometimes!" Charlie Brown says emphatically.

"Here, you could probably use this." I slide my half-beer over to Charlie Brown. "I have to head out anyway." I stand up to leave before Mel can object. "I'll call you tomorrow, Mel. Let me know if you want to go curtain shopping."

The weather is warm and wonderful so I walk home. It's still light outside and not late enough to be considered dangerous. The entire walk home I consider what Mel said and the comment Charlie Brown made. Maybe I am being too hard on Marc. Maybe he did think he was being considerate by not calling. He did show some serious remorse with the flowers. My gut is telling me to run far and fast the other way. Why would my gut be saying that if it's all going to work out perfectly and Marc and I are going to end up together? Maybe its just bad timing and Marc and I just aren't meant to be together yet. Maybe we're meant to be together at a later date. Arrgh. I have no idea what is meant to be but I know I don't like being stood up. What does a phone call take? Ten seconds, maybe twelve? Would it have killed him to let me know he wasn't coming? No. I'm not ready to date yet. I like being in control of my life and not being a victim to the whims of men. The Bastard just up and left and Marc just didn't show. I'm not strong enough to date right now.

I go for a run on Saturday morning. I love the feeling of getting out and letting off steam. When I get back to the condo I'm hot and sweaty and exhausted and too tired to care what men have done to badly influence my life lately. After my shower I turn the coffee maker on. Yes, I've mastered my own coffee maker, and it gives me a sense of accomplishment and satisfaction. I'm a woman in control. I can successfully make my own coffee. I check the caller ID on the phone and notice that Marc has called four times this morning and Mel called once. I haven't turned my cell phone on but assume Marc has left messages there as well. I delete Marc's messages before I listen to them. Mel's message suggests shopping after lunch then a barbecue at the almost finished house. I call Mel back to confirm then settle down on the couch to read my newest

*Vogue* magazine and enjoy my coffee. I know I should be reading proper literature but I find my concentration still isn't back since The Bastard dumped me. I can read magazine articles and look at the pretty advertising photos but anything too deep and my eyes glaze over and I start to daydream, mostly about how awful The Bastard's life is with Muffy, or whatever her name is, and how she's making his life miserable. I know it's wrong but it makes me smile. Smiling is good exercise for your face, so I don't feel too bad about my thoughts.

I can tell by the knocking on the door it isn't Mel; she would never waste that many knocks, although it is almost time to meet her. I open the door and discover Marc. *Arrgh*. I have to get a peephole installed. The door downstairs is a security door but if someone else is coming in, anyone can walk in behind them, and it appears "anyone" has done just that.

"What do you want?" My tolerance for pleasantries with Marc is at an all-time low.

"I just had to see you." Marc gives me his most pathetic, sad look which I'm sure he practised in his illegally parked truck before sneaking in the front door.

"Well, you've seen me. Goodbye." I try to shut the door on him but he holds it open.

"You have to give me another chance. I know I screwed up but I promise I won't the next time. All I want is to be with you. I can't screw up again, I know that. Please. Just one more chance?"

"Marc, if you stand me up again I think it will push me

over an edge I've been teetering on for months. I can't do it. If I'm so bloody important why didn't you call? It doesn't make sense. You say I'm important but your actions show me otherwise. Talk is cheap. The bottom line is you stood me up with no call. You left me sitting here all night wondering if you were alive or dead, so you didn't give my feelings one thought, did you?" I'm tired of this. I just want him to go away.

"I know. I know. I screwed up. Please, give me one more chance. Please."

"Why should I?"

"Because if you don't then I'll shrivel up and die."

"Fine. You can take me out for dinner on Friday night. I want to go to Fred's Not Here. You make the reservations and pick me up here at seven o'clock." If I have to endure a second attempt at dating it might as well be on my terms.

"What is Fred's Not Here?"

"It's a restaurant and it's listed in the phonebook. Look, if this is going to be too much trouble I'm fine to just say forget it!" I honestly hope he does think it's too much trouble because the thought of being stood up again is too much to tolerate.

"No. Fine. Fred's Not Here on Friday. I pick you up at seven." Marc seems a bit afraid of me, and I don't mind at all.

"*Here*. You pick me up here and in the event you are late or heaven help you, you can't make it, you'd better dial the bloody phone." I honestly do not even want to try this again.

Any romantic inclinations I had for Marc were severely cut down with the last date attempt.

"He *won't* do it twice! There's no way." Mel and I are shopping for curtains for the newly renovated house and I've told her about Marc's visit.

"He better not." I'm tired of talking about Marc.

"He is madly in love with you. He won't screw up. He knows it is his last chance; he'll be on his absolute best behaviour. I'm sure of it." Mel presents a white gauzy curtain panel, "What do you think?"

"Not bad, but I don't think it's what you want in the kitchen."

# 48

Friday morning, on my way to work, I bump into Rob at the coffee shop.

"Hey Kit, Minefield Boom is playing at the Bovine tonight. Are you in?"

"Sorry, I have a date." I haven't told anyone but Mel up until now.

"Wow! That's good news, but I didn't think you were ready to date yet? You turned me down twice just last week," Rob laughs.

"I'm not and I turned you down because you cheated on me."

"Good point. But when are you going to date me again?" Rob asks and I think he might be half serious.

"You, sir, are bad news. Oh I might sleep with you again, but I don't think I'll date you," I laugh and try to make light of Rob's question.

"All righty, then!" Rob pauses briefly, "So, about that sleeping together…" Rob and I both laugh as we leave the coffee shop and head off toward our respective office buildings.

It's six forty-five. Only fifteen minutes until my *date* arrives. Will my date arrive? I am positive he will. Mel drove home that point a million times this past week. Little black dress, little black shoes, little black purse and favourite summer lipstick in aforementioned little black purse, check. I'm ready to go. I refuse to meet him downstairs this time. He can buzz up and then I'll go down. I tidy the kitchen again. Six fifty-five. One last makeup check. Looks good, nothing glaringly out of place. Eyebrows, two, that's always encouraging. I'm ready. Check watch again. Six fifty-eight, almost six fifty-nine. Pace. Look out the window. My condo doesn't face the street where Marc would illegally park to buzz the condo so I can't tell if he's here. Twirl. Twirling is always fun. Pace. Check watch. Seven oh-two. Hmm. Well, traffic in Toronto, watches calibrated differently, I must give him the benefit of the doubt. He will be here. He knows this is his absolutely last chance. Check cell phone, on. Press Talk. Yes, getting reception. Land line. Dial tone? Yes. All telephones are working and ready for communication. Seven oh-six. I personally would have been early for an important date, apparently not Marc. I am starting to get nauseous; there will be vomiting if he doesn't show up. He *has* to show up. He would not do this to me twice. Seven ten. Getting dizzy and not from twirling. Sitting down. He's standing me up again. No. Think positively, maybe he's dead. No, not *that* positively. He's just stuck in traffic and not checking the time. How long do I give him before I give up? There must be etiquette for this sort of thing. How long would Ms. Manners give him? Ten minutes seems too long. Okay, I'll give him thirty minutes. Thirty minutes, then what?

Do I call his cell phone and yell profanities? No, that would put me into the "crazy" category and then he could come back and say, "Oh yeah, well you're insane." No, just say no to profanity, although I have several good lines racing through my mind. I should write them down for future use. Seven fifteen. Fifteen minutes late and no phone call. Unbelievable. This man is completely unbelievable! At this point he better be dead. Dead is the only excuse that will save his butt at this point. I think I made myself clear on the not showing up *and* not calling. If you're late, you *call*. I'm in such a state, I don't even want him to show up now. Who goes to all the trouble of sending seven dozen roses, begging and pleading just to *not* show up a second time? I think Marc has some hidden, or maybe not so hidden, mental illness issues. He should really be in therapy. Seven twenty. The phone is ringing. Okay maybe he can save his skin. No caller ID information but it must be him. I pick up, "Hello," I try to sound calm and collected even though I'm churning inside. I wonder if this is the I-can't-make-it call and what his excuse will be? Locusts? Yes, a swarm of locusts has attacked his truck and he can't possibly get here. This ought to be good.

"Kathryn? It's me, Derek." I hear a voice from that past. I don't suppose his timing could be worse. I'm currently being stood up and now The Bastard Cock-Lick is on the phone. My knees buckle and I'm sitting on the coffee table.

"What do *you* want?" I have no ability to make small talk with this person who has completely blindsided me with this call. I feel really nauseous now.

"I have to talk to you. I've made a big mistake. Huge. I need to see you." The Bastard's voice is cracking and I can tell he's upset, but I honestly don't care. I actually get an evil little smile on my face when I hear sadness in his voice. What do you mean? Marrying a bimbo you hardly know isn't going so well? Ah, too bad!

"I didn't check the weather lately but to the best of my knowledge hell *hasn't* frozen over, so no, I won't be continuing this conversation. Please don't call me ever again." I press the Off button on my portable telephone but miss the satisfying thud of the handset slamming down into the cradle like a traditional phone so I set the handset down hard beside me in an angry hanging-up fashion, but it isn't completely satisfying so I toss the phone onto the couch. I can't think about The Bastard right now, I have bigger fish to fry. I'm currently and now *officially*, as it's seven thirty-two, being stood up by the man who has on more than one occasion professed undying love for me. Suffice it to say, all men are jerks.

I'm in a complete state now. I'm hungry, angry and nauseous, not necessarily in that order.

The phone starts to ring again. No caller ID information. *Arrgh*. It's probably The Bastard Derek again. I can't stay here all night. I'll go completely insane. Well, first things first, get out of the dress-up clothes. I throw on jeans, t-shirt and sandals, switch from little black purse to fun over-the-shoulder bag appropriate for dancing at a crowded club. It's seven forty. Marc is officially dead, or will wish he is the next time

I see him. I pick up the phone and dial in-between what I assume are Derek's calls.

"Hey Rob, it's me, Kit. Are you still going to the Bovine?"

"Absolutely. What happened to your date?"

"Well, I've been stood up and I'm having a hell of an evening so far, the loud punk styling of Minefield Boom is just what I need." I try to be upbeat despite my churning insides. I have managed to refrain from vomiting but must get out and do something in order to keep it that way. "Have you eaten?" I ask Rob because I'm hungry.

"Nope. Jump in a cab and meet me at the Rivoli in fifteen minutes. We'll get some Pad Thai and have a beer before the show." Rob is officially my new best guy friend, replacing Marc for now and forever.

"See you there, oh, and this is *not* a date." I hang up the phone and pick up my cell phone and start to drop it in my purse. I then think better of it. I certainly don't want to take calls from either Marc or Derek. No. Cell phone stays here.

# 49

I wake up but I don't open my eyes. I know from the heavy feeling in my head and the dry mouth that I definitely had too much to drink last night. Oh no, I hope I didn't do anything embarrassing. Think. Rivoli, Pad Thai, beer, it's the beer that kills me really, more beer, the Bovine, band, dancing, yelling over the music, more beer. No, nothing too embarrassing. I think I'm in good shape. Oh wait. Damn, maybe not so good. End of the night, there was kissing. Yes, I was kissing Rob. Did I stop kissing Rob? No. Do I have clothes on? No. Am I alone? With my eyes still closed I reach behind me and touch a person. Oh God, I hope it's Rob and not the scary pierced guy who was standing near us at the bar. No, I'm sure it's Rob. I vaguely remember inviting him up to give him back the skateboard I've now carried with me to two different homes. I also remember smooching him in the elevator. It's Rob. Whew! Okay, I apparently slept with Rob last night. Am I okay with this? Yes, I think I am. I don't feel the least bit nauseous, well a bit from the hangover, but not from stress.

I open my eyes. Water and aspirin are priorities one and two. I must try to combat the headache. I get up slowly so as not to wake Rob or move my head too quickly and venture to the kitchen for water, stopping at the washroom for headache medication and a quick brush of my teeth. I hate the feeling of little sweaters on my teeth. Blech! I find a new toothbrush in the vanity and put it beside the sink for Rob. There is nothing worse than crashing at someone's house and not having a toothbrush. I take the whole bottle of aspirin with me back to the bedroom as I suspect Rob is in a similar state and will require medication as well.

Rob opens his eyes when I come back to the bedroom, "Good morning, naked lady," he says groggily and I realize I'm standing in front of him completely naked holding water and aspirins. A sight which might seem funny if my head wasn't pounding so fiercely.

"Good morning, sunshine," I laugh in my hoarse morning-after-drinking-too-much voice, "I brought you a present."

"You are a lifesaver." Rob takes the water and two aspirins from me. I crawl back into bed and slip under the sheet, put my head on Rob's shoulder and throw my arm over him. It's nice to have a man in my bed again. I missed this, even though I didn't realize I missed it.

"Are you okay?" Rob asks as he pushes my hair out of my face.

"I will be when this headache goes away. I honestly don't know why I drink so much," I state numbly as I lightly scratch my nails over Rob's chiselled torso.

"You were stood up, for one, and I kept buying them for you, for two."

"You are an evil man."

"Well, I sorta had an ulterior motive. I wanted to get invited back to see the condo so I could have my way with you," Rob laughs and rolls me onto my back and starts to kiss my neck.

"Really? Well, for the record, I saw through your evil little plot but let you keep plotting because I wanted to bring *you* home and have my way with *you*!"

"I have a new plot. Do you wanna hear it?" Rob says between kisses on my belly.

"Absolutely, if it's half as diabolical as the first one, I might even join in."

"I'm going to go to the washroom and do something with my breath, then I'm going to come back here and do evil unspeakable things to you." Rob starts to push himself up and get out of bed.

"Promise?"

"Oh I promise," Rob laughs as I watch his perfectly toned butt walk toward the washroom.

Rob and I stay in bed for the best part of the morning. The phone rings several times but I don't answer. There's no one I want to talk to at this point besides Rob and his chiselled abs. Around eleven o'clock we have to start thinking about getting up and facing the day. We are both starving, starving as only the truly hungover can be, and we've run out of condoms. Rob suggests we could use a sandwich bag and a twist tie, but we both think that might be tempting fate and we're hungry anyway. The plan is to get up, take more aspirin, get dressed, get some greasy fast food and pick up condoms at the drugstore. The plan is simple yet highly ambitious for two hungover adults. I have a quick shower, careful not to get the mane of hair wet, then check my messages while Rob is in the shower. Six messages from The Bastard which I skip over but don't delete because I probably should listen to them in case he ambushes me at some point. I'll listen to them later. Mel called twice and has left messages indicating she's sure I'm fine and to call me when I surface. Mel assumes I'm with Marc. Zero calls from Marc on either of my phones. Prick. No amount of kissing up or flowers will get him off the hook this time. He'd better be dead.

I call Mel's home phone, I know she's working, and leave a message that I'm fine and I'll call her later. I can't even imagine getting into the Marc story or the Derek update at this point. I'm having fun with Rob and don't want to dwell on what complete idiots I've aligned myself with in the recent past. I'm sure Marc's therapist could explain Marc's insane behaviour but I really just don't care anymore. As for Derek, there's no explaining that guy. No, I'm not cut out for dating. I'm better single and hanging out with Rob. Rob's single, I'm single, we're both adults, no one is committed to anything except having fun. It's perfect, *Sex with the Single Ex*. No one gets hurt, no one gets jealous, no one gets stood up — we're just friends who have sex when it's convenient for both parties.

Having decided that, I turn my cell phone off and set it on the charger. I won't be requiring a cell phone today because there's no one I want to hear from.

Rob and I get Harvey's burgers and fries for lunch. Nothing like a whole bunch of grease to help you feel better the morning after too much beer. As I sip my Coke, I'm really glad Rob is with me today. Rob is fun and normal, he makes me laugh, and he's just what I need. Rob and I decide to take a walk on Queen Street and window shop after our greasy lunch. Even I have to admit a walk is a good idea after ingesting so much of what can't possibly be good for you. Queen Street is bustling on this sunny August day and it's nice to be anonymous and blend with the crowd. Around two o'clock I start to feel tired and really think I'd like a nap. I tell Rob and we decide it's time to call it an afternoon. Rob is going to head home to his apartment because he has plans with other friends for this evening and I head home to the condo. After such a great day with Rob, I feel lonely and annoyed sitting on the subway. I have to deal with the Derek thing, I have to figure out what boots to wear to kick Marc's coffin and I have to fill Mel in on the past twenty-four hours.

I get back to the cool condo, and give a silent thank you to the inventor of central air conditioning, just as the phone is ringing. Caller ID tells me the caller is Mel so it's safe to pick up.

"Hello," I say cheerfully into the handset.

"You sound happy. How were things last night? I'm dying

to know. Was Marc all 'Mr. Romance' now that he's finally dating you?" Mel sounds like a giddy teenager.

"Sorry, hate to burst your bubble, sweetie, but Marc was a no-show."

"*Get out*! No way! He called though, right?" Mel, ever the optimist where Marc's concerned, is still giving him the benefit of the doubt.

"Nope, sorry. Not even a call. Exactly the same as last time, well not exactly." I smile when I remember dancing with Rob at the Bovine.

"What do you mean, not exactly?"

"This time I didn't sit by the phone worrying, I called Rob and went out dancing. Nothing gets you out of a funk like dancing to Minefield Boom at the Bovine!"

"You went to the Bovine? With cheating Rob? Okay, one thought at a time, surely Marc's called by now," Mel, again with the optimism.

"You can come over and check all my caller ID. I assure you he has not called, or hadn't when I went out this morning around eleven. Derek called though." I throw that last bit in to keep Mel on her toes. I never have exciting news and now I have three juicy bits for her to chomp on.

"The Bastard? The Bastard Cock-Lick *called* you?" I love getting Mel going.

"Yep, just before I left to meet Rob last night."

"AND!" Mel is so easy when there's juicy dish to hear.

"And nothing, I didn't talk to him! He's left several messages. I might listen to them later."

"You *might*? Aren't you the least bit curious what he wants?"

"Absolutely not! He left me for an undersexed, large-breasted, *tall*, bimbo! I could give two hoots what he wants. He can't touch the condo or cause me any more grief so what do I care what he's going on about?"

"Well, you've come a long way this past week. I can't believe Marc didn't show. I don't think he is a nice guy after all." Mel seems more upset about Marc standing me up than I am.

"Well, the jury's been out on that since last week. He's just a jerk who doesn't know what he wants. I'm glad his wife finally got the nerve to go and find Dwight or Dwayne or whatever-his-name is. Good for her!"

"I have to get the full story, *with* details, I haven't even heard about the Bovine yet, but I have to get back to work." Mel really isn't truly happy unless she's doing thirty things all at one time.

"Sure. Call me later, I'm staying in tonight," I yawn into the phone.

"Oh wait, better yet, John is having his college friends over for poker tonight. What if I come down and crash at the condo and we'll do a girl's sleepover? No boys allowed."

"Sure, but bring some ice cream. I have one heck of a hangover." I pause and think for a second, "Oh and some..."

"Yeah, yeah, After Eights, I know, I know!" Mel laughs. "You have got to sign up for After Eights Anonymous?"

"I don't need A8A. I can quit any time I want to," I laugh

into the phone before hanging up, kicking off my sandals and crawling into my bed still fully clothed.

I awake with a start in a cold sweat. That was the scariest dream ever. I just dreamt that I walked into a posh restaurant and was seated at a table already full save one chair for me. When I looked around the table all the faces staring back at me are ex-boyfriends and males that I've come into dating contact with. Every single male that I've dated, slept with or smooched is staring at me. Derek, Rob, Boob Man, that red-haired guy from university, what was his name, and Marc. I shudder with the memory and try to shake off the fear of being faced with all my ex's in one room.

I glance at my watch and see that it's four o'clock. I stare at my TAG. How can the guy who gives me this beautiful watch, saves my condo-buying butt, sends me seven dozen roses in one day, and tells me he's crazy in love with me, stand me up? Twice? Better question, why do I care what his clinical diagnosis is? He's obviously completely insane. I think, "I own a condo with a crazy man but hey, it's better than owning it with The Bastard." I smile to myself and stand up and start to the washroom. I need a shower after my nightmare, the actual one as well as the one that is becoming my real existence.

After my shower, I'm dancing around the living room in my camisole and panties to very loud Old 97's, the *Alive & Wired* album, when I hear the knock on the door. I assume from the one knock that it's Mel, who is early — she usually works until six on Saturday. I guess she took off early for girl's night. I pop my last After Eight in my mouth and throw open the door. It's not Mel.

# 50

The fact that I have dripping wet hair, am chewing on an After Eight dinner mint and wearing nothing but my cami and panties doesn't register until I gasp and almost choke on the After Eight. I hadn't given any thought to what I might say to *Marc* if I ever saw him again, and as I stand here half-naked my brain is letting me down. I finish swallowing then manage to say, "Just a second," before I close the door in his face. I throw on a pair of yoga pants and a t-shirt and return to the door and open it again.

"Bastard, what do you want?"

"I thought that was the other guy's name." Marc tries to make light of my anger.

"If the shoe fits, strap it on and go for a stroll. Again, what do you want?"

"I have to talk to you."

"Talk," I say through the crack in the door.

"Can I come in?"

"Nope. Talk or leave." I have found a spine where Marc's concerned and it's making him uneasy.

"I want to apologize…" Marc starts.

"Not necessary. Anything else?" I cut Marc off because his

apology at this point is just words. If he really cared about my feelings he would have called last night.

"I need to talk to you. Please just give me five minutes!"

"You have four seconds to say something I might want to hear. Your apologies are lies and we both know it. You are sorry, but in the sad and pathetic sort of way. So it's a different sorry really, isn't it?" I am fearsome. Mel would be proud of me.

"You're mad." Marc's ability to assess the situation is astounding.

"Gee, do you think?"

"I want to explain what happened." Marc seems sincere and I can tell by the way he looks he didn't get much sleep last night, but I don't care.

"I know what happened, you didn't show up and you didn't call and since you're obviously alive and well, that makes you an insensitive prick!" I slam the door and deadbolt it. I have to get a peephole installed because apparently even the saddest losers can penetrate the fortress that is our building's security system. I walk to the fridge and open it but realize as I look inside that I ate my last After Eight and I didn't even get to enjoy it because Marc showed up. I slam the fridge door and go to the washroom to blowdry my hair and start the taming process. I hope Mel brings the big box of After Eights. Maybe I am addicted.

Mel shows up at seven o'clock and by then I've had time to tame the hair, launder the sheets on my bed and listen to the messages on the machine. The Bastard Derek is relentless. He left seven long-winded messages, each sounding more pathetic than the last, the general idea being he made a huge mistake marrying someone he hardly knew. No shit Sherlock.

Apparently, five days before The Bastard had the misfortune of running into Tiffy, she had been dumped by her previous fiancé (the wedding was already planned) and Tiffy's parents insisted since everything was paid for "there *would* be a wedding." The Bastard maintains he was in the very wrong place at the very wrong time. The Bastard further maintains he wants to see me to apologize and see if we can try again. Again? What do I look like, a complete idiot? He ran off and married a bimbo and told me I was short. He can't honestly think for one nanosecond I'd even be caught in the same room with him, let alone *try again*. I'll try not to kill him if he's within arm's reach but that's where the trying will end for my part. What a bozo! I did the right thing not listening to these messages until now. I need a drink. Thank goodness my headache from last night's drinking is finally gone. It's time to work on tomorrow's headache.

I'm opening the wine when Mel arrives. I yell through the deadbolted door to make sure it's her and not some crazy man like the last time I opened the door. I *have* to get a peephole installed — I can't keep living like this.

"What's the yelling about?" Mel asks as she steps in the door and hands me two grocery bags full of snacks.

"It's just until I get a peephole installed," I laugh as I deadbolt the door behind her and return to the kitchen to pour wine and unpack the snacks. Mel pulled through with the After Eights — she didn't bring the big box but did bring two small boxes, so enough to get me through the next couple of days. I break into the mints before I pour the wine.

"You know what?" I ask Mel but don't wait for her to ask what, "I think I am addicted to After Eights."

"Really?" laughs Mel, "there's a shocking revelation."

"Sarcasm is never becoming," I hand Mel her glass and we settle in on the couch, After Eights within arm's reach. Mel is anxious to hear what has transpired in the past twenty-four hours so I fill her in. I let her listen to The Bastard's messages but she only manages to get through two of them.

"And there's seven of these?" Mel asks in her most annoyed voice.

"Yes. He's a complete idiot."

"So I don't have to beat you and tell you not to go back there," Mel asks, I think half-seriously.

"Absolutely not! He dumped on the verge of buying the condo, makes me deal with everything on my own and now wants to come back! I don't think so!"

"You did care about him a lot." Mel is playing devil's advocate.

"Yeah, I care about After Eights as well, but if I develop an allergy to them, I'll give them up," I explain. "Oh my God! I hope *that* doesn't happen!"

"Well, it's good to hear that you have your priorities in order! And speaking of condos, what are you going to do with Marc?"

"I want to kill him, but I think it will be better punishment to make him live without me. I'm just going to ignore him." I have decided ignoring him is the only way to combat his narcissistic behaviour.

"What makes someone who so obviously is madly in love with you stand you up twice in a row and behave like a total imbecile?" Mel is as confused about Marc's behaviour as I am.

"A personality disorder, that's what! I do not have the strength to deal with his issues. He can deal with them all by himself. I have a life to live. I have wine to drink, meaningless sex to have and After Eight dinner mints calling my name," I laugh as I grab another mint.

"I really thought he'd come through this time. I guess you never really know some people. Besides, you don't want to start a life with someone who has three kids anyway, especially if one is prone to getting in trouble."

"Good point. If I were to get together with someone and decided to have kids of my own, I'd hope they'd be a little more hands on than Marc seems to be." I'd given the kid situation some thought while I was in the shower.

"What if Marc makes a point about the condo and forces you to sell it now that you aren't speaking to him?"

"I call you and you list it. There's nothing I can do about that and if he plays that card he really is a creep and I don't want to live in a condo that he has anything to do with."

"I like the Sex with the Single Ex plan, are you going to have sex with The Bastard now that he's single?"

"Ewww. Absolutely not! Besides, he never said he was single. I'm betting he's trying to ensure he has someone lined up before he gives Ms. Debutante her walking papers. He is truly a dog. I'm just glad now that he did what he did so I got to see his true colours." I actually feel mentally strong for the first time since Derek dumped me. Knowing that he's miserable and is recognizing his mistake is very empowering. The Marc issue is another story. Neither Mel nor I can figure out what Marc is up to, but it doesn't matter, I will just remove myself from his "game" and he can abuse someone else. My life is back on track and stupid men will not derail me.

# 51

I am dreaming. There is a telephone ringing, incessantly ringing, and it's giving me a headache, but I can't find the telephone. I groggily start to awaken and realize the incessant ringing is my real phone. I have to find the phone. What time is it? The ringing stops as I focus on the clock so I know voicemail picked up. Good. Who calls at eight thirty on a Sunday morning? I bet it's my mother. Oh no, the dreaded red wine hangover. I think today's headache will make yesterday's look like a little slice of heaven. Arrgh. The ringing. Who could possibly be calling me? I hear Mel faintly yell "get the phone!" from the guest room. Mel drank more than I did so I suppose I'd better. I stumble to the living room and hit Talk just before it goes to voicemail again.

"This better be good," I mutter half-asleep into the phone. I am not impressed and if it's Marc or Derek I will scream.

"Ms. Jennings? Kathryn Jennings?" I hear a very official-sounding male voice. I immediately wake up fully and my heart jumps into my throat.

"Yes, this is Kathryn Jennings."

"Ms. Jennings, this is Constable Lloyd from the Toronto Police Department. Do you know a Derek Stanford?"

"I knew a Derek Stanford. We haven't spoken in months. He moved away." I am a little bit relieved; at least it's not about my parents or the twins.

"Mr. Stanford was in a car accident late yesterday afternoon and you are his 'In Case of Emergency' contact in his cell phone," Constable Lloyd continues.

"That must be an old entry. His wife should be his contact. He got married a few months ago. Is he all right?" I am very confused and the red wine haze is not helping.

"He's pretty banged up and unconscious. They won't know the extent of his injuries until he wakes up. Do you have any contact information for his wife?" I know Constable Lloyd is just doing his job but he has no idea how ridiculous this particular question is.

"No, I'm the ex-girlfriend. We don't exactly hang out anymore. His wife's name is Tiffany. She's probably in his phone. Oh and his parents live in Richmond Hill and they are listed in the book." I don't particularly care for Derek these days but I'm sure his parents will want to know what's going on.

"Thanks for your help, Ms. Jennings." Constable Lloyd sounds like a nice man.

"No problem, I hope Derek is okay." I don't want to come across as completely callous.

"What was that all about so early in the morning?" Mel is awake now and is starting to make coffee.

"It was a policeman. Seems Derek was in a car accident

and I was listed as his I.C.E. contact. He must not have updated it in the wedding frenzy," I answer with just a hint of sarcasm at the end.

"Oh, is he okay?" I'm sure Mel's just asking because it's the proper thing to do in these situations.

"Apparently he is pretty banged up and unconscious."

"I know he's a schmuck and everything but should we send flowers or something?"

"Hardly. I wouldn't even know about it if Derek had reprogrammed his phone. Besides, I'm sure his wife wouldn't appreciate holding vigil beside a bouquet from us."

"Maybe that's a good reason to send a really big one!" Mel laughs.

Mel and I are sitting down to coffee and discussing what to do for breakfast when the phone rings again.

"This has to be my mother," I laugh as I pick up the handset and check the caller ID. "Nope, the police again." I hit Talk and say, "Kathryn Jennings speaking."

"Sorry to bother you again, Ms. Jennings." It's Constable Lloyd again. "I spoke to Mrs. Stanford and apparently there are some issues there."

"I don't understand." I am confused by Constable Lloyd's statement, mostly because I can't figure out what I have to do with any of this.

"Well, Mrs. Stanford wasn't very happy."

"Her husband's been in an accident, of course she's not happy." I shrug my shoulders and give Mel my I-don't-get-it eyebrow furrow.

"No, not that kind of unhappy. She used quite a bit of profanity and strongly indicated that she would not be coming to see her husband. She mentioned that the next time she sees him it will 'be in hell.'" Constable Lloyd is trying not to laugh.

"Oh." Sadly, I don't have the same control as Constable Lloyd and let out a snicker before I'm able to clamp my hand over the mouthpiece of the phone.

"I also tried to contact his parents and managed to get a housekeeper who doesn't speak much English, but I think Mr. Stanford's parents are RV'ing across the Northwest Territories, something about polar bears. Does that make sense?" Poor Constable Lloyd had no idea what he was in for when he made his first innocent call this morning.

"His parents do travel extensively and his mother does have a soft spot for animals — they have eight cats and three dogs. So yes, that does make sense." As much as I don't care about any of this it is quite amusing.

"Anyway, the reason I'm calling you back is that Mr. Stanford is in Toronto General Hospital and for all intents and purposes, you're his only Toronto contact," Constable Lloyd continues, "and honestly, you seem much nicer than his wife."

"He's in Toronto?" I am confused. "I just assumed he was in New York."

"No. He is here. His car was hit by a concrete truck on the Lakeshore late yesterday afternoon," Constable Lloyd fills me in.

"On a Saturday? It costs a premium to get concrete delivered on the weekend." I'm not sure where that came from. I obviously spend far too much time at work.

"Premium or not," Constable Lloyd laughs, "Mr. Stanford's Saab was hit by a concrete truck." I want to ask what company the truck belonged to but realize it probably isn't appropriate.

"Are you sure you have the correct Derek Sanford? The Derek I know hates Saabs." I am very confused, but Derek driving a Saab isn't any crazier than him marrying a debutante he doesn't know I suppose.

"Well, he was in a Saab convertible which is part of the reason for the head trauma." Constable Lloyd must be getting tired of me.

"Arrgh. I'm really not the right person to do anything. As you can tell, Derek and I don't speak anymore." I really don't like where this conversation is heading.

"I know. It just might be nice for him to have someone with him when he wakes up. I left a message with the housekeeper to have the Stanfords contact me if they call home, but until they do, you're all he's got. You are his I.C.E. contact." Constable Lloyd is laying it on thick and yes, I do feel a bit guilty; I did envision, on more than one occasion, Derek being run down by a concrete truck. Arrgh. Maybe I'm psychic, or wait, maybe all the awful things I think will end up coming true! I must think of some particularly nasty rash to wish upon Marc.

"Okay. Where is he again?" I write down the information that Constable Lloyd gives me. The absolute last thing I want to do is sit vigil by The Bastard's hospital bed but I can't ignore the fact I am his I.C.E. as Constable Lloyd so helpfully pointed out. Constable Lloyd missed his calling; he should be on television asking for money to save the children. I thank Constable Lloyd, while silently cursing him, then hang up and fill Mel in.

"She said she'd see him in hell? Oh, she does sound charming." Mel thinks it's as funny as I did.

"I know! Can you imagine saying that to a policeman — oh you can think it, but you shouldn't say it. I wonder if it was her attitude that held her back in the pageant world?" I laugh.

"So you're going to go to the hospital?"

"I don't know. No. I don't want to. What would you do?"

"I'd probably go. It is the right thing to do." Mel is as big a pushover as I am sometimes. "He could be banged up pretty bad. If you were all alone in New York and this happened to you, you'd want someone there, right?"

"Yes. Fine. You're right, but will you come with me? I don't think I can go alone. Not seeing him the first time since, well, since he dumped me for Ms. Congeniality."

"Sure. I have an open house at one o'clock this afternoon but I'll stay with you until lunchtime."

# 52

I hate hospitals. If you're at a hospital it's generally for a bad reason. The only good thing that happens at hospitals is a baby being born; everything else falls into the "something went very, very badly" category.

Mel and I find The Bastard's room but I almost walk back out when I see him because he doesn't look like The Bastard I remember. He is hooked up to every machine possible, he has two nasty cuts, one across his forehead and one down his cheek that have been stitched, his face is very swollen and his hair is matted with dried blood. Mel and I are both speechless.

"Makes the whole Jetta incident look like a walk in the park, doesn't it?" I finally say quietly to Mel.

"Okay, this is bad. I can see why Constable Lloyd was so anxious to get someone here," Mel whispers back to me.

"Well, what am I supposed to do now that I *am* here?"

"Just be supportive I guess. I think people in comas can hear you. Talk to him." Mel saw that in a movie; I'm sure she hasn't been brushing up on medical journals.

"Well, I don't think I have anything to say that he wants to hear, or that I can say out loud in a hospital! Don't they frown on profanity here?" I am completely stressed out. The idea of making one-sided small talk to the man who dumped me seven months ago isn't very appealing.

"Okay, point. We'll just talk normally and he can listen. We won't mention your panties or the Sex with the Single Ex thing though — it might give him subliminal ideas." Mel is actually serious about the last part.

"You are just too funny!" I start to laugh. If anyone were watching us, huddled by the doorway, whispering about what to talk about in front of a man in a coma, they would laugh. "Fine, we'll just act normal, whatever that means!"

"So, how are you today, Bastard?" Mel asks in a louder but awkward voice.

"He's in a coma, that's how he is! And we probably shouldn't call him that because he won't know who we're talking to." I smack Mel on the arm and give her my best what-the-hell? look.

"Okay, you do better!"

"Hey *Derek*, well you look like hell!" I say as I walk closer to his bed.

"Oh yeah, that's better!" Mel smacks me back as she joins me near the bed.

I continue talking to Derek and telling him what happened to him accidentwise — well, what I know about the accident. Mel says she will investigate it further. There must have been something on the news, which neither of us watched yesterday. I mention to Derek that his wife seems to be a catch, might as well get the sarcasm out of my system while he's comatose. I would smack him, just for being an idiot and dumping me, but I can't find one bit of arm that isn't completely bruised. The smacking will have to wait until he's feeling better. Mel and I actually get used to the idea of talking around a comatose man and we discuss what Mel's doing today at work, how things are going with Sebring III and the fact that gas prices seem completely insane. Mel has to leave around noon and I give her the please-don't-leave-me look, but Mel, always prepared, pulls Helen Fielding's *Bridget Jones's Diary* and a half-empty box of After Eight mints out of her Prada bag and hands them to me.

"Here, I grabbed these at your place when you were getting dressed." Mel is so much more prepared than I am.

"Thank you!" I have never been so happy to see a book I've read fifteen times, and my joy about the mints goes without saying.

"You should read out loud to him. That way he'll hear your voice and you won't be saying mean things to him. Might help you keep things on a happier note."

"Okay. I'll call you later and let you know how things are going. I think I have to have my cell phone off in here with all these machines. The cell phone can't be good for them. I'll slip outside and call you this afternoon." I am sorry to see Mel leave and hope nothing bad happens to Derek while I'm here alone. I wonder if there has been any contact with his parents yet. Surely they will get here soon.

After Mel leaves I spend four hours reading out loud to

Derek. I'm not sure if *Bridget Jones* is actually something Derek would normally read, but let's face it, he's hardly in a position to complain. I for one am glad that Mel picked a book I've read before. My concentration being what it is these days, I don't think I could have managed *The Famished Road* which I have been meaning to read for ages. If Derek doesn't wake up soon I may go through my whole bookcase.

Two different nurses come into Derek's room on separate occasions. I ask a few questions but the common answer seems to be "no one knows anything for sure until he wakes up" and "no one knows when that might happen." I need to stretch so go outside for a few minutes around five o'clock. I also need a drink of some sort so endeavour to find a soda machine. I step outside into the cool air, and it feels refreshing after the stuffy hospital room. I call Mel and give her the update, which is basically no change. I then call Derek's parents' house; Mel looked the number up in the phonebook for me before we left the condo this morning. I get the housekeeper and after a very long discussion, of which I'm not sure how much she understood, I finally get a cell phone number for the Stanfords. I try the number but it's "out of service area." I wonder just how far north they are and if they'll ever get back into a service area. I don't suppose polar bears need a service area, since they probably can't dial with their large clumsy paws; they do well to hold Coke bottles on the Coke commercials but I'm sure they can't use cell phones.

When I walk back into Derek's room it finally hits me.

This situation is very serious. Derek has been unconscious for almost twenty-four hours; he might never wake up, or he might have brain damage or he could die. I don't love Derek anymore but the realization I'm the only one here for him makes me suddenly very nauseous and I have to sit down and put my head between my legs. I vow not to vomit. Firstly, this is no time for a weak stomach. Secondly, the thought of vomiting After Eight dinner mints and Coke Classic, the only two things in my stomach since a bagel this morning, hardly seems appealing. I gather my composure, or what I can of it, and pick up *Bridget Jones's Diary* again. By reading out loud to Derek I can get my mind off the seriousness of the situation. I read into the night and when I finally come up for air it's after ten and I'm exhausted. Exhaustion from worry and doing nothing is much worse than exhaustion from physical labour. A part of me wants to go home, crawl into my bed and never surface but I can't. I really can't leave Derek here all alone. What if he wakes up? How awful would it be to wake up and no one is here to tell you what the hell happened to you? I suppose he might remember being hit by a concrete truck but if I were him, I'd block that memory. I turn on my cell and redial Derek's parents, but they are still out of service area. I turn the cell back off and pull my chair over to Derek's bed and look up at his poor cut-up face. His eyelashes are still lovely and long. I silently hope he wakes up soon, then put my head down on the bed beside his arm, just for a few minutes.

# 53

I wake up at seven o'clock the next morning and I'm very stiff. Sleeping sitting up is not a good idea. I rub my neck and shoulders and look at Derek. Absolutely no change; he looks exactly like he did when I put my head down last night.

"Please just wake up! Please! This is getting ridiculous now!" I squeeze Derek's hand. "I promise I won't yell at you for being a complete idiot. I promise. Just wake up!"

Arrgh. No response. I have to stretch so I head outside and walk down the street to a coffee shop. I turn on my cell phone and try Derek's parents again; still no service area. I then call Joyce's voicemail at work and explain the situation and ask her to tell Mr. Sebring that I'll be away for a few days and that I will call her later. I then call Peter Peterson, because I have no idea who to call in New York, and explain to Pete what happened and ask him to contact the right people in New York to let them know about Derek. I leave Pete my cell phone number and tell him to call me if he needs any further information. I buy a coffee and a bagel and sit down at the coffee shop. I can't go back to Derek's room just yet. I must look a mess and I suspect my twenty-four-hour deodorant, which never lasts more than twelve hours despite all the advertising hype, is failing wretchedly at this point. On the way back to the hospital I stop at a twenty-four-hour drugstore and buy three bottles of water, some deodorant and a magazine. *Bridget Jones's Diary* is almost finished and I need something to read out loud to Derek. I'm not sure Derek is a *Cosmo* reader, but what the heck, he's a Bridget Jones fan now so he probably likes *Cosmo*. I try Derek's parents again just before I get back to the hospital, but still no luck. How many polar bears can one couple save? Or whatever it is they are doing with them.

By nine o'clock Monday night, I've finished *Bridget Jones's Diary*, read *Cosmo* cover to cover including the advertising, given Derek a vivid description of all the sexy women in the advertisements, read the ingredients and nutritional information on the water bottles and let Derek smell the deodorant. I'm completely stir crazy and at a particularly low point in the day around three o'clock in the afternoon I yell at Derek to "just wake up already." I still feel a bit bad about that — it's not his fault he's in a coma, or I don't think it's his fault. He'd better not be pretending or I'll kick his butt. At nine thirty, one of the nurses comes into Derek's room and suggests that I might want to go home tonight. She promises if anything changes she will call me immediately. I have to agree she has a point. Me pacing around Derek's room covered in two days of sweat is probably not good for anyone. I don't want to make the sick people sicker. I confirm the nurse's station has both my phone numbers and I start home.

I jump in a cab because the thought of waiting for the sub-way is too much to bear. When I get out of the cab at the condo, I'm wondering what food I have in the house. My stomach started growling on the way home and I realize that I am quite hungry. I guess it'll be the ice cream Mel brought over on Saturday night. Saturday night seems like it was forever ago.

I'm digging for my keys outside the building when I hear "Hi Kit" coming from the shadow of the pillar beside me and I let out a scream.

"For heaven's sake, Marc! You *have* to stop doing that! What is *wrong* with you?" My patience for Marc and his antics is at an all-time low.

"Sorry." Marc reaches out and touches my arm but I take a step back.

"What are you doing here?" I'm hungry and tired and smelly, and dealing with Marc is the last thing I want to do.

"John told me what happened and I wanted to make sure you're all right and if there's anything I can do?"

"Charlie Brown has a big mouth and if you are serious about doing something you can go to Wendy's and get me a bacon cheeseburger. I'm absolutely starving and I have no food." I don't know where *that* came from. I shouldn't ask Marc to do anything for me, especially in light of having been stood up for a second time. I suppose my stomach worked my brain on that one and I honestly don't have the energy to fight with Marc right now.

"Absolutely. I'll be back in a few minutes." Marc squeezes my arm and starts to walk away. "Do you want fries with that?"

"Surprise me," I yell over my shoulder as I enter the lobby of my building.

Half an hour later, Marc buzzes from the front door right after I've had the most amazing shower and donned my yoga pants and a t-shirt. I don't think I appreciated the body shower fully until today. I could honestly feel some of the tension melting away. I've just hung up the phone from hearing that Mr. and Mrs. Stanford are still in the middle of the bush somewhere when Marc comes in and hands me a Wendy's bag and a Coke.

"Thanks. I appreciate this even though I still think you're a complete ass." I take the bag from Marc and sit down on the couch and break into the burger.

"How's what's-his-name?" Marc asks but winks at me so I can tell he's just being funny with the what's-his-name part.

"Still the same. He just won't wake up," I say, then take another bite of burger. I can honestly say I've never enjoyed a burger as much as I'm enjoying this one. I take some fries as well — Marc pulled through with the fries. I would have been fine without them but they are very tasty.

"He will. I'm sure he'll be fine in no time." Marc is being overly optimistic in my mind but I hope he's right.

"How long were you lurking outside my building?" It has just dawned on me it's almost ten o'clock in the evening.

"A while. I worked late then came over. I would have given up by eleven," Marc states matter-of-factly. I don't venture a comment. At this point I have no idea what makes Marc tick; he stands outside my building for hours waiting to see me but doesn't show up for scheduled dates. There is no figuring this guy out and I'm way too tired to try tonight.

"I want to explain last Friday to you," Marc continues talking as I continue chewing.

"I *really* don't care," I say in-between bites. "You don't show when you're supposed to but you show when I don't want you here. You obviously have some personality disorder but that's between you and your therapist. I'd much rather be left out of it altogether."

"I probably should see a therapist," Marc laughs.

"Don't laugh, you *should*." I try to emphasize the "should" but I think my point gets lost because my mouth is partially full of burger.

"I wanted to take you out for dinner, I did. I do!" Marc starts his explanation and I just roll my eyes at him. "I have been absolutely, wholeheartedly in love with you since the first time I saw you. I have never felt this way about anyone. Ever. Not my wife, not my first girlfriend. No one. But for the past year and a half you've been telling me that you can't date me and that you'll break my heart, so when it comes time to pick you up for a real date, I panic. I absolutely cannot make myself come to your door. Both times I made it to the street but I parked down the block. I couldn't get out of the truck." Marc takes a break, presumably because he realizes how ridiculous this sounds. "Can I have a beer?"

"Knock your socks off," I answer and Marc walks to the fridge. "Okay, let me get this straight. You sort of show up, you park down the street and you don't call. This doesn't make any sense. You asked me out, it's not as if I'm making you take me out." I think I preferred not knowing what is going on in Marc's convoluted, confused little brain.

"I know. I know it sounds crazy. Hell, it probably is crazy. I can't date you because if I date you and we get together we might break up and if we break up, my heart will break and I don't think I'll be able to recover. I know I won't recover. Losing you would be worse than never having you at all." Marc has obviously thought this out but his logic seems slightly askew.

"Work with me here, I'm not completely understanding this. You *love* me more than *anything* but you can't date me in case we break up sometime down the road, be it tomorrow or fifteen years from now?" My head is aching.

"Exactly. You told me you'd break my heart more than once." Marc seems stuck on a statement I made months ago.

"I also said I was getting a sex change and that I had a brain tumour with only six months to live — it was just a game. As far as I know, I'm still a woman and I don't have a brain tumour, or I didn't before we started this conversation."

"I know it was a game, but you were right. I love you way more than you love me. If there's a heart that's going to break in this it's mine. I've never had my heart broken but I know

I won't survive if *you* break it." Marc means what he's saying even though it makes absolutely no sense to me.

"Don't be ridiculous, everyone has had a broken heart. But forget about that. What if we get together and no one breaks anyone's heart? What if we can actually make it work and have a great life together?"

"I know, that's what I am thinking every time I ask you out, but then, the more I think about it, the more the breakup scenario hit home. Neither of us has ever been in a relationship that worked. My marriage worked for almost twenty years but then it failed. I think with our track records we're destined to fail." Marc's logic, or lack of it, is astounding.

"Okay, track records being what they are, maybe you have a point, but are you going to be fine with me dating other people and eventually getting married and having a dozen kids with someone who's not you?" I ask as the memory of the Vera Wang blouse day rushes to the front of my brain.

"No, of course I'm not going to be okay with that!" Marc comes back defensively, "but I'm going to have to live with it, aren't I?"

"Yes you will and I *am* going to go on with my life. I'm not going to stay your single friend forever — God, I hope I'm not your single friend forever." The thought of Marc and me as two grey-hairs drinking beer and punching each other in the arms at the Firkin comes to mind and sends a shudder up my spine.

"I know, but I'll be happy being your friend for as long as

it lasts." Marc finally says something I can understand. I know he loves me. I know every time I look at my wrist and see the TAG and every time I open the door to this condo. I wouldn't have a credit rating at this point without Marc. Marc's friendship has been as important in my world as Mel's has and I can't imagine my life without him in it, even in a small way. Maybe he's right that we shouldn't date. Why spoil a perfectly good friendship? Lovers come and go and get hit by concrete trucks, maybe one good friend is way more important than all the lovers in a lifetime.

"Well, if you stop jumping out of the shadows and scaring the wits out of me, we'll have a better chance of staying friends." I smile at Marc as I gather up my fast-food wrappers and start toward the kitchen. "I need a beer after all this. Do you want another one?"

# 54

I wake up super early, have another shower and tame my hair. I don't want to scare Derek into another coma if he does wake up. I grab a couple of books from the bookshelf, my trusty new deodorant and my freshly charged cell phone. I decide to drive to the hospital in case it's another late night. I stop at the convenience store for some bottled water and a Coke Classic and try Derek's parents again, to no avail. I'm starting to wonder about Derek's mother. Don't mothers have "mother's intuition"? Surely she must sense something is wrong with her only child! Can the polar bears be more important than the son she bore from her loins? Okay, now I'm thinking about Mrs. Stanford's loins. Shudder. I just have to stay focused on the job at hand, which is reading out loud to a man I don't even like who is in a coma. Honestly, does stuff like this happen to other people? I've never overheard a conversation on the subway in which one person says, "Guess what happened to me?" and goes on to explain that her ex-boyfriend is in a coma and she spends days reading to him, or who says "Hey, the guy who loves me can't date me because we might break up someday." These things just don't happen to normal people. Maybe I need therapy like Marc.

I'm in Derek's room just before 9 a.m. When I see him, after I've had a good night's sleep, he looks better. I'm not sure if I'm imagining it or if it's real, but he looks like he has more colour, the cuts look less nasty and the swelling in his face seems to have gone down. I decide that even in his coma he probably feels grimy — I know I did after a couple of days in the hospital. I get a facecloth and fill the sink in his room with water. I might as well try to get some of the dried blood out of his hair, carefully, of course, since it is his head that has him stuck in coma-land.

After I get the grime off Derek I sit down to start *The Edge of Reason*. I'm sure Derek can't wait to hear what other mishaps Bridget gets herself into; besides, I'm picking the books here. If he doesn't like it he can damn well wake up and tell me he doesn't like it. *Please wake up!* I've stopped calling Derek The Bastard, even in my mind. I'm still mad at him but I think ultimately calling someone who's in a coma The Bastard is pretty much just asking for an express ticket on the train to hell.

We're ten pages into Bridget's next adventure when I hear a light knock on Derek's open door. I turn around and it's a policeman. I stand up as Constable Lloyd introduces himself. I shake Constable Lloyd's hand and say it's a pleasure to meet him, which might be true under completely different circumstances, like at the policeman's ball or at crossing-guard school. The reason Constable Lloyd and I are in the same small hospital room is not a good one.

"Good book choice," Constable Lloyd laughs, "my wife's read that book ten times."

"Yes, I decided it was time Derek got a better appreciation for Bridget Jones. I'm hoping he doesn't like it enough to wake up and tell me so." I try to keep it light.

"These are Mr. Stanford's effects from his car, you know, the Saab?" Constable Lloyd smiles.

"Oh yes, the Saab." I take the banker's box from Constable Lloyd.

"The Saab is a writeoff but the plates are in the box," Constable Lloyd explains as I pop the top off the box and see the plates that read "TIFS CR." "So we can probably assume that Mr. Stanford still doesn't like Saabs."

"Also explains where he was going; he must have been on his way to hell to return it to her," I laugh, then realize what I've said and cover my mouth.

"Don't worry about it, I know what you meant," Constable Lloyd laughs again. "How's our guy doing?"

"The same. I'm hoping *The Edge of Reason* snaps him out of it. If that doesn't do it, I'll have to break out the Jane Austen and no man deserves that. I've been trying his parents' cell phone repeatedly but no luck yet," I explain to Constable Lloyd.

"That's one of the reasons I came by. I finally spoke to his mother. Apparently she called home to remind the housekeeper about a vet appointment for one of the cats and the housekeeper had her call me. Mrs. Stanford is going to be on a plane tomorrow morning and will be here by tomorrow evening," Constable Lloyd explains.

"Oh thank God! I was starting to think I'd never reach them." I feel tears welling up in relief.

"You did well." Constable Lloyd pats my shoulder.

"No, I didn't really do anything but sit and worry." I try to laugh through my tears.

"You read him *Bridget Jones*, that's a book he would never have picked up on his own."

"Good point, maybe I can win over more men in comas."

After Constable Lloyd leaves I get back to *The Edge of Reason*. I want to finish it before Derek's mother arrives. I don't want to leave him hanging, wondering what happened to Bridget, because I plan to return to work as soon as I've handed over the vigil reins.

I get through the best part of the book before Mel walks into the room around six o'clock. She's carrying a Harvey's bag and I could just kiss her. I'm starving again but didn't want to leave Derek's room.

"He looks better; you cleaned up his hair." Mel notices my grime-busting.

"Yeah, crunchy hair can't be comfortable, even in a coma," I say as I unwrap the burger. I don't think I've ever had so many burgers in one week.

Mel and I chat while I eat my dinner. I fill her in on the late night visit from Marc and explain my understanding of "Marc and I never dating."

"Okay, that's just funny. John called me today and told me that Marc was in an exceptionally good mood so he guessed Marc had spoken to you," Mel laughs.

"Well, he's nothing if not transparent."

Mel tells me about an offer she put in today and I fill her in on Derek's mother finally arriving tomorrow. Mel stays for about an hour and I get back to reading to Derek. I stay until ten o'clock. I call Joyce's voicemail and tell her that I will be back to work on Thursday provided Mrs. Stanford arrives on schedule.

The next day I'm at the hospital by nine o'clock in the morning and have finished *The Edge of Reason* by eleven. After I finish Bridget's tale I realize how tired I am and how sore my throat is. I've been reading out loud for more than three days. That can't be good for you. I suddenly have a new appreciation for schoolteachers who have to talk all the time. I get up to refill my water bottle with tap water; it's not my first choice but I don't want to leave Derek's room in case his mother arrives. I'd hate for her to walk in and find him all alone. As I'm filling the bottle I notice a movement in my peripheral vision that is coming from Derek. I think he moved his hand. I drop the bottle and leave the tap running and rush to Derek's side.

"Derek, can you hear me?" I'm sure I saw something but he appears to be lying exactly as he was. I guess my eyes are finally playing tricks on me, but what can I expect, I've been drinking Toronto tap water all day. I return to the sink and fill my bottle then settle back down on the chair and stare intently at Derek's hand. I'm sure something moved but I don't want to get a nurse because they'll think I've finally cracked under the pressure, or maybe I *have* finally cracked. Either way, I don't want that to be the consensus. I reach out and start picking up Derek's fingers one at a time and letting them drop, maybe I can get him to move again and prove to myself that I'm not losing it.

"Just wake *up!*" I moan as I look up at Derek's eyes, which are looking back me. Derek's eyes are open. Mother of Pearl! I've been willing him to wake up for days but now that he's looking at me with his clear blue eyes, which appear to have not been harmed in the accident, I'm not quite sure what I should do.

"Oh my God! Oh my God. Don't say anything!" I say to Derek; he probably can't anyway, I decide. "Can you hear me?" I am practically jumping with excitement and I perceive a slight nod from Derek.

"Okay! You stay right here — well, not that you can go anywhere — and I'll get someone," I say over my shoulder as I sprint out of Derek's room and down the hall to the nurse's station. There are two nurses at the station and one follows me back to Derek's room and the other one gets on the phone to find Derek's doctor. Once the nurse is with Derek I just stand back. The second nurse joins us and starts making arrangements to get Derek moved for a CAT scan. Within thirty minutes Derek has been taken downstairs and

I've called Mel and Peter to let them know that Derek woke up. I'm gathering up the books and cleaning up the water bottles when Mrs. Stanford arrives.

"Where is he? Where is he?" Mrs. Stanford says to the empty bed more than to me.

"He woke up! Don't worry, they just took him to get a CAT scan. He will be back soon. He just woke up, not even an hour ago." I touch Mrs. Stanford's shoulder and try to reassure her.

"Kathryn? What are you doing here?" Mrs. Stanford has just realized who I am.

"Oh, my phone number was in Derek's cell phone so they called me to come and be with him until you could get here," I explain without going into too much detail. I have no idea what Mrs. Stanford knows about Derek's marital woes.

"Where's Tiffany?" Mrs. Stanford asks innocently, so I have to assume Derek hasn't mentioned any of those woes to her.

"She's still in New York, she couldn't get away." I think it's prudent not to mention the "see him in hell" part; no mother wants to hear that sort of thing about her daughter-in-law.

"Oh, that's strange," Mrs. Stanford doesn't elaborate and I don't encourage her to.

I stay with Mrs. Stanford until Derek gets back a couple of hours later. The doctor is with Derek and tells Mrs. Stanford that it looks as though Derek is going to make a full recovery. Derek is able to answer simple questions, but seems to have some memory loss from just before the accident. I feel incredibly uncomfortable now that Derek is awake. I haven't seen him since two weeks before he dumped me over the phone. Seeing him awake brings back a flood of feelings I'm not prepared to deal with in a hospital room while standing beside his mother. I stay until there is a break in conversation with the doctor and then say my goodbyes. As I'm walking out the door I hear Derek ask his mother, "Mom, have I ever been in prison in Thailand?"

I return to work the next day and am relieved the hospital vigil is over. Work is easy compared to sitting in a hospital room talking to myself. I call Rob and meet him for lunch. I tell him about the last couple of days and Derek's near miss.

Derek calls me to thank me for the vigil; apparently the nurses filled him in on my being there day and night. He asks me to come and see him at his parents' house once he's discharged but, as glad as I am he's alive and making a full recovery, I tell him that we won't be socializing. I also suggest he reprogram his phone and remove me as his I.C.E. contact. I'm hardly the one who should be called for such emergencies. All in all though, I think I'm making huge strides in the Derek department. Not long ago I wanted him dead and today I'm honestly glad he's alive. I think I'm growing as a human being. Oh, I'm no Mother Teresa, but one of the lesser-known saints maybe. I'll have to ask Mel which saint she thinks I'm most resembling these days. Mel took World Religions at university so she is the most qualified to figure these things out.

After work I meet Mel, Charlie Brown and Marc at the Firkin for a beer and some nachos for dinner because I still haven't picked up groceries with all the drama that's been going on. I tell them about my breakthrough of wanting Derek to live and ask Mel which saint she thinks I most resemble.

"Without a doubt you resemble Saint Arnold. He's the patron saint of beer." I look down at my glass, which contains my second beer of the evening and I have to agree with Mel on this one.

# 55

By the end of November my life is back on an even keel. I'm fully recovered from being dumped for a ditzy debutante but have to admit that process accelerated after I found out Derek married badly. I have food in my refrigerator, other than After Eight dinner mints, and Marc and I are friends who don't speak of dating each other anymore. Derek called a few times while he was in Toronto recovering and I was civil to him but made it clear I do not want to rekindle any sort of relationship with him, including friendship. Derek returned to New York in the middle of November. Rob still has abs of steel and we occasionally have sex after we've seen a great band, and sometimes even after a not-so-great band. My leg is back to normal, or as normal as it probably ever will be, and I'm running longer distances. I'm planning to run the half-marathon in Ottawa in May. My birthday is just around the corner and I've threatened Mel with her life if she plans any surprises. I just want to go to the Firkin with the usual group and have nachos and beer and follow the teachings of my mentor Saint Arnold. My wants are simple and I hope my life stays the same.

I meet Mel for lunch on Thursday and I tell her I won't be

around for the Firkin on Friday because Tia sent me a parcel she wants me to take to Ben when he's setting up for a Kevin show tomorrow after work. Tia and Ben are still dating long-distance and Tia is planning to move to Toronto in the spring when she's finished her course in Kingston. The parcel for Ben is wrapped so I don't know what is in it.

"I'm away Friday as well, at a course in Niagara. I'm not back until late Saturday. What about tonight?" Mel asks.

"Marc is taking me to the hockey game. I'm actually excited. I haven't been to one in ages."

"But it's not a date, right?" Mel laughs.

"No! It is absolutely not a date," I laugh and we both continue together, "because dating might lead to a breakup!" As much as Marc and I don't talk about dating or not dating, Mel and I get endless mileage out of the "might break up" rationale.

Later at the game, Marc seems nervous. He is visibly agitated and jumpy. It's actually making me a little uncomfortable. I'm sure he wants to tell me he's dating someone or something similar but he won't come out and say anything. I've asked him three times if he's okay or if he needs to tell me something and he keeps saying no, so I guess it's just Marc being weird; he does have a precarious mental condition. The game is a sleeper. The Leafs are losing 4 to 0 halfway through the third period so I suggest to Marc that if he wants to we can leave early but he says no, he wants to stay until the end. Which seems strange but his whole demeanour is strange today so I just shrug my shoulders and go with the flow.

The most entertaining part of tonight's game is a Leafs fan sitting two rows behind us who is watching the game through his oversized army-camouflage binoculars and is heckling the players. His advice to the players includes things like "Okay, warm-up's been over for a while ladies, let's get the puck now" and "Let's go! It's time to earn your millions, you lazy bums!" He actually even makes Marc laugh despite the fact Marc is so obviously preoccupied. With eight minutes left in the game, the score is still 4 to 0 for the Thrashers, not the Leafs obviously, and Marc turns to me very seriously and stares at me. I'm trying to watch the game but have to look at him because his staring is making me uncomfortable.

"What?" I have the uncomfortable feeling you get when you're watching a horror movie and one of the group says "I'm just going to go outside and look around."

"You know I love you, right?" Marc says completely seriously.

"Oh God, not this again. Enough already!"

"I have to ask you something but I don't want you to answer. I'm leaving tomorrow to go snowmobiling up north for the weekend and I won't be back until Tuesday. I don't want you to answer until then, okay?" Marc is so melodramatic sometimes. I swear he and Mel went to the same drama queen school.

"Okay. Sure. Whatever!" If he asks me out on a date again I'm going to kill him and that will throw my newfound sainthood into question.

"No really, promise me you'll think about it until Tuesday."

"I promise," I say out loud but right now, this instant, I'm thinking "drama queen" in my head.

"I wanted to ask you this after the Leafs scored but it looks like they aren't about to so I don't want the fact that the Leafs are scoreless tonight to influence your decision. The Leafs' losing is not an omen." Marc is nervous talking now and looks at me with the raised eyebrow, so he seems to want me to respond.

"Okay, the Leafs being losers will not affect my decision on whatever you are going to ask me. They haven't won a cup in my lifetime. I think I can handle this one small loss." I now suspect Marc is going to ask me to another game so I have no idea what all the drama is about.

"Will you marry me?" Marc has produced an open blue-velvet ring box from his pocket that contains the most stunning emerald-cut solitaire I've ever seen. The diamond is well over a carat in size, or I guess it to be with my less-than-experienced eye, and it's set in white gold.

"Pull up your panties ladies, it's time to play some real hockey!" The word *pull* is out of the heckler's mouth just as Marc says "me."

I want to laugh at the heckler, because this is his best line all night, but suspect this is no time for levity. My mouth is instantly dry so I take a gulp of my beer.

"Don't answer, because I know this is sudden." Marc tries to hand me the ring box.

"I'm not taking that. I'll think about the question but I'm not taking that *thing*." I back away from the ring as if it's a snake.

"You have to take it. It's part of the question." Marc's staggering logic is again fascinating me.

"No. Questions are words not things. I am not taking responsibility for an expensive piece of jewellery at a Leafs game." I am seriously having nothing to do with that ring or even the empty box for that matter.

"Okay, I'll keep the ring until I get you back to the condo, but you have to keep it for the weekend because I'm loading my snowmobile tonight and I'll lose it for sure."

"Whatever! Can we go now?" I am suddenly overwhelmed and very confused. I don't say anything as Marc and I make our way through the throngs of people at the Air Canada Centre and outside to his truck.

"I don't get it. You can't date me but you want to *marry* me?" I say as soon as the truck doors slam shut.

"I know. It sounds crazy, well sort of..." Marc starts.

"Sort of, my ass, it *is* crazy!" I cut him off.

"Just hear me out. I can't date you because you'll break my heart but if we get married you won't leave me, therefore you won't break my heart." Marc's logic is completely convoluted and if I didn't know him better I'd suspect serious drug abuse.

"Marc, people divorce every day. *You're* divorced! What is it...half of all marriages that fail?"

"We *won't* fail. I know we won't fail." Mr. Drama Queen has suddenly become Mr. Overly Confident.

"Marc, you can't show up for a dinner date. I'm not holding out much hope that you'd actually show up at a church to marry my ass." I honestly believe getting Marc to a church would be infinitely harder than getting him to Fred's Not Here for dinner, that's just common sense. There's food and beer at a restaurant.

"I promise I'll show up. I want this. I really like your ass. I *want* to marry your *ass*." Marc is being sort of funny and he seems sincere, but he seemed sincere when he asked me out for dinner as well.

"Okay, this wonderful wedding that you've planned aside, we haven't been on one date, *and* a bigger issue, we've never had sex. Marrying someone I haven't dated would be crazy, but marrying someone I don't even know if I'm sexually compatible with would be *completely* insane." I've got him with this argument. If Marc can't show up for dinner, he's not going to show up for sex.

"We'll figure all that out. I promise. I know that if we are getting married I'll be able to finally be 'normal' around you and we'll date and do all that normal stuff. It won't work though unless we have some sort of commitment."

"*Someone* should be committed! How long have you been thinking about this?" I ask. A logic this warped must have taken a great deal of time to formulate.

"Since I explained to you why I can't date you. It sounded

better in my head than when I said it out loud to you. I've been trying to come up with a compromise and I think this is it."

"Well, it's one hell of a compromise and you are one strange little man!" I suddenly have a very large headache and can't wait to get home to my bed.

# 56

I wake up and thank all the angels and saints that Marc is gone for the weekend. Thank you Saint Arnold! All I have to do is get through today at work, drop Ben's parcel off and then I can hide out until tomorrow when Mel gets back. Mel will help me figure this Marc thing out.

"Hey handsome," I say to Rob as I walk into the coffee shop before work.

"Hey you, I was hoping to see you. What are you doing after work?" Rob asks.

"Why, do you have something fun planned?"

"Well, sort of. I leave tonight at nine for that conference in South Carolina, but I'd love to see you before I go. I won't be here for your birthday so I'd like to take you out for dinner."

"Sure, I have to drop a package off to Ben, but I can do that after you leave for the airport."

"Great. Can you come to my office after work?"

"Absolutely. Your office by six, is that okay?"

"Perfect," Rob leans down and kisses me on the lips. Odd. He doesn't usually kiss me in public. I guess he just got carried away. He must have a lot on his mind getting ready for the conference.

The day progresses quite normally after Rob's kiss. Everything else happens as it should and I manage to get caught up on the filing. After I file the last document from the pile that was over a foot tall, I give myself the arm pump and a quiet "yay for me." Having all the filing completed on a Friday afternoon always makes for a happier Monday. Joyce packs up at five o'clock and I tell her to have a great weekend. I'm not meeting Rob until six so I sit down and start to respond to some emails, ignoring the ten from Derek. He is becoming a pain. I'm delving into email when Joyce comes back into my office and hands me a package.

"This was outside the door. I guess the courier didn't know enough to knock or try the handle," Joyce laughs and raises her hand to wave as she walks back toward the door. "Goodbye again."

"Goodbye. Have a great weekend," I shout after her.

I inspect the package. It's addressed to me and it's from Derek's firm in New York. *Arrgh*.

I unwrap the brown outer paper of a package about the size of a small shoebox, and inside, the box is wrapped in beautiful silver paper and has a note on the top that reads "Thank you so much for standing by me when I was in the hospital. Derek."

Okay, that's nice. Oh, maybe it's a nice scarf! I was just thinking this morning I need a new scarf. I hope it's not a joke gift like a stethoscope and a bunch of tongue depressors. I unwrap the silver paper and take the top off the box. The contents are wrapped in tissue paper and there's another note.

*Dear Kit,*

[Derek has recently taken my nickname to a new level and uses it ALL the time]

*On the day of the car accident I was in Toronto because I was coming to see you. My intention was to tell you how much I love you and how sorry I am for what happened last spring. I don't know why I did what I did. The only explanation I can offer is that I was completely overwhelmed with the transfer and long distance. What I did does not change how I felt for you at the time or how I feel for you now. I knew immediately after I was married that I'd made the biggest mistake of my life when I broke up with you. My marriage has been dissolved and I would be honoured if you would give us another chance. Please accept the enclosed as an indication of my love for you and how serious I am about making your life everything you've ever dreamed of.*

*Love always, Derek*

After I read the note, I'm fairly sure there isn't a scarf in the box. I slowly peel back the tissue and it reveals white Styrofoam popcorn. Okay. Popcorn works. I'm hesitant to put my hand in the popcorn but my curiosity will win out eventually so there's no time like the present for a present. I reach in and feel around, maybe he forgot to put it in. I finally feel something in the last corner I check. I pull it out to reveal a red-velvet jewellery box. I close my eyes and say quietly,

"Please be earrings! Please be earrings!" I open the box and half turn my head because I don't want to know. A note falls out that reads "Please say yes and make me the happiest man in the world."

Inside the box is a breathtaking diamond engagement ring. It has a pear-cut centre diamond, roughly the size of a small doorknob, with two rows of tapered baguette-cut diamonds on each side. I realize as I look at it that I've never seen anything so sparkly. Not even the champagne Mel pulls out of her Prada briefcase. I make the mistake of trying it on. It is even more fantastic on. As I'm looking at it and turning my hand so I can see it sparkle I suddenly get a nauseating thought, "*Ewww*, what if this is Tiffy's ring?" *Ewww*. I can't get it off and back in the box fast enough. It is stunning, so surely something Tiffy might have demanded. I find the note that fell out when I opened the box and start to put it back when I notice writing on the back of it: "P.S. This is a new ring. No one has ever worn it." I laugh. I guess I have to give Derek credit for knowing me well enough to know I'd wonder about previous owners.

I can't even think about this right now. I look at my watch and it's time to close up the office and meet Rob. I put the ring and the notes in my purse. I'll deal with this later; right now I need a drink. I'll have a great time with Rob and get my mind off the engagement rings that are piling up in what used to be my nice, calm, even-keeled world.

# 57

Dinner is amazing as it always is at Fred's Not Here and Rob is in a great mood. I'm not sure if he's excited about the conference or if he just had a great day at work, but either way it is nice to be with someone who is so upbeat. Rob makes me laugh; being with him is just fun. This is how life is meant to be, I'm sure of it. Rob and I walk out of Fred's Not Here at eight o'clock so it's perfect timing for Rob to have the cab drop me off at the Kevin show and then get home, get his bags and meet the car that is picking him up at nine o'clock to take him to the airport. I love it when a plan works out perfectly.

In the cab, Rob reiterates a story about one of his clients who has a registered therapy St. Bernard named Tinkerbell. Tinkerbell's owners take her to hospitals and convalescent homes to cheer up the people who are sick and in recovery. I didn't see Tinkerbell when I was in the hospital with Derek for three days but I would have welcomed a visit from a St. Bernard with an oxymoron name, so I assume that the therapy works for family members and staff as well as for the patients.

"How long have I known you?" Rob asks right after the Tinkerbell story.

"I don't know? Three years, maybe a little longer, but we didn't actually speak to each other for a lot of that time."

"I know," Rob laughs, "my bad! I wish I'd been in a better place when I first met you. You are exceptional. I've never met anyone like you."

"Do you mean, 'someone who would sacrifice her favourite lipstick in order to write on your mirror' sort of exceptional?" I laugh.

"Yeah, like that."

"Thanks for the compliment, but you don't have to say anything. We're friends again now, so that's the important thing."

"Kit, will you marry me?" Rob asks just as the cab pulls up in front of the Kevin gig.

"*What?*" I am sure I did not just hear what I think I just heard.

"I mean it. You are the person I want to spend the rest of my life with." Rob starts his explanation and I'm sure this is a joke. There is no way this sort of thing happens to anyone, not even me. I start to look around the cab for signs of hidden cameras. I've been set up. This is some crazy candid camera spoof or I'm being "punked" by Aston Kutcher. I'm going to kill Mel. My newly formulated sainthood be damned. This is so *not* funny.

"Kit!" Rob realizes that I'm completely zoned out.

"Sorry Rob… No. What? We aren't even dating." I'm trying to show no reaction so Mel's little punked ploy will backfire and I don't end up embarrassed on national television. I bet the twins are in on it too.

"No, we just *say* we aren't dating. Are you dating anyone else?"

"Well, no. Are you?" I've never really thought about the truth of my Sex with the Single Ex plan. Damn. I have been dating Rob exclusively without acknowledging it. Curses to his six-pack and amazing smile. The plan was so perfect! I suppose it might have worked better if I'd had more than one single ex. I still think it's a solid plan, despite my mismanagement of the whole thing.

"No!" Rob laughs. "Absolutely not! I know a great thing when I have it. I knew it the last time we dated and I kept hoping I'd get my life in order before you found out how screwed up I was, but we both know how that went." Rob pauses for a second and I realize the cab driver is completely enthralled with our discussion. "I finally figured out my life and I promise I'll never do you wrong again. I want to spend my life with you. Please promise me you'll think about it. Just think about it."

"Okay," I say quietly, mostly because I just want to get out of the cab and away from Rob. What Rob says is true. We have technically been dating and I love being with him but this is just too weird. Three marriage proposals in two days is the making of a bad comedy show, not someone's life.

"You should say yes," the cab driver speaks in a thick accent. "That is a really nice man."

"I know. Thank you." I'm on autopilot. I lean over to kiss Rob on the cheek. "Have a super trip and I promise I'll think about it." I think to myself "you have no idea how much I have to think about!"

I jump out of the cab and am opening the door to the club when I hear Rob behind me.

"Kit." I turn and step into the club and Rob steps in behind me.

"Here." Rob tries to hand me a green-velvet ring box or what I assume is a ring box — it's the same size as two other ring boxes I've seen recently. Doesn't anyone give earrings as gifts anymore?

"Why don't you keep that," I say as I step back slightly. "I'm good."

"Don't be silly," Rob laughs and takes my hand and folds my fingers around the box, "in my mind it's already yours." Rob leans down and kisses me.

"See you next week," he kisses me again and turns to leave.

I'm standing just inside the doorway of the club holding a bag with Ben's package in it in one hand and a green-velvet ring box in the other. My head is spinning. This has to be a joke. Right?

I turn my head to look around the club for signs of a camera crew, Ashton Kutcher or Mel, but realize I never told Mel where I was meeting Ben. Maybe this isn't a joke. Maybe it's just a really bad dream, which would make it a nightmare, and would explain my nausea.

As I turn my head I see Kevin walking up to me. I try to smile but I know it doesn't look natural.

"Hey Kit! I thought that was you," Kevin kisses my cheek.

"Hi, Kevin." I try to act normal but I suddenly feel a little bit faint.

"Are you okay? You look a bit pale." Kevin grabs my arm and holds me up, then grabs me around my waist as my knees start to buckle and leads me to a bar stool. After I'm sitting Kevin asks the bartender for a bottle of water, which Kevin opens. My hands are still full, of bag and ring box.

"Here," Kevin takes the bag out of my hand and hands me the bottle of water in the same motion. I take a large drink of water and then nod at the bag Kevin has put on the bar stool beside me and say, "That's from Tia, for Ben. She asked me to drop it by for him. Thanks for the water." I then start to get off the bar stool and leave. All I want to do is be at home in my bed. This day cannot be over soon enough. As I step down from the stool — why bar stools are so bloody tall and awkward will always be a mystery to me — I stumble because I am still a little bit faint.

"Woe up there!" Kevin says and takes my arm again, "I think you should stay sitting for a bit." Then he leads me to a chair across from the bar and gets me sitting again. I immediately lower my head and put it between my knees. I am going to faint. Or vomit. Maybe both. The ring box is still clutched in my hand. Even in my state of lightheadedness I know I don't want whatever is in the box but I don't want to lose it either.

"What'cha got there?" Kevin asks. I lift my head and look up at him and he's pointing at the ring box.

"I don't know," I answer honestly.

"You don't know?"

"Nope."

"Well, maybe you should look and see what it is," Kevin laughs again.

"I don't think I can."

"Do you want me to?"

"No, not really." Again, honesty is probably the best policy and I'm too faint to come up with anything pithy or remotely interesting. Kevin squats down in front of me and lifts my head so I'm looking at him.

"I have to finish setting up. Why don't you come to the stage with me and sit there for a while? You can give the parcel to Ben and I'll feel better knowing you're not fainting in the street."

"Okay," I answer before my brain even considers the question. I suppose I'm not really in good shape to be striking out on my own at this point. Kevin takes the ring box out of my hand and says, "Why don't you put whatever-this-is into your purse so it's safe." On autopilot I do what he suggests, careful not to let the other ring box, which is already in my purse, fall out. I'm really glad I have a purse with a zipper. I can't imagine my paranoia if I had an open-concept purse and was toting around at least one but what in reality is probably *two* very expensive engagement rings.

I walk with Kevin to the stage and try to act as normal as

possible as I give Ben his parcel, which turns out to be a Queen's Class of '07 t-shirt. Ben seems to be thrilled and changes shirts on the spot, then walks away dialling his cell phone. I assume he's calling Tia to thank her. I sit and watch the band set up and start to feel much better. I am fairly confident at this point, because no one has jumped out and said "gotcha" that I am not being punked or on candid camera. My situation is very real and not an elaborate joke. I'm actually impressed, in light of the fact that the past two days are real, I didn't faint or vomit on poor unsuspecting Kevin. I am making strides. First, I achieve potential sainthood and now no vomiting in the presence of three marriage proposals. True, I almost fainted, but that was only almost so it probably doesn't count.

Once the band is set up they start to warm up by playing a couple of their original songs and I am able to sing along because I've heard them enough times to know them. The third song they play Kevin explains to me isn't new but just added to the playlist recently. The song is the lovely ballad with the amazing lyrics Kevin played for me at my birthday last year. At one point it makes the hair on my neck stand up and sends a shiver down my spine, so I know it must be good. Only great songs do that. One of the lines in the chorus, "I could live forever in the memory of your smile," does make me smile. They really are a very talented group of men.

After they practise I decide it's probably time for me to get a cab and go home and I start to put my jacket on.

"Are you leaving, Kit?" Kevin asks.

"Yes. Sorry, I'd love to stay but I'm not really feeling 'myself' right now. I've had an...," I have to pause before I can continue, "...*interesting* day."

"I could sort of tell that. Are you okay to get home on your own?" Kevin is genuinely concerned and it's really sweet.

"I'll just catch a cab and let the driver do all the work."

"Well, you sound better and you do look a bit better. Let me walk you out." Kevin walks me to the front of the club and just before we get to the door he stops and grabs my arm and turns me so I'm looking at him.

"This might be completely out of line but I have to say something. I don't know what's in that box that you had in your hand, but I have a pretty good idea and I just want to say that I hope you don't feel obliged to...," now it's Kevin turn to pause, "...do *anything*. You didn't look like you wanted to have that box in your possession so you probably don't want to do anything...," another pause, "...hasty."

"Thanks, you're probably right," is all I can say.

"Kit, I know I'm not well off so I don't have much to offer financially, but I do think you're amazing and that last song, I wrote it about you. I've had a crush on you since I first met you when you were on the crutches. I would really like the opportunity to get to know you better and maybe take you out for dinner sometime. I know this is probably the absolute wrong time to tell you this, I mean I can guess what's in that box, and I'm sorry but I think that if I don't tell you now I'll never get another chance."

"You wrote that song for me?" Wow. That is absolutely the sweetest thing ever.

"Yeah, and the guys bug me about it too," Kevin laughs. "Here, I want you to hold on to this for me for a couple of days," Kevin places a well-worn high-school graduation ring with a large blue stone in my hand. "You can give it back the next time you see me but I just want you to know that you have options and you don't have to...," Kevin pauses again as if looking for a delicate way to say get married, "...do anything." Kevin leans down and kisses my cheek, then takes my arm and leads me to the sidewalk and hails a cab immediately. Options? If Kevin only knew the half of it, options are all I have and the very thing I'd rather not have. I miss my straightforward life with no options.

"Thanks for this," I hold the ring up. "I will give it back but I will keep it for a couple of days if you don't mind."

"Absolutely not, I want you to keep it. Hey, sometimes not making any decision is the best decision of all," Kevin laughs and waves, then stands on the sidewalk until the cab pulls away.

# 58

"Then I came home, locked the door and turned off the ringer on my phone," I say to Mel who still looks a bit stunned by the whole story.

"So what are you going to do?" Mel asks me seriously.

"Mel, look at me. Do I look like I'm in control of my life and know what I'm going to do?" I give her the "you've got to be kidding" look.

"Sorry. No, of course not. Look at you!" Mel cuts to the chase.

"Thanks, Mel. Tell me again why I love you?"

"Because I'm so cute and don't let you get away with anything." Mel shows no remorse for the "look at you" comment.

"Whatever! Back to the situation at hand." I stand up and start to pace.

"Okay, we can figure this out." I can see Mel's mind churning. "Marc has loved you madly for a very long time, and you admitted that you had feelings for him as well." Mel pauses and looks at me for feedback.

"Yes, but since then he's stood me up, *without* even the decency of a phone call on two separate occasions and told me we can't date...," Mel joins me in saying, "...because dating might lead to a breakup!"

"And don't forget he comes complete with kids so I'd be an instant stepmonster and his mental state is questionable at best."

"Good points." Mel admits that Marc might not be the most stable choice. "Okay, Derek then. You actually did love him and you almost lived together. Hell you baked for *him*!"

"Until he dumped me for the undersexed ditzy debutante."

"Rob. Okay, let's look at Rob. He has managed to pull his life together and still has abs of steel."

"Yes, but he *also* cheated on me. Seems to be a trend." I voice one of the many thoughts I've been mulling over for two full days. Everything Mel is saying I've already thought, argued against, then re-thought.

"Well, maybe none of them are right?" Mel presents yet another option I've also considered.

"Mel, I've been engaged once and I called the wedding off." I sit down in frustration. "I have three engagement rings before me. Three. Do you think if I turn *all* of these offers down I'll ever stand even the remotest chance of getting a *fifth* offer? Some people wait their whole lives for *one* offer of marriage and I've had four! If the pressure were ever on to get married I think it's now." I stand up at this point and walk over to the ring display. "These are all wonderful sweet men whom I love in some way or other. I really think that if I turn all of them down I'm going to end up a very lonely old lady who lives with nothing but cats and regrets."

"Don't be silly," Mel says as she walks to stand beside me

and puts her arm around me, rubbing my shoulder, "you're allergic to cats."

"Mel!"

"Okay, sorry about that. Well, let's look at the rings, then." Mel points at the scratched-up school ring. "That's Kevin's, right?"

"Right."

"I knew he had a crush on you, by the way, but he's the least of your worries right now." Mel then points at the pear-cut diamond with the baguettes that Derek couriered to me, "That one's huge!"

"Yes, it's the one from Derek. I guess he figured he'd better wow with size since he'd couriered the proposal," I explain my thoughts on the doorknob-sized ring.

"Good point, the courier proposal isn't the most romantic. If you were to pick a diamond, what shape would you pick?"

"Princess. I've always wanted a square diamond." I tell Mel the truth, no point holding back now.

"Okay, no princess. So none of them knows you well enough to know that, but then again it isn't really something that comes up, so no harm no foul." Mel points at the blue ring box, "I guess the emerald-cut is the closest to square so if you were going by the ring, you'd pick...?"

"Marc, who I've never had sex with or even gone on a proper date with for that matter."

"Good point, so the marquee diamond," Mel points at the

one-carat marquise solitaire that Rob gave me and continues, "which is my favourite cut by the way, would be the opposite of square and opposites attract. I bet it looks stunning on your finger, have you tried it on?"

"I tried them all on," I admit to Mel. I had to. You can't have three amazing diamond engagement rings on your table for forty-eight hours and not try them on. I'm only human and they are very shiny and distracting.

"Oh, now we're on to something! Which one fit the best? You know, like Cinderella's shoe!" Mel is very animated. She loves to solve puzzles and this is the biggest one she's ever tackled.

"Seems I'm the perfect size six. They all fit perfectly." I have to admit I had the Cinderella theory myself around four o'clock this morning.

"Oh. Well then, that's not going to work." Mel walks over to the counter, retrieves the almost empty wine bottle and pours the last of its contents equally into our glasses. "Well, I understand the wine so early in the morning now. This is a bit of dilemma, isn't it?"

"Yes, it certainly is." I am just as confused as I was on Friday night and all weekend. My head hurts from thinking and my emotions are all over the board. One minute I'm certain that I love Rob, then I remember standing in the coffee-shop line and hearing the "Who's your daddy?" story repeated in front of me and I feel betrayed. Then I remember how much I loved Derek but the memory of vomiting after the breakup blows it all away. I look at my wrist and am reminded that Marc is the sweetest, most generous person I've ever known and we already own a condo together, but he also seems to be ridiculously unbalanced and comes as a complete — teenagers included — package. I sit down on the couch and put my head between my knees. I discovered late Saturday I feel calmer this way.

"Can I try this one on?" I hear Mel ask and know she means one of the rings.

"Knock yourself out!" I answer without looking up.

I hear Mel's shoes click across the floor and she's standing in front of me. "I'd pick this one." I look up and Mel's left hand is in my face and she's wearing the marquise diamond from Rob.

"The pear-cut from Derek is bigger. I thought you'd pick that one," I laugh.

"Nah, baguettes are a terrible pain to keep clean. You want a solitaire. Besides, I'm a sucker for a marquise."

"I'll be sure to tell Charlie Brown that if he ever asks." I smile for the first time in a while.

"Oh, you don't think I'll let John pick out a ring by himself, do you?" Mel laughs as she puts the marquise back in the green-velvet box then comes to sit beside me on the couch. Mel takes her last sip of wine and puts her arm around my shoulders.

"Sweetie, I can't help you with this one. This is a decision that will change your life forever. If I advise you badly I'll never forgive myself; but whatever you decide, *whoever* you decide, I will stand by you steadfastly and never say one word about the ones you turn down. I promise. I know I can be a pain in the ass, but I'll support whatever you do. I do not envy you the position you're in."

"Thanks," I say quietly as I too finish my last sip of wine.

"Okay, the wine is gone and it's time for you to come back to the land of the living. I can just make my twelve o'clock. I can't get out of it and my afternoon is packed, but I want you to get in the shower, sober up and take the bull by the horns. Only you can figure this out, but you *have* to figure it out soon before it kills you." Mel is back to being in charge.

"I know you're right." And I *do* know Mel is right. Hell, I can't even stand the sight or smell of me.

"I want you to turn on your ringer and check your voice-mail. You can delete all mine — they are mostly all harping anyway — and start living again. I'll be back here around seven o'clock tonight. Will you be okay until then?"

"Yep." I try to sound strong and confident.

"Good." Mel kisses my forehead and stands up to go.

"Mel?" I look up at Mel as she turns back to me, "I don't care what you say and I won't hold it against you in any way, but what would you do?"

"Most people think I don't have one, but I'd follow my heart," Mel says seriously, then walks to the door where she turns around and adds, "or I'd just pick the most expensive ring. Whatever!" Mel laughs maniacally and closes the door behind her.

# 59

By six o'clock I feel like a new woman. After Mel leaves I take control of my life. I am already disgusting and smelly so decide I might as well go for a run. Running is the one thing that always helps me to clear my head and get a better picture of things. I plan to run five kilometres but have run almost ten by the time I get back to the condo. I am tired but feel strong and confident. The fact I can run ten kilometres at all at this point, especially partially hungover, means I'm in a good place.

I stand in the shower for ages and when I finally surface I feel revitalized and, I must admit, about a thousand percent better than I did a few hours ago. It's amazing what a little run and then some shampoo and body wash can accomplish. I'm just starting to tame my hair when the phone starts ringing. I check caller ID and it's Mel from her cell.

"Check your email as soon as you can, I sent you something that will be very helpful. I'll be there soon!" and click she's gone. I honestly wonder if Mel and Charlie Brown have sex like that. Mel says go then gives Charlie Brown three point five seconds before she pulls up her panties and is on the go again. I finish my hair before I check my email. I don't want to ruin the hair-taming momentum I've managed to get going.

When I do get to my email, Mel has sent a note that says "check attachment, this will come in handy for your situation and is some of my best work i might add!" typed in all lower case. Mel does not waste time capitalizing when she emails friends and family. The attachment seems to be a form letter that reads:

> Dear _____ ,
> Thank you so much for expressing the desire to marry my ass. It is with great *sadness / delight* that I *return / accept* the lovely token of your affection. I have chosen to *decline / accept* your generous proposal because:
> *(insert reason)*
> Bye Bye Now! / Let's talk prenup!
> Kit

I laugh out loud for the first time in days. Mel's form letter is very funny and I have to agree, if this wasn't happening to me, I too might have come up with a similar form. I mean, honestly, three proposals at the same time? It's the stuff of fantasy and imagination, certainly not someone's real life. Well, certainly not anyone's life except mine, at any rate.

Mel arrives at seven, right on schedule. I answer her one knock on the door clean and fresh and dressed. I'm wearing my favourite jeans with my cool wide black belt, my black V-necked cashmere sweater and my high-heeled black leather boots. My hair is tame, I smell good, having applied both deodorant and perfume, and I have makeup on. Basically, I look normal and the polar opposite of how I looked just a few short hours ago.

"Much better," Mel hugs me, "is this the 'confident cashmere' sweater? Does this mean you've made a decision?" Mel is pleased to see the cashmere I only ever wear when I'm in complete control, so I don't wear it very often. Well…the complete control thing combined with the dry-clean-only laundering it requires. I guess since Mel knows about the confident cashmere she probably knows about all my other occasion clothing.

"Yep!" I am a bit giddy having finally made the toughest decision of my life so far.

"Tell me, tell me!" Mel must be excited because she never repeats herself.

"Okay, but you have to sit down," I say as I walk to the table and retrieve the two glasses of wine I just finished pouring before Mel arrived. Mel walks over to the table and takes a glass from me. I sit down on the blue Two-Step and Mel gets as comfortable as she can on the white Two-Step.

"Do you remember Tanya Gowling from university?" I continue.

"No! What are you talking about?"

"Work with me! Tanya Gowling? Tall, slim, brunette, modelled in Paris? Lived down the hall from us in residence?" I'm trying to get Mel's memory gland in gear.

"No."

"You remember, she had the gorgeous, three-quarter-length red-leather jacket with the slash pockets and the mink collar." I know Mel will remember the coat.

"Ohhh, yes, I remember her! She dated that football player who dressed head to toe in Tommy Hilfiger. What was his name?" Mel remembers what complete strangers wear but can't remember the name of a girl we went to school with for four years.

"He was a *basketball* player and his name, unfortunately for him, was John Kennedy. Remember we called them John John and Too Tall Tannie? You have to remember we called him John John, like JFK Junior?"

"Hmm…vaguely," Mel pauses. "Okay no, not at all, but what does this have to do with you and the jewellery store?"

"I'm getting to that. In our last year, I took World Politics with Tannie and one day she came to class and she was really bummed out," I start.

"I'm not seeing the connection here," Mel interrupts.

"Just listen. Anyway she was totally bummed so after class I took her to the student union for a coffee and she told me that she and John John broke up. You *do* remember that they broke up just before we graduated, right?"

"John John and Too Tall broke up?" Mel seems shocked about an event that was well publicized over a decade ago.

"Honestly Mel, did we even go to the same school? Yes, they broke up and when I asked Tannie what happened she said that they broke up because John John had asked her to marry him." I pause for a sip of wine.

"I still don't get what this has to do with you."

"Tannie told me that her grandmother had given her a wonderful bit of advice, which was, 'If the answer to *that* question is not an absolute resounding yes that comes from the whole of your heart and the deepest part of your soul, then the answer *has* to be no.' Needless to say, when John John asked Tannie to marry him, Tannie knew she didn't love him like her grandmother had described so the answer had to be no and they broke up instead of getting engaged." I finish my John John and Tannie story.

"Wow. That's some pretty persuasive advice and it makes sense I guess. Marriage is a huge commitment, and if you don't have that undying love it could be one heck of a long life." Mel finally sees the light but I still strongly suspect she has no memory of John John or Too Tall Tannie.

"Let's go out for dinner tonight. Oh, let's go to the Rivoli. I feel like Pad Thai," I say as I stand up from the table.

"Hold up a minute! Thanks for the stroll down memory lane, but what did you, Kit Jennings, decide to do with your 'sticky situation'?" Mel puts on her best affronted look.

"Here," I laugh as I hand Mel three pieces of paper.

Dear <u>Rob-the-bike-courier slash real estate lawyer,</u>
Thank you so much for expressing the desire to marry
my ass. It is with great *sadness / ~~delight~~* that I *return / ~~accept~~*
the lovely token of your affection. I have chosen to
*decline / ~~accept~~* your generous proposal because:

*You make me laugh and I absolutely love and adore you but I'm*
*not in love with you in the way you have to be in love with*
*someone to marry them. I want you in my world forever and hope*
*we can still be friends.*

~~Bye Bye Now! / Let's talk prenup!~~
Love Kit

---

Dear <u>Marc,</u>
Thank you so much for expressing the desire to marry
my ass. It is with great *sadness / ~~delight~~* that I *return / ~~accept~~*
the lovely token of your affection. I have chosen to
*decline / ~~accept~~* your generous proposal because:

*You are my strongest supporter and my most ardent admirer but I*
*can't marry you. One good friend is more important than all the*
*lovers in a lifetime. If it's okay with you, I'd rather keep the*
*status quo on this one.*

Bye Bye Now! / ~~Let's talk prenup!~~
Love Kit

Dear **The Bastard Derek**,

Thank you so much for expressing the desire to marry my ass. It is with great ~~sadness~~ / delight that I return / ~~accept~~ the lovely token of your affection. I have chosen to decline / ~~accept~~ your generous proposal because:

*Well honestly, you had to see this coming! You did dump me to run off to marry a spoiled, undersexed debutante with large breasts whom you'd just met. You didn't really think I'd overlook <u>that</u>, did you?*

Bye Bye Now! / ~~Let's talk prenup!~~
Kit

"So you didn't pick *anyone?*" Mel can hardly formulate the words. I reach into the V of my sweater and pull out my twenty-inch box-link chain that has Kevin's scratched-up class of '92 high-school ring on the end of it. "Kevin goes on at ten o'clock Friday night! You and Charlie Brown should come along. Now grab your coat, I'm starving!"

"But…"

"Mel, sometimes not making any decision is the best decision of all." I take Mel by the arm and coax her up from the Two-Step, "Come on, did I mention I'm starving?"